'What do you... ...d slammed her eyes shut aga...

A taste was thundering toward them across the desert, vast and ancient and bitter, tumbling over itself in a rushing wave. It grew stronger as it advanced, like an avalanche pulling down more snow from the mountainside, burying everything in its wake.

Then it struck, washing through the gymnasium, sweeping away the puny energies of the pep rally, obliterating the surrounding mind noise of Bixby leaking in through the walls. It consumed everything. Only Melissa's connection with Rex remained, his shock and alarm reverberating through her like the echoes of a gunshot.

She opened her eyes and saw what had happened. The blue light, the frozen bodies, a leaping cheerleader hovering suspended in the air. The whole world struck by . . .

Silence.

Melissa looked at her watch in amazement. It was just after 9 A.M.

But the blue time was here.

By Scott Westerfeld

Midnighters
THE SECRET HOUR
TOUCHING DARKNESS
BLUE NOON

PARASITE POSITIVE
LAST DAYS

THE RISEN EMPIRE

MIDNIGHTERS

BLUE NOON

SCOTT WESTERFELD

www.atombooks.co.uk

ATOM

First published in the United States in 2005 by Eos, HarperCollins Publishers Inc.
First published in Great Britain in 2006 by Atom
This edition published in 2010 by Atom

A CIP catalogue record for this book
is available from the British Library.

ISBN 978-1-90741-005-5

Typeset in Baskerville by M Rules
Printed and bound in Great Britain by
Clays Ltd, St Ives plc

Papers used by Atom are natural, renewable and
recyclable products sourced from well-managed forests and certified
in accordance with the rules of the Forest Stewardship Council.

Mixed Sources
Product group from well-managed
forests and other controlled sources
FSC   www.fsc.org Cert no. SGS-COC-004081
© 1996 Forest Stewardship Council

Atom
An imprint of
Little, Brown Book Group
100 Victoria Embankment
London EC4Y 0DY

An Hachette UK Company
www.hachette.co.uk

www.atombooks.co.uk

To John and Jan, and Niki,
for making me part of the family

Acknowledgments

Like all books everywhere, this series has been shaped and supported by a host of readers, editors and friends. Most especially: Liesa Abrams, Holly Black, Gwenda Bond, Eloise Flood, Claudia Gabel, Justine Larbalestier, Ursula K. Le Guin, Garth Nix, Christopher Rowe, John Scalzi, Jonathan Strahan, Tui Sutherland, Kathleen Thomas, and Sean Williams, among others.

1

PREDATOR

Bixby High's late bell shrieked in the distance, like something wounded and ready to be cut from the herd.

Rex Greene was always late these days, stumbling in confusion from one class to another, late with his father's pills or forgetting them altogether. But the worst was getting up for school. It didn't help that he'd unplugged his clock a few nights ago, unable to sleep with the soft buzzing sound it made all night, like a mosquito hovering just out of arm's reach. His newly acute hearing had turned every electronic contraption into something whiny and annoying.

But it was more than just the clock's noise; it was what it *meant*, with its false day of twenty-four hours. Since what had happened to him in the desert, Rex had started to feel time as something marked out in the sky – the rise and fall of the sun, the spinning stars, the interlocking ratios of the light moon and the dark.

The rest of the world still had their clocks, though, so Melissa had banged on his window again this morning, dragging him rudely out of his strange new dreams.

'Smells like . . . assembly,' she said as they pulled into the school parking lot, her head tipping back a bit, nostrils flaring.

All Rex could smell was crumbling vinyl – the upholstery of Melissa's crappy Ford broken down by thirty-odd Oklahoma summers – and gasoline fumes leaking up through the floorboard from the car's rumbling engine. Humans loved their oil, a flash of darkling memory informed him. They scoured the desert for it, used it to make clever things like plastic and gasoline . . .

Rex shook his head to clear it. On mornings like these, when he'd dreamed of Stone Age hunts all night, he had more trouble concentrating than usual. The old knowledge inside him seemed more real than his sixteen years of human memories. Sometimes Rex wondered if he would ever recover from what the darklings had done, the half change they'd effected before Jessica had rescued him.

Was he gradually healing from the experience? Or was the darkness they'd left inside him like a virus, slowly growing stronger?

As Melissa maneuvered the Ford into a parking place, Rex spotted a few stragglers making their way into the gymnasium entrance. The sound of an amplified voice echoed out from the propped-open double doors.

'Crap, that's right,' Melissa said, gripping the steering wheel tighter. 'Pep rally today.'

Rex groaned and closed his eyes. He hadn't faced anything like this since the change, and he wasn't looking forward to it. The thought of all those bodies pressed in close around him, chanting together, brought a trickle of nerves into his stomach.

'Don't worry,' Melissa said, reaching across to take his hand. 'I'll be there.'

At her touch, with no more insistence than a cool breeze, a calmness fell across Rex. His stomach stopped roiling, his mind growing still as Melissa's serenity poured into him.

A shudder passed through Rex; her strength became his.

Funny. A month ago it had been Rex who'd had to talk Melissa through the beginning-of-football-season pep rally. Now she was the sane one, and he was . . .

What, exactly?

He didn't know yet, and Rex hated not knowing. There were no halflings in the lore, much less recovering halflings.

Bad dreams last night?

Rex smiled and turned to face Melissa. The words had come through as clear as speech. They could have whole conversations now without her uttering a sound.

Her control was almost perfect, not a leaked thought anywhere, so different from the vomited rush of fear and pain that had struck him when they had first begun to touch each other. Although sometimes Rex missed those early experiments, the terrifying moments when he saw all of Melissa at once.

When his mind was focused, he hardly had to speak himself; Melissa simply pulled the words from him. But this morning he was too much of a wreck.

'Yeah, some bad dreams,' Rex said aloud. 'But not all of them.'

The hunting dreams had been sweet – the cold, patient hunger as he tracked prey for days across the plain, anticipation building as the weakest were cut from the group, and then the burning rush of the kill.

But of course, there'd been those *other* dreams as well, memories of when the clever little monkeys had started hunting back. The beginning of the end.

'Jeez, lighten up,' Melissa said, pulling her hand away and rubbing it, as if to wring out the ancient horror she'd felt in his mind. 'I think someone forgot to drink his coffee this morning.'

'Sorry, Cowgirl. Yeah, I guess I could use a cup. Or six.' Rex shook his head again. His brain felt stuffed full, his own thoughts almost crowded out by the memories that the darklings had implanted to make him one of them. 'Sometimes I wonder if I'll ever get back to normal.'

Melissa snorted. 'When were you ever normal, Rex? When were any of us?'

'Well, maybe not normal,' Rex admitted. 'But I'd settle for human.'

She laughed and touched his shoulder, and he felt a spark of her pleasure even through the fabric of his long black coat. 'You're totally human, Rex. Trust me on that one.'

'Glad you think so,' he said, smiling.

Melissa's fingers stayed on his shoulder, drumming out a nervous rhythm, and her glance strayed to the open gymnasium door. Rex realized that however much her control had improved, the thought of enduring a pep rally still made Melissa anxious.

'You'll be okay,' he said softly, pulling her closer.

She turned to him, and their lips met.

At first Rex felt serenity in the warmth of their kiss, her new calmness and self-control flowing into him. But then Melissa allowed her composure to slip, and it was like their first time. Everything inside her crashed out in a torrent: the enduring wounds of all those years alone, memories of the constant hammering of other minds, the old fear of being touched. She let it well up and spill over, pouring into him.

Rex was overwhelmed for a moment, but then he felt his damaged surety rallying, responding to her need. He twisted in the car seat to take her shoulders, and the kiss built, his strength becoming hers, until he felt Melissa's mastery of herself return.

She sighed as they separated. 'I say again, Rex: fully human.'

Rex leaned back into his seat, smiling. The heavy dread that he had felt since waking and realizing that it was a school day – and a Monday at that – had lifted from him at last.

Melissa's fingers played across his cheek, and she grinned. 'You taste electric now, like you do after a jolt of coffee.'

'Hmm. Maybe kissing is sort of like nature's coffee.'

'Actually, Rex, *coffee* is nature's coffee. It is a plant, you know.'

'Ah, right. Good point, Cowgirl.'

He looked at the gymnasium door. A pep rally couldn't be *that* bad, could it? Better than the hated first-period math class it would replace, and he could use the time to cram for his upcoming English test. One thing about carrying ancient memories of an elder species around in your head, it could royally screw up your interpretation of *Catcher in the Rye*.

Rex checked his backpack. No English book. 'Listen, I have to go by my locker. Save me a seat?'

'Back row?'

'Of course.' He snorted. 'I haven't changed that much.'

She nodded slowly, then her eyes narrowed. 'Should I come with you?'

'Don't worry about me.' Rex ran his tongue across his teeth. They never felt as sharp as he expected them to, the canines never as long as they should be. Phantom limbs itched sometimes at night, as if parts of his body were missing.

But Rex took a deep breath and forced those thoughts from his mind. He couldn't complain about every discomfort. He'd been granted something that any seer would die for: a chance to learn more about the darklings than the lore could ever teach, to understand them from the *inside*. Maybe his kidnapping and transformation had been a gift in disguise.

As long as his human half stayed in control . . .

'It's okay, Cowgirl,' he said. 'I can take care of myself.'

The hallway was as unpleasantly bright as always, sunlight spilling through the doors, the fluorescents buzzing overhead in a constant drone.

Rex squinted in the light, reminding himself to buy sunglasses. That was one advantage since the change: his vision was much sharper. Rex didn't even need his eyeglasses at school anymore. A strange kind of Focus clung to everything here: the marks of human passage and invention, a million prey trails piled on top of one another, making everything crystal clear and somehow . . . appetizing.

It was almost too much. Sometimes he wished that school could be blurry and soft again, distanced behind the thick glasses he'd worn since third grade. Everything was so sharp now. It wasn't just the buzzing fluorescents that annoyed him; Rex could feel the fire alarms and public address system behind the walls, those razor-fine wires that clever humans always laced their buildings with. It felt like being in a metal cage with electrified bars.

And human places were so ugly. Rex noticed for the first time in his two years at Bixby High that the tiled floors were the exact same yellow hue as his father's nicotine-stained fingers. Whose idea of interior decorating was that?

At least the halls had been emptied by the pep rally.

As he headed for his locker, Rex ran a hand across his scalp, feeling it prickle his palm. When Jessica's white flame had freed him from the darkling body, big patches of his hair had burned away, his gothy haircut totaled. So Rex had cropped it to a half inch all over with the electric clippers that his father had once used to shorten the thick coat of their dog, Magnetosphere, for summer.

Rex's own reflection still brought him to a halt when he passed shop windows, and he found himself touching his scalp all the time, fascinated by the hairs standing up so straight, as hard and even as Astroturf under his palm. Maybe this meant that Melissa was right, that he was still human: even after all the other changes that had racked his body and mind, a new haircut still took some getting used to.

Rex reached his locker, letting his fingers open it by feel. The tricky part was not thinking of the numbers, that cleverest and most dangerous of human inventions. Fortunately, there weren't any multiples of the Aversion in his combination. It was hard enough already when his fingers faltered, and Rex had to start over, forcing his way through the sequence number by number, like some freshman on his first day of school.

When he looked at the locker's dial, he hardly even saw the Aversion anymore – it appeared as a wavering blurry spot between twelve and fourteen, edited out by his mind, like an FBI informant's face on the news.

He was thinking of taking Dess up on her offer to pull

apart the lock and hack it, changing the combination to a smooth string of twelves and twenty-fours. She was already doing his math homework these days. Too many combinations awaited on every page that could paralyze the darkling half of his mind, leaving him with a snapped pencil and a pounding headache.

Math was deadly now.

Success on the first try. He heard the tiny click of the last cylinder lining up and pulled the locker open happily. But distracted by his thoughts of numbers, Rex realized too late that someone had crept up behind him. A familiar scent swept through him, setting off old alarm bells, fearful and violent memories suddenly rising up.

A fist struck the locker, slamming it shut again. The sound echoed through the empty hallway as he spun around.

'Hey, Rex. Lost your specs?'

Timmy Hudson. That explained the trickle of fear in Rex's stomach – the boy had beaten him up almost every day back in fifth grade. As strong as any flash of darkling memory, Rex recalled being trapped behind the school one day by Timmy and three friends, punched in the gut so hard that for a week it had hurt to piss. Though it had been years since Timmy had done anything worse to Rex than slam him against the wall, the tightening in Rex's stomach remained as knife-edged as it had ever been.

'Didn't lose them,' Rex answered, his own voice weak and plaintive in his ears. 'Don't wear glasses anymore.'

Timmy grinned and stood closer, the smell of sour milk sharp on his breath. 'Contact lenses? Huh. The funny thing is, makes you look like even more of a retard.'

Rex didn't answer, struck with the sudden realization that

Timmy Hudson was looking *up* at him. At some point he had grown taller than his old nemesis. When had *that* happened?

'You must think you're getting pretty cool these days, huh?' Timmy punctuated the last grunted word with a hard shove, and a combination lock rammed into the small of Rex's back, hard as the barrel of a gun. The feel of it focused his mind, and he felt his lips begin to twitch, pulling away from his teeth. His mouth felt suddenly dry.

Something was moving through Rex, something stronger than him.

He shook his head *no*. He was Rex Greene, a seer, not an animal.

'What's the matter? Too cool to talk to me these days?' Timmy laughed, then squinted up at Rex's scalp. He reached out and ran one hand across its bristly surface.

'And a new 'do?' Timmy shook his head sadly. 'You trying to look tough? Like everyone doesn't remember what a little pussy you are?'

Rex found himself staring at Timmy's throat, where the blood pulsed close to the surface. One shallow rip through the frail skin and life would spill out, warm and nourishing.

'Think your little extreme makeover makes you Mr. Cool, don't you?'

Rex found himself smiling at the words. What had happened to him was so much more extreme than anything Timmy could imagine.

'What's so funny?'

'Your weakness.' Rex blinked. The words had just popped out of his mouth.

Timmy took half a step back, blank-faced with shock for a

moment. He looked one way down the empty hall, then the other, as if checking the reaction of some invisible audience.

'My *what*?' he finally spat.

Rex nodded slowly. He could *smell* it now, he realized, and the scent of weakness had triggered something inside him, something that threatened to spin out of control.

His mind grasped for some way to master himself. He tried to think of the lore symbols, but they had all flown out of his brain. All he had left were words. Maybe if he could keep talking . . .

'You're the kind we cut from the herd.'

Timmy's eyebrows went up. 'Say what, retard?'

'You're weak and afraid.'

'You think I'm afraid, Rex?' The boy tried to put on an amused smile, but only half his face obeyed. The left side seemed frozen, taut and wide-eyed, his fear leaking out into his expression. 'Of *you*?'

Rex saw that Timmy's pulse was quickening, his hands shaking.

Weakness.

'I can smell it on you . . .' The words faded as Rex finally lost control. He watched the rest of what happened like a passenger in his own body. He took a step forward until his face was as close as Timmy had dared come a moment before.

The fear in Rex's stomach had changed into something else, something hot and cruel that surged through his chest and up into his jaw. His teeth parted, lips pulling back so far that he felt them split, baring his teeth and half an inch of gums. His whole body grew as taut as one long trembling muscle, swaying for balance like a snake ready to strike, arms out and fingers locked in rigid claws.

He made a noise then, right in Timmy's face, a horrific sound that Rex had never heard before, much less produced himself. His mouth still open wide, the back of his throat cinched tightly closed, a breath forcing its way out with a long and shuddering *hisssss* – a mix of fingernails on a chalkboard, the shriek of a hawk, and the last rattle of a punctured lung. The noise seemed to coil in the air for a moment, wrapping around Timmy's shuddering frame, squeezing the breath from him.

The hiss lingered in the empty hallway like the echoes of a shout, disappearing into the buzzing of the fluorescent lights.

Timmy didn't move. The twisted half smile stayed on his face, muscles frozen, as if some careless surgeon had snipped a nerve and he was stuck with the half-formed expression for the rest of his life.

'Weakness,' Rex said softly, the hiss still ringing in his voice.

His body softened then, whatever demon had slipped into him departing as swiftly as it had come. His jaw relaxed, and Rex's muscles lost their inhuman rigidity – but Timmy still didn't move. He looked thoroughly frozen, like a rat that had just lost a staring contest with a python.

He didn't make another sound as Rex walked away.

Halfway to the gym, Rex's heart was still pounding with the weirdness of what had just happened. He felt elated, confident, and powerful, finally cleansed of the fear that had stalked him through the halls of Bixby High School every day for the last two years.

But he was also afraid. He'd tried to fend off the darkling part of him, but it had taken control nonetheless.

Still, the experience had left him feeling so *good* – purposeful and somehow more complete. And he hadn't really lost it, had he? The predator had drawn its claws, but it hadn't used them. He hadn't struck for the pulse in Timmy's throat, the easy kill of the straggler.

Maybe the darkling side of him maintained a balance with his human half. Perhaps Rex Greene was still sane.

For now.

2

PEP RALLY

She watched the pep rally with awestruck fascination.

Melissa had been forced to attend dozens of these things before, of course, but she'd never really *seen* one. Battered by the mind noise, huddled in the back with eyes closed and fists clenched, the old Melissa had understood pep rallies about as well as a bird sucked through a jet engine comprehended aircraft design.

But the crowd no longer terrorized her, the horde of other minds no longer threatened to erase her own. Using the memories Madeleine had given her, the generations of technique passed on among mindcasters, she could rise above the tempest, ride its swells like a buoy in a storm.

Finally she could *taste* it all . . .

The football team strutting in Lycra before the crowd, their testosterone and bluster mixed with a bitter backwash flavor – the growing realization that once again, they were going to lose every game this year. The clique of pretty girls clustered together a few rows down, surrounded by a force field of disdain for all the nobodies around them – unaware of how much the nobodies hated them right back. The bored minds of teachers stationed around the edges of the gym, jonesing for cigarettes and more coffee, quietly relieved that first period had been superseded. The group of freshman boys camped on the first row of bleachers, watching the cheerleaders' skirts fly up, their horny thoughts as sharp as sweat licked off an upper lip.

Melissa found it all hysterically funny. Why hadn't she ever understood this simple fact before? Why hadn't anyone told her? High school wasn't a trial by fire or some ordeal that had to be survived.

It was all a big joke. You just had to provide the laugh track.

Through the crowd noise the minds of the other mid-nighters reached her, their various flavors coming through loud and clear. The three of them sat together – about as far away from Melissa as they could. In particular, she tasted every cold glance from Dess, who was glowering behind dark glasses, her mind still full of acid hatred for what had happened ten days ago.

Melissa did feel bad about that – no one knew better than she how vile it was having your mind wrenched open against your will. But there hadn't been any choice. If she hadn't gone in and dredged up Dess's secrets, Rex would be a full-fledged darkling now instead of . . .

Well, instead of whatever he had become.

Jonathan and Jessica sat close to each other, their fingers intertwined, separated from everyone around them by their coupleness. Of course, they would turn and talk to Dess every once in a while, throwing her a bone. Jessica had witnessed what Melissa had done to Dess and felt almost as bad as if she'd done it herself. Her thoughts were often layered with a sickly survivor's guilt: *If only I had stopped Melissa, blah, blah, blah* . . .

Of course, Jessica's indignation wasn't nearly as bad as what lurked in Jonathan's mind. Ever since he'd touched Melissa and felt what it was like to be her, a rancid pity polluted him from head to toe.

Of course, the joke was on him. Because being Melissa *didn't* feel like that anymore.

It felt sweet.

'Sucker,' she whispered, and let herself be buoyed again by the chanting crowd.

Loverboy made his way in about fifteen minutes late, slipping easily past the teacher monitoring the door.

Melissa tasted his mind through the chaotic energies of the pep rally. Despite all the confusion he carried now, Rex's thoughts still reached her on their own special channel, even clearer than those of the other midnighters'. She knew instantly that something unexpected had happened to him in the empty hallways of the school. His mind was bright and buzzing, like just after they'd kissed.

But whatever had happened had also unnerved him. Melissa felt him scan the crowd anxiously, relaxing only when he spotted her atop the closest bleachers to the door. He made his way up with soft, effortless steps, as fluid as a cat across a rooftop.

Melissa smiled. Watching Rex show off his new feline grace was one of her great pleasures.

'Get what you wanted?' she asked as he settled beside her.

'Oh, my English book.' He shook his head. 'Forgot all about it, actually. Had some trouble on the way.'

'Yeah, I figured that.' She could taste it more clearly now: Underneath his excitement Rex was bubbling with the darkling flavor he sometimes had now – the sour lemon of a young hunter's mind jazzed by the smell of prey. 'Hmm. Didn't eat anybody, did you?'

'Not quite. But it was a pretty close thing.' He held out his hand, palm up. 'Want to see?' His eyes flashed.

'Of course, Loverboy.' She smiled and placed her hand over his.

The darkling taste redoubled, shuddering through her acid and electric, like kissing an old car battery that still carried some juice. The surging taste of it blotted out the insipid flavors of the pep rally.

She felt Rex's new predatory confidence, his worries about losing control, the fading buzz of his wild transformation. Someone had threatened him, she realized, had actually dared to get into his face. Sucker.

And there was something else . . . an unexpected cluster of memories carried on top of Rex's spinning thoughts. Not a darkling flavor, but something fearful and human.

Melissa pulled her hand away, staring into the whorls of her palm to puzzle over the strange images: a rattler cut in two by someone's dad in a backyard, its fangs snapping together in its death throes. The two snake halves squirming for thirty minutes on either side of the shovel that had bisected them, as if trying to rejoin each other and wreak revenge.

Melissa blinked. 'Someone's afraid of snakes?'

'Timmy Hudson is.' Rex smiled, showing too many teeth. 'Very.'

She shook her head. 'What the hell?'

Rex stared down at the cheerleaders, who were piling themselves into a shaky pyramid. His glassy eyes gazed straight through them, into some new mix of midnighter lore and implanted ancient memories.

'Well, you know how darklings take our nightmares and use them against us?'

'Of course I do, Rex.' Every night Melissa tasted the old minds out across the desert. And she had personally witnessed their shape-shifting into all creatures vile and hideous – worms, spiders, slugs. 'That's why they always pull the tarantula trip on you.'

'Yeah, tarantulas.' He nodded thoughtfully. 'Well, Timmy Hudson was bugging me. And he's afraid of snakes, it turns out. Ever since he was little, when his dad killed a rattler in the backyard and then brought Timmy out to take a look at the results. So I sort of got . . . snaky.'

He glanced at her, his tongue darting out for a split second. Then he smiled.

Melissa noticed that Rex's chapped lower lip was split, his chin a little reddened with wiped-off blood. She reached up and touched it, felt the fading tension in his jaw muscle. 'Okay, Loverboy. But how did you know that? About Timmy? You and he were never exactly friends.'

Rex shook his head. 'I just knew.'

'But *how*, Rex? I'm the mindcaster here, remember? How did *you* get into someone's nightmares?'

He turned away again, staring at the pep festivities without seeing them. His mind radiated a quiet confidence, an intensity Melissa had never felt from him before, not during daylight hours. His strength was flavored, though, with tremors of uncertainty, bitter as the dregs of Madeleine's tea.

Rex felt a lot like a young trucker Melissa had once tasted on the highway, driving an eighteen-wheeler for the first time with no one else in the cab – heady with an overdose of power, but nervous that the rig was about to hurtle off the road.

Finally he answered. 'That's what darklings do.'

The pep rally dragged on for ages. Announcements were made about bake sales and car washes and school plays. Team banners were raised. The members of last year's district-winning chess club got a few seconds of applause – a token suggestion that being smart might actually be a *good* thing. And gradually the rally began to lose its pep. Even the cheerleaders started to look bored, pom-poms wilting in their hands.

Then came the part when everyone chanted together.

'Beat North Tulsa. Beat North Tulsa,' the gnomelike principal began. He stepped back from the microphone, raising his tiny fist in rhythm with the words. Gradually the chant built, louder and louder, until the gymnasium thundered with the sound.

This ritual was supposed to channel the whole school's 'spirit' into the football team, transforming them from a bunch of seventeen-year-old boys into the champions of Bixby High.

The funny thing was, the concept wasn't total nonsense. You could see it on the team's faces as they listened: it did affect them, as if a gathered mass of humans really could lend its strength to a few zit-faced boys. Melissa often wondered if the daylighter who had invented pep rallies actually knew something about how mindcasting worked.

This part of pep rallies had always terrified Melissa in the past – the assembled minds uniting their energy in the chant, every strand of individual thought swamped by the animal imperatives of the pack: *Stay with the herd. Safety in numbers. Kill the enemy. Beat North Tulsa.*

She looked down across the fists rising and falling in rhythm, felt the beat of stomping feet resonating through the bleachers. The clique of pretty girls had lost the force field around them, dissolving into the crowd. The freshman boys in the first row were taking it seriously, no longer ogling the cheerleaders. Even Jessica Day and Flyboy had joined in, trying to act halfhearted but overtaken by the power of the mob.

Melissa nervously took a few deep breaths. This pep rally was a joke, she reminded herself. The crowd didn't know what they were doing, and not one of the minds in this gymnasium matched hers for sheer power. Just because they'd found a meaningless football game to channel themselves into didn't make them stronger than her.

She steadily gained control again.

Then Melissa noticed Rex sniffing the air, eyes twitching as his nostrils flared.

The chant was making him anxious as well.

'It's like a hunt,' he hissed. 'This is how they got themselves ready in the old days.'

Melissa touched Rex's hand and for an awful moment felt the crowd as he did. Little humans, weak and frail – but *so many of them.* It had been rituals like this one that had helped them conquer their fear of the darklings. And one day they had begun to hunt their own predators, packs of humans armed with fire and their sharp, clever stones.

Finally a band of them had gotten lucky, taking down a young darkling that had thought itself invulnerable. And some of the dread that the master species had always depended on was lost forever. The oldest minds still remembered that moment, when the balance had begun to shift. Humans had slowly become more confident, scratching pictures of their kills onto rocks and into mud, the first hated symbols of their mastery.

Melissa pulled her hand away, burned by the memory.

Maybe this pep rally wasn't such a joke. After all, high school was all about the oldest human bonds – the tribe, the pack, the hunting party.

Rex's hands twitched. He was struggling with the part of him that wanted to flee.

'You need to leave?' she whispered.

He shook his head grimly. 'No. This is important. Have to learn to keep control.'

Melissa sighed. Rex could be a moron sometimes.

She often remembered a line she'd read once on a bathroom wall: *That which does not kill us makes us stronger.* As Melissa watched the sweat building on Rex's upper lip, she knew that he was making the same mistake as the bathroom wall guy.

Not everything made you stronger. It was possible to survive, yet still be crippled for your trouble. Sometimes it was okay to run away, to skip the test, to chicken out. Or at least to get some help.

She firmly took his hand, not letting him pull away, and reached inside herself for a place that Madeleine had shown her, an old mindcaster trick for chilling out. Melissa closed her eyes and entered Rex, gently pushing the crowd's chant out of his mind.

She felt him relax, his fear of the crowd – and of the beast inside him – slipping away.

'Whoa,' he said softly. 'Thanks, Cowgirl.'

'Any time, Loverboy.'

'Okay. How about tonight?'

She opened her eyes. 'Hmm?'

'Maybe later we can – ' Rex's voice choked off, his grip suddenly tightening. 'Something's coming.'

'What do you—?' she started, but then she felt it too and slammed her eyes shut again.

A taste was thundering toward them across the desert, vast and ancient and bitter, tumbling over itself in a rushing wave. It grew stronger as it advanced, like an avalanche pulling down more snow from the mountainside, burying everything in its wake.

Then it struck, washing through the gymnasium, sweeping away the puny energies of the pep rally, obliterating the surrounding mind noise of Bixby leaking in through the walls. It consumed everything. Only Melissa's connection with Rex remained, his shock and alarm reverberating through her like the echoes of a gunshot.

She opened her eyes and saw what had happened. The blue light, the frozen bodies, a leaping cheerleader hovering suspended in the air. The whole world struck by . . .

Silence.

Melissa looked at her watch in amazement. It was just after 9 A.M.

But the blue time was here.

3

BLUE MONDAY

Midnight gravity flowed into Jessica.

She clenched Jonathan's hand harder. 'What the . . .?' Her voice trailed off into the sudden and overwhelming silence, her heart pounding as her eyes scanned the frozen pep rally.

Everything was blue.

The shiny Lycra uniforms of the football team, the Bixby town seal in the center of the basketball court, the motionless tendrils of a pom-pom thrust into the air – it had all turned the color of midnight. And everything was perfectly still.

'Jonathan?' Jessica looked into his face, hoping to catch some glimmer of comprehension. Maybe this had happened before here in Bixby, a weird hiccup of the blue time, and Rex had simply forgotten to tell her about it.

Jonathan didn't answer. His eyes were wide with shock.

'This is messed up,' Dess confirmed in a quiet voice.

Jessica gripped the edge of the bleacher she sat on, felt the grainy reality of the wood. This was not a dream – this was the blue time.

Her eye caught movement across the gym. Rex and

Melissa were slowly rising, looking strangely isolated among the frozen human forms.

His paralysis suddenly broken, Jonathan let out a cry and sprang out of his seat. Jessica instinctively clung to his hand, and as he left his feet, he pulled her softly into the air after him – they were both light as feathers.

'Jonathan!'

'What the hell?' His voice faded as midnight gravity carried them helplessly up and over the crowd, spinning around each other like two balls on a string. 'Is this really . . .?'

'Yeah, really happening,' Jessica managed, gripping his hand still harder. The floor looked miles below, and she flashed back to Climbing Day in gym class – peering down from the top of the thick, knotted rope, terrified of falling.

As their flight peaked and they began to descend, reflexes honed by countless hours of flying together kicked in. Jonathan twisted to bring their spin to a halt, and as they settled back onto the gym floor – right on the Bixby seal, as if they'd been aiming for it – Jessica's knees bent for a soft landing.

She looked back up at the bleachers and swallowed. The frozen crowd were all staring right at her and Jonathan. It reminded Jessica of her least-favorite recurring nightmare: being in a play she hadn't rehearsed, the motionless audience waiting for her first line. It was stunning to see so many people captured by midnight. Their faces were waxy and pale, their eyes lifeless, like an army of plastic dummies.

'Never seen this many stiffs before.' Melissa's soft words carried across the gym, echoing Jessica's thoughts.

'Outside, quick!' Rex called. He was running down the

bleachers, jumping over the frozen bodies like hurdles. Dess and Melissa followed him toward the door to the parking lot.

Jessica looked at Jonathan, who shrugged. 'Might as well see what's in the sky,' he said.

'Oh, right.' If this were midnight, the dark moon would be up there, bathing the world in its cold blue light.

But this *wasn't* midnight. This was a Monday morning pep rally, which was just about as far away from the magic of the blue time as you could get.

'Come on,' Jonathan said, his knees bending.

They jumped together, covering the distance to the door in one easy leap, landing just as Rex got there. The three of them burst out into the parking lot together, staring up at the sky.

Behind a few frozen and wispy clouds, the dark moon was huge and fully risen. Its vast bulk seemed perfectly centered, blotting out the whole sky except for a thin sliver around the horizon, hiding the sun. A few white stars glittered at its edges, their light dulled, as if they were being squashed down against the earth by the huge moon's weight.

Suddenly Jessica needed the feel of solid ground under her feet. She slipped her fingers from Jonathan's hand, letting normal gravity fall back across her. Dizzied by the weird, absent light of the moon, she dropped her eyes down to the asphalt.

Its cracked surface shone uncanny blue.

Dess and Melissa charged through the door, staggering to a halt as they stared upward.

'This can't be happening,' Rex murmured.

'Yeah,' Dess said, gazing at her own blue hand. 'But it kind of . . . *is.*'

For a long moment they all stood there in silence. Jonathan

pushed off from the ground nervously, rising a few feet into the air.

Jessica checked her watch. The numbers were still pulsing: 9:05 A.M. Just like during a normal midnight hour, her flame-bringer's magic kept its electronic numbers flashing.

How many minutes had it lasted so far? Two?

'The moon isn't moving,' Rex said.

'Isn't what?' Dess asked.

His skyward gaze stayed steady, his eyes flashing violet. 'It's just stuck up there, halfway across.'

'How can you tell?' Jessica asked, glancing up at the huge, baleful eye above them. The dark moon crossed the sky much faster than the sun, taking only an hour to rise and fall, but it was still like watching a minute hand move on a clock. 'Isn't it sort of too slow to see?'

'For you, maybe.' He smiled. 'But I *am* a seer, you know.'

'Oh, right.' Jessica glanced at Jonathan, who shrugged back at her. These days it was easy to forget that Rex was gifted with special sight and deep knowledge of the lore. The transformation out in the desert had left him . . . different. Lately his gaze was so freaked out and wild-eyed that he seemed more like a stoner than a seer.

'So the moon didn't rise?' Dess asked. 'It just appeared out of nowhere?'

'Or it rose really quick.' Rex glanced at his own watch; on a midnighter's wrist, windups worked in the blue hour. 'We got out here in less than three minutes.'

'Why is it such a big deal what the moon's doing?' Jessica asked quietly. 'I mean, isn't this all completely screwed up anyway?'

'The moon makes the secret hour, as far as we know.' Rex

looked up again as he answered her, staring at the sky with a frown. 'If it's not moving, there's no way to tell how long this will last.'

'Oh.' Jessica glanced at Jonathan, who had jumped to the top of a school bus to look around. 'Um, then maybe . . .'

'Spot the problem, Rex,' Dess said. 'Let's do some math: zero velocity multiplied by *any* amount of time equals zero movement. What if the moon's just *stuck up* there?'

'Stuck?' Jessica said softly. 'Like, forever?'

'I didn't say forever.' Rex dropped his eyes from the sky. 'That would be . . . crazy.'

'This whole thing is crazy, Rex!' Dess cried. 'It's not midnight, except in Australia or somewhere, but it's *blue*.'

'Yeah, what's happening, Rex?' Jonathan said as he bounded softly back to the group.

Rex raised his hands. 'Look, there's nothing like this in the lore.' His voice stayed calm. 'So I don't know why you're asking *me*.'

For a moment no one said anything, stunned by his words. Jessica realized that her jaw had dropped open. After all, that's what you did when things got weird: you asked Rex what was going on.

With a cool seer's gaze, he stared silently back at them for a moment, then smiled, his point made. 'Okay, everyone, calm down and give Melissa some head space.' He turned to the mindcaster. 'Can you feel Madeleine?'

'No, she's staying hidden. But I bet you she's just as freaked out as we are.'

'What about the darklings? Are they awake?'

Melissa stood in silence for a moment, eyes closed and head tilted back, casting her mind across the desert.

Jessica looked around at the others. It had been a while since the five of them had all been together. Probably since that night on the salt flats when everything had gone haywire – Rex kidnapped, Melissa thrown through the windshield of her car, and Dess . . .

Dess seemed the worst for it. She ate lunch with Jessica and Jonathan or alone these days – never with Rex and Melissa. She hadn't forgiven the mindcaster for pillaging her memories that night.

Not that Jessica could blame her. Or blame Rex for being freaked out by his transformation into a halfling. And the scars on Melissa's face from her accident still carried pink stitches.

But everyone seemed to have forgotten that Anathea, the young seer who'd been turned into a halfling back in the old days, had *died* that night. Which was a lot worse than anything that had happened to the rest of them.

Sometimes when Jessica watched the other midnighters interact, she felt like wearing a T-shirt with big letters on the front: GET OVER IT.

'They're awake, all right,' Melissa said slowly. 'I'm surprised you guys can't hear them.'

'Hear them?' Rex glanced over his shoulder toward the badlands. 'You mean they're coming this way?'

Jessica reached for Disintegrator in her pocket, but it wasn't there; she'd never expected to need the flashlight during the day. She had only Acariciandote, the bracelet Jonathan had given her. She reached to touch it, feeling the thirteen tiny charms dangling from her wrist.

Melissa shook her head. 'Not coming, not moving much at all. Just so *loud*.' She winced, her face twisting into the pained expression she wore whenever too many people were around.

'Melissa,' Rex asked, 'what do you mean by "loud"?'

'I mean screaming, howling, raising a ruckus.'

'As in afraid?'

Melissa shook her head. 'No. As in celebrating.'

Jessica's watch said 9:17 A.M., but it seemed like hours since the blue time had begun. The minutes seemed to drag along, as if time itself had become a formless, limping thing.

How could she even be sure if her watch was working right or not? It felt like they'd all been standing out there in the parking lot for hours.

'Get down from there!' Rex yelled again.

Jessica looked up and sighed. Jonathan was still on the roof of the school.

'I thought you said this could go on forever,' he shouted down.

'Yeah, or it could end any second!'

'Nah, midnight only comes in one-hour slices, Rex. You know that.' Jonathan laughed and took an arcing hop up to the top of the gym. From there he scanned the horizon, as if the Bixby skyline might hold some clue as to what was going on.

Jessica saw how high he was and swallowed. But she knew yelling at Jonathan was pointless. He always flew until the last moment of midnight, squeezing out every second of weight-lessness; it hadn't taken him long to convince himself that this unexpected blue time would last a solid hour. For Jonathan this wasn't a terrifying mystery to be solved – it was a double helping of dessert, an extra recess, a free period spicing up an otherwise crappy Monday.

Jessica wanted to scream at him to quit being stupid, but if she sided with Rex in front of everyone else, Jonathan would probably stay up there until the world ended.

Unless, of course, it already had.

'Come on, Jonathan,' Melissa called up to him. 'There's nothing to see, and you really could get hurt.'

Jonathan frowned at her, but a moment later he stepped from the roof's edge and floated down.

Jessica glanced sidelong at Melissa. The mindcaster had sounded so concerned, *and* Jonathan was listening to her. This was definitely too much weirdness for one Monday morning.

But at least Jonathan was safely on the ground again. She crossed the parking lot to grab hold of his jacket.

'Sorry,' he said when he saw her expression. 'But it seems like a waste, just standing around.'

'You could get killed.'

'But what if this really does last a long time?' He frowned. 'Or forever.'

She took his hand, but the feeling of his midnight gravity flowing into Jessica didn't help her mood. It would be just like the world to end on a Monday, especially *this* Monday, the day she was theoretically going to become ungrounded.

Only theoretically, of course. There had been a fierce debate this morning about what day was exactly one month from the night Jessica had been brought home by the police, tonight or tomorrow. Finally she'd given up arguing about it. Tuesday's promised freedom wouldn't take forever to come, after all.

Except now it might.

Standing here with the dark moon overhead, it made perfect sense that time had been halted, the darklings decreeing that Jessica Day would remain grounded forever. That's what she got for being born the flame-bringer.

'Hey, look! It's Sanchez,' Dess cried suddenly. She was pointing at a stiff just outside the gym entrance. The frozen Mr. Sanchez was huddled close to the wall, out of sight from anyone coming through the door, a motionless geyser of smoke spewing from his mouth.

Jonathan pulled his hand away from Jessica and bounded across the lot. 'Oh my God – he's sneaking a cigarette. I didn't know he smoked!'

'Well, well, Mr. Sanchez,' Dess said. 'Your secrets are revealed at last.' She stepped into the smoke and laughed, waving it away. Released from the dark moon's spell by her touch, it drifted slowly upward in the still air.

'Get away from him, you two,' Rex shouted. 'Don't stand where he can see you. What if time starts up again?'

Jonathan got out of Sanchez's face, but Dess just stood there giggling. Rex sighed.

The sight of the frozen teacher caused a trickle of nerves to crawl up Jessica's spine. If time did start again, there was a good chance they could be caught out here, busted for skipping the pep rally. Then, like the seasons, the mighty grounding cycle would begin again . . .

'Maybe we should wait inside?' she said quietly.

'Were you talking to someone in there?' Rex asked. 'Or in front of anyone who'll notice if you suddenly disappear?'

'No,' Jessica answered. 'We were in the back row, like you guys.'

'So what's the problem?'

'Well, you know,' Jessica said. 'Just in case time starts again, we don't want to get busted for cutting.'

Rex looked at her like she was crazy. 'Time is frozen during broad daylight for the first time in recorded history, and you're worried about skipping a *pep rally*?'

'Um, well . . .'

'Hey, maybe this is like an eclipse!' Dess called across the parking lot.

'How do you mean?' Jonathan said.

Dess stared at Mr. Sanchez as she spoke, as if drawing inspiration from the trig teacher's harried expression. 'You know, an eclipse looks like a little bit of night that happens in the middle of the day. But it's not really night, it's just the moon blocking out the sun.'

'And a long time ago,' Rex added, 'people used to freak out about eclipses, like it was the end of the world.'

'Exactly. But it's not a big deal, just a totally random thing – two objects lining up. Doesn't even last that long.' Dess crossed the lot as she spoke, Jonathan bounding along beside her. 'The trick is not to have a heart attack about it.'

'Can't you go blind from eclipses?' Jonathan said.

'Yeah, true.' Dess glanced up at the dark moon. 'If you're stupid enough to stare at the sun for too long.'

Rex thought about this for a second, then shook his head. 'But you can predict eclipses years in advance, right?'

'Centuries, Rex,' Dess said, rolling her eyes, as if eclipse prediction was something she did for fun in study hall. (Of course, Jessica realized, it probably was.) 'Thousands of years, even. You just do the math, and they happen right on schedule.'

'So where's the schedule, then?' Rex said. 'I repeat: nothing like this has ever been recorded in the lore.'

'The lore's not perfect, Rex,' Jonathan said, bouncing a few feet into the air. 'You can't look up everything. I thought by this point you'd have figured that out.'

Jessica waited for an outburst. Those were fighting words as far as Rex was concerned. And a big fight was *just* what they needed right now.

But Rex only nodded and scratched his chin. 'Yeah, you could be right. Maybe it is just an eclipse or something like that. Totally random.' He looked up into the sky, squinting as his eyes flashed purple.

Jessica dared a quick glance at the dark moon, which was giving her a headache as usual. As far as she could tell, it hadn't moved an inch, or a degree, or whatever. When an eclipse happened, didn't the regular moon keep going across the sky?

'Well, the darklings must have known this was coming.' Melissa spoke up. 'Or at least, they must know something. They're still rocking out, like it's darkling Fourth of July.'

'I guess maybe they've got the schedule, then,' Dess said quietly.

Jonathan pushed himself softly up into the air ten feet or so, staring out across the desert. 'Hey, Rex, could they have *made* this happen?'

'The darklings? Maybe.'

'But it was daylight when it happened, Rex,' Jessica said. 'How could the darklings do anything? Aren't they, like, frozen during regular time?'

Rex nodded slowly. 'Yeah, frozen. And buried deep in the desert to escape the sun. But still . . . maybe.' He shrugged.

Jessica sighed. She didn't know which was freakier, the complete rupture of time itself or Rex acting like he didn't know everything.

The way he'd changed was hard to pin down. On the one hand, he moved with much more confidence, like he was stronger, no longer afraid of the daylight world. But at the same time he could seem sort of dislocated, as if Earth was a new planet to him and every passing car something astonishing to behold.

At times like this she missed the old Rex, who could be depended on to at least *pretend* like he knew what was happening.

What if they were stuck here? What if this really was the end of regular time, at least for the five of them? What were they supposed to do? Spend the rest of their lives scavenging for canned food and being hunted nonstop by the darklings?

The secret hour was magical, but it could also be a trap; Jessica had already experienced enough since moving to Bixby to understand that. If they really were stuck here, she would never see her parents or sister again, except as pale, waxen statues – stiffs. She would never talk to anyone again except the other four midnighters or feel the sun on her face.

And she would never . . .

'Oh, jeez, would you knock it off, Jessica!' Melissa cried. 'You're bumming me out, and I think something's happening.'

Jessica felt a hot flush rising in her face. 'Were you reading my mind?'

Melissa sighed. 'It's not like I have a choice. Just chill out for a second. The darklings are doing something . . .' Her eyes closed, her expression changing from concentration to puzzlement, then suddenly to alarm. 'Flyboy! Get down!' she shouted.

Jessica spun around and saw Jonathan hovering eight feet or so in the air. He had been bouncing up and down with nervous energy, still thinking of this extra blue time as an invitation to fly to his heart's content.

He waved his arms uselessly, still drifting softly upward, powerless to change his course. Falling that far wouldn't be fatal, but the parking lot's asphalt surface was hard enough to twist an ankle or break a leg.

Above him the dark moon was dropping, sweeping across the sky faster than a second hand. The sun peeked out from behind it, a cold and lifeless eye against darkness.

As she ran toward him, Jessica remembered her lessons from flying and from physics class. Jonathan's midnight touch made things almost weightless, but the rest of the laws of motion still applied. If she could throw something heavy up to him, and he caught it while it was headed downward, its momentum would carry him quickly back toward earth.

But Jessica's backpack was still in the gym, and she didn't have anything heavier than loose change in her pockets.

All she could use was her own body.

She ran three steps and leapt up onto the hood of the car nearest him, then jumped from it toward Jonathan's dangling feet. Her fingers grasped his ankle, giving it a yank earthward.

She expected lightness to flow into her, Jonathan's midnight gravity to take the sting out of her fall. But Jessica still felt heavy, tumbling like a brick toward the asphalt.

Then she realized that she wasn't touching Jonathan's skin, only the leg of his jeans. With only seconds before they hit the earth, there was no way to reach up to his bare hands, to share his acrobat's weightlessness. She was dragging him down too fast.

Jessica let go . . . and the ground rushed up.

The blue time ended just as she hit, the Oklahoma sun suddenly blinding as she stumbled across hot, black asphalt. One ankle twisted under her, and she crashed shoulder-first against the side of a car. The collision knocked the breath out of her.

Jessica fell to her knees, clutching her ankle and wondering why an earsplitting shriek had filled the air.

Suddenly Jonathan was crouching beside her.

'Are you okay?' he shouted above the noise.

'Ow. I don't know. What's that . . .?' Jessica's voice trailed off as she realized that the wailing sound was coming from the car next to her. Crashing into it just as the blue time had ended, she'd set off its burglar alarm. 'I did that, didn't I?'

'Don't worry about it. And thanks for saving me.' Jonathan raised up a little from his crouch, peering over the hood of the car. 'Dess is talking to Sanchez. It looks like he's more embarrassed than anything else. I think she's lecturing him about the evils of smoking.' He ducked. 'He's looking over here, though, wondering about the car alarm. Just stay down.'

Jessica tested her sore ankle, wincing as pain shot up her leg. 'No problem with that. So you're okay?'

He nodded. 'You pulled just hard enough; perfect timing. I wound up with only a few inches of regular-gravity acceleration. And I was falling straight down, so I didn't stumble like you did.' He smiled. 'Plus I do have a couple more years' practice at landing than you.'

'Oh.' She sighed. 'Guess I was stupid, trying to save you.'

He took her hand. 'Not stupid at all, Jess. I would have been at least ten feet up if you hadn't given me a yank. That's a long way to fall onto concrete, believe me.' He leaned over and kissed her, then pulled away, smiling. 'That was really fast thinking and excellent use of the laws of motion.'

'Really?'

'Yeah. Like I said, thanks for saving me.'

'From a sprained ankle. Brave me.'

'Could have been worse than a sprain.' He rose slightly and peered over the car again. 'They're all sneaking back into the gym now, Mr. Sanchez too. Looks like no big deal.'

'What about this stupid car alarm? Someone's going to check it out.'

He shook his head. 'I doubt anybody inside can hear it over that chanting. Can you walk?'

Jessica tested her weight on the ankle. '*Ow.*'

'Okay, let's just stay here a few more minutes. The rally's almost over anyhow. We'll blend in when it breaks up, get our stuff, and go to physics.'

'Sure, great.' She winced. 'Only I think I've already had my physics lesson for today.'

'Guess you have,' Jonathan said. He knelt and began to rub her ankle tenderly. At first she flinched at his touch, but then the wrenched muscles began to loosen. 'Guess I have too.'

'How do you mean?'

He sighed. 'Well, it was kind of stupid, flying around when we didn't know what the hell was going on.' Jonathan looked up at the gym roof. 'I could've taken a *real* fall.'

Jessica reached out and brushed his hand with her fingertips. 'That would have sucked.'

'Yeah, well, the next time that happens, I'll listen to Rex.'

She smiled, amazed to hear words 'listen to' and 'Rex' coming out of Jonathan's mouth in the same sentence. But then her mind played back the first half of what he'd said, and she frowned.

'Hang on. The *next* time it happens?'

Jonathan looked at her blankly, then laughed as he worked on her ankle. 'Do you really think that whole thing was just an eclipse or whatever? That it means nothing and will never happen again?'

'Yeah, well.' She swallowed. 'I mean, it *could* be like Dess said. A totally random event . . .'

He chuckled.

'*What*, Jonathan?'

He stopped his massage and looked up at her with a wry smile. 'Yeah, sure, could be totally random. Just like all the other totally random stuff that's happened since you arrived in Bixby.' He started counting on his fingers. 'The darklings go crazy and try to kill you, the Broken Arrows kidnap Rex, Madeleine reappears after fifty years in hiding . . . How much more random could things get?'

The car alarm next to them switched off with a two-syllable *dweeping* sound, finally running out of steam.

'Great,' Jessica said softly into the sudden, ringing silence. 'The flame-bringer rides again.'

4

MAJORETTE

'Don't worry, I'll take you over to Madeleine's at midnight.'

'Yeah, sure,' Jessica answered. 'After you guys have already talked about all the important stuff this afternoon.'

Both Dess and Jonathan sighed and looked away, apparently tired of her whining.

Jessica rubbed her ankle, which wasn't helping her mood. It had been getting gradually better all day, but it still twinged with pain. The three of them were sitting on the school's front steps. Around them students were spilling out of Bixby High, slowly sorting themselves among the line of idling school buses. The lawn was dotted with clusters of people saying goodbye or arranging rides home. The sound of a tuba warming up for band practice drifted across the football field.

Jessica, of course, was waiting for her father to pick her up for a final night of being grounded.

'You won't be missing anything, Jess,' Dess said. 'Madeleine probably doesn't know any more about what happened this morning than we do. I doubt this is a mindcaster issue.'

'But she's all old and stuff,' Jessica said.

'Yeah, but if anything like this ever happened before, it wasn't fifty years ago. More like five thousand, if Rex doesn't know about it.' Dess nodded slowly, rubbing her hands together. 'My guess is, this is a job for a polymath.'

'But doesn't she have all those memories in her head?' Jessica said. 'All that stuff passed on from mindcasters in the olden days?'

Dess seemed to shiver a bit, and Jessica cursed herself for bringing up the subject of mindcasters and memories. Madeleine had also messed with Dess's brain, trying to keep her existence a secret from the darklings.

After an uncomfortable silence, Dess answered. 'Anything this big would be in the lore. They wouldn't just use memory, would they?' She shrugged. 'But maybe she did scoop some info from the darklings this morning. I can't wait to ask her if that blue time was shaped funny.'

'Shaped funny?'

Dess's eyes lit up. 'Yeah, like, did it go all the way to the edge of Bixby County? Or was it smaller than a normal midnight? Like . . . focused in some particular places.'

'Why would it be?'

Dess shrugged. 'That's just the way the blue time is: it has a shape.'

Not for the first time, Jessica tried to wrap her head around that concept. These days Dess talked about the midnight hour more like it was a place than a time. She was always playing with maps, and even as they sat there, she was fiddling – as usual – with her electronic gadget that spat out coordinates.

To Jessica it seemed weird that the blue time only went so

far, then just stopped, like the edge of the world the way people imagined it before they realized it was round.

'So, Dess,' she said. 'What would happen if you went all the way to the edge of Bixby at midnight and then went just a *little* farther?'

'You mean go past the midnight boundary? You wouldn't . . . or couldn't. Time's frozen out there. So from your perspective, midnight would end as you took that step. But if another midnighter was watching you, they'd see you freeze up for the rest of the hour, just out of reach.'

Jessica's head spun with that image for a moment. 'So midnight's, like, a bubble around us?'

'You mean a sphere? Well, it's lumpy and uneven, but yeah.'

'But say you were right on the border when midnight fell. Would, like, half of you keep moving and half of you freeze up?'

'And then you'd slide into two pieces,' Jonathan added. 'Like those guys in samurai movies?'

'Um, I guess I don't know.' Dess laughed. 'Why don't you try it and tell me?'

'Here they come,' Jonathan said.

Rex and Melissa were making their unhurried way through the throng, their fingertips touching lightly, their expressions tranquil. As usual these days, the crowd seemed to have no effect on Melissa. She ignored the stares of the few freshmen who were freaked out by her scarred face, gliding past them as serene as a movie star on a red carpet.

Dess sighed. 'I can see why you're bummed, Jess. You don't get to spend the afternoon drinking skanky tea and putting up with *two* mindcasters.' She rose to her feet, her long skirt rustling. 'See you.'

'Yeah, really,' Jonathan said. 'You're lucky to miss this.' He gave Jessica's hand a squeeze and stood.

'Yeah, *so* lucky,' Jessica said. 'If only I could be grounded all the time.'

She watched the four of them walk away, chewing her lip and cursing her parents' calendar logic. Didn't they know she had more important things to do than be grounded these days?

For the first time ever, her dad was late.

He had faithfully picked up Jessica every day of her grounding, on the theory that left to ride the school bus, she would fall back into her criminal ways. But Don Day's car wasn't anywhere to be seen among the crawling traffic of parents picking up their kids.

Maybe after all the debate about exactly how long her grounding should last, he had gotten confused about whether it ended today or not.

For this morning's argument Jessica herself had gone with the werewolf model: a month was twenty-eight days, which meant that she should have been ungrounded *last* night. But her parents had cruelly opted for the calendar month, and as her father liked to repeat: 'Thirty days hath September (April, June, and November).'

Of course, it *still* wasn't fair that she was grounded tonight. Jessica had been detained and returned to parental custody (technically not arrested) on a Saturday night. So thirty days later should be a Monday night, to any sane person. But both her parents had raised the technical point that she'd been brought home Sunday morning, and so her grounding really hadn't begun until Sunday night, which meant that it was Tuesday before her sentence would be served.

Jessica had kept arguing until her dad had gotten angry and threatened to invoke the fact that most months were thirty-one days, which meant he could in good conscience extend her grounding until Wednesday. Even Mom had rolled her eyes at that one, but Jessica had finally realized she was beaten.

She looked at her watch, which she'd reset to regular Bixby time – it had gained twenty minutes during the eclipse. Her bus would be leaving soon. If she got on it and her father showed up looking for her later, he would go ballistic and ground her again. Of course, maybe this was all a trick to make her miss the bus, forcing her to walk home so then she could be re-grounded for showing up late.

Unless she'd forgotten something. Jessica searched her memory for any change in plans. Since the weird events of this morning, her mind had been a little vague. All day she'd kept expecting time to freeze again and blue amber to capture everyone around her. Every lull in the noise of lunchtime had made her jump as she'd wondered if the world of motion and sunlight and other human beings was fading out for good.

Finally Jessica spotted the familiar car, Beth's head visible in the front seat next to her father's, and suddenly she remembered why he was late. Beth had demanded to be picked up at the junior high school on the other side of town so she wouldn't have to walk home in her humiliating new marching band uniform.

'Oh, right,' Jess said, smiling. Her little sister was a majorette again.

She ran through the horde of cars, opened the door, and slid herself into the backseat.

Beth whirled around. 'Not *one* word.'

Jessica smiled at her. 'I was just going to say that you look ravishing in purple and gold.'

'Dad! She's making fun of me!' She turned to him. 'You said she wasn't supposed to make fun of me!'

'Jess . . .'

'I just said *ravishing*. Ravishing is not a bad thing. Dad, explain to Beth how poor kids in Bangladesh would love to wear such a ravishing costume.'

'Stop talking about it, Jess!' Beth cried.

'*Girls* . . .' Don Day's tone was still only vaguely threatening as he concentrated on guiding the car out of the traffic jam.

'Could you just ground her again and get it over with!' Beth shouted.

'Beth! That is *so* not cool!'

'Will both of you please be quiet!' their father pleaded. In an attempt to be scary he fixed Jessica with a stern look as he backed the car up into the clear, then put it into forward gear, and stared at Beth for a meaningful second before accelerating out onto the road.

Jessica settled back into her seat, unbeaten. 'Anyway, I'm not even really grounded right now.'

'Yes, you are,' Beth said.

'Okay, I am.' Jessica waited for a moment, then played her final trump card. 'So, Dad, you know my one night a week off from my grounding? Could I have it, say . . . tonight?' She sat back and smiled. Her parents had granted her this limited reprieve a few days after she'd been brought home by the police. One day a week – a solemn promise. It had been a little suspicious, Mom agreeing to change a punishment once it had been meted out, especially now that Jessica knew what Rex and Melissa could get up to with people's minds.

But at the moment Jessica was willing to use the exception for all it was worth.

'That is so lame,' Beth said. 'Dad, tell her that's lame.'

'That is pretty lame, Jess.'

'But you said one day a week.'

'And you've taken four free days. And you were grounded a month, which is four weeks.'

Jessica's jaw dropped open at this unjust change of definition. 'But you said, and I quote, 'Thirty days hath—''

'That's *enough*, Jessica.' His voice had suddenly moved to fully threatening mode. 'Or September will have *sixty* days this year.'

Jessica swallowed. For once, he sounded like he really meant it.

Beth turned from the front seat and gave Jessica a worried look, hostilities briefly suspended by their father's outburst. Since coming to Bixby, Don Day had been jobless, a condition that had gradually turned into shiftless, then shirtless, and finally spineless. It had been a while since he'd gotten up the energy to raise his voice.

In fact, Jessica realized, it had been exactly thirty days – he'd yelled a lot when the police had brought her home for breaking Bixby's curfew with Jonathan. Maybe the end of the grounding was freaking him out and the concept of her being free to wander the streets of Bixby between the hours of three and 10 P.M. was too much for him. He wasn't like Mom, too tired out from having to impress her new bosses to obsess over anything but work.

Maybe it was time to change the subject.

'So, Beth, how was band practice?' she asked.

'It was lame.'

'You used to like it.'

Beth turned toward the front of the car again and didn't answer.

Jessica frowned, wishing she hadn't made fun of Beth's uniform. It was an old habit, from the days when Beth could take being teased without exploding.

Two years ago, back in Chicago, Beth had been a champion majorette. She could stick a three-turn every time and do a hundred thumb flips per minute, and she came home from camp every summer with tons of ribbons. But halfway through being eleven years old, she'd declared majorettes totally lame and exchanged marching band for being Ms. Social. Since the move down to Bixby, she hadn't even unpacked her baton-twirling trophies. Jessica had found herself missing the little silvery majorettes lined up on their marble pedestals, just like she missed the younger, happier Beth of the old days.

But having made zero friends in Bixby had apparently changed Beth's mind about majorettes. Maybe being in the marching band was a big deal at Bixby Junior High. Or maybe at this point she simply didn't know what else to do.

Seeing Beth in a gaudy costume after two years was so strange, as if time had broken down completely this morning and was heading backward now.

'Listen, you want to practice together later?' Jessica said. 'I mean, I *think* I'm allowed to go in the backyard.'

'Sure,' her father piped up.

'Yes, Jess, that would be great.' Beth turned around to face her again. 'Because it's *so* important to have an assistant while baton twirling.'

'All right. Fine. Just trying to be helpful.'

'And mature. Don't forget mature.'

'I said fine.'

Beth kept looking at her, the gold piping around her collar flashing in the sun.

'What's your problem?' Jessica finally asked.

'Why do you think I had Dad pick me up today?'

Jessica sighed. 'Because you look so ravishing?'

'No, retard. I could have changed at school.' She dropped her voice. 'It was because of you.'

Jessica shot a puzzled look toward the back of her father's head. Was Beth talking about Jonathan? Since Jess had introduced the two of them, she'd figured Beth was on her side on the secret boyfriend front. At least Beth hadn't told Mom and Dad about his late-night visits or how Jessica skipped out at night sometimes.

'What do you mean, Beth?'

'Just to make sure you know.'

'Know *what*?'

'That even though you're not grounded anymore, I've still got my eye on you.'

Jessica sighed again. 'Beth, quit being weird. Dad, tell Beth to quit being weird.'

Don Day was silent for a moment. Finally he said, 'Well, Jessica, I kind of know what she means. After all, I've got my eye on you too.'

5

DREGS

'Milk, no sugar, correct?'

'Yes, please.' Dess smiled politely, but the bitter taste of Madeleine's tea was already trickling through her imagination, the acid flavor of betrayal on her tongue.

By rights, this secret place should have been *her* playground. Dess was the one who had found Madeleine, after all. She'd struggled through sleepless nights to decode the weird dreams the old mindcaster had sent her; she was the one who'd *done the math*.

But it had all been in the service of Melissa and Rex. They were the ones really enjoying themselves here in Madeleine's crepuscular contortion, her little secret hideaway. Rex finally had all the lore he could possibly want. Years of reading awaited him in this house, every document the surviving midnighters of the last generation had managed to salvage when they'd been forced into hiding.

And Melissa . . . she had *totally* scored.

Dess noticed that as Melissa took her cup and saucer from Madeleine's hand, the two mindcasters' fingers brushed for a moment. Then they both smirked at some shared, silent joke.

The sight made her flesh crawl. The two of them communicated mostly by mindcasting, rarely uttering a word to each other. Dess wondered what they were saying to each other right now.

On the other side of the big dining table, Rex was also watching them. Besides Rex, Madeleine was the only person whom Melissa allowed to touch her – not that anyone else would *want* to – but he didn't seem jealous of little moments like this one. It was those long sessions, when the two mindcasters sat for hours at a stretch with eyes closed and fingers interlocked, that made Rex start to get all territorial.

Of course, Melissa did have some catching up to do. Growing up as a lone mindcaster, she'd never learned the old tricks that should have been taught to her by the previous generation. A trove had awaited her inside Madeleine's brain – the thousands of years of memories, techniques, and gossip accumulated since the first mindcasters had learned how to pass knowledge from hand to hand.

Dess wondered how *that* math worked. If every generation of mindcasters took all their memories and forwarded them onto the next bunch, who then passed theirs onto the next, who added *their* memories, and so on . . . wouldn't the pile get too big at some point? Wouldn't all that knowledge become less and less stable, like building blocks stacked higher and higher, until the whole thing collapsed at once?

Maybe the memories got fuzzier as you went back in time, a blurry aggregate of thoughts and feelings, like the symbols that meteorologists used to represent weather. Dess imagined a big *H* hovering over Madeleine's house, warning of a high-pressure center of bitchiness.

'Don't rattle the cup when you stir, Jonathan!'

Speaking of which, Dess thought as Jonathan exchanged an eye roll with her. He kept stirring his tea, adopting a sarcastic little spoon twirl that Madeleine didn't seem to notice.

At least they didn't have to edit their thoughts here. Madeleine's house was built on a whopping big crepuscular contortion, a wrinkle in the blue time that made it almost impossible to plunder anyone's mind without physical contact. It was like living next to a power line that screwed up your TV reception.

This contortion was the only thing that had protected Madeleine for the last five decades. She was invisible to the darklings here, hidden along with her antiques and books, all the leftovers from the days when midnighters had ruled Bixby instead of skulking in the shadows.

Dess looked at the junk piled in the corners of the room, her mind automatically dissecting the angles of tridecagrams in rusted steel, all the patterns of thirteens and thirty-nines that had once guarded the town's key citizens. Some of the junk was pretty interesting, engraved with old-timey tridecalogisms like *accelerograph* and *paterfamilias*. She had to admit: Rex and Melissa weren't the only ones who'd found stuff to play with here.

Still, it bugged Dess that those two had gotten anything at all out of *her* discovery. Especially since the sweaty work of protecting Madeleine had been left to Dess, Jessica, and Jonathan. The three had spent hours making a big pile of the least-rusty darkling defenses. Then Dess had made sure every piece had its own brand-new thirteen-letter name and mounted them all around the house as a last line of protection should the darklings ever find Madeleine's hiding place.

And what thanks had they gotten? Mostly getting yelled at for making too much noise.

'So, now that we all have tea,' Madeleine pronounced, 'perhaps we should discuss the little incident this morning.'

'About time,' Dess muttered. Her fingers traced the deep scratches in the wood of the table. It had been completely covered by big, *heavy* iron tridecagrams before she'd cleared the room to make it habitable.

Madeleine arched an eyebrow. 'Well, then, Desdemona. Since you're feeling feisty, perhaps you'd like to start.'

'Me? What do I know about it? We were sort of hoping you could tell us something.'

'But surely you have something numerate to contribute?'

Dess sighed. 'Well, we checked Rex's fancy watch after the eclipse was over. He resets it every morning to the time on Geostationary, which is *always* perfect.' She felt the comforting weight of the GPS device in her pocket. 'Turns out it had gained twenty-one minutes and thirty-six seconds – that was the total length of time the dark moon was up. That's nine times 144 seconds, which is a very darkling number. Must mean something.'

'But you don't know what?' Madeleine said.

'Not yet.' Dess sipped at her tea. Maybe the bitter taste of it would focus her mind on the problem.

'There's nothing like this in the lore,' Rex piped up. 'Not that I've read. You don't have any old memories that would help, do you?'

Madeleine took a long while to respond, as if she was filtering out an answer from the centuries of thought echoes in her head. *Voices in her head* . . . That didn't sound particularly sane. Maybe the weight of all those piled-up memories had driven Madeleine madder and madder as she'd hidden in this house, alone. Maybe what mindcasters really passed on was a trick for acting serene and knowing when all of them, including Madeleine and Melissa, were actually as nutty as bat guano.

Dess smiled to herself. Maybe Madeleine could use a new mental nickname.

'No, Rex,' Maddy finally said. 'Like the lore, our memories reveal nothing of these events. I'm certain this is all quite unprecedented.'

Dess allowed herself a smirk. Of course history wasn't going to be any help. This was a job for numbers, maps, and GPS precision.

'That's what I was afraid of,' Rex said glumly.

'Afraid, Rex?' Madeleine snapped. 'Chicken-fried baloney! In my day, seers didn't speak of being afraid. They spoke of action!'

It was Rex's turn to roll his eyes. He covered the expression by raising his own teacup and wincing at the acid taste.

Some mind reader, Dess thought. Maddy didn't even know that everyone hated her tea.

'Well,' Jonathan said. 'You must have sensed something while the eclipse was happening. Melissa said the darklings were celebrating. You think they were expecting this to happen?'

'Ah, now you're headed in the right direction,' Maddy said.

Rex shot Jonathan an annoyed look for asking the obvious next question and scoring extra Maddy credit for it.

Very clever, Dess thought. The old mindcaster was good at playing the boys against each other. Dess had found a few old photographs of a youthful Madeleine around the house, and she'd been quite the 1940s cutie.

Of course, it was worth remembering that Maddy had been the one to spill the beans back then, coughing up the secrets of the blue time to a daylighter, Grandpa Grayfoot (probably one of her boyfriends). So in theory she could be blamed for the whole mess since: the creation of the halfling, the extermination of the previous generation of midnighters, and the fact that the five of them had been left orphaned and clueless.

'So what did you taste?' Rex asked.

Maddy paused dramatically, then looked across the table at her pupil.

Melissa stopped chewing her lip and said, 'We aren't sure yet. We haven't had a chance to' – she glanced at Rex – 'compare notes.'

'But there were some ruptures,' Maddy said. 'Places where the false midnight felt very thin.'

'Places?' Dess asked, her ears perking up. Places could be expressed as longitude and latitude – sweet numbers. 'You mean like this crepuscular contortion?'

Maddy nodded. 'Yes, but not hiding places. Spots where the barrier between the blue world and ours seemed almost to disappear.'

'Oh.' One hand inside her jacket pocket, Dess gripped Geostationary harder. 'You mean like Sheriff Michaels?'

'Sheriff Michaels?' Jonathan asked. 'That guy who disappeared?'

Everyone was quiet for a moment.

Some time ago – before Jessica, or even Jonathan, had moved to Bixby – the town sheriff had vanished out in the desert. Only his gun and badge had been found, along with his teeth and all their fillings – the darkling-proof, high-tech alloys of dentistry.

The rumor was he'd been killed by drug dealers, but between Rex's lore and her careful mapping of the blue time, Dess understood what had really happened.

She cleared her throat. 'Well, you know that darklings have to eat, right? Even if they only live one hour in twenty-five, predators still need prey to stay alive. Normal animals can step through into the blue time if they're in the wrong spot at exactly midnight. So darklings mostly eat unlucky rabbits and cows, but every once in a while a human being slips through.'

'Hmmph,' Madeleine said. 'In my day, people knew where not to be at midnight.'

'Yeah, well, your day got canceled,' Dess said.

'Wait a second,' Jonathan said. 'I thought darklings couldn't hurt normal people.'

Dess shook her head. 'Once you poke through into midnight, you're part of that world for that hour. And eligible to join the darkling food chain.'

Madeleine nodded. 'We sometimes brought daylighter allies through so that they could see the blue time for themselves. A special treat. The strange thing was, once that midnight ended, they became frozen, just like darklings during normal time. They stayed that way until the sun struck them.'

'Like Anathea,' Jonathan said softly. 'Trapped in midnight.'

'Great, so we could have civilians running around in the blue time,' Rex muttered. 'And you said the eclipse was focused around these contortions?'

Slowly Madeleine's wrinkled hand drew shapes on the scratched table. 'Not exactly, Rex. What the eclipse seemed to do was make more of them.'

'*Make* them?' Dess said. The wrinkles in midnight were baked into the map with numbers. 'You can't just change longitude and latitude like they're property lines!'

'And the darklings moved toward the ruptures,' Melissa added quietly. 'They could feel them too.'

Maddy stood, walking around the table to place a hand on Melissa's shoulder. 'But we haven't compared experiences yet. We'll tell you when we know more. I'm sure you can amuse yourselves.'

The two headed up to the attic together.

Rex looked screamingly jealous for an ill-concealed moment, then got all official. 'Okay. I'll check some of your older lore books,' he said to Maddy's departing footsteps. 'Just in case.'

Dess sighed. 'And while those two are having mindcaster time, I'm going to take a look at some maps.'

Rex looked at Jonathan, raising one eyebrow. Without Jessica around, Flyboy was sort of hopeless – couldn't read lore, couldn't do math, and here in the afternoon couldn't even fly. Dess felt sorry for him. What was he supposed to do? Wash the curtains?

'Um, I was wondering,' Jonathan sputtered. 'Does she have a TV?'

The house was starting to smell less old and musty, as if having its first visitors in half a century had breathed some life into it. But whenever Dess moved anything, pulled a book or map from the shelves, dust rose into the air, threatening to make her sneeze. Going home from a long night's work here, her fingers always felt dry and brittle, as if the ancient, thirsty dust had sucked the moisture from them.

While cleaning out the dining room, Dess had discovered a cache of Maddy's maps, yellowing rolls of heavy paper that practically crumbled in your hands. The oldest were annotated in Spanish, which gave Flyboy some translating to do, though he found the spindly, old-time handwriting hard going. Of course, what Dess was after wasn't really the words. The secret hour was centered at exactly 36 degrees north latitude and 96 west longitude, and all the weirdness of Bixby flowed from those coordinates. This was all about the numbers.

Dess's most interesting discovery was how the early midnighters' maps compared with more recent efforts. For one thing, in the old days they hadn't invented GPS or decent clocks yet and had to rely on star readings and guesswork to plug the numbers in. So as you went further back, everything looked more and more warped and distorted, as if they'd been looking at the world through a Coke bottle. And of course, as time had passed, the early midnighters had explored more of the secret hour. Every century the maps of midnight's domain grew to cover a greater part of southeastern Oklahoma, or Indian Territory, or Mexico – depending on who'd stolen what last.

She'd been happily sitting at the dining table for an hour, absorbed in the slow progress of midnighter cartography, when a voice, joined by a cool hand on her shoulder, almost made her jump out of her skin.

'Desdemona?'

'Jeez! Scare me, why don't you?' Dess stared at Maddy's hand accusingly. At least the mindcaster hadn't touched her bare flesh.

'Pardon me, then.' The wrinkled hand withdrew. 'I just thought you might want to see this.'

Madeleine placed a roll of paper on the table. It was a map from the 1930s, the first map Maddy had ever shared with Dess, back when it had just been the two of them. But it was covered now with a layer of colored swirls, as if some kid had stuck red and blue pencils to a Ouija board pointer and let it roam freely.

'You guys drew on this?' Dess said angrily, but after a few seconds of staring, the map's new eddies and whorls began to engage her brain. The mindcasters' marks seemed to flesh out the usual contortions of midnight, adding another dimension to the map. It was like seeing the latest version of a familiar video game, the same old characters suddenly rendered in high resolution. 'Oh,' Dess added.

'You were right, you know,' Maddy said softly.

Dess didn't take her eyes from the map. 'About what?'

'I don't think the lore or memories will help us much. As you suspected, this is a riddle best solved by a polymath.'

Dess swallowed. Had the old woman sneaked a quick peek into her brain when she'd touched Dess's leather jacket? 'Gee, Maddy, I don't remember saying anything about that.'

Madeleine only smirked at the nickname. 'Sometimes, Dessy, it doesn't require mind reading to know what someone is thinking.'

Dessy? Jeez. Maddy's revenge hadn't taken very long.

'Well, thanks. I'll take a closer look at this when I get a chance.' Like, the moment Madeleine was out of sight.

The old mindcaster smiled. 'Let me know what you find, Desdemona.'

'Hey, there's something wrong with your TV!' Jonathan called. He was hunched over the giant set in the living room, a wood-paneled monstrosity that he'd spent the last hour freeing from a pile of thirty-nine-patterned fire grates.

Dess looked over at the machine and smirked. She was glad to see that Maddy didn't harbor any grudges against television. Last Dess had heard, Madeleine blamed TV – and air-conditioning, of course – for the destruction of the midnighters fifty years before. Something about watching the tube instead of the kids.

Madeleine stared archly into the weirdly rounded screen. It looked more like a goldfish bowl filled with murky water than a TV.

'Chicken-fried baloney, Jonathan. It's working fine.' She turned and strode from the room, adding over her shoulder, 'Just takes a while to warm up. In my day, young people were more patient.'

Jonathan looked dubious, but something was definitely happening in the television's depths: a flicker of light had appeared in the center of the screen. It grew slowly, like a fire spreading through a pile of damp leaves, until it filled the dark glass with a blurry image.

'Man,' he said softly. 'Black and white.'

'Looks more like gray and gray,' Dess said. The screen was mostly full of snow. You could barely make out the weather guy standing in front of a map, the sweeping Doppler radar circling behind him looking very out of place on the ancient TV.

Jonathan turned a big dial that went *ka-thunk*, and the screen filled with static. As he searched in vain for a channel with a better picture, or any picture at all, Dess watched the little gray pixels dance. She remembered some weird factoid about those little dots of static, how they were the remnants of the most perfectly random thing in all of nature . . .

Finally Jonathan sighed and *ka-thunked* his way back to the local news.

Dess tuned out the anchor's voice and took the last sip of her lukewarm tea, a tiny glob of leaves catching in her teeth. The details of the factoid came back to her now: there'd been something on the Discovery Channel (the only television that Dess ever watched) about how the snow on old TVs actually showed leftover radiation from the big bang, the explosion that had made the universe. That's why the dots were perfectly random – they were the result of a perfect explosion.

Well, *almost* perfect. The big bang, after all, had left a few billion clumpy bits of matter that had turned into galaxies and clusters of galaxies. The universe was lumpy, sort of like . . . tea leaves.

Or the blue time.

Dess's eyes lit up. She looked down at the map Madeleine had given her. The new shapes scrawled across it were spirals and pinwheels – like galaxies, the dregs of the big bang.

Maybe the secret hour had been created by some sort of explosion, or at least something violent and big bangish, with a similar mix of chaos and order, randomness and patterns.

Dess looked down into her cup. Cosmology was like reading tea leaves, figuring out the future by looking at the remnants of the past. Except unlike tea leaves, telescopes actually *worked*. You could tell where the universe was headed based on the dregs of the big bang.

Maybe she could look at these old maps and figure out what the future of the blue time was.

'Oh, right,' Dess said suddenly. Math happiness wavered in her mind as she remembered something else from that same Discovery Channel show.

The universe hadn't been created stable. It was still expanding from the bang, all its parts moving gradually away from the center. She looked at her old maps – and saw again how as the centuries passed, the secret hour always seemed to cover a larger area. Maybe it wasn't just that the old midnighters had explored more . . . maybe the blue time had actually grown *bigger*.

Dess swallowed, suddenly remembering one more thing about the universe. One day it would end, scientists said, either by spreading out into mush, a big whimper, or when gravity pulled it all together again into a big crunch.

Nobody knew which way it was going yet, but someday there would definitely come a big Game Over.

'Hey, Dess, check this out.'

Jonathan's voice cut through her reverie, and Dess snapped from the end of the universe back into late-afternoon light and musty Maddy-house smells. Jonathan was standing beside her, pointing at the TV. A blurry older woman was talking about how her granddaughter had disappeared.

It cut back to the anchor, who started yammering about a police hotline, an ongoing search, state troopers bringing in dogs. Dess hardly listened, but that word kept being repeated in various forms . . . *disappearing girl, strange disappearance, she just disappeared*.

'Right in front of her grandma's eyes,' Jonathan said. 'As in, she was there one moment and gone the next.'

'Crap,' Dess said. 'When?'

'This morning,' Jonathan whispered. 'Around 9 A.M.'

'Where?'

He leaned over the map Maddy had brought down, outstretched hand sliding across to a cluster of whorls in the northwest corner. 'They said it was near Jenks, on the railroad tracks.' His fingers found the hatched path of the rail line, old enough to be included on an eighty-year-old map. The tiny town of Jenks was labeled there too.

Dess pushed his hand away, and her pencil moved to the spot, scribbling calculations. Rough and hand-drawn though they were, the new shapes that Maddy and Melissa had scrawled possessed their own logic, were ruled by their own patterns and laws. It *was* sort of like mapping the stars, seemingly random points of light that added up to show you the big picture – as long as you did the math right.

The whorls and eddies seemed to rise up from the paper and enter Dess, running like sugar-rushing hamsters on all the wheels of her brain. They made her dizzy, made her fingers tremble as they tried to record her intuitive leaps.

But finally they began to come into focus . . .

After five long minutes she leaned back exhausted, pointing. 'This is where it's broken.'

'Where what's broken?'

'The blue time. It's starting to snap, Jonathan, probably to break down completely. But some coordinates will go quicker than others. And anyone who's standing around in the wrong place when they do . . .'

Jonathan sat down next to her, staring at the map with its chaos of scribbled numbers and mindcaster swirls. 'So what happened to that girl?'

'*Midnight* happened to her, Jonathan. It opened up and swallowed her.'

'So she's where now?'

'Well, she should have come out of it when time started again, when the sun hit her. Unless she was taken somewhere.'

'Melissa said the darklings were headed that way.'

Dess blinked. 'They only had twenty-one minutes and thirty-six seconds.'

'So she might still be okay?'

'Yeah, probably. Unless . . .'

Part of Dess's brain wanted to explain the whole thing to Jonathan: about snow on TV screens, the big bang, and the shapes of galaxies and tea leaves. About how you could know how something was going to happen in the future by looking into the dregs of the past, so maybe the darklings had predicted *exactly* where it would happen, exactly where their young prey would fall between the cracks of time. They could have lured her away to someplace dark and underground . . .

She didn't have a chance to say a word before another set of images rushed into her mind – also straight from the Discovery Channel – and Dess found herself silent and shivering in her chair.

She wasn't thinking about the big bang anymore.

She was thinking about the food chain.

6

11:36 P.M.

SPEED BUMP

Jonathan sat in his father's car, drumming on the steering wheel. Jessica was late. Halfway down the block, he could see her window still glowing. She hadn't even turned her lights off yet.

What was she waiting for? Tonight every second counted.

On the phone with Jessica this afternoon, the five of them had planned everything to the minute: Jonathan had driven here instead of flying during the secret hour. Jessica was supposed to sneak out at eleven-thirty, leaving time to get within a mile of the spot where Cassie Flinders had disappeared. Then when midnight fell, they'd be at most a few jumps away.

Dess, Rex, and Melissa were already there, which made it doubly important to stay on schedule. Jenks wasn't exactly the badlands, and the three were well armed with clean steel, but the spot was too far from the city's center for them to survive forever without the flame-bringer's protection.

He looked at his watch – 11:38. 'Where are you, Jessica?'

The words echoed in his mind, and Jonathan remembered what they'd kept saying on the evening news: *Where is Cassie Flinders?*

If Dess was right, the lost girl had slipped into the blue time.

Jonathan let out a breath through his teeth – a daylighter walking around in their private world. Just when he thought he understood the secret hour, it threw another curveball.

Of course, it was nothing like the curveball that reality had thrown Cassie Flinders.

Rex and Madeleine kept talking like she might be okay. Cassie could have wandered off during the eclipse and wound up somewhere out of the sun's reach, frozen in darkness, like the darklings were during daylight hours. And once midnight fell, she would awake again, and Melissa would find her, no problem. All they had to do was protect her until the secret hour ended, when a blast from Jessica's flashlight or – if that didn't work – the eventual arrival of sunrise would push her back into regular time.

Of course, there was also the possibility that Cassie hadn't wandered off – that she'd been taken. If the darklings had actually known in advance where the blue time was going to wrinkle, they could have flown straight to the spot and taken her away, deep into the desert where no one would ever find her again.

There was a third possibility as well: they could have simply eaten her on the spot, right in front of her grandmother's frozen, unseeing eyes.

'Come *on*, Jessica . . .' He tapped one fist against the hard, cold metal of the dashboard.

An endless, whispered count of sixty later, Jonathan swore, checked the rearview mirror for any sign of curfew-sniffing cop cars, and stepped out into the cold autumn air.

*

New flower beds edged Jessica's house, her father's latest project. He was getting into gardening in a big way, she'd said, trying to grow all the vegetables the family ate. Apparently he hadn't noticed that the season was changing into fall, the ground turning cold and hard at night.

Jonathan tried to step lightly on the overturned earth, wondering if Don Day's gardening efforts weren't just an excuse to look for footprints under Jessica's window. Jonathan cursed his Flatland heaviness; in the blue time he could have just floated over to the sill.

Voices. He ducked down.

He could hear Jessica speak, then someone answering. Muffled through the window, the voice's high-pitched insistence reminded Jonathan of a mosquito trapped under a glass.

His heartbeat settled a little. Probably only Beth. He eased his head up to peer inside.

They both sat on the bed, no parents in sight. Jessica was dressed, her little sister huddled in pajamas. Beth was still talking, waving her hands around frantically, as if warding off an attack of houseflies. Jonathan saw Jessica glance over at her bedside clock, where the approach of midnight was clearly displayed.

Why didn't Jessica just get rid of her? On a school night it had to be past Beth's bedtime by now.

Jonathan raised a fist to the glass, steeling himself to knock. Jessica wouldn't appreciate him announcing his presence in front of the little sister, especially on the very last night of her grounding. But Beth wouldn't tell her parents – Jessica's sister wasn't that uncool.

Besides, there were more important things at stake here.

According to the news, Cassie Flinders was thirteen, about the same age that Anathea had been when the darklings had taken her. Jonathan remembered how small she had been, almost disappearing into the darkling body they had grafted to her.

Of course, Cassie was no seer. She couldn't read the lore; the darklings wouldn't bother to make a halfling out of her. She wouldn't last very long in the blue time, except maybe for the fillings in her teeth.

He knocked.

Both sisters jumped at the noise, the sound of Beth's voice choking off mid-sentence. She stared at Jonathan's face in the window for a moment, then focused a cold gaze on Jessica.

As Jonathan pushed the sash up, he heard her whisper, 'I *knew* it!'

Jessica just stared at him.

'Hey, guys,' he said.

'Well, hey there, Jonathan,' Beth said sweetly. 'Just dropping by?'

'Jonathan!' Jessica groaned. 'Couldn't you have . . .' Her voice trailed off.

He climbed in and looked from one sister to the other. Beth's eyes were narrowed, and Jess was staring at the floor and shaking her head. He sighed. 'Look, I'm really sorry to interrupt, Beth. But something's come up. Something *important.*' He looked at Jessica to emphasize that last word.

'You're sneaking out *tonight?*' Beth said, her whispering only making the words harsher. 'You've only got one more day, Jess. Do you want to get grounded again?'

'Believe me,' Jessica said. 'I really don't.'

'Listen, Beth, I only need to borrow your sister for . . .'

Jonathan glanced at the clock. 'Eighteen minutes. I promise she'll be back by then.'

Jessica closed her eyes as Beth's stare swung across to the clock.

'Eighteen minutes?' Beth said.

Jonathan swallowed. Jessica's little sister didn't know anything about the blue time, of course, but she had an uncanny way of making you think she did. 'Yeah. More or less.'

Jessica stood, pulling her jacket from the bed. 'Come on. Let's just go.'

'*Jessica,*' Beth whined.

'Look,' Jessica said tiredly. 'If you're going to tell Mom and Dad, go ahead. I don't have time for this.'

'Jess, I don't *want* you to be in trouble,' Beth whispered, tears welling up in her eyes. 'I just want to know what's going on with you.'

'I'm sorry, okay?' Jessica paused, as if struggling for words. 'But I need to get out of here *right now*, and I can't explain why.'

'And you're going to sneak out right in front of me?' Beth crossed her arms. 'So I'll be in trouble too when you get caught?'

'That's *your* fault, Beth. I told you to leave half an hour ago.'

'Can you at least explain when you come back . . . in eighteen minutes?'

Jessica sighed. 'Sorry, Beth, I'd love to. I just can't.'

'Got your flashlight?' Jonathan said, one foot already out the window.

She thumped a bulge in her jacket. 'Yeah, right here.'

They slipped out, dropping to the soft earth of the garden.

Jonathan heard one last complaint cut off by Jessica's sliding the window closed and thought again how he couldn't wait for midnight gravity to arrive. Finally he would be unstuck from Flatland, able to fly again, and all little sisters would be mutely frozen.

And the darklings will come to life, he realized, checking his watch as they jogged toward the car.

Midnight was coming, all right. Way too soon.

'Why did you have to say that?'

'Say what?'

'That thing about eighteen minutes exactly,' Jessica said. 'It was kind of obvious, don't you think?'

Jonathan shrugged. The clock had said 11:42, and he could fly Jess back here by the end of the secret hour, midnight on the dot. He did see her point, though. Maybe he had been a little too precise about exactly when Jessica would return.

He sighed, watching a flattened armadillo flash past on the road. Listening to Dess talk math all afternoon had crowded his brain with numbers. 'What's the difference, anyway?'

'Beth's starting to figure out that midnight's important.' Jessica was staring out the passenger window. 'She's noticed that I'm always getting ready to leave around twelve, and she's started showing up just before the secret hour starts. If I kick her out, she'll probably just go get Mom and Dad. It's like she *knows*. Ever since that night I shoved her in the closet – right at the stroke of midnight.'

Jonathan chuckled. 'Well, maybe you shouldn't shove her in closets.'

'You're lucky – nobody but your father, and no hassle from him.'

He winced a little at that and took one hand off the wheel, reaching out to her. She was nervously playing with Acariciandote, the bracelet he'd given her, and he stilled her hand. 'That was my mom's, remember?'

'Oh. Sorry, Jonathan.'

'It's okay. She ran off all the time, so it wasn't a huge surprise when she didn't come back. But you're lucky to have family.'

She was quiet for a moment. 'Yeah.'

Jonathan wished he hadn't brought it up. Talking about this kind of stuff never helped. 'Anyway, Beth probably isn't going to guess that time freezes at the stroke of twelve and a secret blue world full of monsters appears.' Jonathan laughed. 'She might be smart, but she's not that smart.'

Jessica turned toward him. 'You don't really mind her that much, do you? You *like* her.'

'Sure. Don't you?'

'Yeah. But she's my sister. I sort of have to.'

Jonathan chuckled again. 'Listen. You guys used to get along before you moved here, right? You will again, once Beth gets used to the weird ways of Bixby. And yeah, I *do* like her. Since you introduced us, I feel like less of a stalker when I'm sneaking around.'

Jessica drew closer, leaning her weight against him. 'Yeah, it's been better since she got to know you. I think she trusts you. At least, she doesn't think you're a serial killer anymore.'

Jonathan smiled, but the expression faded as he glanced at his watch: only ten more minutes before the blue time fell, and they were about that many miles from Jenks. He stepped on the gas, the old car shuddering as it accelerated. They had more important things to worry about tonight than little sisters.

They zoomed passed an old Chevy that was lumbering down Creek Turnpike. This far out of town the roads were almost empty, which meant that his father's car would be easy for his old friends in the sheriff's department to spot. He was sure that by now, they'd recognize it from halfway across the county.

Jonathan didn't know what he'd do then. Get stopped for breaking curfew, maybe go to jail again, and risk Cassie Flinders disappearing forever? Or do a grand theft auto, get the cops into hot pursuit mode, and get Jessica and himself into more trouble than Beth could ever have imagined?

Not a great choice.

Jessica cleared her throat. 'Um, I hope you're not planning on going this fast when time freezes. Don't want to fly through the windshield, personally.'

'Midnight's not for ten more minutes. Unless there's another eclipse.'

She pulled away, sitting straighter in her seat and checking her seat belt. 'Oh, right. Thanks for reminding me. Midnight can come at any time now.'

'Yeah. Cool, huh?'

'Uh, no, Jonathan. *Not* cool. What if it keeps happening?'

He shrugged. 'Then we get to fly around more.'

She sighed. 'You'd love that, wouldn't you?'

'What? *More* midnight? The whole world belonging to just us five? Less time in Flatland? Sure, I would.'

'But we don't understand what's happening, Jonathan. On the phone Dess said something about the blue time changing completely. And today we didn't know if the eclipse was ever going to stop. It felt like the world had ended.'

'Yeah, right. Like that's going to happen.' He snorted. 'And anyhow, look at it this way: if the world ends, you won't have to worry about Beth anymore.'

Jessica just turned away, staring out the passenger window and not saying another word.

Jonathan frowned, wondering what he'd said wrong now.

7

PREY

Melissa's eyes rolled back in her head, her nose wrinkling. Rex saw a shudder pass through her body from toes to fingertips.

'What, did they stop already?' Rex asked.

She shook her head. 'No, Flyboy's still got his pedal all the way down. They'll get here in time, more or less. But the flame-bringer's not in a very good mood.'

Dess glanced up from her GPS device and snorted. Rex shook his head. Great time for a lovers' quarrel.

He swept his eyes across the railroad tracks again. This place was wrapped in Focus, inhuman marks corrupting every piece of gravel in the rail bed, every blade of grass shooting up through the wooden cross-ties. Darklings and slithers had danced here. Even the steel spikes in the iron rails bore the traces of their claws and snouts and slithering bellies.

All this Focus couldn't have been laid down in twenty-one minutes. They must have come here before the eclipse.

Of course, Rex thought, there were always a few midnight

places on the outskirts of town. Perhaps it was only a coincidence that this weak spot had been visited before.

He knelt to take a closer look at a slitherprint, a sinuous line that wound down the railroad tracks as far as he could see. It didn't look especially fresh, not like a trail left only fifteen hours ago.

But Rex frowned; his new hunter's nerves were twitching with all the metal around him. Why would a slither travel down a railroad line that reeked of iron rails, steel bolts, and buried telegraph lines? Most darkling places on the city's edges were open fields and empty back lots, places where little patches of the wild still clung – stands of native plants, snake holes, or small creeks not yet erased by buildings and concrete. But this iron path was an artery of the rail system, an old and powerful symbol of human cleverness and dominance. Only a hundred years ago it had represented the highest technology that humanity possessed, yet the darklings had embraced this spot. They must have come here with a purpose.

Rex saw how far the Focus stretched up and down the track, how it trailed off into the brush and extended even to the ramshackle houses backed up against the right-of-way. He wondered how far into the mesquite trees it went. The small town of Jenks was close to the Arkansas River, and the scrub in these parts was impenetrably dense, hiding much of the landscape from his new predator's eyes.

But old darklings had been here, of that Rex was sure. He could see deep, clawed footprints in the soil and a broad tree branch that had almost cracked under the weight of something huge and winged. There were slither burrows scattered throughout the underbrush; darklings young and old hid from the sun out in the deep desert caves, but some of their little minions nested closer to town, buried under the earth.

It took time to layer a place with this much Focus, this many signs. They must have begun months ago, maybe a lot longer than that. Melissa and Madeleine had felt their celebrations out in the desert: the darklings had somehow known that the eclipse was coming and exactly where it would happen. Which meant they'd probably also known what Dess had discovered today, that this first tear in the blue time would spread like a rip along the seam of an old T-shirt.

Maybe it had always been their plan that the blue time would one day come apart. But what would happen then?

Suddenly something caught Rex's eye. One of the railroad track cross-ties stood out, a halo of red surrounding it. He looked closer and smelled the inherent strangeness of the spot. The blue time was paper-thin here.

The old wood of the cross-tie was marked with a sliver of Focus, looking out of place here among the stains of darklings. He drew closer and saw in the half-moon shape the distinctive tread of a sneaker.

That was why it looked different – that *other* kind of Focus clung to it, the kind Rex had only learned to see over the last couple of weeks.

'Prey,' he said softly.

'Five minutes,' announced Dess, nervously rocking the long piece of steel pipe that rested on her shoulder. 'How's the flame-bringer doing?'

'Close,' Melissa said. 'But they're slowing down. Wimps.'

'Not everyone appreciates the subtle pleasures of flying through a windshield, Melissa,' Dess said.

'They've got five whole minutes before midnight, and Flyboy's already parking it!'

'How far are they?' Rex interrupted.

'A few miles.'

'Not good.' He followed the trail of human Focus with his gaze. The glimmering footprints left the rail bed and headed down into the dense undergrowth. 'She went this way. On foot, not being dragged.'

'Who? Cassie?' Dess asked.

Rex nodded.

'You can *see* that?'

'I can see the traces of humans now,' he said, pointing at the trail. 'And these footprints look like they were made in the blue time. Cassie must have left them during the eclipse.'

Dess's face twisted into a skeptical expression. Other than Melissa and Madeleine, none of them yet understood how different he had become.

Rex knelt on the tracks and sniffed. He could smell the uncertainty of the lost girl, could see her fear in the tentative distance between the steps. It made his mouth water, his palms sweat. This was a young one, weak and ready to be cut from the herd.

'Get a grip, Rex,' Melissa said softly.

He shook the hunting thoughts from his head. 'Okay, I'm going to track her. She might still be close by. You guys stay here. But yell out a countdown for the last thirty seconds, Dess.' He slid down the loose gravel bank of the rail bed and plunged into the thick bushes.

'Rex!' Dess shouted. 'There's only four minutes left! Get back here.'

'Quit showing off, Rex,' Melissa called. 'Once midnight falls and her brain starts up again, I'll find her right away.'

Rex glanced back. The two of them were standing inside Polychronious, a large and complex tridecagram that Dess had laid down on a patch of clearing, using a spool of fiberoptic cable stolen from Oklahoma Telecom a few midnights ago. The cable smelled bright and buzzy to Rex, like cleaning detergent fumes going up his nose, and the thirteen-pointed star Dess had woven with it made his head spin. They would be safe from darklings inside it, even if the flame-bringer was a few minutes late.

'Just give me that countdown,' he called back.

'Rex!' Dess wailed.

He noticed that she and Melissa were standing as far apart as they could inside the tridecagram, like two rival cats locked in a small room together.

Whatever. They'd live.

Rex pushed his way deeper into the underbrush, fighting the bare, brittle branches of mesquite. He could see in the dark better than ever now, and the spaces between leafless trees and scrub seemed to open up before him. He soon realized that his prey's slender marks of Focus followed a narrow path, probably an old animal trail.

As Cassie's footsteps went deeper into the brush, they began to grow more sure and purposeful, as if after the first few minutes of confusion in the blue time, she'd headed for someplace where she felt safe.

A branch caught Rex, bending taut, then whipping backward, leaving a long rip in his shirt. The girl must have grown up around here to move so easily through this overgrowth. He could tell she was much shorter than him – from her footprints, she had walked almost upright underneath branches that he was forced to crouch beneath.

Her footsteps grew farther apart; moving more swiftly now, as if coaxed forward by some goal. Rex swore – he wasn't going to find the girl before midnight fell. She'd had twenty-one minutes to get wherever she'd disappeared to, and he had only . . .

'Thirty seconds, Rex!' Dess's voice called through the trees.

He paused. To make it back to safety, he should turn around now and start running. Inside Dess's ring of protection, they could wait for the flame-bringer. In the blue time Melissa would be able to taste the lost girl's thoughts even if she were miles away.

Of course, Cassie couldn't have actually gotten that far in twenty minutes unless the darklings had swooped down and carried her off. And if that had happened, she probably wasn't alive and certainly wouldn't survive the long minutes it would take Jonathan and Jessica to reach her.

Rex sniffed the trail before him. An electric trickle of fear still lingered in the human scent, mixed with excitement and wonder. It made something within him grow hungry. This was the smell of those young, adventurous humans who tended to stray too far from their villages – the call of easy meat.

Part of Rex knew that he should do the sensible thing. He should head back to safety and get everyone organized: keep Dess and Melissa from fighting with each other, tell Jonathan and Jessica what to do when they arrived, maybe fly along with them to the rescue. No one but he could be the leader that the group needed.

But the smell of the lone girl drew him forward, calling his entire body down the narrow path. Cassie Flinders felt *so close*. His hands tingled with how near she was, and a raw imperative filled him . . .

Reach her before the others do. She's yours.

Rex took an unsteady step forward. He had to get there first.

'Fifteen!' Dess's distant cry reached him. 'Where the hell are you, Rex? *Ten.* You're-an-idiot-*nine*, get-back-here-*eight*, you-dimwit-*seven* . . .'

Rex plunged deeper into the undergrowth.

Seconds later the earth shuddered under his feet. Blue light swept through the brush and across the sky, dulling the stars and bringing every branch and blade of grass into sharp relief, his vision suddenly seer-perfect.

He breathed in the hungry essence of the blue time, the mental clarity of midnight.

Ahead of him in the distance Rex's sharp ears caught a small cry of surprise and fear . . . Cassie waking up in the blue time.

It made him hungrier.

Only a minute after midnight's fall, things were beginning to stir in every direction. Slithers were worming their way up out of the deep burrows that protected them from the sun, signaling one another with their strange, chirping calls. It was like first light on some weird spring morning, the birds waking up and making a ruckus.

There were *lots* of slithers out here. Suddenly the steel hoops around his boots didn't feel like enough protection. He swept his eyes back and forth nervously across the dense brush, searching for the sharp Focus of their burrows, imagining the icy sting of a slither strike catching him on the leg. Rex had once worked on his grandfather's farm in Texas during harvest season; every step through these burrows reminded him of the anxious moment of lifting a hay bale and not knowing if an angry rattler lay underneath.

Another cry reached his ears, and Rex tore his eyes from the forest floor. Through the trees he saw a wedge of stone jutting up from the earth, cut in two by a narrow fissure. It was a tight fit even for a little kid but enough cover to hide Cassie from the sun.

Why had she gone in there? It seemed like incredibly bad luck to have wandered into a cave hidden from the sun's rays.

Unless she had somehow been coaxed into coming here . . .

Rex pulled his gloves on. These days the touch of stainless steel made his bare flesh itch during the secret hour, but leather gloves allowed him a solid grip on his new weapon. Dess had decorated the hunting knife's blade with a superfine guitar string wound in patterns that made his eyes burn and water. The knife had the clever human smell of a finely tooled bicycle part – all modern alloys and precise proportions – buzzing with a thousand ingenious angles.

It make his head hurt to look at it, even to think its name, which meant that the weapon could fend off any darkling, at least for the short time it would take for Jessica and Jonathan to get here. The secret hour had begun almost three minutes ago – they had to be on their way.

From just outside the mouth of the fissure, he stared into the gloom. A blue glow emanated from the rocks, revealing layers of slither Focus in the cave, plus one slender trail of human footsteps. The crevice went deeper than he'd thought, the Oklahoma shale crumpled into zigzags by some ancient earthquake.

He paused to listen. The short, raspy breaths of a panicking thirteen-year-old reached his ears.

'Cassie?' he called.

The breathing caught, then a voice answered softly, 'Help me.'

The girl sounded much younger than thirteen; probably she was frightened out of her wits. 'Are you okay?'

'My grandma froze.'

'She's better now, Cassie,' he said calmly. 'But she's worried about you. Are you all right?'

'It hurts.'

'What hurts, Cassie?'

'My foot. Where the kitty bit me.'

A cat. Rex remembered the slither that Jessica had followed on the first night the darklings had tried to kill her. It had disguised itself as a black cat and scratched on her window, then led her out onto Bixby's empty streets to where a darkling awaited. They must have used the same trick on Cassie Flinders. With the whole world transformed into a frozen, empty place around her, she had innocently followed the only other living creature she could see.

'It's okay, Cassie. My name's Rex. I'm here to take you home.'

She didn't answer.

'Cassie, you have to tell me: is there anything else in there? Anything besides the kitty?'

'It went away.'

'That's good.' The slither must have struck as the eclipse had ended, just before heading back to its burrow. It had hobbled Cassie to make sure she didn't wander out of the cave, out to where the sunlight would free her from the blue time.

Cassie had been frozen for the fifteen hours since the eclipse – to her the cat had only run off a few minutes ago.

'But there are snakes in here, Rex,' Cassie said. 'They're *looking* at me.'

He tried to ignore the fear in her voice, the way it made him react. He could tell from her breathing that she was sick and remembered from the news that she'd been home from school with a head cold. Easy prey.

It was going to be tricky coaxing her out of the cave. In his darkling dreams Rex had seen humans paralyzed by their own fear when cornered.

Standing sideways, he tried to push deeper into the fissure, but after only a few feet, teeth of sharp stone closed on his spine and ribs. 'Cassie? Try to come toward me.'

'I can't.'

'I know your foot hurts, Cassie. But you can still walk.'

'No. They won't let me.'

Crap, Rex thought. The slithers had her trapped in there. He wondered whether even the beam of Jessica's flashlight could reach back to where Cassie was. He reached out with his hunting knife and struck the stone a glancing blow. A single blue spark flared blindingly, illuminating the jagged walls of the fissure for an instant.

'Did you see that, Cassie?'

'That flash?'

'Yeah. Good girl. I'm not far from you.' Rex leaned his weight against the stone and stood on one leg, pulling the metal hoops from his boot. Then he reversed his stance and yanked them off the other. 'I'm going to throw some things, Cassie. They're going to scare the snakes. You have to run this way when you see sparks.'

'I can't. They're looking at me.' Her voice had gone flat, as if hypnotized by the lifeless stare of the slithers.

'They won't bite you if you're fast, okay? I'm going to count to three, then scare them.'

'Rex. I can't. My foot.'

'Just get ready. One . . .' He held the hoops almost to his lips and whispered their names – Woolgathering, Inexhaustible, Unquestioning, and Vulnerability – the Aversions sending a shooting migraine through the darkling half of his brain. 'Two . . . three . . . *run!*'

He threw the handful of hoops as hard as he could, and they careened deep into the cave, raising up a shower of sparks as they clanged off the walls. The bright, ringing sound of metal striking stone cut painfully into Rex's ears.

'You scared them!' Cassie announced.

'Well, *run* then, dammit!'

As the echoes of his shout died, Rex heard her sneakers' squeaky footfalls carrying her through the sharp angles of the cave. She came into view a few seconds later, limping and white-faced as she pulled herself down the narrow channel of stone. Rex reached out a gloved hand and pulled her from the crevice after him, out under the rising bulk of the dark moon.

Outside he stumbled to a halt. An army of slithers surrounded them. A host of the creatures covered the ground, and their winged forms filled every tree branch.

'Snakes . . .' Cassie said softly.

Melissa, Rex thought as hard as he could.

In the depths of his mind he heard the faintest word – *Coming* – and wondered if that meant Melissa and Dess were coming, or Jessica . . . or if something else was on its way.

'It's all right,' he said, drawing Cassie closer and thrusting the knife out before them.

Then he saw the darkling.

It seemed to uncoil from the ground, its eight legs spreading out from its bulbous center like the blooming of some horrific flower. A tarantula, the desert spider of his nightmares.

Rex wondered where it had come from, whether it had flown here swiftly from the desert or crouched in some rocky warren out of the sun, waiting since the eclipse for this ancient delicacy – a rare meal of human flesh.

'Rex . . .?' Cassie said softly.

That had been the plan, of course: the slither-cat leading her to this spot, trapping her in the cave until its master arrived at midnight. Next the slithers inside would have driven her into its jaws . . . if Rex hadn't already coaxed her out himself.

'Go back inside,' he whispered.

She only clung to him tighter.

'Go back in the cave, Cassie!' he shouted. 'That thing can't fit in there!'

'But the snakes!'

Rex turned to look. The blue-lit depths of the cave were dotted with the eyes of slithers staring back at them.

'Here, take this,' he said, pressing the hunting knife into her hand. 'They're scared of it, and help is coming.'

She held the knife loosely, looking down at it with wide eyes.

'It's name is Animalization,' he said. His fists clenched in pain as Dess's pointed little tridecalogism passed his lips. 'Keep saying that, and they'll be really scared. *Animalization*.'

'But—'

'Go!' He shoved her into the fissure, hoping she would find the courage to go deep into the cave, far enough to escape the thin, reaching arms of the darkling.

He whirled back around to face the creature, crouching down into a fighting stance. Its eight legs had extended to full length, pressing against the ground to lift the central body mass up into the air. The legs were covered not with hair, but with glistening spurs, like thorns on some vast and hideous rosebush. The entire beast was dripping with a viscous black substance, as if it had been dipped in crude oil.

Rex flexed his empty hands, realizing that he was completely unarmed. He had no knife, no metal on his boots, and yelling thirteen-letter words would hurt him more than it would any darkling.

'Where *are* you, Jessica?' he whispered, daring a glance at his watch.

His heart sank. Only six minutes of the secret hour had passed.

She wasn't going to make it here in time.

The darkling's two forward legs raised and its body rested on its rear, the posture of a tarantula facing an enemy. Rex could see the fangs in its oily maw, shivering with the creature's hunger.

He remembered being forced to stand still at ten years old as his father's pet tarantulas crawled across his bare flesh. The weird slowness with which they moved, the interlocking motions of their eight legs, the sickening fascination that they compelled.

His father's voice came back to him: *Relax, boy! They're not poisonous. They can't hurt you. Be a man!*

Hairy spiders had crawled through every one of his child-hood nightmares.

Rex waited for the darkling to strike. Its two forward legs made slow circles in the air, like the arms of a dog paddling in water. The sinuous motion threatened to hypnotize him, and he tore his gaze away.

He stared at the ground, his heart pounding, every muscle tensed, ready to fight a hopeless battle. But somehow, Rex realized, something in his reaction was missing. The gnawing fear in his stomach hadn't come yet; the spider didn't terrify him as it should have.

In fact, he couldn't remember having a single dream since the darklings had changed him that had included his father's tarantulas. He and Melissa had killed them after the accident had left the old man helpless, but Rex had always known their ghosts were lurking beneath his house, waiting to wreak revenge.

He looked up at the giant spider again and realized that the cold sweat of those childhood traumas had disappeared. His arachnophobia (his brain twinged at the word's thirteen letters) was gone.

Another moment passed, and still the creature didn't strike.

Rex bared his teeth at the beast, and a sound gurgled up from his throat – the same hiss that had turned Timmy Hudson into a puddle of melted bully.

Of course, the darkling before him wasn't so easily scared. It stood firm on its six hind legs, the dance of its spurs still mesmerizing, its bulk glistening in the dark moon's light. But as the long seconds stretched out, it didn't strike.

Slowly the reason dawned on him. The beast hadn't taken a hunting stance at all – Rex wasn't prey. This wasn't the kill at the end of a chase; it was a ritual between two predators, like a standoff over some carcass. The spider's dance was posturing and bluster, a challenge made, hoping that another hunter would back down. But Rex had gotten here first to claim the kill.

He stood his ground.

Wolves didn't eat other wolves, after all.

For a long minute he faced the creature, letting the motions of the contest move through him. His fingers clenched into rigid claws, slowly cutting the air like a familiar ceremony unfolding. Neither he nor the darkling advanced, held apart by mutual respect and fear.

Then Rex felt a flavor in his mind, not Melissa's familiar taste – but something ancient and arid, like dust on his tongue, hardly words at all.

Join us.

He swallowed, his throat parched, staring back at the darkling.

We will hunt again soon.

Rex tried to hiss again, to ward off the murmurings inside his head.

Then he felt a rush of fear from the beast, its cold heart suddenly pounding, driving its bloated body like a lash. The darkling turned away and twisted quickly into a new shape, growing thin and long and sprouting wings. Then with one last hiss of its own, it leapt into the air, a host of slithers whirling around it. A great dark cloud of them gathered as the darkling disappeared into the sky, the local burrows emptying, running for fear of the flame-bringer.

As the creature left his sight, a last thought trailed from it . . .

Winter is coming, halfling. Join.

Rex fell onto one knee, exhausted and shaking. His head was throbbing, one half of his mind warring against the other. The world around him seemed to flex and bend, his seer's Focus overwhelmed by the warped vision of a darkling.

He'd actually heard the thing in his mind – not just caught fleeting tastes and emotions like Melissa casting across the desert. He could *talk* to them now.

'You scared it.'

The small voice sucked him back into reality and the cool light of the blue time, and Rex whirled around to face its source. Cassie clutched the hunting knife with both hands, staring back at him, her eyes wide with amazement. The patterns woven onto the knife stung his eyes.

'How did you do that?' she asked. 'It was so big.'

Speechless, Rex found himself watching Cassie's heartbeat pulsing in her throat, the blood close to the surface. The awe on her face was like the hopeless gaze of paralyzed prey, caught and cornered by its pursuers. Helplessly he felt the hunger rising inside him.

The other darkling had left this prey for him, small and alone.

Join us, Rex heard the beast's words echo in his mind, and realized that he could end the awful struggle within himself now, with just one easy kill.

8

NIGHTMARE INTERRUPTED

'There they go,' Jessica said.

A cloud of slithers was swirling up from the dense trees in the distance, like a flock of birds sent into flight by a gunshot. She and Jonathan were at the top of their arc, the straight line of the railroad track below them leading off toward the deep desert.

'Never seen that many before,' Jonathan said. 'Not since . . .' His voice trailed off.

Jessica saw that the swarm had split, half of them wheeling around, heading toward her and Jonathan.

'What are they up to?' she said. The darklings had mostly steered clear of Jessica since she'd discovered her talent. But this flock of slithers almost looked intent on attacking. The creatures were spreading out, flying low, rushing toward them like oil spreading across the treetops.

'Not sure.' Jonathan squeezed her hand. 'And I think we're lost. Hold up a second.'

They were descending into a small clearing near the railroad tracks. She bent her knees on landing, the soft grass absorbing their momentum.

'Which way?' she asked. From the ground the trees looked the same in every direction.

Jonathan shook his head. 'Don't know. And we're taking way too long.'

The trip from the car had eaten up precious minutes, but at least they'd been moving fast, bounding straight down a dirt road, then through a neighborhood of shabby houses set on large, junk-strewn lots. At the rendezvous point Melissa had pointed in the direction Rex had wandered off, saying he was only half a mile away. But the dense brush had forced them to take small jumps from clearing to clearing, weaving their way toward him. This was the worst kind of terrain to fly across; mesquite trees were dangerous, with their razor-sharp thorns.

After all this aimless bouncing around, Jessica figured that the other two were probably there already, charging straight through the trees under Melissa's guidance. She just hoped they had enough Dess-made weapons to protect Rex and the lost girl – and themselves – until she and Jonathan finally managed to discover a flight path.

'I *think* it's that way,' Jonathan said. 'But what were those—?'

Suddenly a wave of silent shapes surged through the trees. The slithers' wings were furled into their snakelike bodies, like black arrows launched by invisible archers. Jessica's arms shot up just in time to ward off one flying toward her face. Acariciandote exploded with blue sparks, its charms glowing white-hot, but the icy needles of a slither bite shot all the way up into her shoulder.

'Jess!' Jonathan pulled her to himself, shielding her with his body. She heard the *thunk* of a slither plowing into his back, and he let out a grunt of pain.

With her good hand Jessica pulled Disintegrator from her pocket and turned it on, the beam of white light cutting through the blue time, turning a few of the darting shapes into flaming streaks of red fire.

She played her flashlight through the trees in all directions, the familiar glow of power moving through her. But the beam connected with nothing. The swarm had passed through the clearing in seconds flat.

Jonathan pulled away, groaning and stretching to reach the middle of his back. 'Ow! Right on my spine! Little creeps.'

'What was that all about?' Jessica cried, flicking off the flashlight.

Jonathan opened his eyes, blinking away the white light. 'Who knows? Maybe they didn't realize it was you . . . *Down!*' He wrapped his arms around her, pulling her to the ground.

Jessica heard the whistle of more slithers passing just overhead; they'd shot from the trees again, coming from a new direction, fearless of her flame-bringer's power. She turned Disintegrator on and waved it randomly, missing completely as the last slithers disappeared into the trees.

'We need to jump!' Jonathan cried, his eyes shut tight against the white light. 'They're using the trees for cover!'

He pulled her up from the ground by her numbed hand, jumping straight up into the sky. They spun slowly around each other, their flight unbalanced from the uncoordinated jump.

Nothing was in the air with them, but Jessica saw another flight of slithers slicing from the trees and through the spot where they had stood a moment before. She angled Disintegrator's beam downward, and soon the clearing floor was dotted with screaming, burning bodies.

'What are they doing? Don't they know I'll just kill them?'

'I think they're trying to delay us.'

As they reached the peak of the jump, Jessica whipped the flashlight around, but nothing flew nearby. In the distance, though, the rest of the slither cloud had gathered itself around a rising black nucleus, a single darkling on the wing.

'That's not good,' she said. The rescue plan had assumed it would take a while for anything big to reach Jenks from the deep desert. But apparently a darkling had come early, while she, the flame-bringer, had been late.

'Can I open my eyes?' Jonathan said as they began to descend.

She swept the flashlight across the trees below them one more time, but nothing sparked to life, and she flicked it off. 'Sure.'

As they began to descend, Jonathan swept his gaze across the horizon swiftly, then pointed with his free hand. 'That's it over there.'

Among the low, gnarly mesquite trees a spike of rock thrust into the air like a rude finger. It was in the general direction Melissa had indicated, and she'd said that Rex had found the lost girl in some sort of cave.

'Come on. Let's try to make it in one jump,' Jonathan said. 'If they're risking white light to slow us down, we should probably get there fast.'

Instinct took over as they dropped, Jessica twisting in midair to reorient herself for a last jump toward the stone spire. They landed in the high grass and rebounded without any pause.

They rose above the trees again, and Jessica spotted two tiny figures standing close together by a fissure in the stone. 'That's them!'

'They look like they're in one piece,' Jonathan said softly. 'Any slithers down there?'

'Close your eyes.'

She switched the flashlight on again, playing it across the small clearing, the rocks, and the treetops. Nothing burst into flame; no slithers hurtled screaming from the undergrowth. Jessica did catch, however, the dark purple flash of Rex's eyes as he glanced up, then turned away, his expression of pain visible even from the air.

'Oops.' Jessica turned the flashlight off. 'Okay. You can look now, Jonathan. Landing in five, four . . .'

They came down softly in the thick grass, about ten feet from Rex and the small, thin girl who stood next to him, clinging to his arm. She was about Beth's age, wearing a ragged sweatshirt and pajama bottoms. Her eyes bulged as she stared at Jonathan and Jessica. She'd probably seen some pretty astonishing stuff tonight, but two people flying hand in hand was still pretty jaw-dropping.

'Are you okay?' Jonathan asked.

'Sorry about blinding you, Rex,' Jessica said.

His eyes still covered, his hands shaking, Rex answered, 'No, that's fine. It cleared my head. You got here just in time.'

Jessica raised an eyebrow, wondering what that meant. There weren't any slithers here. Why had they been frying themselves just to delay her another minute?

Jonathan dropped Jessica's hand and crossed to the girl. 'Cassie, right?'

She nodded dumbly.

'I'm Jonathan. Hey, your elbow looks ouchy.'

Cassie looked at the red mark, then pointed into the cave. 'Banged it in there. But you should see my ankle.' She pulled up one pant leg, revealing the dark bruise of a slither bite. Jessica winced, shaking out her own hand, which was still tingling with icy needles.

'Ow!' Jonathan said. 'I hate snakes.'

'No. It was this stupid cat.'

Jonathan glanced back at Jessica.

She remembered that night, only her second time in the secret hour, when the black slither-cat had transformed horribly into a snake before her eyes. Then another dozen slithers had shown up, along with a darkling in the shape of a giant panther. And then the biggest surprise of all: finding out that the whole thing hadn't been a dream, but an entire new reality opening up.

Jessica frowned. On the phone this afternoon no one had mentioned what was supposed to happen *after* they rescued Cassie from the blue time. How would they keep her from spilling the beans to everyone in town?

Of course, maybe the answer was obvious. Melissa would reach into the young girl's mind and erase what had happened here. She had done it more than once before – to Jessica's own parents, probably. And back when her talent was young and unformed, Melissa had forced herself into Rex's father's mind, leaving the old guy half crazy. The thought of his milky, empty eyes made Jessica shiver again.

But maybe it didn't have to be that way.

'This is a pretty crappy dream, huh?' she said to the girl, rubbing her slither-bitten hand.

Jonathan raised an eyebrow, and even Rex, who still looked pretty shaky, snorted out a short laugh.

'What?' Jessica shrugged. 'I'm just saying, as nightmares go, this one's on the weird side. Right, Cassie?'

The look of dazed confusion gradually faded from the girl's face, her expression turning more thoughtful. 'Well, I was kind of wondering: what's going *on* here?' She looked up at the dark moon. 'What happened to everything? And who are you guys?'

'You've got a fever, right?' Jessica asked.

'Not a fever. My grandma said it's just a cold.'

'Oh. Right. Okay,' Jessica said slowly and deliberately. 'But sometimes when we're sick, we have funny dreams.'

Cassie crossed her arms. 'Yeah, maybe. But people in those funny dreams don't usually bring it up that I'm dreaming.'

Jonathan laughed. 'Nice try, Jess.'

'Yeah, this kid's smarter than that,' Rex said. 'And tougher than she looks too.'

'Smarter?' Jessica cried. 'What's that supposed to mean? *I* thought the blue time was all a dream, remember?'

'Oh, yeah.' Rex chuckled. 'Well, feel free to tell her whatever you want until Melissa gets here.'

Jessica frowned and glanced at Jonathan, who shrugged, a helpless look on his face. He didn't much like the idea either, but he clearly couldn't see any other way of keeping the secret hour secret.

A crashing sound reached them through the trees.

'Speaking of which,' Rex said.

Dess emerged first, a long metal pipe balanced over one

shoulder, like a spear ready to be thrown. She stumbled into the clearing and came to a halt, looking at them one by one. Then she lowered the spear with a disgusted noise. 'No monsters left, are there?'

'All under control,' Rex said.

'Rats,' Dess said. 'Jessica, I haven't slain jack squat since you became the flame-bringer.'

Jessica sighed. 'Yeah. My bad.'

Melissa came into view, yanking on her long black dress, the hem of which was tangled with twigs and trailing branches.

'Jeez, Rex. That was freaky,' she announced.

'You tasted it?' he asked quietly.

'It was pretty hard to miss,' Melissa said, running a finger along one of her scars. 'I mean, I already knew you were having an identity crisis. But I didn't think a darkling would *agree* with you!'

Jessica glanced from one of them to the other. Rex had a funny look on his face, and she noticed that his hands were still shaking, his fingers bent stiffly into claws. Melissa was staring at him like he'd grown antlers.

'Are we missing something here?' Dess asked aloud.

'Yeah, what happened?' Jessica said. 'I saw a darkling running away.'

Melissa took a step closer to Rex and the girl. 'The darkling was here, but it seemed to think Rex was a—'

'Don't!' Rex interrupted.

There was a long silence, the two of them staring at each other.

'Not now,' he hissed.

'Wow,' Cassie Flinders said. 'Maybe I am dreaming because you guys are really weird.'

Everyone looked at the girl. She stood there, staring defiantly back at them. Jessica decided that she had a point.

'Okay, kiddo,' Melissa said after another awkward moment of silence. 'I think it's past your bedtime.'

'But it's morning,' Cassie answered, then looked up at the sky and frowned. 'Or it *was* . . .'

'Either way, I can't believe your grandma let you out of bed,' Rex said. 'You being sick and all.'

'She always lets me play in the backyard,' Cassie said huffily. 'Says it's good for a cold to get out in the cold.'

'Well, I'm putting you back under the covers,' Melissa said, reaching out a hand. 'Come with me.'

'Said the spider to the fly,' Dess muttered.

Jessica looked across the clearing at Jonathan. There had to be some other way to keep the secret than messing with people's brains. She was just a kid, after all. Who would believe her?

As Melissa's hand closed around Cassie's, the girl seemed to relax. Then she yawned, her eyes growing sleepy.

Melissa turned to the others. 'Chill, guys. I'm a lot better at this than I used to be.' She shrugged. 'Besides, I'm only going to calm her down and put her to sleep and maybe *suggest* that this all was a nightmare. When it comes to radical memory overhaul, I only work on stiffs. Which, you may have noticed, Cassie isn't. Anything else will have to wait.'

'What are you guys talking about?' Cassie asked sleepily.

Melissa smiled, leading Cassie back toward the railroad tracks. 'We're discussing how you're going to remember this crazy dream tomorrow.' She winked at Rex. 'But probably not the next day.'

'So she'll tell people about it?' Jonathan asked. 'And then

just forget the next day? Won't that seem funny to everyone else? I mean, she'll probably be on the news tomorrow.'

Rex shrugged. 'She's a kid, she's sick, she wandered off. So what if she talks crazy for a day? And after we pay her a visit tomorrow at midnight—' He raised his fingers and snapped.

The sound sent a shiver through Jessica. Maybe they were right, and mindcasting was the only way to keep the secret. In the old days, when Bixby had practically been ruled by mid-nighters, they'd probably done it all the time. But still, the idea didn't make her very happy.

'So, Rex, should I leave her out in the sun?' Melissa asked from the edge of the clearing.

'No reason to,' he said. 'Jessica already gave us both a blinding dose of white light. It worked for me when I was half-darkling; it should work for her. Meet you at the car?'

'Sure thing, Spider-Man,' Melissa called, waving goodbye.

Jessica watched the two of them disappear into the trees, wondering at how pliant and sleepy Cassie had become after Melissa had taken her hand. Maybe it was only shock, the poor girl overwhelmed after everything that happened. But Madeleine had suppressed Dess's memories with only a touch too.

Melissa was growing in power every day. Jessica wondered what she could do if she got really pissed off at someone.

'So, Jessica, you ready to fly home?' Jonathan asked.

She looked at Rex. He still seemed shaky, as if it had been a close thing tonight.

'Will you guys be safe, Rex?'

He nodded. 'Sure. I'll stick around and see if there's any lore sites around here. Or any other clues about this place. I think you ruined the darklings' party, for the rest of the hour at least. And Dess here has . . .'

'Magisterially Supernumerary Mathematician,' she said, hefting the spear proudly.

'But what about your car, Jonathan?' Jessica said.

He shrugged. 'I'll get it tomorrow.'

'I can drive it into town!' Dess offered.

'I don't think so,' Jonathan said.

Dess snorted and prodded his ribs with the point of Supernumerary.

Jessica stood there, rubbing her wounded hand and thinking glum thoughts. They had saved a young girl tonight, but in payment for the rescue the memory of the most amazing experience in Cassie's life would be erased forever. And Cassie Flinders was only the beginning. If the blue time was tearing, more unlucky people were likely to step into the secret hour, where hungry monsters waited for them. And possibly normal time itself was coming to an end.

Worst of all, Beth was probably waiting in Jessica's room right now, ready to unleash holy fury when she got home.

'You know what?' Jessica said. 'You can drive me back after the secret hour's over.'

Jonathan frowned at her, rubbing at the middle of his back. 'What about curfew?'

'I'll risk it. You guys do all the time.'

'What about Beth? I told her eighteen minutes.'

'I'll risk her too.'

'But what—?'

'Jonathan, you *don't* have to take me home yet, okay?' She took his hands, felt weightlessness flow into her. 'This whole night has sucked so far. Maybe we could just do some flying?

Real flying, out in the open. We can take our time getting me home.'

His frown faded, and a smile spread slowly across his face.

'Take our time getting home?' Dess said with a smirk. 'Is *that* what they're calling it these days?'

Rex chuckled softly.

Jessica ignored them. The heart-pounding panic of the slither attack had erased the mutual irritation between them on the subject of little sisters. And although what he'd said about liking Beth had been maddening at the time, right now it seemed kind of sweet.

'Come on. Let's fly somewhere together,' she said. She massaged her shoulder. 'Now that we're not getting pelted with slithers.'

'Well,' he said after a moment's thought, 'have you ever seen the river?'

'The Arkansas?' Jessica shrugged. 'Just from the bridge on the way over here.'

'You haven't seen the Arkansas River till you've seen it in the secret hour,' Jonathan said. 'Motionless water, excellent for skipping rocks.'

'Oh, cool.' For a moment she tried to figure out how the laws of motion would apply, but her new physics lobe quickly gave up. 'So how does that work?'

Jonathan smiled again, his brown eyes flashing in the light of the dark moon. 'It's kind of tricky to explain. But you get a lot more skips than on regular water. Swimming's fun too.'

'Okay,' Jessica said. 'I could use some fun.'

'Come on, then. I'll show you.'

Jonathan offered her his hand, and she took it.

'You kids have fun now,' Dess called.

'Okay,' Jessica said. 'See you, Rex.'

The seer only nodded, his hands still shaking. Even in the blue light she could tell his face was ashen. What had happened to him before they'd arrived? And why had the darkling run away while she was still finding her way here, if its minions were sacrificing themselves to hold her up?

She shook her head. Evidently Rex and Melissa were still keeping secrets from the rest of them.

They leapt up and over the trees, finding their way back to the railroad bed and then across Jenks, until Jessica could see the glimmer of the river in the distance. From the air it looked like a giant slither winding its way down from the black hills, glowing with the cold light of the dark moon.

'You know,' Jonathan said as they flew. 'Maybe it's better for Cassie. Forgetting about all this.'

'Maybe. Doesn't seem fair, though.'

'Sure, but think about how much it would scare a kid like that. Knowing about all these weird creatures crawling across her while she's frozen for an hour every night?'

'Yeah, I guess so,' Jessica said. 'I mean, it scares me, and I'm the all-powerful flashlight-bringer.'

'And on top of the fear factor, everyone would think she was totally crazy. Eventually, since she'll never see the blue time again after all, she'd probably decide they were right.'

They landed on a stretch of not-quite beach, a narrow strip of dry earth dotted with patches of scrubby grass. The river stretched out before them, motionless wavelets glittering like scales made of diamond, reflecting a shattered image of the dark moon.

It was beautiful, but Jessica shivered.

'Not cold, are you?'

'No. It's always warm here.' She shook her head. 'I was just wondering if Cassie might see the blue time again. I mean, what if Dess is right? What if the secret hour swallows all of Bixby – or even the whole world – forever? And *everyone* gets sucked through, like Cassie was? Suddenly cars and electricity don't work, and people can't even make *fires* anymore. Only five of us on the whole planet know anything about using thirteen-letter words and stainless steel to protect ourselves. What happens then?'

He squeezed her hand. 'Then I'll come get you, wherever you are when it happens. We'll be okay.'

'But what about everybody else?'

He stared out across the river, nodding slowly. 'My guess is, everybody else is in big trouble.'

9

MISS TRUST

At the kitchen door the next morning Jessica breathed a sigh of relief. She was safe for a few more minutes – Beth wasn't up yet.

'Morning, Jess. Toast?'

Jessica checked for signs of imminent re-grounding in her mother's expression but saw only sleepiness and the usual lines of stress. Apparently Beth hadn't raised any alarms last night.

'Sure, Mom. Thanks.' Jessica sat down at the table. Maybe Jonathan was right, and the trick to dealing with Beth was to call her bluff.

Somehow, though, Jessica didn't think it was going to be that easy.

Her mother popped two slices of bread into the toaster, then turned her attention back to the coffeemaker gurgling happily on the counter. 'Any plans tonight?'

'Um, no.' Jessica frowned. 'Hang on, was that question a subtle recognition of the fact that I'm not grounded any-more?'

'Not exactly subtle,' her mother said. 'I don't do subtlety before coffee.' She splashed milk into an empty mug, her eyes remaining fixed on the black brew now dribbling into the pot.

'Well, you're tons more subtle than Dad. Yesterday afternoon he said he was keeping an eye on me.'

'He is.' Mom looked at Jessica. 'But I'm just going to say that I trust you. How's that for good parenting?'

'It's great. But didn't you used to be the bad cop?'

'Yeah, I think so.' Her mother gave the coffeepot a look of intense concentration. 'Takes too much energy, though. At least your father's taking up the slack somewhere.'

'Well, thanks anyway. I won't let you down.' The words came out automatically, but Jessica felt a twinge of guilt as they left her lips. She had crossed a new line just the night before. It was one thing sneaking out during the secret hour, which hardly counted as breaking curfew; when every clock in the world was frozen, surely time was a meaningless concept. Plus there were darklings to slay and lost kids to rescue.

But last night she hadn't gotten home till about 2 A.M., cutting solidly into school-night real time. Crusty sleep still caked her eyes, and red Oklahoma dust had spun around the drain for a solid minute while she'd showered.

Not that she regretted it. Their visit to the motionless river had been worth any amount of lost sleep. Just like air during the blue time, the water had been as warm as a summer day. Jonathan said that you could go swimming in the middle of winter. With the current arrested, the broad river was like one big heated swimming pool. The water had seemed to wash away the pain in her slither-bitten hand, not to mention all the tension between her and Jonathan.

'That's Jessica, all right: Miss Trustworthy,' Beth said from the kitchen door.

Jess wondered how long she'd been standing there. Maybe she had been waiting for the sounds of Jessica getting up and had followed her down the hall.

Not much fun, having a spy in your own house.

Jessica cleared her throat. 'That's me.'

Beth came in and flopped down on a chair, smiling sweetly at her sister. 'Get it?' she asked. 'Miss Trust?'

At the exact same moment Jessica's toast popped up and the coffeemaker's gurgling ended with a final sigh.

'I got it, Mom.' Jessica jumped up and pulled a knife and fork from the drawer, wielding them like chopsticks to remove the toast.

'Put some in for me?' Beth asked.

Jessica glanced at her mother, who was giving Beth a puzzled look with her sleepy eyes, the pot in one hand, mug in the other. The coffeemaker let a last few drops fall onto its hot metal plate, which hissed like angry slithers as they boiled away.

'Be polite, Beth,' Mom finally said. 'Say "please."'

'I'm very polite. Aren't I, Jessica?'

'Amazingly polite.' Jessica depressed the toaster's handle and stared down into its double maw, watching as the elements glowed red. 'For example, you'd never hang around when you're *not wanted*.'

'Yeah, and always *on time*. That's me.'

'*What* are you two talking about?' their mother said.

Jessica glared at her little sister, daring her to go ahead and blab to their mother about everything: her sneaking out the night before, Jonathan, whatever she wanted. It gave Jessica pleasure to think that no matter how much Beth snitched about, she didn't know half of what was really going on.

And for that matter, what difference did being in trouble make? Yesterday Jessica had discovered that everything she knew could disappear at any time – maybe in a week, maybe this morning – her whole reality swallowed by the darklings. She definitely wasn't going to let a little twerp like Beth push her around in the meantime.

Besides, her boyfriend could fly. Grounded was a relative state of affairs.

She stared at Beth and thought, Go *right ahead*.

'Nothing,' Beth finally said. 'We're just fooling around. No big deal.'

Their mother raised an eyebrow but then just sighed and looked at her watch. 'Okay, whatever. I'm late. You guys try to have a good day.' She looked at Jessica and held up her cell phone. 'Call me *and* Dad if you do anything after school, okay?'

'Sure, both of you. No problem.'

Beth's toast popped up, and Jessica carried it to her little sister on a plate. 'Here you go.'

'Thank you, Jess. See, Mom? Totally polite.'

'That's nice, Beth. 'Bye, you two.'

The sisters said goodbye, then waited silently as their mother hoisted her heavy bag onto her shoulder and walked, footsteps fading, to the end of the hall. The door opened and closed.

Jessica turned to her sister, who was chewing toast thoughtfully. 'Thanks, I guess.'

'For what?'

Jessica swallowed. 'Not telling Mom about . . . everything.'

Beth shrugged.

'Like I said, Jess, I don't want you in trouble. I just want to find out what's going on here in Bixby.' She gave her older sister a sweet smile. 'And I will too . . . one way or another.'

10

MEMORY FIX

The mind noise of Jenks rumbled softly at this time of night. A fair percentage of the locals seemed to be awake – most watching the late-night dreck of unemployment TV – but this area was sparsely populated compared to Bixby. The thinly sprinkled minds dotted the mental landscape like lazy fireflies.

'Anybody near the tracks?'

She opened her eyes, licked her lips, and shook her head. 'No, Rex. Nothing bigger than a squirrel.'

Her old Ford was parked in the same field as the night before, facing the long hump of the railroad line. Melissa couldn't taste any human minds among the trees, which was one less thing to worry about.

Rex was almost being his old self, getting anxious over everything. He'd been worried that Cassie Flinders had told her friends everything she'd seen last night – or worse, spilled the beans to the local news channel.

Of course, Melissa had to admit, a bunch of thrill seekers showing up to dare 'haunted' railroad tracks would be a pain.

It was bad enough out at the snake pit, having to crawl over frozen teenagers playing games with so-called magic rocks. But this rip in the blue time was actually dangerous – they didn't need any more Cassies crossing over and causing all kinds of inconvenience.

As Melissa cast her mind across the contortion, she realized that she could faintly taste the rip. There was something unnatural and vaguely *wrong* about this place, like the smell of chlorine on your own skin after swimming. She wrinkled her nose, wondering if the rip had grown since last night or if it only got bigger during eclipses.

'Maybe it's too soon,' he said. 'Any rumors Cassie started haven't had much time to spread.'

'Well, we can come out here again tomorrow night if you want.' She flexed her fingers. 'Scare the hell out of them. Of course, it does seem like a waste of effort.'

'What do you mean?'

'Saving every little kid who wanders into darkling land when all of Bixby's fixing to get turned into one big buffet.' She saw his fists tighten, felt the tension course through him, and sighed. '*Kidding*, Rex. You know me, always happy to rescue people.'

He relaxed, took a breath. 'Well, you rescued me.'

She smiled. The great thing about Rex was, he'd never forgotten the night she'd walked across Bixby to find him, back when they were kids. Even after all these years, all the mistakes they'd made, he was still that eight-year-old, forever grateful to her for showing him that the blue time was real, not just some recurring nightmare.

But what was he so nervous about tonight? Even with her new and improved skills, Melissa still couldn't tease out the details sometimes. Not without physical contact, anyway, and Rex had been very edgy about touching today.

'Maybe Cassie hasn't told anyone,' he said. 'Maybe she really does think it was a dream.'

'I don't know. She tasted really . . . clever.' Melissa paused, unsure if *clever* was what she meant. The kid was tough, and Melissa had detected a crafty streak in her that was a mile wide. Cassie Flinders might not have said much last night, acting very much like a kid in shock, but she'd listened to everything the midnighters had said in front of her, recording it all. The sooner Melissa rejiggered her memories, the better.

'Just don't push too hard, Cowgirl.'

Rex's guilt washed over her, sour milk mixed with battery acid, and she groaned. 'That's all behind us, Rex. No more screwups. I'll be light as a feather in there. Just trust me, all right?'

'Okay.' He looked at his watch. 'So what do we do for eight minutes?'

'Jeez, Loverboy, if you have to ask . . .'

He smiled and turned to her, leaning across the car seat. But his movements were tentative.

What are you hiding, Loverboy? she wondered.

As they kissed, she felt Rex's nervous energy buzzing across his lips. She ran her tongue lightly across them, transforming their flavor from anxiety into desire, drawing him closer. Melissa's own excitement – her anticipation of midnight, of using her new skills to manipulate Cassie's frozen mind – began to build. It overwhelmed Rex's tension, mixing with his arousal like two sharp tastes colliding in her mouth.

He reached to grasp her shoulders, his hands gloved against the accidental touch of steel, and pulled her closer.

She ran a hand inside his jacket, feeling her mind begin to spin. She could taste the ferment of Rex's ongoing transformation and wondered at its sweet electric taste, like Pop Rocks under her tongue, fizzing as it trickled down her throat.

Usually when they touched, her generations of mindcaster technique ensured that Melissa kept herself under control. But tonight Rex's newfound confidence, the strength in him that grew every day, threatened to overpower her. She caught glimpses of what had happened the night before, saw through his eyes the darkling in its dance, acknowledging him as another predator. *Talking* to him, almost.

And then the real cause of his guilt and anxiety came through: how close he had come to letting his darkling side boil over. She wondered what would be left of Cassie Flinders if *that* had happened . . .

Her ancient memories cautioned Melissa that Rex was becoming something no mindcaster had ever kissed before. There were shadows in him, ancient and terrifying.

But she ignored the warnings – this was *Rex*, after all. He was the only reason she had survived this long. All through those years while her mind had been untutored and undefended, *this* was all she'd wanted: to be able to touch him. Melissa felt herself let go of everything Madeleine had given her, all mastery and control, and allowed herself to sink into the darkness inside him.

Like the old minds across the desert, the things down there didn't have words, just images she could barely grasp – lore signs, a pile of bones, the smell of burning . . . the glorious rush of taking prey.

There was a moment of sharp pain, and then he pulled away, his body shuddering.

Melissa sat for a moment, watching his eyes flash violet in the moonlight, the echoes of what she'd felt in him subsiding slowly. She tasted salt and wondered for a moment what sort of mind noise it was, then realized that the taste was real – blood in her mouth.

'Crap,' she said, putting a hand to her lips. 'I bit my lip. How lame is that?'

'It wasn't you.' He turned away. 'Sorry . . . if that was weird.'

'It's okay, Rex.' Melissa touched her wounded lip tenderly. 'I had some spooky stuff in me too the first few times we touched. Remember?'

He turned back to her and pulled off one glove. He reached out, his fingertips lightly touching her mouth.

A shudder traveled through the car at that moment, all the random mind noise around them extinguished at once. Blue light swept across the world, and against the suddenly quiet mental landscape, the visions she'd taken from Rex's mind grew clearer.

She saw a piece of paper covered with the spindly symbols of the lore and knew that those unreadable signs were what had made him so edgy tonight.

Melissa squinted in the dark moon's light. 'What the hell?'

'I found it this morning.' Rex's voice was rough.

He reached into his jacket, pulling out a folded piece of paper. He opened it, revealing the same scrawled symbols she'd seen in his mind.

'So this is what's got you spooked?' She settled back onto the driver's side, sighing. 'Ancient seer wisdom about the end of the world?'

He shook his head. 'Not exactly ancient. Look.'

She peered closer. The symbols were written on lined paper, three-hole punched, with a confettied edge from being torn out of a spiral notebook.

'I don't understand. These are your notes?'

'I didn't write that. I found it on my kitchen table this morning.'

'Wait a second.' Melissa's mind spun. 'But it's written in lore signs, Rex.'

He nodded. 'That's right, Cowgirl. A slightly odd dialect, but readable.'

'And it just showed up on your kitchen table? But no one knows how to write the lore besides you. And . . . oh, crap.' Melissa placed the nail of her ring finger between her front teeth and bit down on it furiously. Her teeth slipped from the fingernail with a jarring *snap*. 'Those dominoes that the Grayfoots used to communicate with the darklings – they had lore symbols on them.'

'That's right. With the same slight differences as this one. It's even signed.' He pointed to the bottom right-hand corner of the page, where a cell phone number was written next to three spindly symbols grouped by a circle. '*Ah-nu-gee.*'

'What the hell is *ah-nu-gee*?'

'Each lore sign usually stands for a word, but when you put a circle around them, they turn into sounds, like using the alphabet. It's a way to spell out names and write about objects that didn't exist a few thousand years ago.'

She raised her eyebrows. 'And people back then didn't have *ah-nu-gee*? I repeat: what the hell?'

He laughed softly. 'What they didn't have back then were certain sounds. It was a Stone Age language, after all. "*Ah-nu-gee*" is as close as they could get to "*Angie*."'

'*Angie*.' Melissa's blood ran cold at the name. Angie, last name unknown, was one of the Grayfoots' agents. She'd translated the darklings' messages, had been in the desert that night Anathea had died, and it was her – Melissa was certain – leading the party that had kidnapped Rex. 'She *wrote* to you?'

He nodded. 'She wants to meet me.'

'*Meet* you? What the—?' Melissa pressed herself back against the car seat and growled, fists tightly clenched. 'Is she crazy?'

Rex gave that question a shrug. 'More scared than crazy, sounds like. The Grayfoots are up to something, and she doesn't know what. She says that after Anathea died, they cut her out of the loop because she's not family.'

'Oh, poor Angie,' Melissa hissed, her fingernails cutting into her palms. 'This is such crap. They just want to kidnap you again!'

He shook his head. 'Why? The darklings can't turn me into anything. Jessica burned away their special halfling-making spot.'

'So they just want to kill you, then. Spiteful little creeps. Finish what they started fifty years ago.'

'Melissa,' he said with maddening calm. 'They left it on my kitchen table, while I was *sleeping*. If they wanted to kill me, I'd be dead, right? What she wants is to exchange information. Like I said, she's scared.'

Melissa got herself under control, concentrating on her heartbeat until it slowed. 'Okay, then, Rex, an exchange of information sounds like fun. Why don't you offer to meet her at your house, say, around eleven fifty-five at night?' She felt her lips curl back from her teeth. 'I'll show her what *scared* really means.'

'I thought you were all featherlight these days.'

She snorted. 'Come on, Rex. It's a win-win situation. We'll know everything about the Grayfoots that she does, and she'll be left a drooling vegetable.'

He just stared at her, the old guilt of what they'd done to his father spreading through the car like a gas leak.

Melissa held his gaze for a moment but then let out a sigh. 'Sorry.' She turned away. 'Why did you keep this a secret from me, anyway?'

'Because it gave me an idea. Something you won't like.'

'You are *not* going to meet with her, Rex,' she hissed. 'Not unless it's in the middle of Bixby right before midnight and I'm there to rip that bitch's mind inside out. I don't care if the darklings can't make you a halfling anymore – Angie's a psycho. What's to stop her from trussing you up and giving you to the Grayfoots just to get back on their good side!'

'Don't worry. Meeting with her wasn't the idea I'm talking about.' He scratched his chin. 'I'm not even tempted to call. But something big is happening. And the information we need isn't in the lore. I may have to go directly to the source.'

'You're going to talk to Grandpa Grayfoot *himself*? He's an even bigger psycho than Angie. This is a guy who had a hundred people killed in one night!'

'Not him. When Anathea died, he was cut off from the darklings. He's probably panicking too.'

'So who else is left, Rex?'

He reached out and let his fingers stray across her lips again. She felt them glide across the sticky trickle of blood, tugging at the wounded skin beneath. Then an appalling thought drifted into her mind from his. She saw the desert, the light cool and flat and blue . . .

'No,' she said.

'They know what's going on. You said so yourself.'

'They'll eat you, Rex.'

He shook his head slowly. 'Wolves don't eat other wolves.'

'Um, Rex?' She cleared her throat. 'Maybe you're right. But I'm pretty sure that wolves do *kill* other wolves.'

'Hmm, good point.' He took a breath. 'But you felt what happened last night. It *talked* to me.'

She shuddered, recalling the images that had come from Rex's mind during their kiss – that huge spider practically doing the two-step with him, like they were old friends. The taste of its forelegs in their sinuous salute was still in her mouth. 'That was *one* darkling, Rex. You're talking about the deep desert. Dozens of them, maybe hundreds. We don't even know how many.'

'I haven't decided yet, okay?'

She looked out at the sliver of dark moon on the horizon, checking for winged shapes against it. When Rex had first suggested coming out here tonight without Jessica, she'd wondered if it was a good idea. They'd faced darklings on their own together, but this place had drawn huge clouds of slithers, and the taste of old minds lingered here.

But during their kiss Melissa had realized that she was safe here with Rex. Safe from darklings, anyway. He had become as much one of them as he was human.

Suddenly something odd caught her eye – a few leaves were falling near the tracks, giving off a soft red glow that looked completely strange here in the blue time. It was the rip, the sliver of unfrozen time. It must have been there that Cassie Flinders had been standing the morning before.

Melissa sighed. They had to deal with that girl tonight, not sit around talking. 'Okay, Rex, maybe you really can talk to darklings. But tell me before you do anything.'

He laughed. 'Think you can change my mind?'

'I'd never do that to you, Rex.'

'Do you swear, Cowgirl? No more of that, on me or anyone else, unless I'm there.'

'Absolutely.'

He took her hand, and Melissa let the surety of her promise flow into him. Whatever Rex was turning into, whatever crazy risks he decided to take, she would never twist or change a single thought in his brain . . .

Not even to save your life.

They crossed the tracks, pausing to look at the rip in the blue time. A red glimmer ran along its boundaries. It was about the size of an eighteen-wheeler now, much bigger than when Cassie had stepped through while her grandmother, only a few yards away, had remained frozen. The leaves from two trees caught within it were drifting down.

Rex stepped into the rip and caught a leaf. He dropped it, and it fell again.

'Feels different in here somehow.'

'Is it spreading all the time? Like, right now?'

He shook his head. 'Only during the eclipse, Dess says. It's like a fault line shifting during an earthquake.'

She pulled him away. This whole rip business gave her the creeps. The last thing Melissa needed was a bunch of annoying human minds invading midnight. 'Come on.'

Cassie Flinders's house was an old double-wide trailer, its concrete teeth sunk deep into the hard soil, gripping tenaciously against the Oklahoma wind. Halloween decorations were already up on the door – a grinning paper skeleton with swinging joints, orange and black bunting that glowed blue.

Rex stared at the skeleton for a moment.

'Friend of yours?' Melissa asked.

'Don't think so.' He pushed open the screen door, and its rusty hinges rang out in the blue time. The wooden door inside was unlocked. Rex smiled. 'Good country folk.'

They pushed into the blue-lit home, the floorboards creaking as they walked. Melissa wondered if the old wood stayed pressed down until the end of the secret hour, then popped up with a final complaint – letting out a sudden chorus of creaking just after the stroke of midnight. Flyboy was always wondering about stuff like that. If she was ever on normal speaking terms with the rest of them again, she'd have to ask him.

An old woman sat at a kitchen table, a bowl of something glowing an unappetizing blue in front of her. Her eyes were locked on a blank-screened TV. Melissa avoided her and the motionless cloud of smoke that rose from the cigarette clutched in her fingers.

Cassie's room was in one corner, the door plastered with drawings and more Halloween decorations. Rex pointed at the black cat. 'Funny, even after last night she didn't take that down.'

'Cats.' Melissa snorted. 'Smug, self-centered little beasts.' Then she remembered to add, 'Except yours, of course.'

'Daguerreotype's smugness is part of his charm.' He pushed the door open.

The room didn't reek of thirteen-year-old. No boy band posters, no dolls. The walls were covered with more drawings, crayon landscapes of Jenks, the Bixby skyline, and oil derricks, all drained of their color.

'Not bad,' Rex said. He pointed to a music stand, a clarinet leaning against it. 'Creative kid.'

'Good. Nobody believes the artistic ones.'

Cassie was lying on her bed, eyes closed and sheets tangled around her – a bad night of sleep in the making. Melissa wondered if being frozen for fifteen hours had given the girl some sort of jet lag and cracked her knuckles. She could fix that.

Even Rex's crazy plan to visit the darklings hadn't taken the edge off her excitement. This was her first serious mind-casting since Madeleine had started tutoring her.

'Featherlight,' she murmured softly.

She rested her fingers lightly on Cassie's waxy skin, her hands like a pair of pale blue spiders splayed across the girl's face. Melissa closed her eyes, entering the cool domain of a mind frozen in time.

Low-level nerves were scattered throughout Cassie, lingering shock from her trip into the secret hour. The taste of dread stung Melissa's lips, anxiety that the black cat would return, terror that the spider thing was still out there in the woods.

The girl had an artist's eye, Melissa had to admit. The slithers, the old darkling, the midnighters' faces were all in there, as crisp as if she'd snapped photographs. As she soothed the fears away, Melissa blurred the memories into shadowy figments.

This was so *easy* now, she thought. Not like the clumsy attempts she'd once called mindcasting. Thoughts and memories stood before her like chess pieces awaiting her command.

She remolded the images trapped in Cassie's mind, erasing

the words they'd said in front of her, turning everything into the sort of nonsense mush remembered from a dream. Melissa softened the sense of danger, made it all vague and formless, divorced it from the reality outside the double-wide's doors.

But she left intact one perfectly shaped bit of terror, a phobia a few yards across and a thousand miles deep . . .

Stay away from the railroad tracks at midnight. Something nasty *lives under them.*

'Done.' Melissa smiled as she withdrew her hands from Cassie's face. 'Now, *that* was some awesome, featherlight mindcasting.'

'That's it?' Rex asked. 'You were so fast. Like thirty seconds.'

Melissa smiled. It had seemed like long minutes. 'Bada-bing, bada-boom.'

'Has she talked to anyone? Told anyone what she saw?'

Melissa took a breath, stretching her muscles. 'She's been right here since I put her down, sleeping it off and doodling. Grandma didn't even let her talk on the phone. Her whole day was bedsores and boredom.'

'But what if she told—'

'Relax, Rex. Even if Cassie made a full report to the National Guard, when she wakes up tomorrow morning, she won't remember what she was babbling about. This is a done deal.'

'Maybe you should check her grandmother.'

'Rex, it's not a problem. Trust me. We've been doing this for thousands of years.'

His breath caught, and Melissa felt a twinge of jealousy from him; she had reminded him of all the knowledge she'd received from Madeleine. He'd finally gotten over that time when she'd touched Jonathan, and he understood about Dess, but when Melissa and the older mindcaster went up to the attic, he lost all rationality.

Funny, he was the one who knew the history. How mindcasters used to pass on information with a handshake, silently spreading midnighter news and gossip throughout Bixby. Compared to those days, Melissa was hardly some sort of mind slut.

She took a step closer to him. 'Come on. Let's go back to the car. I'll show you everything.'

'She saw what I almost became last night. Are you sure she—'

'Everything.' She drew him closer, silencing his lips with hers.

GOODBYE, BIXBY

'So the *weirdest* thing happened yesterday.'

Jessica nodded. She'd been expecting Constanza Grayfoot to tell her all about it. 'Yeah, I heard.'

Constanza came to a sudden halt in the hall, letting lesser mortals flow around them. 'You did? From who?'

Jessica shrugged. For once she'd known what everyone would be talking about way ahead of time. 'I don't remember who told me. Wasn't it on TV last night or something? How that lost kid just turned up in her bed yesterday morning, totally okay?'

'Oh, that. *Ancient* news, Jess. Pay attention here, please. I'm talking about something much weirder and much more likely to affect our, lives. Especially my life.'

Jessica blinked. 'Okay. What are you talking about?'

'My grandfather called me last night.'

Cold, dry fingers walked down Jessica's spine. 'He did what?'

'Called me, with the most incredible news. Come on, let's get to study hall. And I hope you don't have any stupid trig homework today because I'm going to need everyone's full attention.'

'You've got it.'

As they made their way up to the library, Jessica's heart pounded. Any mention of Constanza's grandfather definitely got her attention.

Grandpa Grayfoot was like anyone else not born at midnight – frozen during the secret hour. But as a kid he'd been a sort of super-evil version of Beth, spying on everyone and uncovering Bixby's secrets. He'd figured that the darklings were ghosts, or ancient spirits, or something equally creepy and had tried to communicate with them in secret midnight rituals. Eventually the darklings had answered, exchanging messages with him through a half-human, half-darkling creature – a translator between the two worlds.

Years of doing the darklings' bidding made his family rich and powerful, but the things that the midnight creatures asked him to do got more and more hideous. Fifty years ago the Grayfoots and their allies had been ordered to wipe out an entire generation of midnighters. They had all but succeeded; only Madeleine remained.

Just two weeks ago the translator who had made the whole thing possible had been close to death. The Grayfoots had tried to kidnap Rex so the darklings could turn him into a replacement, another halfling.

But the other midnighters had rescued Rex, and Anathea – the halfling – had died, destroying the old man's link to his masters. If he and his pals were still trying to contact the darklings, they were leaving messages that would never be returned.

Jessica followed Constanza into the library, wondering what on earth the old guy was up to now.

'Okay, this is absolutely top secret. I'm not even supposed to be telling you guys, so everyone here must swear never to tell a soul. Well, at least not until this is all final.'

'Until what's all final?' Liz asked.

'Whatever she's going to tell us,' Maria said. '*Duh.*'

'So, do you all swear?'

They went around the library table one by one, promising to keep the secret: Jen, Liz, Maria, and finally Jessica. By the time it got to her, Jess managed to get away with just a nod. She was pretty sure that she was going to have to tell the other midnighters about this in a big way, promise or no promise.

'Okay,' Constanza began once the ritual was complete. 'Remember when my house got trashed by those weirdos?'

Everyone nodded, eyes wide. Jessica tried to put on her not-guilty face. She'd witnessed the aftermath of Rex and Melissa burgling Constanza's house, back when they'd first been looking for evidence about the Grayfoot-darkling conspiracy. Not that the damage had all been their fault; there was nothing like a horde of midnight monsters showing up to leave a mess.

'Well, you probably remember how that totally freaked out my grandfather. He's always had this thing about not living in Bixby.'

'You guys stayed with him in Broken Arrow after that happened, right?' Liz asked.

'We did. And let me tell you, I was totally sick of commuting to school. So . . .' Constanza leaned closer, indicating that the top secret part was coming up, and Jessica dared a glance at Dess, sitting in her usual corner. Dess held her trig book up to cover her face, which meant she was listening to every word. She needed to study trigonometry about as hard as a darkling needed to study scary.

'Well, Grandpa must have had a slow leak about me coming back to Bixby,' Constanza continued. 'You know, he cut my dad out of the family oil business when he and Mom moved here, ages ago. He still hardly talks to them, even when we were staying out there. So anyway, he called me last night, trying to convince me to leave town.'

'What's his problem with Bixby, anyway?' Maria asked.

Constanza shrugged. 'He never tells anyone what happened. He grew up here, but something weird went down when he was a teenager. I think the Anglos chased the family out of town during the oil boom because we're Native American and everything. He hasn't set foot in Bixby in, like, fifty-something years.'

Except for slipping across the edge of the midnight border to leave his little messages, Jessica thought. Then a horrible notion occurred to her.

'He wants you to go live in Broken Arrow?' Jessica asked. She'd always wondered if the old man knew that Constanza and she were friends. Maybe he planned to finally bring his granddaughter into the real family business – working for the darklings.

'Excuse me, Jess? Me, living in puny little Broken Arrow?' Constanza shook her head and snorted. 'No way.'

'So where, then?' Liz asked. 'Tulsa?'

'No.' Constanza lowered her voice still further, and Jessica saw Ms. Thomas, the librarian, straining to hear. 'You know how I'm going to be an actress?'

Everyone nodded, a few of them exchanging glances. You only had to know Constanza for about ten minutes to hear about that aspiration.

'Well, my grandfather said that if I wanted to start right now, I could come stay with him. Because in a couple of weeks he and a whole bunch of my cousins are moving to . . . now get this . . . *LA!*'

'Los Angeles?' Maria cried.

'No, Maria,' Liz said with a sneer. 'Lower Argentina. That's the new LA. Haven't you heard?' She turned to Constanza. 'Los *Angeles*? I hate you. You are *so* lucky.'

'You've got to be kidding,' Jessica said. Her mouth had gone dry.

'Grandpa's got it all worked out,' Constanza said. 'He's already found a school for me there, and this movie agent who's a business friend of his wants to meet me. And he says I can have an awesome allowance to pay for acting lessons and stuff.'

'I can't *believe* you!' Liz said. 'I'm going to *kill* you. After I come visit, of course. I can come visit, right?'

'So why exactly is he going to LA?' Jessica asked.

Constanza shrugged. 'I don't know. There must be oil wells there. Right?'

'In Los Angeles?' That didn't seem likely. Nor did it seem very likely that the old man was concentrating on his oil business anymore. He seemed more focused on getting himself and his family as far away from Bixby as possible.

'Who cares *why* he's going there, Jess? As long as the result is' – Constanza pointed both her index fingers toward herself – 'movie star!'

'Girls!' Ms. Thomas called from her desk. 'Could you *please* keep it down to a dull roar?'

Jen turned to the librarian. 'But Constanza's going to—'

'Shhh!' Constanza hissed. 'Could we please all remember about the top secret thing?' Then she turned and called out in a normal voice, 'Sorry, Ms. Thomas. We'll try to be more quiet.' She glared at Jen. 'Especially you.'

'Wait a second,' Jessica said. 'Why is this all a big secret?'

'Well, believe it or not,' Constanza said. 'I haven't mentioned the weirdest part of this yet.' She paused, waiting until all eyes were on her again. 'It's like this whole moving-to-LA thing just appeared out of nowhere. Grandpa hasn't even talked to my parents about it yet. But in the meantime he says that there's this agent who needs somebody like me right away, for some new TV show or something. So first I'm going to go "visit" Grandpa out there, supposedly just for a week or so. I can audition then, and if I get the part, I'm not coming back!'

Everyone was quiet for a moment as Constanza's words gradually sank in. Jessica felt her own pulse pounding in her fingertips and saw Dess lower her book slowly so that she could see the other girls. Even Ms. Thomas shot them a glance, intrigued by their sudden silence.

Liz spoke first. 'Right away?'

'Like . . . when?' Maria asked.

Constanza shook her head, her mouth slightly open, as if she still couldn't believe it herself. 'Well, they're holding auditions in a couple of weeks, right about when Grandpa and my cousins are all moving out there. So he said I have to be there before the end of this month or the whole thing's off. So in a couple of weeks or so, it's goodbye, Bixby!'

'You're kidding!' said Jen.

'You are so psychotically *lucky*!' said Maria.

'I repeat: I *hate* you!' said Liz. 'And you've *got* to have a going-away party!'

Jessica didn't say anything. Suddenly the library's fluorescent lights were buzzing too loud for her to think clearly. The old man and his family moving, this agent for Constanza – all of it was happening way too fast for any innocent explanation to be believed.

Constanza's last words rang in her ears: *Goodbye, Bixby . . .*

Jessica glanced over at Dess and saw the polymath drop her trig book onto her lap and pull out a few pieces of paper. She hunched over them, scribbling furiously, filling page after page with grids drawn in blue ink. One of the pages fell to the floor . . .

Jessica squinted and saw that it was divided into seven squares across and five down, like a wall calendar. Each of the squares was filled with cryptic formulas in tiny, manic handwriting.

She closed her eyes and did a few simple calculations herself.

It was the eighth of October today and she knew from her father's annoying little rhyme that October had thirty-one days.

The end of the month was just over three weeks away.

12

LUNCH MEAT

'Okay, guys,' Dess said. 'There's some good news and some bad news.'

The others looked at her tiredly, already shell-shocked from the weirdness of the last fifty-three hours. Dess was glad she'd waited until all five of them were here; no sense explaining this twice.

Dess found it oddly comforting to be sitting here at the old corner table, the one farthest from the windows, where she and Rex and the Vile One had always eaten together, back before Melissa had revealed her totally evil side. The lunch-room rumbled along around them in its familiar state of chaos, daylighters jockeying for prime table space, unaware of the major trouble that was on its way.

Rex, of course, spoke up first. 'Okay. What's the bad news?'

Dess shook her head. 'Sorry, Rex. But it's one of those things where the good news has to come first. Otherwise there's no punch line.'

'Come on, Dess,' Jessica said. 'This is serious. Don't you think this is serious?'

'Good question.' Dess stared down at her pile of extremely rough calculations. On the one hand, all their information had come from Constanza Grayfoot, which made it inherently suspect. Her instant TV-star status had sounded more like a psycho-cheerleader wet dream than a prophecy of the end times. Dess often wondered how the same family that had managed to undo thousands of years of midnighter rule in Bixby had also produced Constanza.

But as the girl's revelations in study hall had gotten weirder and weirder, Dess had stopped smirking and done her own calculations. The numbers were grim.

The four of them stared at her expectantly, but she just waited. That was the good thing about being the one who actually did the math. Other people had to play by your rules.

Finally Jessica sighed. 'Okay, Dess. What's the *good* news?'

Dess allowed herself a victorious smile. 'Well, it doesn't look like the *whole* world is going to end.'

That got a reaction. Rex raised both eyebrows, and Jonathan managed to stop eating for five whole seconds. Jessica was already freaking out, of course, but her expression angsted up a notch. And Melissa . . . Well, the bitch goddess looked like she always did at lunch: a bit pained by all the mind chaos of the cafeteria, even though she was supposedly in control these days.

'Of course, the math isn't 100 percent sure at this point,' Dess admitted.

'So wait,' Rex said. 'What's the *bad* news, then?'

'The bad news is that Bixby County, including the whole area of the blue time as we know it, plus definitely a big chunk of Broken Arrow and probably Tulsa, and possibly the top half of Oklahoma City – and hell, let's just throw in everything from Wichita to Dallas to Little Rock while we're at it – might very well get sucked into the blue time. In about three weeks.'

Dess took a deep breath, feeling a rush of relief now that the proclamation had been made. It was sort of like being the first astronomer to spot one of those big dinosaur-extermination-sized asteroids on its way toward Earth. Sure, this was majorly unpleasant news for everyone, including Dess personally, but at least *she* got to announce it. Doing the calculations always gave Dess a feeling of control. After all, it was better to be one of the astronomers headed for the hills than, say, one of the dinosaurs.

'And you just found this out,' Rex said slowly, 'in *study hall?*'

'The library is a wonderful place to learn new things, Rex.'

'It was Constanza,' Jessica said.

'You got this from that cheerleader?' Jonathan snorted. 'Well, that makes me feel a *lot* better.'

Jessica gave him a nasty look. 'This isn't about Constanza. Her grandfather – who's definitely *not* a cheerleader – knows something. He's evacuating his whole family.'

'Evacuating?' Rex said. 'But they don't even live in Bixby.'

'That's the point, Rex.' Dess spread her hands. 'Remember when I said the blue time might be expanding? Well, it looks like Broken Arrow isn't far enough away from the darklings anymore. So the Grayfoots are bailing out, running away, heading for the hills. Got it?'

Rex paused for a moment before saying, 'That's . . . interesting.'

'And how far away is the old guy going?' Dess continued. 'Tulsa? Nope. Oklahoma City? Sorry, too close. What about Houston, oilman's paradise? Five hundred miles away but still not far enough, apparently. Because he's taking himself and his whole extended family, including his annoying grand-daughter, all the way *to California*.'

'Yeah,' Jessica added. 'And there's not much oil business in LA.'

Dess leaned back and crossed her arms, waiting for their tiny little brains to catch up. She wished she had a map to show them. When astronomers in movies had to explain that the world was getting clobbered, they always had those fancy computer simulations to make the disaster come to life, or at least a whiteboard.

'But how does he know anything?' Flyboy asked, his jaws still working on a peanut butter sandwich. 'Anathea's dead. There's no other halfling to translate for them. So the Grayfoots are cut off from the darklings, aren't they?'

'Exactly,' Rex said. 'And probably *that's* why Grandpa's freaking out. Maybe since the darklings have stopped answering his messages, he believes those words we left for him: YOU'RE NEXT.'

Jessica shot Dess a puzzled look. Apparently she hadn't thought of that one.

Dess had, though. 'I admit he's afraid of the darklings, Rex. You made sure of that. But he's not just nervous; he's working on a schedule.'

'A schedule?' Rex leaned forward. 'How do you mean?'

'Okay: history lesson.' She leaned forward, addressing Rex directly. 'Grandpa Grayfoot kicked Constanza's parents out of the clan when they moved to Bixby, right?'

'Because he knew about mindcasters,' Melissa said. 'He didn't want anyone in the family business here, where we could rip their memories.'

A shudder went through Dess. 'Lovely choice of words, Melissa. But basically, yeah. So maybe he doesn't care what happens to her parents because they disobeyed the no Bixby rule.'

'But Constanza's still his favorite granddaughter,' Jessica said.

'Mystifyingly,' Dess muttered.

'She's really nice,' Jessica said defensively. 'And it's true, he really likes her. He buys her tons of clothes.'

Melissa nodded. 'We've seen the closets.'

'Lucky you,' Dess said. 'But closets full of tacky clothes are nothing compared to what the old guy's bribing her with now. He's invited her to come live in Los Angeles and *promised* that she's going to be a TV star. But there are two catches. One: she can't tell her parents about it.'

A guilty look crossed Jessica's face. 'Actually, she wasn't supposed to tell anyone at all.'

'Yeah.' Dess chuckled. 'Good move, telling Constanza to keep a secret. It would've been smarter to just come by in a van and grab her. Worked on Rex, after all.'

'Like I said, he thinks the darklings are coming after his family,' Rex said. 'But that doesn't prove the world's ending.'

Dess shook her head. 'No, it doesn't. Which brings us to catch number two: Constanza has to get her butt out to Hollywood by the end of the month or, and I quote, "the whole thing's off." And Grandpa's moving the rest of his clan out there in two weeks – from *Broken Arrow*, Rex, where the darklings can't reach. Not yet anyway.'

She let that sink in for a moment. The noise of the lunchroom seemed to grow around them, like the rumble of a coming storm.

'But how would he know the blue time's expanding?' Rex said. 'There's no halfling to tell him.'

'Maybe he already knew,' Melissa said suddenly. She squinted, chewing her lip. 'The oldest darklings did.'

Rex shook his head, still unconvinced. Dess realized what the problem was: he refused to believe that the Grayfoots knew something he didn't.

Jessica spoke up. 'It's so sad. Constanza thinks that she's going to an audition and that she'll get an agent and acting lessons and stuff. But she's leaving her parents behind forever.'

'She's one of the lucky ones,' Dess said. 'At least she'll be out of town before October 31.'

'Hey,' Flyboy said. 'That's Halloween!'

'Um, yeah.' Dess raised an eyebrow. 'I hadn't thought of that. It's kind of . . . interesting, but it's not numbers.' She frowned at Rex. 'Anything about Halloween in the lore?'

'Of course not.' He shrugged. 'There was no Halloween in Oklahoma until about a hundred years ago.'

Dess nodded. 'Fine, enough with history. Here's the math: when you boil it into numbers, October 31 seems like no big deal at first. I mean, the sum is forty-one, and you get three hundred-ten when you multiply. No relevant numbers there. But in the old days October wasn't the tenth month, it was the eighth. You know, *Oc*tober, like an octagon, with eight sides?' They all looked at her blank-faced, and Dess suppressed a groan. Next time she was definitely bringing visual aids. 'Come on, guys. Eighth month? Thirty-first day? And eight plus thirty-one is . . .?'

'Thirty-nine?' Jessica said.

'Give the girl a prize.'

'Wait a second, Dess,' Flyboy said. 'I thought thirty-nine

was a major *anti*darkling number. Like all those thirty-nine-letter names.'

'Magisterially Supernumerary Mathematician,' Dess supplied. 'An instant classic. And yes, the number thirty-nine is totally antidarkling. The real problem is the *next* day.'

'Isn't that All Saints' Day or something?' Jonathan said.

Dess let out an exasperated breath. This wasn't about spooks or ghosts or saints; it was about *numbers*. 'Don't know. Don't care.'

Melissa brought her fingers up to her temples. 'Hang on, guys.'

Dess ignored her. 'But November 1, here in the modern era, is the *first* day of—'

'Guys!' Melissa cried out.

They were all silent for a moment, and Dess thought she heard the hubbub of the cafeteria fade for a few seconds, as if a chill had spread through the room. Her fingertips were tingling, and a trickle of nerves filtered their way down to the pit of her stomach.

'Something's *coming*,' Melissa whispered.

As the words passed the mindcaster's lips, a tremor rolled across the room, the shudder of the spinning earth halting in its tracks. The roar of the cafeteria was sucked away all at once, leaving the five of them surrounded by almost two hundred stiffs, faces blue and cold and waxen, caught throwing food and picking their noses and chewing with their mouths open.

'What time is it, Rex?' Dess's own voice sounded small in the awesome, sudden silence.

Rex looked at his watch. 'Twelve twenty-one and fifteen seconds.'

Dess wrote the number down and stared at it, wondering how long this one was going to last.

Jonathan bobbed weightlessly up from his chair. 'Cool, this again.'

'What are we supposed to do?' Jessica said softly.

'We just sit here,' Rex said. 'We wait it out. And get *down*, Jonathan!'

'Why?' Jonathan said. 'I can fall from here, no problem.'

'There are people all around, Jonathan. If you fly off someplace and the blue time ends, they'll see you disappear.'

'Come on, Jonathan.' Jessica reached up and took his hand. 'Plenty of time to fly when the world ends.'

'All right, whatever.' Jonathan sighed, settling back onto his chair like a deflating balloon.

No one said anything for a moment. Dess's eyes were drawn to the tray in front of Rex, whose cafeteria lunch had already been left to congeal during the discussion. Its waxy layer of interrupted time made it look even more unappetizing, his Jell-O glowing blue, its wobble arrested.

Melissa held her head tipped back, tasting the air to her heart's content, and for once Dess was glad that the mindcaster was around. At least they'd know if an army of darklings was on its way.

Of course, this wasn't the end of the world, not yet. You could tell just by looking. If the secret hour had snapped completely, all the stiffs around them would still be moving, having been sucked into the blue time along with everything else within a few hundred miles.

Dess didn't have to do any math to know what the result of that would be. All those predators suddenly escaping from their midnight prison, unleashed on their prey –

maybe millions of people, if the blue time really expanded across the whole state. No phones, no cars, not even fire, and only the five midnighters knew how to defend themselves.

Dess fixed her gaze on a constellation of french fries hovering over a motionless food fight across the lunchroom. She wondered if what she'd told Jessica yesterday after school was really true. Could you make it to the border of the blue time, freezing yourself at the edge until the long midnight ended?

Not too many people would be lucky enough to make it that far. Not with all those hungry darklings pouring in from the desert. And what if the blue time *never* ended? What if everyone on the outside was permanently frozen and everyone in the inside was lunch meat – most of humanity gone with a whimper, the rest with a bang?

'So, Dess?' Jessica said, finally breaking the silence.

She pulled her gaze from the hovering french fries. 'Yeah?'

'In study hall, what were you scribbling on those papers? You said Halloween was safe. What's wrong with the next day?'

'Oh, yeah.' Dess looked down at the papers before her, tinged blue by the eclipse. 'Well, the weird thing is what happens at midnight, Halloween, if you switch from the old system to the new. October 31 was an antidarkling fiesta back when October was the eighth month. But now November's the eleventh month. Right?' Dess spread her hands. 'Man, you guys are hopeless. So it's November 1. And eleven plus one is *twelve*, as in midnight. As in darklings.'

They were all silent for a moment.

Finally Jonathan asked, 'How long is that from now?'

'Twenty-three days, eleven hours, and thirty-nine minutes,' Dess said. 'Minus fifteen seconds.'

'Three weeks.' Jessica looked at Rex. 'So what should we do?'

Dess was glad to see him scratch his brow, at least pretending like he was coming up with a plan. However messed up Rex's head was, the coming end of the world might screw it on a little bit tighter.

'I'm not convinced yet, Dess,' he said after a minute. 'But I guess we have to find out more about what the Grayfoots are up to.'

'How are we supposed to do that?' Jonathan said. 'Just drive over to Broken Arrow and ask them?'

He smiled. 'Maybe it's better if we get them over to Bixby.'

Everyone stared at him, but Rex didn't blink.

Dess leaned back into her chair, wondering what Rex was smoking. When the last bunch of midnighters had gotten in Grandpa Grayfoot's way, he'd made a hundred prominent citizens disappear overnight. Less than two weeks ago the Grayfoots had kidnapped Rex right out of his own house, then left him in the desert to have his humanity stripped away.

But for some reason he wasn't scared of them. Dess might not be a mindcaster, but she could see that. What the hell was happening to him?

It was funny, but ever since the bitch goddess had gotten under control, Rex had gone six kinds of crazy. It was like the five of them only had so much sanity to go around.

'Rex, be serious,' Jessica said softly.

'I am serious.' He reached into his jacket and threw a piece of paper on the table. It was covered with scrawled lore signs. 'This is a message from Angie.'

'That psycho who kidnapped you?' Jonathan asked.

'That's the one.'

'Um, Rex.' Dess shook her head. 'Why didn't you mention this earlier?'

'Sorry. It only showed up yesterday morning, and I wasn't sure what to do about it – until now.'

'Burn it, maybe?' suggested Dess.

Rex ignored her. 'From what Angie says, the family is closing ranks, leaving outsiders like her in the dark. She's just as freaked out as we are.' His fingers drummed the table. 'Which means that Dess might be right.'

'About burning it?' Dess said.

'No, about what's going to happen in three weeks and that the Grayfoots know more about it than we do. So I guess I should meet with her.'

Jonathan stared at the piece of paper with a horrified expression, like a live rattlesnake had flopped onto the table. 'What the hell, Rex? You're actually going to trust her?'

'I don't trust her at all. But I've been wondering about this message and figuring out a way to get Angie over to Bixby, whether she wants to come or not. We'll all have to work together, though.' He looked around at them, a seer-knows-best expression on his face.

Dess sighed, wondering if anyone else had noticed how every time all five of them did anything together, things went totally haywire.

'Hang on, guys!' Melissa said suddenly. 'It's ending.'

Rex snatched the scrawled paper from the table. 'Get ready.'

Jonathan pulled himself firmly down onto his seat. Melissa put her fingers back on her temples, the way she'd been when the eclipse had hit. Dess tried to remember what she'd been doing – probably looking at Melissa and wondering what the hell she was yelling about.

She turned toward the mindcaster and gave her a suitable look of contempt.

A few seconds later the world shuddered again. The cold blue light was swept from the cafeteria, which exploded around them into a mass of motion and sound and sunlight. The seventeen french fries sailed on their various trajectories, two hundred mouths resumed their chewing, and Rex's Jell-O began to wobble once more.

Dess pulled at Rex's arm and looked at his watch, comparing it with the time on her GPS device. This eclipse had been shorter than the first one, lasting only seven minutes and twelve seconds. But it had followed a similar pattern: three times 144 seconds.

Now that it was over, Dess allowed herself a long sigh. However certain she'd been that the big event was three weeks away, it was a relief to know the end hadn't come.

Not this time, anyway.

13

BRILLIANT PLAN

Broken Arrow hadn't changed much, as far as Rex could see.

The town was still Bixby's little sister, with no buildings over a few stories marking its skyline. Clanking oil derricks and mesquite trees went right up to the city's edge, and instead of green lawns most people had dirt front yards. The native desert scrub they planted to keep the soil from eroding needed a lot less water than grass – and looked better, Rex thought – but in Bixby not having a real lawn meant that you were poor or lazy, which most people figured was pretty much the same thing.

He drove carefully, checking the street signs, following the exact route that Dess had used for her calculations. She'd complained about that part of the plan because too many things could mess with the math – how fast Rex drove, the air pressure in the tires, even the temperature outside. She spent a lot of time complaining about something called 'fumes.'

Rex couldn't think about all that. It was all he could do to drive this rumbling, smelly, *human* machine. His reflexes were much faster now, but the plastics and metal in the car put him on edge.

Besides, there were lots of ways this plan could go wrong. The precisely measured gas in the Ford's tank was only one.

It was strange being in Melissa's car without her along, but Angie had demanded three things: that they meet no later than 11:00 p.m., that they didn't go *anywhere* near Bixby, and that Rex come alone.

He remembered how nervous Angie's voice had sounded on the phone. But Rex didn't want her too anxious. He wouldn't get any information from the woman if things got violent.

He found the corner Angie had named, two narrow back alleys that intersected among dark and looming warehouses, the prey marks of humans scant – the perfect place for Rex to disappear, if that's what Angie had in mind. Of course, if Rex were still relevant to the family's plans, they probably wouldn't have gone to this much trouble.

Still, he was glad it was just him here in the car and not all five of them. The Grayfoots were old hands at making people vanish.

Angie was already there, smoking a cigarette and wearing a leather coat that reached her knees. She gave him an angry glare, checked her watch, then cast a wary glance around. As she walked toward the Ford, Rex realized that he'd never seen her in normal time before. In motion and without the waxy pallor of the secret hour laid across her skin, she didn't look that much older than a college student.

He remembered to turn off the Ford's engine; Dess's calculations didn't include any idling time.

'You're late,' she said.

'Sorry. My mom came over. Had to sneak out – school night.'

Her eyes narrowed with suspicion, but then she let out a smoke-tinged sigh. Nothing like being reminded that the latest person you'd kidnapped was still in high school. Rex hoped that seeing Anathea dead out in the desert had made Angie think twice about her employers. Hopefully she was fed up with the kid-snatching business.

'Fine, let's talk,' she said. 'But in exactly twenty minutes I'm out of here. You're not going to pull any of that spook crap on me.'

Rex laughed. 'What sort of "spook crap" are you expecting? We're miles from Bixby.'

'Yeah, I know where the edges are,' she said. 'But before the Grayfoots stopped talking to me, Ernesto said that things were changing.'

Rex nodded. Ernesto was Constanza's cousin – the family definitely knew something.

'They are,' he said. 'Get in and I'll tell you what we know.'

'What? Get in that car with you?'

He gave her a bored look. 'Don't be so paranoid, Angie. Midnight still comes at midnight, not . . .' He checked his watch, as if he hadn't planned this all out to the minute. 'Eleven-fifteen. And I'm not standing around in the cold.' He tugged on the front of his T-shirt; not wearing a jacket had been Jessica's idea. 'So get in.'

Her nervous eyes scanned the buildings around them again. 'Okay, but *my* car.'

'Forget that,' he said. 'My wheels or no deal.'

Rex held her suspicious gaze, wondering if that last line had been too much. He'd rehearsed it on the way over here, trying out various inflections, settling on a dramatic pause between 'no' and 'deal.' But maybe he'd blown it. The rest of the plan wouldn't work unless Angie got into Melissa's car.

But as he watched her think about it, Rex felt something else replace his jitters – the same calm he'd experienced just before he'd turned Timmy Hudson into jelly. He could smell Angie's fear now, could see it in the play of lines on her face, and he realized that she'd been telling the truth about the Grayfoots cutting her off. She carried the anxious scent of a human rejected by its tribe, left to its own devices on the harsh desert.

A trickle of anticipation went through Rex, the same excitement he'd felt tracking Cassie Flinders across the blue time. He was the hunter here, not this human.

'Take it or leave it, Angie. But don't make me sit here.' He drew his lips back from his teeth. 'Like I said: it's a school night.'

A long moment later she said, 'Okay. But if you start that engine, I'm sticking this between your ribs.' Steel flashed in the darkness.

At the sight of the knife Rex felt some of his predatory confidence slip away. He could smell that the blade was tungsten stainless; its very touch would burn him. Rex couldn't imagine what the weapon would feel like thrust into his side.

Angie walked the long way around the car, checking the backseat for any surprises. Finally she opened the passenger door and slipped inside, bringing in the scents of anxiety and cigarette smoke.

'You know,' he said. 'Seeing as how you kidnapped me, you've got a lot of nerve acting like I'm the bad guy.'

She snorted, running nervous fingers through her blond hair. 'Spare me. I know what you midnighters are.'

'What? High school students?'

She turned away to stare through the front windshield, watching the empty alley. 'It doesn't matter how old you are. A monster is still a monster.'

'*Me?* A monster?' For a second the word made him shudder. Did she know about the way he was changing?

Angie turned to him, her words spilling out with furious speed. 'Listen, Rex, the family may have shut me out after what happened two weeks ago, but I know a lot about the history of Bixby. Probably more than you do.'

Rex's jaw dropped open. 'I doubt that.'

'Right, I'm sure you think you know everything.' She smiled. 'You may know a few tricks, like how to read fifty-year-old propaganda, but you don't know what things were really like in Bixby back then. You weren't there. The old guy I work for was.'

'What? He's a . . .' Rex started, but he was too indignant to finish. This traitor to humanity, this Grayfoot lackey, this *daylighter* was lecturing *him* about the lore? Rex's amazement sputtered out of him like an old car engine giving up the ghost.

He'd made Melissa swear to take it easy on Angie's brain, but Rex doubted it would be tough to make her break that promise.

'After they freed Bixby,' Angie continued, 'the Grayfoots discovered a lot of what you midnighters call "the lore." That's how I learned to read the symbols, practicing on all that old rubbish about how the great midnighters kept everyone happy and safe.'

'The Grayfoots *freed* Bixby?' was all Rex could manage. 'From what?'

'Come on, Rex. What do you think it was really like back then? A small, unelected group of people running a tiny town in the middle of nowhere. People who could play God with time, who could ruin the brain of anyone who disagreed with them. Doesn't that sound great, Rex, growing up in a place like that?' She paused, giving him a disgusted look. 'Of course, you would have been one of the people in charge.'

'But midnighters aren't about controlling people's minds.'

'Are you kidding?'

'Well, they only did it to keep the secret hour hidden, to keep the town safe.'

Angie barked out a single-syllable laugh. 'Sometime, Rex, you should read some *real* history. Everyone who abuses power says exactly the same thing: "We only do nasty, secret things to keep everyone safe. Without us in charge, you're all doomed."'

'What are . . .?' He growled, unable to organize his thoughts. 'You *kidnapped* me!'

She looked away, letting out a slow breath, and Rex thought for a moment that he had finally quieted her madness. But after a moment she turned back and said, 'It was the only way to stay in contact with the darklings. Without them we couldn't keep you from re-creating the old Bixby.' She shrugged, the thick leather coat creaking. 'Besides, do you know how many hundreds of children the old midnighters kidnapped over the years?'

'What?' Rex cried. But then he remembered the ancient tales: when mindcasters detected newly born midnighters nearby, war parties had been dispatched to steal them. More recently, offers of jobs and money had been sent to their parents. Rex found himself wondering, though – if those inducements hadn't worked, had the old midnighters resorted to stronger tactics? There wasn't anything like that in the lore, but what if they had just pretended it hadn't happened?

'Well,' he said, 'maybe a long time ago they did some things that seem weird now, sort of like . . . George Washington having slaves or whatever.' Rex shook his head firmly. 'But *we're* not like that!'

'I've seen your father, Rex,' she said calmly. 'Did a stroke leave him that way?'

'That was . . .' His voice broke. 'We were just kids.'

She rolled her eyes. 'Yeah. Born monsters, like I said.'

They were silent for a moment, Rex's head spinning from everything Angie had said. When he'd seen her name in lore symbols at the bottom of the note, there had been a moment of curiosity; even if she wasn't a seer, here was someone else who could read the lore, who knew the signs of midnight. But after just a few minutes of talking to her, he felt his oldest sureties in danger of crumbling.

Was she making all this up? Could there really be a secret history *behind* the secret history?

He took a deep breath, checking his watch. The only way to find out was to stick to the plan; Melissa could get to the bottom of this.

'In any case,' Angie said. 'I didn't come here to debate midnighter ethics. Just don't sit there pretending like I'm some kind of demon, all right?'

'Fine.' Rex forced himself to calm down. This was nuts, sitting here questioning what was what. It was probably the new predator part of his mind, willing to believe anything said against the humans who had dared to challenge the darkling kind.

He just had to let the plan unfold. Keep stalling and make sure that Angie stayed nervous.

'Just one quick question,' he said. 'Your employers? The nice people who "freed" Bixby. What would they do if they knew you were here talking to me?'

She let out a short, dry laugh. 'Probably cut me into small pieces. Maybe you too.'

Rex allowed a grim smile to show on his face. He'd been hoping she would say something like that. 'Talk about monsters.'

'I never said they were perfect. Far from it.' She crossed her arms. 'All right, since it's a school night and everything, shall we move on from the mutual recriminations? I told you some of what I know in my note. Maybe I'll have more to tell you later. But you go first.'

'Okay.' Rex glanced at his watch. He still had fifteen minutes to kill. 'There have been signs of change in the blue time.'

'Blue time?'

'You know, the secret hour.' Rex blinked. He'd forgotten that 'blue time' had originally been Dess's term – not part of the lore. 'Everything turns kind of blue when time freezes.'

Angie just looked at him.

'What?' he said. 'You didn't know that?'

'Yeah, I've read the accounts. But I never got used to the idea of you midnighters,' she said. 'It's one thing that spooks live in the secret hour, but *human beings* walking around while the rest of us are frozen?' She shivered. 'It's so creepy.'

He snorted a laugh. 'Trust me. They're the creepy ones, not us. Whatever you've read about the darklings, I've *seen* them.'

'But you haven't read their words,' she said. 'And I have.'

Rex was silent for a moment. It was true – Grandpa Grayfoot had managed to do something that no seer had ever done before. He'd communicated with the enemy.

But now Rex had gone one better – he'd actually communicated with a darkling face-to-face. He thought again about heading out to the desert, meeting with the old minds there, hearing what *their* perspective was about all this history.

Now, that would be a brain bender . . . if they didn't kill him first.

As Rex stared out the window, he saw a car flash past at the end of the alley. He swallowed, glancing at his watch again. They were early.

Angie hadn't seen it, though.

'Well, whatever,' he said. 'When time freezes, it's blue. But this last week something really strange happened. Something that's not in any lore I've ever read.'

'A timequake.'

He looked at her. 'A what?'

'A spontaneous fluctuation of the prime contortion Releasing the energies built up over the centuries.'

'Um, yeah.' He drummed his fingers on the seat. *Prime contortion?* Maybe Angie really had read a few things that Rex hadn't. 'We've been calling it an eclipse. But it might be more like a tremor, a warning of bigger things to come.'

'And that's why the Grayfoots' houses all sprouted For Sale signs last week?'

He nodded. 'We think that the blue time is going to expand, suddenly and without much warning, getting big enough to swallow Broken Arrow.'

She stared at him for a moment, then said, 'Jesus. No wonder they're running. When?'

He shook his head and smiled. 'I think I'll save that piece of information until you tell me more. Such as, when are the Grayfoots leaving Broken Arrow?'

'Well, I'm not a hundred percent sure,' she said. 'But there is something they've all been talking about for a while.'

'What is it?'

Suddenly lights swept through the interior of the car.

'What the . . .?' Angie said, turning to look back.

Rex winced as he glanced in the mirror. A pair of headlights loomed at the other end of the alley. *Jonathan and Dess, you morons*, he thought. *Can't you read a clock?*

They'd come way too soon.

But there was only one thing to do: stick with the plan. He started the engine.

'What the hell are you doing?' Angie shouted.

'They're coming for us,' he said. The headlights were closing fast. 'They must have followed you!' He put the car in gear and rolled down the alley.

'Oh, Christ! Let me out!' She started to open her door. Rex accelerated, and the door crushed a trash can with a sickening sound, swinging closed with a thunk. *Sorry, Melissa*, he thought.

'You'll never make it to your car!' he shouted. 'Just hang on. I'll get us out of here.'

He accelerated down the alley and out onto the first street on Dess's route map. As he turned right, the Ford's freshly filled tires screeched across the asphalt.

The headlights swept out of the alley behind them, clinging to his tail.

Very convincing, Flyboy.

'I don't know if I can outrun them,' he said. 'This car's pretty old.'

'Oh, great! You know, my car goes plenty fast!'

'I didn't know you were going to bring company!' he shouted. 'I'll head for the highway.'

He hit Highway 75 and turned west, bringing the Ford up to eighty miles per hour. This was the diciest part of the plan. Going over the speed limit was bad enough, given that it was curfew time back in Bixby, but if another eclipse – or time-quake, or fluctuation of the prime contortion – suddenly struck, Rex would plow through the windshield like a bullet.

'Hey! You're headed to Bixby!' The knife flashed in the corner of Rex's eye – he smelled steel inches from his face.

'Oh, crap.' He swallowed, finding it easy to sound scared. 'Just headed home by reflex. Sorry.'

He heard a growl rise in her throat, but no burning blade of steel pierced his ribs just yet.

'Listen,' he said. 'There aren't any exits before Bixby except the access road. We can follow it through Saddleback.'

'Don't try to mess with me, Rex. That's inside the contortion!'

'Yeah, but we can go straight through to the other side of the county. You'll be in and out of the blue time inside ten minutes.'

'Dammit, Rex . . .' She looked at her watch.

'Maybe the Grayfoots will be afraid to follow us in!'

Angie's voice suddenly grew very calm. 'Okay, keep driving. It's before eleven-thirty, so you can get me out by midnight. But if you stop *anywhere* in this county, Rex, I swear I'll kill you.'

'Hey, don't threaten the driver. I won't stop, okay?'

Unless of course, I happen to run out of gas.

There was movement in his peripheral vision, and the glimmer of the knife disappeared. 'All right, then,' she said.

Rex breathed a sigh of relief. Things were going more or less according to plan. Jonathan and Dess might have shown up a bit too early, but at least Angie hadn't stabbed him yet.

'They're catching up,' she announced.

He looked in the rearview. *Idiots.* They weren't supposed to overtake them or force Rex to drive over seventy-five, which would draw cops like flies.

Couldn't Jonathan and Dess do *anything* right?

'Like I said, the Grayfoots probably won't follow us into Bixby. Right?'

'If they know I'm meeting with one of you midnighters, they might make an exception.'

'But maybe not.' Rex pushed the accelerator a bit farther down, trying to make it look convincing. The old Ford's engine began to make a grinding sound, and Rex hoped he wasn't screwing up Dess's calculations too much.

Of course, the most worrying question was whether Angie would go crazy when his car ran out of gas right smack in the center of the emptiest, least traveled part of the county.

Rex swore under his breath. It would have been better if Dess and Jonathan had shown up ten minutes later. As it was, Angie would have too much time before midnight to wonder if this had all been arranged. Or she might get lucky and have a passing car pick her up.

Still looking backward, she swore. 'There's two of them now.'

'Huh? Two of *what?*'

'Two cars following us, you pinhead.'

'How could there . . .? Oh, crap!' he shouted. It had to be the police. 'Does one of them have a flashing light on top?'

'No, they're both black Mercedes. Standard Grayfoot issue.'

'Mercedes . . .?'

A few seconds later Rex let out a strangled little laugh of pure amazement. On the other side of the highway, headed into Broken Arrow right on schedule, was Jonathan's father's car, complete with him and Dess in the front seat, their expressions of surprise briefly visible as they flashed by.

'Oops,' Rex said softly.

'What?'

'You actually let the Grayfoots *follow you*!'

'I thought we already covered that,' Angie said. 'They're closing in! Doesn't this thing go any faster?'

'I guess it does,' said Rex, and pushed the pedal to the floor.

He looked down at the gas gauge, which hovered just above *E*.

But not for much longer.

14

CHANGE OF PLAN

'So, Flyboy – clue me in here. Was that *Rex* we just saw speeding down the other lane?'

Jonathan's eyes swept the highway frantically. Now that the shock was wearing off, he'd realized they needed to turn around. Fast. 'Yep.'

'And that was Angie sitting next to him?'

'I don't think it was his mom.'

'And – now this was the confusing part – there was this big black car chasing them, right? Like we were supposed to be doing? I mean, this isn't one of those time travel things where we just saw ourselves in the future, is it?'

'Not unless ten minutes in the future we've got a pair of Mercedes between us.'

'There were *two* of them?'

'That's what I saw.' Although at this point Jonathan wasn't completely sure what he'd seen.

Then he spotted a familiar exit, a mile up. He could pull off here and head back west without getting completely tangled in downtown Broken Arrow's web of warehouses and alleys.

Dess tapped her fingers on her window for a few seconds. 'So that means Rex's plan isn't going very well, is it?'

'Nope. Hold on.' Without slowing at all, Jonathan brought the car off the highway. Dess crushed against his shoulder as she leaned into the turn.

'Seat belt?' he suggested. He heard the slithering sound of vinyl as Dess scrambled to secure herself, then the click of a metal clasp.

He found himself glad that Melissa and Jess were still back in Bixby. Rex hadn't wanted them all inside Broken Arrow together in case this whole thing was some kind of Grayfoot trap.

Frankly, Jonathan had never thought much of the plan. It was pretty complicated, which always meant there were lots of things that could go wrong. Being involved in Rex's schemes had taught Jonathan that someone was always late (usually Jessica) or didn't pass along the message (usually Beth) or simply didn't do what they were supposed to do because they didn't feel like it (typically Melissa). And even if all the midnighters decided to play their parts, there were always cops, or parents, or teachers to screw things up.

Of course, even with all his doubts, Jonathan hadn't actually thought of this particular possibility.

'So wait,' Dess said as they zoomed through the dark underbelly of a cluster of overpasses, huge concrete columns flashing past on either side. 'The Grayfoots really *did* know that Angie was meeting with Rex?'

'Yeah. They must have been following her or something.'

'Stupid cow.'

'That's usually the problem with brilliant plans: not-so-brilliant people.'

Dess shook her head as they climbed onto an entrance ramp and shot back up onto Highway 75. 'WOW. So this afternoon, when Rex made us siphon most of the gas out of Melissa's tank? That was kind of a waste of two hours.'

'My guess is that Rex feels the same way,' Jonathan said. 'When's he supposed to run out?'

'At exactly eleven forty-seven and . . . oh, wait. We're ahead of schedule here, aren't we?'

'About ten minutes.'

She looked at Geostationary. 'Well, they were supposed to come to a stop right when they got to the middle of Saddleback. Of course, Rex looked like he was driving a little faster than we figured, which is less fuel efficient, especially in an old beater like Melissa's car. So . . .'

'Pretty soon, right?'

'Yeah. About eleven-forty. Unless those guys in the Mercs have guns and shoot out their tires or something.'

'Oh, right. Good point.' Jonathan realized that he had been going a bit slower than maximum, not wanting to send Dess through the windshield if an eclipse sneaked up on them. But the more he thought about it, the worse trouble he figured Rex was in. He pressed the accelerator down harder.

'So, Dess, if you see any blue sweeping across the sky, you know what to do, right?'

'Grab your hand. No problem.'

Jonathan nodded. If he was sharing his midnight gravity with someone, they probably wouldn't carry their momentum into the blue time. Two weeks before in the desert, Jessica and Dess had been whacked against their seat belts when his car had frozen and Melissa almost killed when she'd been, but nothing had happened to Jonathan.

Of course, no one had been crazy enough to test this hand-holding theory yet.

This zooming along at seventy-five miles an hour was another reason he was glad Melissa and Jess weren't here. He only had two hands.

They shot along the highway, the lights of central Bixby glowing before them, a great mass of darkness all around.

'Can you see anything?'

She leaned forward, squinting through the windshield at the dark road ahead. 'Barely. I think that little cluster of tail-lights is them.'

'So what are we supposed to do now?' Jonathan said. 'Try to catch up and help Rex? Or stick to the plan when we hit the county line and head out to pick up Melissa and Jess?'

'Crap, I don't know. I hate all this plan stuff.'

'Me too,' Jonathan said.

'Maybe we should keep following Rex. We can swoop in and pick him up after he runs out of gas.'

Jonathan swallowed. 'You do realize that'll be trickier than it sounds, right, Dess? Remember what you said about them maybe having guns?'

'Absolutely. But we can't just leave him out here with *real* Grayfoots chasing him. Who knows what they'll do to him?'

Jonathan couldn't argue with that. Melissa's car couldn't outrun those two Mercedes even if it wasn't about to conk out. 'I guess I could fly over and get Jessica after midnight falls.'

'What about Melissa?' Dess said. 'We'll need her if we're going to get into Angie's mind. You actually going to hold *her* hand?'

Cold fingers stroked Jonathan's spine at the thought. He'd

touched Melissa exactly once before, for an emergency jump across a hundred yards of angry tarantulas. In those few seconds her tortured mind had flooded into him like a wave of nausea; it was something he never wanted to repeat.

He sighed. 'I guess I'll have to. But what about you and Rex being alone in Saddleback? It'll take me ten minutes to get Jessica there, and that's the deep desert – darkling country.'

'Don't worry about me.' Dess kicked the duffel bag on the floor in front of her, which let out a clank. 'I think our big problem right now is Rex staying alive *until* midnight.'

'Yeah, you got that right. Those guys in the Mercs looked pretty pissed.' Jonathan took a deep breath. 'Okay, we go after Rex and save his sorry ass from the Grayfoots.'

He accelerated still more, squeezing every drop of speed out of his father's car.

Dess scrunched down into her seat. 'Sounds like a plan to me.'

15

OUT OF GAS

As they crossed the county line, Rex kept his eyes locked on the road ahead. 'Are they giving up?'

Angie turned to stare through the back window, then let out a string of curses. 'No, still with us. And if they're risking Bixby at this hour to catch us, that means they're in a really bad mood.'

Rex gripped the steering wheel, trying not to scream with frustration. In all his detailed planning, it had never once occurred to him that the *real* Grayfoots would show up. 'How did they know we were meeting?'

'No one followed me, Rex, I'm positive.'

'What about your phone?'

'They couldn't have tapped it. That number I gave you was a disposable cell phone I bought last week at the Tulsa Mall. Never used it before you called, so they couldn't have . . .' Her voice turned cold. 'You didn't call me from *your* house, did you?'

Rex didn't answer for a few critical seconds, and by the time he found the right words, it was too late to lie.

'Was I not supposed to?' he finally managed.

She let out a groan.

'You mean, my phone is tapped?' he cried.

'Only for the last two years. Pinhead.'

Rex drove on, waiting for the burning sensation of a knife slipping between his ribs, but all he heard was Angie muttering beneath her breath. 'Jesus. Maybe you really are just a bunch of kids.'

The pursuers drew closer, filling the old Ford with their headlights. They were easing up on either side now, like wolves shepherding wounded prey away from the herd, out to a nice, private killing ground. This abandoned stretch of the access road was probably just the sort of place they'd been waiting for. Rex's plan had brought them to a perfect spot.

Angie pulled out a phone. 'All right. I'm calling the police.'

'It won't work out here,' Rex said softly. He and Dess had picked this route to make sure Angie couldn't escape the blue time after the car ran out of gas. Since the new highway had been built, hardly anyone ever drove through Saddleback. There were no cell phone towers, no houses, no cops – just rattlesnakes, slither burrows, and plenty of places to bury a couple of bodies.

Rex checked his watch. If Dess's calculations were on target, they'd be sputtering to a halt in about three minutes. He had to think of something soon or they were both dead.

But what could he do, trapped on a road with no turnoffs, no choices but to keep driving straight?

Suddenly Rex felt something deep inside himself laughing at his own paralysis. Why was he thinking like prey? Why was he letting his pursuers dictate the terms?

Why not make *them* take some risks?

He gritted his teeth and pulled the wheel sharply to the left. The Ford slid from the road and onto the sandy shoulder, where it swerved like a sidewinder for a few seconds. Then the tires gripped the hard-packed desert floor, and the car straightened, rattling like an old washing machine as it crashed through mounds of scrub grass and rumbled over prairie dog holes.

For a moment the pursuing headlights angled off into the distance behind them. But then the two Mercedes swerved from the road, turning onto the desert in pursuit.

'What are you *doing?*' Angie cried, her teeth snapping as the car shook.

'Out here there's a chance one of them will get a flat.'

'Isn't there also a chance of us getting a flat?'

Rex only nodded, deciding not to explain that one way or another, the Ford was about to stop moving. 'Have you got a better idea?'

'My better idea was not using *a tapped phone*!'

'You could have mentioned that in your note!'

'It was so obvious we were watching you! Jesus. How did you people ever take control of a whole town?'

'That wasn't us who . . .' Rex's words trailed off. Up ahead was a cluster of glistening humps, like a field of spiky basketballs glowing in the moonlight. He smiled at the sight. If all three cars were disabled, he and Angie might stand a chance of escaping on foot.

He aimed toward the humps, ignoring the Ford's rattling complaints and building up as much speed as he could. Gas or no gas, tires or no tires – once Melissa's car got going, it took a while to come to a stop.

'Rex? What is that ahead?'

'Big patch of rainbow cactus.'

'What the hell? Are you *trying* to get us killed?'

'No. But we're about to run out of gas.'

'What?'

'Long story. This way at least we've got a chance.'

'Of *what*? A quick death?'

His answer was cut off by a sudden *bang* beneath the car, a sound like a watermelon hitting concrete at eighty miles an hour. More collisions rocked the Ford, Angie crying out as each cactus struck. The shock of the impacts shot up through the car seat, jolting Rex like a series of kicks in the butt.

Behind them a pair of headlights dropped back. One of the Mercedes had ground to a halt, with either a tire burst or an axle busted. As Rex watched in the shuddering rearview mirror, the car was overwhelmed by its own cloud of dust.

Only one to go.

Then, with a parting *bang*, the cactus patch fell behind them. Melissa's Ford was wobbling, its right-front tire making a sound like a rubber flag in a strong wind. But the engine kept rumbling underneath Rex, and the desert still flashed past in front of their headlights.

'They'll be getting nervous now,' Angie said, looking back.

'Nervous?'

'If they lose the other car, they'll have no way to get out of the county in time. They're Grayfoots, brought up so they'd rather die than be in Bixby at midnight.'

Rex blinked. After all his careful planning for tonight, would his insane, wildly improvised idea of barreling through a cactus patch be the one thing that actually worked? Inside him, the darkling half of his mind was quietly pleased.

'Rex, did you say something about running out of gas?'

'Well—' he started, but suddenly another explosion shook the car. The steering wheel jerked out of his hands, and the car began to swerve out of control across the desert floor, swinging into a bootlegger's reverse, tipping so far to the right that Rex thought it was going to roll over. The horrible screeching of bare metal skimming across rocks and hard-packed sand filled his ears, and a cloud of dust rose up to swallow the world around them.

Somehow the Ford didn't roll over, but when they finally skidded to a halt, it was listing to one side like a sinking ship. Rex was pretty sure that both right tires had been reduced to rubber confetti.

The engine died then with a cough, finally realizing that it had run out of gas.

Rex waited for a pair of headlights to lance through the dust swirling around them. The other Mercedes couldn't be far behind.

The view gradually cleared, revealing a starry sky, the dark mountains in the distance – and a pair of red taillights receding into the desert.

'What the hell?' he said. 'They totally *had* us.'

Angie took a while to catch her breath, her hands slowly releasing their grip on the upholstery. 'It's too close to midnight.'

Rex looked at his watch. 'But they still had fifteen minutes. Plenty of time to kill us and get to the county line.'

'Yeah, but first they had to drive back around the cactus to pick up whoever was in the other car.'

'What? They're too nice to just leave them out here?'

'Those were all Grayfoots.' She let out a snort. 'And they'd never leave family behind.'

He looked at her. 'Just you.'

Angie nodded slowly. 'Just me.' Her dazed eyes took in the slowly clearing dust, the empty desert, and finally dropped to stare at her watch. 'I guess I'm screwed. Your little mindcaster friend will be here soon, won't she?'

The smell of terror from Angie had become almost overwhelming. Her hands were shaking now, as if she were even more afraid of a mindcaster entering her brain than of the Grayfoots catching her.

Rex let out a slow breath, willing his thudding heart to calm down. With Angie's fear scent filling the car, a hunting frenzy threatened to take over his mind. But he needed to keep control, to keep talking to her.

'Let me be honest, all right?' he said through gritted teeth. 'It was always my plan to trap you in Bixby for midnight. That's why I only had so much gas.'

'So you *knew* the Grayfoots were going to show up? And you came anyway?' She whistled. 'You've got guts.'

'Well, not exactly. Things didn't quite go the way I planned.' He sighed. 'But listen, Angie, have you really been telling me the truth about the past? The way the old midnighters—' Rex's voice choked off as his nose suddenly caught the sharp smell of stainless steel. Angie's knife flashed in her hand. 'Hey, what the hell?'

'Listen, Rex, I know that in fifteen minutes you can do anything you want to me, make me drooling and stupid like your father, maybe turn me into your slave. But that doesn't mean I can't even the score.'

'Hold up, Angie! No one's going to turn you into a vegetable!'

'Yeah, right.' She snorted. 'So you lured me out here to steal my bank card password?'

'No, to make sure you were telling the truth!' The knife came closer, and his darkling mind writhed at the smell of steel. 'We had to do this! If the world's ending, we had to know for sure!'

Angie paused, her eyes narrowing. 'What did you just say? If the *what's* ending?'

'The world . . . or at least a great big chunk of it.' Rex spoke quickly, his eyes never leaving the knife. 'We think the blue time is expanding far enough to swallow millions of people. They'll be defenseless against your darkling pen pals.'

She shook her head. 'That's crap, Rex. Darklings can't hurt normal humans.'

'Not usually. But the barrier between normal time and the secret hour is weakening. In certain spots daylighters can slip through. You know that girl on the news this week, the one who disappeared in Jenks? She walked into the blue time.'

'Come on, Rex,' Angie said. 'Didn't she turn up the next day?'

'Yes, because we saved her . . . from a huge, hungry darkling, I might add.'

Her eyebrows raised. 'I don't remember that part being on the news.'

'Well . . . no.' Rex swallowed. 'We may have asked her not to say anything about the, uh, incident.'

'You erased her memories,' she said coolly.

He narrowed his eyes. 'We *had* to.'

The knife drew closer, the tip barely touching his cheek, where it burned like a spent match tip. Rex's eyes focused on the pulse in Angie's throat, the darkling part of his mind set on edge by the steel against his flesh, thinking killing thoughts. He knew that if he lost control, the short, brutal fight between them would be more evenly matched than Angie would expect, knife or no knife. But that wouldn't accomplish anything. They had to communicate, not kill each other.

'And what will you do to my memories?' Angie said softly.

Rex tore his eyes from her throat. Would she believe that he'd wanted to change as little as possible inside her mind? Just find out what she knew about the Grayfoots leaving town and maybe introduce a strong phobia about kidnapping people in the future. Unless, of course, Melissa lost her temper in the middle of the whole thing and forgot her promises . . .

If that happened, Rex wouldn't want to be in Angie's shoes.

Maybe there was another way to do this – one that didn't involve any mindcasting.

Rex tried to ignore the knife in his face. 'Do you really believe all that stuff? About how the old midnighters were totally evil?'

'I don't believe it, Rex, I *know* it. I'm a real historian, not some amateur. Before I found out about the secret hour, I was researching a book on Oklahoma's early statehood. I've documented everything the old man told me about his childhood. I've found the court records in Tulsa, from when they got his parents.'

Rex's eyebrows rose. He'd collected old newspapers and handbills from Bixby's past but not court records, and nothing from as far away as Tulsa.

'What are you talking about?' he asked.

'It was a big case in the nineteen-forties. Old Man Grayfoot's parents contested an oil claim made on Indian

land by some of the town fathers – seers like you, pillars of
the community. Normally the trial would have been rigged so
the midnighters would win, no problem. But the case wound
up in a court in Tulsa, a judge that they couldn't control.'

Rex frowned. 'So what happened?'

'One day all the Native American parties involved decided
to back down. They gave up the case, then sold their houses
to pay the town fathers' court costs. They lost everything they
had.'

He swallowed. 'That sounds . . . unfair.'

'Doesn't it? And you know what's worse, Rex?' she said.
'After that day, Grayfoot's parents never showed another
ounce of backbone, except to agree with whatever the town
fathers said. Just like a whole lot of other people always did. So
the old guy got to thinking that things weren't right in Bixby.'

Rex blinked. He'd spent his whole life learning this history;
how could there turn out to be a completely different side?

The odd thing was, whenever Rex read normal daylighter
history, he never took the word of just one historian. You had
to check with several sources – everybody knew that. But until
Angie had gotten into his car tonight, he'd never had another
viewpoint to compare against the lore.

But after all she'd done, how could he trust her to tell the
truth?

'Okay,' he said. 'I want you to pull that knife back a few
inches.'

'Why should I?'

'Because now you're going to tell me what happened
between you and the Grayfoots,' he said. 'Are they really
blowing you off just because you're not related?'

The knife wavered. 'Well, that night in the desert, the night we gave you to the darklings, none of us expected that little kid to appear. She was the first halfling, wasn't she?'

'Her name was Anathea,' Rex said.

'I mean, I know she was a midnighter, and she would have become a monster like all the others. But Jesus, she didn't look any older than twelve.'

'She wasn't, much,' Rex said. 'She spent those fifty years mostly in frozen time. Afraid and alone, surrounded by *real* monsters.'

Angie sat silently for a moment. 'So I started wondering out loud if it was worth it, making another halfling. I thought the old man would listen to me. But the darklings weren't even talking to us. So the Grayfoots started getting cagey around me and nervous about the future.'

'How do they know what's going to happen?'

She shook her head and lowered the knife still further. 'The last thing Ernesto told me is that there was something coming up, something that had been planned for a long time. The Grayfoots had been looking forward to it, but now that the darklings weren't talking, it might be dangerous for them.'

'Not just for them,' Rex said. 'You should leave town too.'

'I'd love to. Except in about . . . five minutes I'm going to get my brain turned to mush.'

Rex shook his head. 'No, you're not. I'm not going to let Melissa touch you.'

Angie snorted. 'You're just saying that so I won't slit your throat.' She let out a deflated sigh and put the knife back into her coat pocket. 'Well, you can relax. I think maybe my child-sacrificing days are over.'

As the knife disappeared, a cool sensation went through Rex. Not just a feeling of relief, but a decision. 'No, I mean it.

We're not like that. Melissa doesn't need to touch you at all. It's quiet out here, mind-noise quiet, and she can tell if you're lying to us, even in normal time. After midnight – when you unfreeze – just tell us everything Ernesto said.'

'And you're going to trust me?'

Rex shrugged. 'Like I said, Melissa will know if you're lying . . . *without* having to touch you. But once midnight passes, you can just walk away if you want. So yeah, I'm trusting you.'

She narrowed her eyes, glancing at her watch. 'And after midnight I'm not going to find myself suddenly mush-brained or wanting to give you my bank account?'

'Bank account?' He shook his head. 'Did you get a look at this piece of crap? It's not exactly a Mercedes, like your buddies' cars back there.'

'I guess not.' She took a slow breath. 'All right, I supposed I don't have much choice about . . . Uh-oh. Speaking of cars.'

Rex followed her gaze through the front windshield. Headlights had reappeared on the horizon, making their slow way through the ravaged cactus patch.

'Crap!' he cried, reaching for the Ford's dashboard and killing the headlights. 'I hope that's not the cops.'

She squinted. 'No, it's not a police car. Or a Mercedes, either. Looks like . . . I don't know. Looks about as crappy as this piece of junk.'

Rex breathed a sigh of relief – it was Jonathan and the others.

'Okay. It's just friends.'

A shudder went through Angie. 'Including the mind-caster?'

'Yeah, but I promise she won't touch you.' He leaned

forward and turned the headlights back on, then blinked in disbelief as the car rolled to a stop a few yards away.

Jonathan and Dess were visible through the front windshield, but there was no one in the backseat. They'd followed him and Angie here without picking up Melissa and Jessica, expecting to be heroes.

He let out a frustrated sigh. Had they actually thought they were going to *save* him from the Grayfoots? Didn't they know how full of darklings this part of the desert would be in two minutes?

'What's the matter?' Angie asked. 'You said they were friends, right?'

'Don't worry. It's not a problem . . . for you.' He shook his head. 'Just the rest of us. If we all disappear after midnight, don't bother leaving any more notes. We'll all be dead.'

'Dead? Why?'

'Because your darkling pen pals are very nasty, Angie, much worse than you'll find in any court records. And because my brilliant schemes don't seem to be working very well tonight.'

Rex leaned back in the driver's seat, waiting for the last few seconds of normal time to tick away. He'd been following his darkling instincts when he'd turned the car onto the flats, and they'd led him out here – miles into the deep desert, farther than he had ever been before at midnight.

Maybe part of him had wanted this.

It looked like his meeting with the old ones had come sooner than he'd planned.

16

FLYING LESSONS

'Well, as of now this plan officially sucks,' Melissa said. 'No way is Jonathan getting here before midnight.'

'We should have gone along with them.' Jessica groaned, huddling in her coat against the chill wind. 'I told Rex I wasn't afraid to.'

'It's not your fault, Jess,' Melissa said. 'Rex didn't want all five of us in Broken Arrow. You heard him.'

Jessica nodded sullenly. He'd said something about a Grayfoot trap catching them all at once – the end of the midnighters. It seemed unlikely to her.

'He probably just figured I was worried about getting busted for curfew violation,' she said. 'And was trying not to make me feel like a weenie.'

She sighed. So now they were stuck here at a cold, windy roadside picnic stop just outside the county line, sitting on their butts. Next time she was going to announce to Rex that she was the new, non-weenie Jessica, unafraid of official, parental, or even sisterly punishment.

'No, Jess. I happen to know it wasn't you he was trying to protect.'

'What do you mean?'

'It was me.' Melissa held out her hand, palm down. It was quivering in the cold. 'The thought of driving fast gives me the shakes.'

Jessica looked at the mindcaster, wondering if she was kidding. Of course, flying through a windshield at eighty miles an hour might make you not want to repeat the experience.

'And they might not be here yet because they really did get busted by the cops,' Melissa continued. 'In which case, we're both lucky we didn't go along.'

Jessica sighed. 'That's a lovely thought.' Jonathan wasn't a big fan of spending the secret hour trapped in a jail cell, bouncing off the walls.

'Just trying to make you feel better. There are worse things than being arrested.'

'I suppose so.'

'I mean, you've got kidnappers and high-speed car chases involved,' Melissa continued.

'Jeez, Melissa. Who elected you Miss Sunshine?'

'I'm just saying is all.' The mindcaster looked at her watch. 'Anyway, we'll know for sure in five, four, three . . .'

The secret hour struck, spilling toward them across the desert floor like a sudden tide of blue ink. The picnic table shuddered beneath them, the air grew warm and still, and the stars turned ghostly pale above.

'Yeah, that's the stuff.' Melissa sighed, tipping her head back to sniff the air. A few moments passed, then a faint smile broke across her face. 'You can relax. Everyone's okay.'

Jessica breathed a sigh of relief, glad that Melissa was here.

When Rex had put the final touches on his plan, she'd been nervous about spending a whole hour in the middle of nowhere with Melissa. But actually, it hadn't turned out so bad. Melissa wasn't the bitchy snob she used to be.

The mindcaster fixed her with a cool glare. 'Gee, thanks, Jess.'

'Oops. Sorry.' Jessica reminded herself to censor her thoughts, especially now that midnight had fallen. 'But I mean . . . it's true, though,' she sputtered. 'You are much nicer these days.'

'Whatever.' Melissa looked skyward again, closing her eyes. 'Okay. They're all together, way out in the desert for some reason, miles off the access road. Something got screwed up – tastes like Rex and Flyboy have been arguing.'

'Funny, but I could have guessed that last part.'

Melissa smirked. 'Now Jonathan's on his way here. In a big hurry . . .' She frowned. 'Things are waking up out there.'

Jessica drew her flashlight, whose new name was Enlightenment, from her pocket. 'Are they going to be all right?'

'If we get out there before anything big jumps on them.'

'We?'

One of Melissa's eyes opened a slit. 'As in me, Flyboy, and you.'

Jessica realized it was pointless to hide her dismay. 'That's right, you'll have to fly along with us.'

'You got it, Jess. I don't *want* to, but the whole point of this plan is for me and Angie to have a little face time. And it's not like I'm going to walk.' Melissa spread her hands. 'Look, don't worry about it, Jessica. I'm not going to spew my crippled mind into your boyfriend's, all right?'

'I didn't say you were.'

'You thought about it. Don't tell me that little twinge was you worrying about a dentist appointment.'

Jessica shook her head. 'It's just that Jonathan told me—'

'*I know* what he told you, Jessica. I can taste the way he pities me. I pretty much know how you guys feel about me, got that? And the more you worry about offending me, the *more* I know it. And frankly, I really don't *want* to know about it anymore, so just give . . . it . . . *a rest*!'

Melissa's voice broke on the last words, the awful sound disappearing into the flat, echoless desert. She sighed then, shaking her head.

'I'm sorry—' Jess began.

'Yeah, well.' Melissa waved her silent. 'I'm sorry too. Didn't mean to rant, but I thought maybe you might want to know what *I* was thinking for a change.'

Jessica swallowed, a dozen apologies tumbling through her brain. But of course, Melissa wouldn't want to hear any of them. So Jessica concentrated hard, trying to banish all excuses and regrets and pity from her mind.

She cleared her head with thoughts of flying – imagining weightlessness rushing into her at Jonathan's touch, the rolling quilt of Bixby's streets from midair, the pleasure of a perfectly timed jump taking them directly to a target, the desert floor passing below . . .

The images crystallized, erasing the bitter aftertaste of the argument, and on an impulse Jessica reached out and touched Melissa's wrist lightly.

Melissa didn't respond at first, but she didn't pull away. Jessica could feel the struggle in her not to flinch from human contact, fighting reflexes trained by years of isolation. And then the connection took hold.

Images and emotions spilled from Jessica's mind – the sheer exhilaration of soaring at top speed across the badlands, scrub and sand and salt all reduced to a blur – and Melissa drew in a breath, amazed by the visions shared between them.

Jessica realized she was the only midnighter who had never touched the mindcaster before. It wasn't like Jonathan had said; there was nothing twisted and pitiable about Melissa's mind now. Through her eyes the blue world was suffused with a stately calm. And under that an old sadness, and worry about Rex.

After a long moment Melissa pulled her hand away.

'Flying . . .' she said softly.

Jessica smiled. 'It'll be fun.'

Melissa turned away, looking down at her hand as if Jessica had somehow marked it. Finally she said, 'Just as long as we get there fast. Rex needs us.'

'Is he scared?'

Melissa's head tilted, like that of a dog listening to a far-off sound. 'Not really. He's not afraid of darklings anymore.'

Jessica frowned. 'Shouldn't he be?'

The mindcaster shrugged. 'I guess we'll find that out soon enough.'

Jonathan came skimming over the desert like a rock flung across frozen water. His flying shield flashed, warding off a pair of fast slithers who were buzzing around him like gigantic flies.

Jessica stood and aimed Enlightenment.

'Don't. You'll blind him,' Melissa warned.

Jessica lowered the flashlight, sighing. Jonathan would

probably rather deal with the slithers himself anyway. Why ruin his fun?

'I know what you mean, Jess,' Melissa added. 'He's enjoying all this way too much.'

Jessica looked at her, suddenly wondering if their brief physical connection had made her thoughts permanently easier to read.

But Melissa shook her head. 'It's pretty obvious, Jess. I used to hate daylight too, you know? But I never loved midnight as much as that boy does.'

An explosion pulled Jessica's gaze back out to the horizon. One of the slithers had glanced off Jonathan's shield, blue sparks arcing across the sky as it fell, and the other turned and fled. Jonathan bounded to a halt a few yards away, raising a cloud of pale blue dust that froze in midair – his acrobat gravity working its strange magic.

'Come on!' he cried, holding out both hands.

Jessica was glad to see that he didn't flinch as Melissa grasped his hand, just looked at her, and said, 'Do you know how this works?'

'Yeah, Jessica just taught me.'

A look of surprise crossed Jonathan's face, and he shot a glance at Jessica. She could only shrug. She hadn't thought about it that way, but all the techniques of flying were recorded in well-used grooves in her mind, honed by long hours at Jonathan's side. Even those nights they didn't fly together, she dreamed about it or puzzled over the mechanics of midnight gravity when she was supposed to be doing physics homework.

Had Melissa really taken all that in so quickly?

'Let's go,' Melissa said, bending her knees.

The three of them jumped together, a small tentative leap at first. Melissa didn't send them spinning or stumbling when they landed thirty feet away. They pushed harder on the second jump, launching into a low, fast trajectory across the desert. They built up speed, growing in confidence, dodging scrub and cactus bulbs without any exchange of words, as if Melissa had been flying with them a dozen times before.

Jessica wondered what was going on in Jonathan's mind, if he was thinking about Melissa reading his thoughts as they flew. Or remembering his horror at their first contact, before Melissa had gotten herself under control. Or perhaps the emergency was too great, his mind too focused on flying . . .

Maybe that was the trick when dealing with mindcasters; maybe you just had to give your head a rest.

'Halfway there,' Melissa said, breathing hard.

Jessica asked, 'Are they okay?'

'Dess is fine. Rex . . . he's with the others.'

'With *what* others?'

Melissa stumbled on the next landing, and the three of them twisted in the air, spinning once all the way around before they set down again. Jonathan dragged them to a halt as they landed.

On the horizon ahead, a flicker of blue sparks rose up from the desert.

'What's happening out there?' he asked her.

'Dess is holding them off. And they'll scatter once they taste the flame-bringer on her way.'

Jessica frowned. 'What about Rex?'

'Don't worry about him. Moron – he said he'd warn me before he tried anything like this.'

'Anything like what?'

Melissa shook her head. 'We should keep moving if we're going to get there before Dess blows a fuse.' She looked at them both, pleading with them not to ask any more questions. 'Let's just keep going, okay?'

Jonathan glanced at Jessica, then bent his knees again. 'Okay.'

They jumped again, eating up the landscape in long, bounding leaps. Melissa flew as if she'd practiced for months.

Half a mile from Dess they passed over a patch of small, stubby cacti. Jessica spotted a big black car with blown-out tires at its edge.

'That's not Melissa's, is it?' she asked.

'No. Grayfoots',' Jonathan said. 'Real ones.'

'Oh.' No wonder things had gotten messed up.

At the height of their next jump Jessica saw a huge black cat rising onto its haunches among blue sparks, surrounded by a whirling cloud of slithers. A thirteen-pointed star was traced out on the desert floor in glowing wires, Dess inside it, the darkling just outside. Melissa's car sat nearby, looking battered and broken.

'That cat smells blood, Jess,' Melissa said. 'It's too young to be afraid of you.'

'Blood?' Jessica said as they landed, but the mindcaster didn't answer.

They jumped again, hurtling toward the struggle. Jessica saw Dess's long spear swing through the air, the panther batting at it with its claws, catching the spear point with a flash. The weapon spun out of Dess's grip as the creature screamed, leaping backward from the contact through its entourage of winged slithers. It rolled across the desert, salt and sand flying into the air.

But like a cat, it sprang to its feet in an instant and bared its fangs.

Dess stood glaring back at it.

'Close your eyes,' Jessica warned through clenched teeth.

Enlightenment's beam shot across the blue desert, reaching the darkling at the limit of its power. White fire played across its fur, bringing another howl of anger. All around it slithers burst into flame, wheeling to escape the scorching light.

But the darkling didn't flee. Its purple eyes flashed as it glared at Dess, directing all its wounded fury toward her.

It readied itself to spring.

Jessica kept the flashlight steady as they flew, squeezing it with all her strength, sending every ounce of her will through it. The white fire grew stronger as the darkling leapt, enveloping it in a hissing ball of flame. Jessica felt the blue world shudder around them, the mountains in the distance seeming to warp as her power surged through Enlightenment.

The beast screamed one last time, disintegrating in midair like an exploding meteor, scattering glowing white coals across the desert floor.

'Eyes open,' Jessica said hoarsely. Another jump took the three of them into a skidding landing near the circle of singed earth and metal stakes. Dess stood inside, dusty and scared-looking, blood running from her forehead.

'Are you okay?' Jessica cried, dropping Jonathan's hand and running toward her, leaping over the strewn and blazing remains of the darkling.

'I'll live. But Rex went out there!' Dess cried, pointing into the desert. 'I couldn't stop him!'

'I know,' Melissa said.

'Jessica, Jonathan, go get him!'

'No, don't.'

The other three looked at the mindcaster in disbelief. Her eyes were half open, rolled back in her head, nothing visible of them but two pale slits of glowing purple.

'He wants us to stay here,' she said softly.

'But you should see the thing that came for him!' Dess cried, wiping the blood from her forehead.

'I *can* see it, Dess.' Melissa slowly moved her head from side to side, like a drunk piano player grooving to her own music. 'He's okay. And he'll be back soon.'

'He'll be dead!' Dess said.

Melissa opened her eyes, which flashed as she stared straight at Jessica. 'Trust me – don't go out there. Rex is in the middle of a big crowd of wicked-old darklings. If you spook them, you'll only get him killed.'

Jessica noticed that the other three were all looking at her too, waiting for her answer. She was the flame-bringer, after all; only she could save Rex.

She looked at Melissa again. The mindcaster wore an expression of absolute certainty. Jessica remembered the calm she'd felt when they'd touched, as well as how she sensed Melissa's love for Rex, and found herself suddenly certain about what she had to do.

Nothing.

No matter how screwed up Melissa was now or ever had been, whatever she had done to Dess or anyone else, she would never, ever hurt Rex. Not in a million years.

Jessica nodded. 'Okay. We'll trust Melissa.'

'Jessica!' Dess cried. 'She's a psycho!'

'No, she's not. We wait here.'

Melissa smiled, her eyes drifting closed again. 'It won't be much longer. They know the flame-bringer's nearby, so they won't be in the mood for a long conversation.'

'Conversation?' Jonathan said. 'Are we talking about dark-lings here?'

'Old ones. Smarter than this turkey,' Melissa said, kicking at the sputtering embers near her feet. 'By the way, Jess, you were right.'

'About what? You not being psycho?'

'No. About flying. That *was* fun.' She opened her eyes and turned toward her old Ford, inside of which Angie's frozen form could be glimpsed, and cracked her knuckles. 'But not as much fun as getting a shot at that bitch's brain.'

Dess shook her head. 'Before he walked off, Rex said for you to wait. He said it's totally important you don't touch Angie until he comes back. And he said that if you were a pain about it, I get to hit you with that.' She pointed to where the darkling had flung Flabbergasted Supernumerary Mathematician, its tip blackened by ichor and fire. 'So, go ahead.'

Melissa gave Dess a sneer but stayed where she was. 'That bastard. He made me promise.' She clenched both fists as she looked across the desert, swearing. Finally she spat out, 'Fine. Seer knows best, even if he is nuts. Maybe I can stand to wait for a few more . . . *whoa*. What the *hell* happened to my car?'

THE OLD ONES

They hovered overhead, like spiderwebs suspended from the air itself. Their tendrils snaked out into the sky, silhouetted against the midnight moon as if sucking energy from its dark light. Other strands anchored them to the desert floor or were wrapped around the necks of darklings, like leashes on giant panthers. The beings seemed to have no head or body, just a matted center where the grasping arms converged.

Rex wondered if this was the darklings' original form before they had taken the shapes of humanity's nightmares. These were certainly the old ones Melissa had always felt across the desert; just as she described, he tasted musty chalk, as if his mouth were full of the remains of something long dead and crumbled to dust.

One of them had come for him across the desert, its arms like glistening threads, resplendent in his seer's vision even from miles away. He'd known he had no choice but to follow – the thing could reach its long arms through Dess's defenses, and it called to the darkling part of him irresistibly.

For that matter, he'd *wanted* to come, even his human half.

After everything Angie had told him, Rex realized how imperfect and incomplete the lore really was. If there was a way to stop what was happening, these old minds would know.

There were three of them, each twenty yards across, and an entourage of another dozen creatures in nightmare shapes: pale snakes and bloated spiders, slugs that dripped black oil, all of them unmoving, as if in thrall to the old ones hovering overhead. Wingless slithers pulsed in the ground beneath his feet, like an eruption of earthworms turning the threadbare soil.

Rex had never felt so small.

How wrong he'd been, thinking he was *half* darkling. Only a tiny fraction of him had changed, a sliver of strength gained, enough courage to express his paltry human anger. These creatures were so much more powerful than he would ever be. Rex found himself unable to move or speak, his humanity shrunk into a terrified corner of his mind, their darkness lying across him like a blanket of lead.

And what was he supposed to do, anyway? Say *hi?*

A liquid motion caught his eye. One of the creatures' long tendrils was approaching, sliding across the desert floor like a snake. As Rex watched in horror, it stretched toward his boot, wound around his leg as soft as feathers. Every muscle in his body strained against it, but he couldn't move.

Cold swept through him then, and an arid voice . . .

Winter is coming.

Rex tried to open his mouth to speak, but his teeth were clenched so hard it felt like they would shatter. He let out a growl, pulling his lips apart, forcing his tongue to form words in his captive mouth.

'What will happen?'

We will hunt again. Join us.

'No,' he said.

We are hungry.

Images exploded in Rex's mind, every bully who had ever taunted him, all his father's beatings, the spiders making their way across his pale, bare flesh. Every old fear came surging out of his memories, tearing at the foundations of his human side. Suddenly he knew he was a failure. The lore he had taught himself to read was nothing but lies. All along he had been a blind seer, a fraud.

Laughing, the old ones showed him the coming change, how the blue time was tearing open, unleashing the darklings' ancient hungers.

'No,' he said, already exhausted. 'I'll stop you.'

There was a shudder from the beasts.

You are not the one who threatens us.

Rex's body suddenly went rigid, as if something was stretching him, prying his mind wide open. All his senses grew a thousand times. The world was suddenly crystal clear all the way to the dim stars on the horizon, even more perfect than in his seer's vision. He could hear the sound of his own blood rushing through his body, like freight trains pouring past. And he tasted the blue time itself, ash and corruption on his tongue.

More images poured into him – the world moving at darkling speed, the seasons flashing past, only one hour in twenty-five visible, every day almost a month. He saw the prime contortion that the old ones had made, the secret hour itself, groaning under the weight of all that missing time. It was beginning to fray, a steady drumbeat of eclipses until it shattered, and then the hunt would begin.

Unless . . . Rex saw a bolt of lightning, the ancient pressures released and spreading across the earth, the rip diminishing.

'We can stop this,' he whispered.

She can. You must take her.

'No.'

More images, like his hunting dreams but a thousand times more vivid. He saw a pile of burning bones, human forms wearing horned masks. He felt the rush of galloping pursuit, smelled the fear of the prey, tasted the warm vitals of the kill. Rex felt himself gorging on flesh.

His stomach clenched against the vision, but what horrified him most was how complete it made him feel, how sated. And how powerful. As Rex Greene, he was trapped in a body that was weak and small, that would sicken as it grew old and certainly die in a laughably short time. But the old ones were offering him millennia.

All he had to do was let his humanity slip away. He could join in the feast.

Just take her. You alone can bring her down.

He shook his head, fighting back with his shredded humanity. Then a long-buried Aversion rose up in his memory, one Dess had taught him long ago.

Join us, they coaxed him.

'Unconquerable,' Rex spat at them hoarsely. His mind almost split from the effort, but the grip of the old ones shuddered again, disgusted with him.

Then away with you.

With astonishing suddenness his mind was released from the creatures' awful grip. Rex felt his muscles unlock, and he was falling like a dropped rag doll, every ounce of will expended in the struggle. They had given up, he realized. Somehow he had beaten them.

Rex opened his eyes and found himself lying facedown on the desert floor, dirt in his mouth, his jaw muscles aching. But he managed a smile. The darklings had shown him something about the coming hunt . . . something important.

But as the cluster of nightmare shapes moved away, leaving him there exhausted and spent, Rex felt his mind contracting, his senses turning back to merely human. Like a great maw closing around him, darkness consumed the new knowledge, leaving only disjointed images and scents and the taste of dust in his mouth.

By the time the old ones had disappeared on the horizon, he hardly remembered what had happened at all.

18

12:00 A.M.

MONSTER

Rex shambled back across the desert like a zombie.

His face was pale, his hands shaking as they had immediately after his transformation weeks before. He looked strangely like his father – eyes glazed and milky, his gait barely a shuffle.

He wasn't bruised or bleeding, and his clothes weren't torn, but the empty expression on his face made Jessica's skin crawl.

'Are you okay, Rex?' she said.

He didn't answer, just turned to Melissa. 'Did you touch her?'

'No, I waited. I promised, didn't I?' Melissa reached toward him. 'Loverboy, you look like crap.'

'Feel like it too.' Rex took her offered hand and shuddered, then straightened, as if taking strength from her. 'Thanks.'

'What the hell, Rex?' Jonathan said. 'Are you *trying* to get yourself killed?'

Rex thought about the question for a few seconds, like it was a tricky one, but finally he shook his head. 'I'm just trying to get all points of view. I think I've been a pretty crappy historian.'

'Pretty crappy *driver*, more like!' Melissa cried. She pointed at the old Ford, which was listing to one side; both tires on the right were reduced almost to bare metal rims. 'The first time I let you take my car somewhere without me, and you totally kill it?'

'Yeah. Looks that way.'

'I can't believe you, Rex! Mr. Responsible, who always gets his library books back on time, but when it comes to *my car*, you don't even bother to use the *road*? The front axle's busted!'

As Jessica watched Melissa continue her tirade – holding Rex tighter with every insult, their fingers intertwining, their bodies leaning against each other for support – she realized how well the mindcaster had concealed her fear that he might never return. Even when they'd touched, Jessica had only caught a glimpse.

Finally Melissa's diatribe sputtered to a halt. Rex held her in silence for a moment, then said, 'I'll always remember the old beast fondly. It died saving me and Angie.'

Melissa pulled away and turned to stare at the frozen figure in the wrecked car, her voice lowering to a growl. 'Well, she's my consolation prize, then. She *really* owes me now.'

'Wait a second,' Rex said.

'No way. I've already waited too long for this.'

He drew Melissa back to him, placing one palm against her cheek.

After a moment her eyes widened. 'What? Why *not?*'

'I made a deal.'

'Well, I didn't make any deal!'

'You did. With me.' He shook his head. 'We have to wait for midnight to end.'

Jessica wondered if anyone else was having trouble following this. 'What are you talking about?'

'Yeah,' Dess added, still holding a bloody rag to the cut above her left eye. 'Could those of us who aren't psychic at least get some subtitles?'

Melissa yanked herself out of Rex's arms, stumbling back a few feet and glaring at him. 'He doesn't want me to mindcast Angie.'

'Excuse me?' Dess said.

'Angie's told me some things about the past,' Rex said. 'About midnighters and Grayfoots. And we made a deal. We're going to wait till midnight ends, then we'll talk to her. Just talk.'

'Hang on,' Jonathan said. 'Are you saying we all risked our lives tonight to have a *chat*?'

'No way!' Dess cried.

Rex looked at Jessica, his exhausted eyes asking for her help. 'We don't have to use mindcasting,' he said. 'We can trust her.'

'To what?' Melissa spat. 'Kidnap us less often?'

'I'm not saying Angie's our friend or anything,' he said, his gaze not wavering from Jessica. 'Far from it. But she is like us in one way: she wants to learn the truth about midnight. We don't have to take her thoughts against her will.'

Jessica drew in a slow breath. The night they'd rescued Cassie Flinders, she'd tried to talk them out of erasing the girl's memories, and they'd basically ignored her. But if Rex himself was actually having second thoughts, maybe this time it wouldn't have to work out that way.

'I agree with Rex,' she said. 'I think.'

The other three stared at her, and Jessica half expected one of them to shout, *Who cares what you think?* But as the silence stretched out, she felt something shift within the group. Even Melissa's manic energy seemed to fade a little, like a child's tantrum left unanswered.

Jessica crossed her arms. Apparently they did care what she thought.

After a long moment Dess said quietly, 'So let me get this straight. I'm bleeding here. An inch lower and psycho-kitty would have taken out my eye. And we're just going to talk to her, which would imply that we could have done this with a *phone call?*'

'Possibly resulting in less damage to my car?' Melissa said.

'Not really,' Rex said. 'Here in person you can make sure Angie isn't lying. I believe her, but the rest of you also have to be certain.' He let out a short laugh. 'And frankly, I don't think it would have worked this way on the phone. Sometimes a little shared danger helps.'

'Well, no problem then, you two wrecking my car,' Melissa said, 'as long as you *bonded.*'

'No, no.' Rex shook his head tiredly. 'My bonding tonight happened out there. Angie's just confused.'

'Confused!' Melissa groaned. 'She's a kidnapper, Rex. She should be in jail forever! And *nothing* happens to her?'

He smiled, his eyes flashing with the dark moon's light.

'I didn't say that.'

As the dark moon set, real time swept across the desert, followed by the sudden return of the cold autumn wind. Next to Jessica, Rex jumped a little, like dishes left behind by a yanked tablecloth – as if he didn't belong in normal time anymore.

He had refused to answer their questions about what had happened to him out in the desert, saying he couldn't remember. Not yet, anyway.

In that same instant Angie's face sprang to life, emotions fluttering across it like a TV flipping through channels: confusion, fear, suspicion, and finally *lots* more confusion. She touched her own head gingerly with her fingertips, as if checking to make sure her ears hadn't fallen off at the stroke of midnight.

The five of them were standing in a row in front of the car, arms crossed – sort of like a band posing for an album cover, Jessica thought. Even the still-seething Melissa had decided to join them, once she realized that this little moment of surprise was the only revenge she would get to wreak on Angie.

The woman's eyes widened as she saw them through the front windshield.

'Come on out,' Rex called. 'Let's talk.'

Angie slowly pulled herself out from the battered Ford and stood facing them, staying behind the protection of the open car door.

'Wow,' she said softly.

Jessica guessed that people appearing out of nowhere might be a lot more impressive than a few dominoes jumping around.

'How's your mind doing?' Rex asked. 'Still feel like yourself?'

Angie puzzled over that one for a moment, then shrugged. 'I guess so.'

'Like I would dirty my hands with your rank little brain,' Melissa said.

Jessica gave her a sidelong glance. *So* not true.

'Then let's talk about the history of Bixby,' Rex said.

'I thought we already covered that.'

'Maybe I want to hear it all again.' He patted Melissa's shoulder. 'And this time I can be sure you're telling the truth. Or at least, if you *think* you're telling the truth.'

'It's all true,' Angie said. 'I can show you the documents.'

'Just talk,' Rex said.

Angie nodded and began telling them all about the early midnighters, the Grayfoots' revolution, and the rest of the *other* secret history of Bixby. She started slowly and softly, her baffled expression at their sudden appearance taking a while to fade. But gradually her voice gained in strength, and soon she was declaiming with the utmost confidence.

Rex had already explained most of it to them while they'd waited for the blue time to end, but as Jessica heard the revelations repeated in Angie's methodical tones, the story began to settle in her bones alongside the desert chill of the Oklahoma autumn night.

If this was all true, then how much had Madeleine known about everything that had gone on back in her day? She'd only been seventeen when the Grayfoots had swept the midnighters from power, but she carried the memories of generations of mindcasters. Wouldn't she know about it if midnighters had been doing creepy things for thousands of years?

And would any of them have the guts to ask her what she thought about all this? Of course, Melissa wouldn't have much choice in the matter the next time the two of them touched. Jessica was just glad it would be Melissa, and not her, doing the asking.

By the time Angie drew her lecture to a close, she didn't seem scared of them anymore. She was smoking now, looking at them like they were just kids.

'So now that I've explained reality to you,' Angie finished, 'what are you going to tell me in return?'

Jessica narrowed her eyes at the woman. She was glad Melissa hadn't turned her into a drooling idiot, but that didn't mean she *liked* Angie. Not at all.

'Here's the main thing you need to know,' Rex said. 'As far as we can tell, all hell's going to break loose on November first.'

'The midnight before, actually,' Dess added. 'When October 31 rolls over into November.'

Angie smirked. 'Midnight on Halloween, huh?'

'It may sound cheesy,' Dess said coolly. 'But numbers don't lie.'

'I don't know if I believe all that numerology stuff.'

'Numerology?' Dess's jaw dropped open. 'This is *math*, you dimwit.'

The woman stared at Dess skeptically for a long moment, but then a troubled look crossed her face. 'You know, before they cut me off, Ernesto Grayfoot kept saying that something was arriving soon. And after the darklings stopped answering, everyone started getting anxious about it. He said it had to do with the flame-bringer.' She looked at Jessica. 'That's you, right?'

Jessica nodded.

'But the Grayfoots never got all their instructions before the halfling died.'

'What exactly did Ernesto say?' Rex asked.

'All he told me was a name – the old man was nervous

because "Samhain" was coming.' She shrugged. 'He never told me who that was.'

Melissa shook her head. 'Not "who," dimwit, *when*. Samhain is the ancient name for Halloween.'

'Spot the goth,' Dess muttered.

'Like *you* should talk,' Melissa answered.

'Halloween again.' Rex sighed tiredly. 'Can't seem to get away from it.'

'Come on, you guys. Don't be stupid,' Angie said. 'Halloween's just pop culture nonsense. It didn't exist here in Oklahoma until a hundred years ago, and as I've explained to you, the monsters got here a lot earlier than that.' Her gaze drifted across the five of them. 'They're still here.'

'Monsters?' Rex said. He took a step toward Angie, then another, and Jessica felt a nervous tingling in the bottom of her stomach. Something was changing in Rex, exhaustion leaving his frame. He seemed suddenly taller, his expression harder, a threat implicit in every line of his face. Then the most astonishing thing – Jessica saw his eyes flash violet, though the dark moon had long set.

He was arm's length from Angie, but the woman stumbled backward, shrinking against the broken car. The cigarette dropped from her fingers.

'Maybe you're right, Angie,' he said. 'Maybe monsters have lived in Bixby for a long, long time. But you should just remember one thing.'

His voice changed then, turning dry and cold, as if something ancient was speaking through him. 'Monster or not, I'm what *you* made me when you left me out in the desert. I'm *your* nightmare now.'

A hissing sound came from him then, and his neck

stretched forward, as if his head were straining to leave his shoulders. His fingers seemed to grow longer and thinner, cutting the air in mesmerizing patterns. The hiss sliced through Jessica's nervous system like a piece of broken glass traveling down her spine.

Angie's smug confidence melted, and she slumped down, only her back against the Ford holding her from sinking to the dirt.

The hissing faded until it was lost in the wind, and then Rex's body seemed to fold into itself again, back to its normal human size and shape. Jessica wasn't sure if she'd really seen him change so completely or if the whole thing had been a massive psych-out.

He turned away from Angie. 'Come on, guys.'

'But she knows more,' Melissa said.

'Not anything important. *They* told me what I really need to know.'

His voice was normal again, and as Rex strode toward Jonathan's car, he looked tired, the energy that had coursed through his body during the sudden transformation now gone.

Jessica and Jonathan cast a wary glance at each other, then followed Melissa, who was trailing worriedly after Rex.

'What about her?' Dess called. Jessica paused and glanced over her shoulder; Dess was looking down at Angie as if she were a particularly interesting bug found smashed against the ground.

Rex didn't turn back, just spoke to the empty desert in front of him.

'She's walking. She knows the way out of town.'

SPAGHETTI SITUATION

'The rule is in force tonight,' Beth announced.

Jessica glanced up from her physics textbook. 'Um, Beth? I'd like to point out that I am in my own bedroom, not in the kitchen. Therefore there is no *possible* way that I can be found in violation of the rule.'

'I'm just warning you,' Beth answered.

'Warning me?' Jessica said with a look of annoyance.

It was Beth Spaghetti Night, which meant that her little sister was cooking dinner. Over the last four years, since Beth had turned nine, the ritual had been held every Wednesday night, interrupted only in the first few tumultuous weeks after the family had arrived in Bixby.

The one rule of Beth Spaghetti Night was simple: Beth cooked, and everyone else had to stay away from the food.

Even now, the scent of reducing onions was already drifting through Jessica's open door. The familiar smell had been making her happy until this interruption.

'Warning me about what exactly?'

'That I am enforcing the rule in its maximum form tonight,' Beth said.

'What does that mean? That we all have to leave the house while you cook?'

'No, but just . . .' Beth wrinkled her nose and checked over her shoulder, as if the smell of something burning had reached her. 'Just stay in here. Okay, Jess?'

'*Why?*'

Beth smiled. 'It's a surprise.'

Jessica considered getting Mom to pass judgment on this new and irksome interpretation of the rule, but it probably wasn't worth the effort. Jessica had been planning on studying until dinner anyway, and maybe the threat of Beth's irritation would keep her from winding up in front of the TV.

Physics was Jessica's only test scheduled before Halloween, and it seemed a shame for the world to end on a D+.

'*Please?*'

'Sure. Whatever,' Jessica said, making sure to roll her eyes.

'Good. You'll like my little surprise.'

'Okay.' Beth's smug expression didn't reassure Jessica. 'Can't wait for it.'

'Can I close your door?'

Jessica groaned. 'Don't I smell something *burning*, Beth?'

Her little sister spun on one heel, an expression of alarm crossing her face. Something really *was* burning. But she still managed to slam the door closed behind her as she fled.

Jessica listened to her footsteps thundering back toward the kitchen, wondering what this 'surprise' was. Beth had been much easier to get along with in the last week, snooping a lot less, talking about her new friends at marching band, and practicing her twirls. Maybe she really did want to surprise them all with something special.

And even if she wanted to make trouble, Beth could hardly have anything up her sleeve that would really make things worse.

There hadn't been any more eclipses – or timequakes, or whatevers of the prime whatever – since lunchtime a week ago. But as far as Melissa could tell, the darklings were expecting another one soon. After the last eclipse the rip in Jenks had grown to roughly the size of an oval-shaped tennis court. One of them checked it every midnight now, just to make sure that no more normal people had fallen through. Along with the usual blue glow everything inside it was tinged with red and nothing was frozen – autumn leaves fell, earthworms crawled, mosquitoes buzzed and bit. Too weird for words.

According to Dess, every eclipse would make the rip larger, like a tear traveling down a set of old stockings. Finally on Halloween the fabric of the secret hour would fall apart, and everyone for miles in all directions would find themselves engulfed in a world of red-blue.

As Jessica scanned her physics textbook, trying to focus on a chapter called 'Waves and You,' images of last Wednesday night kept popping into her mind – the way Rex had looked as he stumbled back across the desert, as pale as a prisoner released after years in a tiny, lightless cell. The way he had transformed into something inhuman in his anger.

Rex said he still couldn't remember what had happened to him out in the desert, and even Melissa hadn't gotten far enough down into his mind to dredge up anything. He said he was having weird dreams, though, like ancient darkling memories running through his head in high definition. All from one conversation with the old ones in the desert.

It had been more of a brainwashing session than a conversation, as far as Jessica could tell. Or maybe a whole *body*washing – his freaky transformation seemed to make Angie's accusations come true, as if Rex really was a monster now.

Jessica shivered at the image and gave up trying to concentrate on toroidal and sinusoidal waves. Instead she closed her eyes and drew in the smell of tomato sauce filtering under her door. If everything was about to change, Jessica wanted to relish these few last slices of normality.

Only two more Wednesdays before Samhain. She might as well enjoy Beth Spaghetti Night while it lasted.

'Dinnertime!' Beth shouted from right outside the door.

Jessica jerked out of her reverie, blinking. 'Thanks for scaring me.'

'No problem.' Footsteps scampered down the hall.

Jessica smiled. Spastically enthusiastic Beth she could deal with. Rolling off the bed and to her feet, she paused to stretch away the muscle kinks of too much studying, then opened her door.

The mouthwatering scent of Beth's tomato sauce rolled toward her from the kitchen, and the house echoed with the sounds of her whole family in animated conversation. Just for tonight, she could pretend that everything was normal here in Bixby.

But as Jessica made her way down the hall, a stranger's voice spoke up, gentle but certain of itself – and somehow vaguely familiar.

'No way,' she said softly. Beth was talking again now; she must have misheard.

But dread grew in Jessica as she reached the kitchen doorway and looked down at the empty table – for the first time since they'd arrived in Bixby, the dining table had been set.

Which meant that company was here.

She went through the kitchen and into the dining room until she found herself facing the four of them: Beth, Mom, Dad . . .

And Cassie Flinders.

'Hey, Jess!' Mom said. 'Beth brought a friend home from school today.'

Jessica managed only a zombified, 'Oh, yeah?'

'Cassie's in marching band with me,' Beth said, an amused smile playing on her lips. She turned to the girl. 'I told you about my sister, Jessica.'

Cassie Flinders looked her up and down, as if comparing her with some mental checklist.

'Hi,' Jessica squeaked, her voice gone all tinny and her mind racing.

Hadn't Rex and Melissa gone back out to Jenks and dealt with Cassie's memories? Wasn't this kid supposed to have only the vaguest recollections of her moments in the blue time?

'I think we've met,' Cassie finally said.

'Really?' Mom said, all smiles. 'Where was that?'

'Yeah, where?' Jessica said, taking her seat in front of the empty plate, trying to keep her voice normal and her expression only mildly puzzled instead of totally flabbergasted. 'I don't think I remember.'

'I don't remember either, exactly.' Cassie's eyes were still scanning Jessica's face, as if recording her features in great detail. 'But I drew a picture of you.'

'You did what?'

Cassie shrugged. 'Drew a picture, with a pencil. The other day when I was sick.'

'Yeah,' Beth said. 'And it's a really good one. She brought it in to show around. You can really tell it's you, Jess. Cassie draws all the time.'

'But you two don't remember meeting?' Mom asked.

'No, not at all,' Jessica said. 'I mean, I've never even been to Jenks.'

'Jenks?' Beth said, smiling radiantly. 'How did you know Cassie lived out there?'

'I don't know . . . how I knew that,' Jessica said slowly. Now even Mom and Dad were looking at her funny. She realized that it would be better if the conversation moved along. 'So, um, are you a majorette too?'

'No. I play clarinet.'

'And she's a really good artist,' Beth repeated.

'Yes,' Jessica said. 'I got that.'

'She also has this other drawing of this guy,' Beth said. 'What was the name you wrote on it? Jonath—'

'Oh, hang on!' Jessica said, playing the only card she could be certain would change the subject. 'Aren't you, like, Cassie *Flinders*?'

No one answered for a second, then Cassie nodded slowly.

'Now, Jess,' her mother said. 'I'm sure Cassie doesn't want to talk about that stuff last week, okay?'

'Sorry.' She shrugged. 'But I mean, it *was* on the news and everything.'

'*Jessica.*'

She didn't say anything more, just let Beth serve the pasta, slithering spaghetti onto their plates and glopping sauce on top of it as the awkwardness stretched out.

Uncomfortable silences were fine with Jessica, definitely better than the uncomfortable noises coming out of Beth's mouth. The pause in the conversation gave her a few minutes to figure out what had happened.

According to Rex, Melissa had checked Cassie's brain to make sure she hadn't spilled the beans. But maybe instead of blabbing about what she'd seen, she'd *drawn* it.

Jessica wondered what other pictures Cassie had made before her memory had been erased. One of Jonathan, apparently, and probably she'd sketched the other midnighters as well. And she might have written their names down too.

Had she drawn the black cat slither or the darkling she'd seen?

Everyone started eating, and soon Beth and Cassie were telling stories about how geeky the rest of the marching band was, acting like nothing weird or unexplained had been mentioned at the table.

Jessica wondered if the drawings would jog Cassie's memories, pulling them out of whatever corner of her mind Melissa had stuffed them into. Or if seeing Jessica in person would make her recall more of what had happened that night.

Still, Cassie didn't have much to go on – just a few names and half-remembered faces and maybe a black cat or monstrous spider straight out of a nightmare. She had no way to connect Jessica and Jonathan to the other midnighters, no more clues about what had really happened that day.

Cassie Flinders wasn't really the problem.

As usual, Beth was.

She had already recognized Jonathan's face and probably remembered from taking phone messages that Jessica had friends named Rex and Dess and Melissa. Worst of all, Beth knew that Jessica liked to sneak out at midnight – the time when the growing rip in Jenks was at its most dangerous.

And – as Jessica knew from long experience – if anyone could turn a small amount of information into a big pain in the ass, Beth could.

Jessica wondered about Rex's new policy against mind-casting. He hadn't let Melissa mess with Angie's brain, but Angie had known all about the secret hour for years. This was a different matter entirely. If rumors started to spread around Bixby Junior High that weird things happened near the Jenks railroad line at midnight, Rex might make an exception for little sisters.

Jessica decided not to mention any of this to him or even *think* about it too hard around Melissa. A quick look into Beth's brain would reveal that she knew more about midnight than was safe.

Way more, now that she was friends with Cassie Flinders.

Jessica kept eating, trying to enjoy the mingled tastes of long-simmered tomatoes, number 18 spaghetti, and almost-too-many reduced onions. But as dinner continued – Beth glancing at Jessica knowingly whenever she got a chance – the familiar flavors turned bitter in her mouth.

'Mom?' Beth said as the meal drew to a close.

'Yeah?'

'Can I go spend the night with Cassie sometime?'

Jessica watched as her parents' faces broke into smiles.

Marching band had paid off, big time. Beth had finally made a friend here in the new town. Everything would be much easier from now on.

'Of course you can,' Mom said.

Beth smiled, and her gaze turned to her older sister, making sure to show that she knew there were more clues to find, more trouble to make, out there in Jenks.

Jessica tried to put on an innocent expression, as if nothing tonight had disturbed her, but she felt the smile wither on her face.

It was just too depressing. Even Beth Spaghetti Night had been touched by the blue time.

10:30 P.M.

MINDCASTERS

'Give it one more chance, Loverboy. Please.'

Rex didn't answer, didn't even stop climbing the stairs toward the attic. His expression didn't change, as if he hadn't heard her plea at all. Not that she'd expected him to sit down for a chat about it. Since that night in the desert, Rex put up a normal front for the others, but around Melissa he often let his not-so-human side show.

Even here in Madeleine's house Melissa could taste the darklings inside him, as dry as a mouthful of chalk dust leeching the moisture from her tongue. Might as well talk to the desert sand as try to reach that part of him.

But this was Rex, after all. She wasn't letting go that easy.

Melissa dashed after him, far enough up the stairs to grab his left ankle from below. She sank her nails into the leg of his jeans, bringing him to a halt with all her strength.

'Wait a damn second, Rex!'

He turned, looking down at her, emotionless. His eyes flashed in that creepy new way they did, somehow catching the dark moon's light even in normal time.

His lips curled away from his teeth, and for a horrible moment Melissa thought she'd gone too far. He would turn into a beast once and for all and devour her right there, leaving Madeleine's staircase littered with her bones.

But then the expression on his face turned into a wry smile.

'What's the matter, Cowgirl?' he said. 'Jealous?'

'Just wait a minute, Rex. Please?'

He looked down at his captive boot and raised one eyebrow.

Melissa turned his ankle loose, realizing that she was half kneeling on the stairs, like some drunk trying to crawl up to bed. She took a deep breath to calm herself and turned away from Rex, sitting down on the steps. Then she pointed one black fingernail at the spot next to her.

After an infuriating pause, as if his oldest friend in the world was *so* hard to deal with, the staircase began to creak and shift under his weight as he descended. He sat down beside her.

'I'm not jealous of Madeleine,' she said. 'But you used to be, remember?'

'Vividly.'

Melissa snorted. 'Glad to hear that. I'd hate it if you gave up jealousy. It's probably the only thing in the world everyone's good at. Everyone besides me, of course.'

'Of course.'

'This isn't about me, though. It's about us.' Melissa winced at her own words and glanced up at him. His eyes had gone back to normal, at least. She had the foul feeling in her stomach that she'd tasted so many times in Bixby High girls, that sour paranoia that their boyfriends' interest in them was evaporating. Melissa had always written them off as dorky and contemptible; she'd never realized that rejection was so *painful*.

Of course, things were bound to be awkward when your boyfriend was changing into a different species.

She took his hand, and his taste filled her. She focused on the surface of his mind – the steady, calming thought patterns of Rex Greene. Even during all those years she'd been unable to touch him, his surety and seer's focus had always been something Melissa could cling to. The old Rex was still in there.

Of course, that familiarity only made the other part of him more disturbing. How could something so comforting and reassuring be wrapped around such darkness?

'Let me try again.'

'We already tried. It's useless.' He shrugged. 'And who knows? Maybe Madeleine can't get inside me either. But it's been a week; I don't want what I got from the darklings to fade before she has a chance to look for it.'

'Believe me, Rex. It isn't fading.' The blackness at his core was as solid as tar.

'Well, it isn't any clearer either, Cowgirl, no matter how many times we've done this. We need Madeleine's help. Samhain is only sixteen days away.'

Instead of answering, Melissa pushed herself farther into him, letting her thoughts flow across the human surface of his mind.

This time she didn't try to crack the darkness at his center. Rex was probably right: whatever the darklings had left behind was too inhuman for her to reach. Melissa instead offered her own store of implanted memories, the accumulated legacy passed from hand to hand across the generations.

Before he went up to the attic, Rex had to know what mindcasters were capable of.

Melissa took Rex to a place in the core of those memories, an event that mindcasters had shared since the old days. A long time ago, back even before the earliest Spanish settlers had come to Oklahoma, long before the Anglos and the eastern tribes, there had been a gathering. Mindcasters from several tribes had met before a large fire to exchange images of far-off places they'd seen – east to the still waters of the Gulf of Mexico, north to where the Rockies reared up; one had traveled as far as the Grand Canyon. Since that first meeting the memory had been added to, layered with more images as it had been passed from generation to generation. It was as if the gathering had grown to a thousand mindcasters, all of those who had ever come to Bixby and discovered their power, until finally it had made its way to Melissa.

'Wow,' he said after a moment of marveling at it all.

'And not a hint of guilt,' Melissa said softly.

'What do you mean?'

'None of them thought that mindcasting was a bad thing, Rex. Of those hundreds of minds, not one thought it came with any cost.'

Rex pulled his hand away, shaking his head to clear it. 'So you're saying Angie's wrong? That the Grayfoots fooled her somehow?'

'No.' Melissa glanced over her shoulder toward the top of the stairs, reassuring herself that Madeleine wasn't within listening range. 'Since Angie gave us her little lecture, I've been sifting through the memories for the kind of thing she was talking about – destroying people, altering minds for profit, mass manipulation. But I haven't found them.' She drummed her fingers on her knees. 'For some reason, though, I still think she's telling the truth. Does that make any sense?'

Rex nodded. 'Maybe they passed down an edited version.'

'What they passed down was unbelievable smugness, Rex. They never questioned what they were doing. I don't think they *could* question it.'

'How do you mean?'

She reached for his hand again and showed him an unpleasant memory from only a few weeks before – the moment when she had touched Dess against her will and pried the secret of Madeleine's existence from her. Melissa forced herself to linger over how Dess's mind had been locked by the old mindcaster, effortlessly twisted to hide what she knew. And how Melissa had torn it open.

When she felt a chill run through Rex, she released his hand.

'Why did you show me that?' he asked.

'Because you have to remember what we're capable of,' she said. 'Mindcasting doesn't just affect normal people. It can be used against other midnighters too.'

'I know.' His eyes narrowed. 'But what does that have to do with Bixby's history?'

She looked up at him. 'Before us five orphans came along, every midnighter grew up surrounded by mindcasters, all of them sharing thoughts every time they shook hands. But what if it wasn't just news and memories they were passing on? What if they were passing on *beliefs*? And what if at some point they all decided to believe that midnighters never did anything bad?'

'*Decided* to believe?'

Melissa leaned closer, speaking softer now, imagining the old woman upstairs listening from just around the corner. Melissa had chosen Madeleine's house to have this conversation with Rex for one simple reason: inside its crepuscular contortion, their minds couldn't be overheard.

'Over the centuries,' she said, 'midnighters started to believe whatever they did was okay, just like people who owned slaves used to think they were being 'good masters' or whatever. Except unlike slavery, nobody from the outside ever questioned what the midnighters were up to in Bixby. It was all secret, and anytime doubts cropped up, there were mindcasters around to squash them. It was like some clique of cheerleaders going through high school together, all thinking the same way, talking the same way, believing they're at the center of the universe . . . but for *thousands of years*.'

She looked into his eyes, hoping that he would get it.

'Until we came along,' Rex said.

'Exactly. We're more different from our predecessors than we thought, Rex. Maybe they really did all that evil stuff, but they didn't *know* they were being evil. They *couldn't* know.'

'You haven't asked Madeleine about this yet?'

Melissa shook her head. 'No way. I haven't let her touch me since Angie gave her little speech.'

Rex smiled softly. 'So you're an Angie fan now, are you?'

'Not really, but she has the same good point that most scumbags have: she makes me feel a lot better about myself.'

'Because you never kidnapped anyone?'

'Oh, much better than that.' She placed her palms together, hoping that the realization would still make sense once she'd said it aloud. 'Madeleine always says I'll never be a *real* mindcaster – I started too late. Those memories are just figments to me; to her they're like real people.' Melissa shook her head. 'But what if it's a *good* thing that I never got indoctrinated? What if I'm not the first crazy mindcaster in history, Rex? What if I'm the first *sane* one?'

'Sane . . .' he said, not quite understanding yet.

Melissa pressed on. 'Because no matter how screwed up I happen to be, no matter what I did to your dad, at least I can see that ripping the minds of a whole town for a hundred generations is *not* cool.'

He took her hand, and all of Melissa's thoughts, which had tumbled out in clumsy words, seemed to order themselves at his touch. They flowed into him, along with the thing she hadn't said aloud.

I'm sorry about your father, Rex.

'You saved me from him, the best you knew how,' he answered.

Melissa looked away, her emotions churning. Her shame at her own past, her worries that she'd already lost Rex to the darklings, her fear of what Madeleine might do to his mind – all of it squeezed into a single tear. It traveled down her cheek like a drop of acid.

Rex sat there thinking, then finally said, 'I think you're right. Madeleine's going to find my new view of history . . . challenging.'

'Then let me go up there with you, Rex. I don't care what a badass darkling you are these days. You need my protection.'

He smiled again, and she saw a violet spark in the depths of his eyes. 'You have no idea what I am.'

She let out a short, choked laugh. 'Whatever, Rex. Even if you are a monster, I don't want to lose you to *her*. And don't think all those creepy old midnighters in her brain won't give you a run for your money.'

Unexpectedly he leaned forward and kissed her – the first time their lips had met since last Wednesday night. His taste hovered on the edge between bitter and sweet, like chocolate that was almost too dark.

But what scared her most was that she tasted no fear in him at all.

'We'll see about that,' he said. 'Come on, Cowgirl. She's waiting.'

Madeleine sat in her usual spot in the corner of the attic, tea things arranged around her. 'Both of you, is it?'

'Maybe I can help,' Melissa said.

The old mindcaster gave a little snort but didn't send her away. Like Rex, Madeleine had no fear.

'Well, sit down then, both of you. Tea's getting cold. In my day, young people didn't keep their elders waiting.'

The more I hear about your day, Melissa thought, *the more I'm glad the Grayfoots came along.*

She and Rex sat down in the corner, the three of them forming a triangle around the tea service. Melissa had never done this before – held two midnighters' hands at once – but she knew from her store of memories that mindcasting circles were an ancient practice.

No wonder they all thought the same way. All those minds tuned together and reinforcing one another's beliefs – add a few pom-poms and they'd be just like the pep rallies of Bixby High, except without anyone sneaking out the back to smoke.

Melissa took a sip of tea. It had indeed grown cold, bringing out its bitter taste even more than usual.

'What you did last week was very dangerous, Rex,' Madeleine scolded. 'I watched from this very spot. No one has ever survived anything like that before.'

'We didn't have anywhere else to turn,' he said.

'I've worked hard the last sixteen years to keep you alive, Rex. You could have thrown away all that effort in a matter of minutes.'

Melissa took a slow breath. In their training sessions Madeleine never tired of reminding her why she and Dess had been made – to help Rex, the only natural midnighter in Bixby's recent history. The old mindcaster had subtly manipulated hundreds of mothers during their labor, trying to create babies born at the stroke of midnight. And all to make sure Rex had a posse to lead, like a proper seer should.

Melissa understood all too well now what the five of them really were: Madeleine's attempt to re-create the Bixby she had grown up with, a paradise for midnighters ... at the expense of everyone else.

'I'm still alive,' Rex said in a flat voice. The human softness he'd allowed himself to reveal on the stairs had disappeared again.

'They could have eaten you,' Madeleine said.

'The things I was talking to don't eat meat,' he said. 'They eat nightmares.'

She raised an eyebrow.

'But they wouldn't have eaten me anyway. I carry their smell.' Rex gave the old mindcaster a cruel smile. He must know how much it offended her, Melissa thought, to have her little seer infected with the darkness.

Madeleine's face twitched. 'You taste more like them every

day. But do you really think they would tell you something useful? Why should they?'

'The darklings didn't *tell* me anything,' he said. 'They share their thoughts naturally, like animals crying out when they've spotted a kill. You know that, Madeleine. You hear them thinking all the time.'

'If you can call it thinking.' She made a face, as if fifty years of her own bitter tea was finally hitting her taste buds. 'Well, let's see if your little experiment accomplished anything other than almost giving me a heart attack.'

She held out both her hands, palms up.

Melissa caught Rex's eye, and they joined hands first with each other, waiting for a moment until their connection was complete. Her heart was pounding, and even though she was certain that the memory was all part of a big lie – propaganda, like Angie had said – Melissa recalled that long-ago mindcaster gathering, letting her wonder at those ancient images shared around the fire calm her.

As her mind stilled, she felt herself drawing strength from Rex's dark confidence. Whatever the horde of old mindcasters inside Madeleine had in store for the two of them, at least they were facing it together.

'Come now. Don't lollygag,' Madeleine snapped.

As one, they raised their other hands and let her grasp them, completing the circle.

As Madeleine stilled herself, she changed, becoming a congress of minds.

Melissa was always awestruck at the vastness of it: memories stretching back to shadowy recollections of the ice age, when glaciers could be reached in a month's walk to the

north. Ten thousand years of history, hundreds of generations, thousands of mindcasters.

She squeezed Rex's hand. Facing that accumulated mass of
minds, she was glad for his dark presence beside her.

'What have they done to you?' Madeleine murmured. She
was probing the black sphere of Rex's darkling half, searching
its smooth surface for purchase. As the fingers of her mind
settled in and began to pry, Rex's hand flinched in Melissa's.

'It's for your own good,' the old woman muttered. Her
concentration deepened, her raspy breathing slowing in
Melissa's ears.

After a long moment the darkness inside Rex began to
swell, like something viscous and heavy coming slowly to a
boil. The muscles in his fingers twitched again in her hand, a
dry taste stirring among the patterns of his mind.

Eyes closed, Melissa watched the changes shifting through
him and wondered if Madeleine really knew what she was
doing. Melissa could taste arrogance in the mass of memories, their certainty that they could control anything and
anyone. But they'd never faced something like Rex.

Then bitter metal filled her mouth, like old pennies on her
tongue.

A seam had begun to open in Rex's mind, his darkling
inner core shivering, its surface cracking. Melissa tasted
Madeleine's satisfaction.

Rex made a pained sound.

Melissa sent calming thoughts toward him, but Madeleine
pushed her back. *You don't know what you're doing, girl. Stay clear*.

The old mindcaster turned her attention back to Rex,
pressing harder, and the darkness inside him began to split –
a black and radiant shaft spilled across the mental landscape,

bleeding color from it like the dark moon's light. Images of an ancient Samhain flowed from his mind: masked humans piling up the bones of cattle and setting them alight, fires dotting the landscape for miles, raising up a slaughterhouse smell. Melissa felt a twitch of hunger at the scent and realized that the reaction was a darkling's. Soon she was ravenous, feeling the call to hunt, to kill.

Abomination, whispered the mass of memories.

They meant Rex – seer and darkling mixed; he horrified them.

Madeleine grew bolder, her mind prising into the cracks of Rex's darkling half. He let out a short cry, and his fingernails dug into Melissa's hand.

'Stop!' Melissa whispered hoarsely. 'You're hurting him.'

Abomination, a thousand voices hissed. The mindcasters' memories had known nothing like him before; he had to be constrained, controlled.

But the darkness inside Rex only grew, swelling into a huge black storm cloud in Melissa's mind, spilling more visions: Bixby as the old ones had seen it fifty years ago, a psychic spiderweb of midnight glittering across the desert. In the darklings' eyes the town was an infected organism, the tendrils of a parasite extended into every fiber of its host – mindcasters quietly toiling, spreading obedience across the city, certain that it was only natural for them to rule.

Even the darklings knew what you were, Melissa thought.

Madeleine made a choking noise, the mass of memories inside her roiling as it beheld its own reflection in Rex's mind. He was an abomination, and his thoughts were an insult to ten thousand years of history.

He had to be destroyed.

A shudder of horror passed through Madeleine at the thought, but she couldn't pull her mind back. She couldn't go against the mass.

'No,' Melissa whispered. *Egotistical morons!*

They ignored her. She tried to wrench her eyes open, to reach over and separate Madeleine's hand from Rex's, but her muscles were locked rigid.

Melissa felt hatred rising up in her, disgust at the conceited, clueless pride of her predecessors. She focused all of her loathing – everything Angie had said about the reign of the midnighters, their greed and child-stealing and brain-ripping – and hurled it at Madeleine as hard as she could.

The mass of memories reared at the insult and turned on her in a flood of contempt and arrogance. They had borne the secrets of midnight for thousands of years; Melissa was an upstart, an orphan, a nothing.

That which sticks up must be pounded down.

But before the mass could do any pounding, Melissa's mouth filled again with the taste of darkling. She'd distracted them just long enough.

The thing in Rex was *really* boiling now . . .

Like a predatory cat, it sliced straight through the mass, down into Madeleine's own memories, her deepest secrets. With a hunter's instinct it found her fears . . . and ransacked them.

'No, Rex!' Madeleine gasped, but he was a wounded animal now, pitiless and rabid. Melissa watched aghast as fifty years of terror erupted from the depths of the old woman's mind, every nervous minute of hiding since the Grayfoots' revolution.

You gave them Anathea, he hissed, and decades of guilt surged up in Madeleine. The mass of memories spun in a tempest, unable to order themselves in her churning mind, like rats in a house on fire.

Melissa tried to focus her mind. *Rex . . . that's enough!*

'We're knocking at your door!' he said aloud, his voice inhuman. 'We've found you at last. We've come for you!'

A single choked scream of terror came from Madeleine's lips, darklings from a thousand nightmares shredding her mind; her hand jerked once, then slipped from Melissa's.

Suddenly the mass of mindcasters was silenced, Madeleine's mind gone; Melissa found herself alone with Rex in the blackness behind closed eyes. The darkling thoughts moved through him, still powerful, still hungry. Melissa watched in horror as her oldest friend transformed, the darkness consuming still more of his humanity.

She wondered if she was next.

Rex, she pleaded. *Come back to me.*

'Unconquerable,' he said softly, his voice dry.

The storm began to subside, and what remained of Rex's humanity settled over the boiling darkness. She felt his sanity return.

With a *snap* her muscles were her own again. Melissa pulled her hand from his and opened her eyes.

Madeleine lay on the attic floor unmoving, shards of her shattered teacup strewn about her. Her face was locked in an expression of horror.

'It worked,' Rex said, his voice calm.

Melissa stared at the stricken woman on the floor. She was still breathing, but her eyes were glazed over, her fingers twitching.

Melissa looked up at Rex, and his eyes flashed violet. 'You call that *working*?'

'I remember now.' His lips curled into a smile. 'I know what Samhain really was.'

Melissa tried to gather her wits and tore her eyes from Madeleine's twisted face. The darklings were coming, and thousands of lives were at stake. 'Can we stop it?'

Rex shuddered for a second, as if one last memory remained fugitive in his mind. But then he nodded slowly.

'We can try.'

21

SAMHAIN

Every night it seemed like the secret hour took longer to come.

Jonathan drummed his fingers on his windowsill, waiting for the cold wind to be silenced, for colors to blur together into blue, for weightlessness to pour into him. He didn't look at the clock, which never worked. Knowing how many minutes of Flatland were left only made the torture worse.

These stretches right before midnight were always the hardest. Jonathan wanted to be out there *now*, soaring over the still cars and softly glowing houses, feeling his muscles propel him across town.

To pass the time – to force the time to get *moving* – he counted off the coming days on his fingers. It was Thursday night, tomorrow was Friday, exactly two weeks until Halloween. If Dess was right, he would only have to endure this wait fifteen more times, including tonight.

And then he would be free of gravity altogether.

His eyes closed. Jonathan realized, of course, that the weakening of the blue time was a disaster; it would give the darklings free rein to hunt down thousands of people, maybe a lot more than that. His father, his classmates, everyone he knew was in terrible danger.

But he couldn't keep his mind off one fact: for however long the frozen midnight lasted, Flatland would be erased, and the world would have three dimensions. For a guilty moment Jonathan let himself feel the pleasure the thought gave him – being able to fly for days on end, however far the blue time expanded.

Maybe it would swallow the whole world.

At last midnight came, almost surprising him in his reverie. The earth shuddered, dropping its claims on his body, the chains of gravity finally falling away. He drifted upward, sucking in a deep, rib-cracking breath. Only at midnight did his lungs feel like they filled completely, no longer constrained by the suffocating weight of his own body. The weight of Flatland.

It was crazy to feel guilty about the joy this gave him. It wasn't his fault the world was ending.

Jonathan launched himself out the window, passing over his father's car and up onto the neighbor's roof with one well-practiced bound. There his right foot landed on its usual spot, a circle of cracked shingles marking where so many nightly flights began.

Then he pushed off toward Jessica's and – as he watched for flying slithers and power lines, calculating the best course down empty roads and across newly harvested fields – his mind kept returning to one thought . . .

Only two more weeks of gravity, and then I'm free.

'Okay, everyone,' Rex said. 'Madeleine went into my mind last night.'

Jonathan frowned. The five of them were meeting in Madeleine's house, seated around her scuffed dining table surrounded by the clutter of tridecagrams and other tangled shapes. But the old woman hadn't appeared tonight, and Rex had started talking as if she wasn't coming down. Wasn't she home?

Where else could she be at midnight?

'You actually let her *touch* you?' Dess asked.

'Melissa was there to protect me,' Rex said.

Jonathan glanced at Jessica, and they both flinched, waiting for the nasty response they knew was coming, but Dess just coughed into her fist and rolled her eyes. Eerily, the scar the darkling had left over her eye was shaped just like one of Melissa's.

Jonathan was glad she kept quiet. Tonight Rex was scary enough without anyone provoking him. His expression seemed vacant somehow, as if there were some other creature inside him, showing off the Rex mask it was going to wear while trick-or-treating.

He looked weird enough in daylight, but in the secret hour the new Rex was almost too much to face.

'The darklings remember Samhain,' Rex said.

'So that goth holiday is the real thing, huh?' Dess asked, shaking her head.

'It isn't a Gothic holiday,' Rex answered. 'The Goths were from Asia. Samhain was Celtic.'

'From Asia?' Dess said, then groaned. 'No, Rex, not the guys who conquered Rome. I mean the kids in black.'

'Um, Dess?' Melissa said. 'Mirror check.'

'This dress is *charcoal*,' Dess said.

'Probably the Goths had something like Samhain too,' Rex

kept going. 'A lot of cultures have festivals at the end of October. The Feast of Souls. Something called Shadowfest. The Death of the Sun.'

Jessica raised an eyebrow. 'Shadowfest? That sounds . . . festive.'

Dess let out a long sigh. 'Why are we even talking about this? All that pagan stuff is from the Old World, but here in Oklahoma, Halloween is just an excuse to sell a bunch of candy and costumes to little kids. Like Angie said, the darklings hid themselves way before any Europeans got here.'

Jonathan cleared his throat. 'Actually, Dess, it's not just a European thing. You know the Day of the Dead down in Mexico? Even though it's the same day as All Hallows' Eve, the natives already had a holiday around then.'

Rex nodded. 'And some Native Americans had festivals celebrating the Old Crone around this time.'

Dess laughed. 'Excuse me, Rex. The *Old Crone*?' She looked around at the others. 'And what were those other ones? Shadowfest? Death of the Sun? Dawn of the Dead? Is it just me, or do all these holidays have a trying-too-hard-to-be-creepy ring to them?'

'Of course they do,' Rex said, his scary mask unruffled by her teasing. 'Look at the bare trees outside, the gray sky, the dead grass everywhere. The word *Samhain* is Celtic for "summer's end." The beginning of winter.' Suddenly Rex's voice sounded dry, like he'd been out in the desert without water for a few days. 'The dying of the light, when warmth turns to cold.'

Everyone was silent for a moment, even Melissa looking a little spooked by Rex. Jonathan heard a creaking noise above his head. So Madeleine *was* here. But why was she hiding upstairs?

He glanced at Melissa, wondering what exactly had happened between the three of them the night before.

Dess broke the mood, letting out an exasperated breath. 'This isn't about spooks and ghosts, Rex, it's about *numbers*. The eleventh month plus one is twelve. That's all it is.'

Jonathan frowned. Back in Philadelphia, his mother had always taken him to church on All Hallows' Eve. Even the Catholic version of Samhain had given him the willies.

'So tell us, Rex,' he said. 'Way back when, before Halloween got all cutesy, what was the point of Samhain?'

'Well, believe it or not, people did wear costumes,' Rex said. 'But the most important ritual was building bonfires. They burned everything they could, even the bones of their slaughtered cattle, hoping to drive away the night for a little while longer. Of course, they knew winter was going to win sooner or later. Samhain recognizes the coming of darkness.'

'Hey,' Dess said. 'Now there's a snappy greeting card: "Hope that you and yours have a lovely coming of darkness."'

'I agree,' Rex said. 'It doesn't seem like the best time of year for a holiday. But for some reason, the coming of darkness wasn't a bad thing.'

'Like I said, it's a *goth* holiday,' Dess muttered.

'Yet during all of recorded history, it was a time of celebration,' Rex continued. 'But what were they celebrating? Think about it. Back then winter must have been a pretty scary time of year.'

'Because everyone starved?' Jonathan said.

Rex's face curled into something resembling a smile.

'Everyone but the darklings. Remember, even before the secret hour was created, darklings hunted at night. In winter, nights get longer and longer. So originally those bonfires weren't symbolic; they were designed to keep the predators away for as long as possible.'

The rapturous expression on Rex's face made Jonathan shiver; his eyelids were fluttering, as if he was mainlining darkling memories. Jessica reached over and squeezed Jonathan's hand beneath the table.

He coughed. 'Sure, Rex. That's not something a normal person would celebrate.'

'No. But one Samhain a long time ago, everything changed. The darklings never showed up again, even after the bonfires burned down. They had retreated into midnight. So those bonfires changed in meaning. Instead of a last-ditch survival maneuver, they were now an act of celebration. Halloween is the anniversary of the beginning of the secret hour, the day humanity finally reached the top of the food chain.'

Dess sat up straighter. 'Huh. So maybe this whole history thing does actually make sense. I mean, if the darklings really did disappear on October 31, that's why it was such a good day in the old system. It was the day when everyone was finally safe from them forever.'

'Not forever,' Rex said.

'Oh, right.' Dess's voice softened. 'November 1 is going to be a darkling holiday from now on, isn't it?'

He nodded. 'They're going to turn the food chain around again. But the good news is this long midnight won't last forever – just for twenty-five hours, a single day by the old reckoning.'

Jonathan knew he should be relieved, but somewhere deep inside him, he felt a little spark of disappointment.

'Okay, Rex,' Dess said. 'What's the bad news?'

'The long midnight will happen every Halloween, the rip getting bigger and bigger every time. From now on, humans are the candy.'

Jonathan's disappointment lifted a little. A *whole day every year*.

'So what do we *do* about this?' Jessica said. 'Wasn't that the point of you talking to the darklings? To find out some way to stop it?'

Rex didn't respond for a while, his face strangely unmoving. Jessica looked over at Jonathan, who only shrugged. He realized that some part of him was scared that the seer already had a plan, something that would shove the secret hour back into its bottle. Which would be a *good* thing, of course, saving thousands of lives at least.

But it would also mean Jonathan would never fly for more than one hour a day . . .

Finally Rex spoke. 'We'll try to stop it, to do whatever we can. When it comes, we'll gather people together and teach them how to fight for themselves.'

'Um, Rex?' Jessica said. 'What about keeping the secret hour a secret?'

'We don't anymore. After the long midnight we won't be able to.' He looked down at the table. 'And after what we saw in Madeleine's mind last night, I'm pretty sure I don't want us midnighters to stay in shadows anymore.'

Everyone was silent for a moment as the idea that the blue time wouldn't be secret any longer slowly sank in.

Jonathan wondered again why the old mindcaster wasn't

down here with them. But there were more important questions right now, he supposed. 'So how do we organize a whole
town in one night?'

Rex shook his head. 'I don't know yet.' He turned to
Jessica. 'But you remember how Angie said Samhain had
something to do with the flame-bringer?'

'Yeah,' she answered. 'That was kind of hard to forget.'

'Well, I've got a few ideas about how the rip works. And
they have to do with you. But we need to do a few experiments. I want all of you to meet me in Jenks tomorrow
morning. At six-thirty.'

Dess let out a snort. 'Hold on there, Rex. There's a six-
thirty in the *morning* now? No one told me about that.'

'Yeah, really,' Jonathan said.

Rex rose from his seat, suddenly inhumanly tall, his bulk
seeming to crowd against the ceiling. His features shifted on
his face, the eyes growing as long and wide as a wolf's and
burning violet. His hands slammed down onto the table,
crooked like claws, then scraped across the wood in one slow,
deliberate movement, his fingernails catching every imper-
fection.

Jonathan swallowed – the creature had come out from
behind the mask.

'Do you think we have time to waste *sleeping*?' Rex said, his
voice gone cold and dry and ancient. 'Thousands will be
killed, and for some it will be worse than dying. The old ones
will suck them dry first, wringing out every drop of fear.
They're coming for you, don't you see?'

He stood there, glaring at them all, while the old house
filled with the echoes of his words, like whispers coming from
every corner. Jonathan thought he saw the piles of junk

around them glow brighter for a moment, their soft blue metal rimmed with cold fire.

A vague, choking noise came from Madeleine upstairs, as if she was crying out in a dream, but Jonathan didn't dare look up. The four of them just stared at Rex in stunned silence. Even Melissa looked bowled over by his sudden transformation.

A long moment later he sat back down, taking in a slow breath. 'I know this is hard. But you can catch up on your sleep after Halloween.'

His voice had gone back to normal, but they all still sat there, dumbfounded. Jonathan wished he could think of something to say, anything at all to break the silence. But the whole concept of language – hellos, goodbyes, jokes, mindless banter – it all seemed to have fled from his brain.

Rex was suddenly so *alien*. It would be like making small talk with a snake.

Finally Dess cleared her throat. 'Okay, then. Six-thirty A.M. it is.'

Jessica looked up at Jonathan, mouthing the words, *Let's go*.

Jonathan didn't have any problem with that. Some serious flying was what he needed right now, stretching his limbs and soaring away from the earth, as far as he could get from Rex's weirdness.

But he remembered to ask, 'So, Melissa, will you guys need a ride out there? I mean, since your car's all busted.'

She looked at Rex, who shook his head no but didn't say anything more.

Great, Jonathan thought. *Maybe they'll fly out with one of his darkling pals.*

*

There was still time, so the two of them headed toward downtown.

'So what the hell is up with Rex?' Jonathan said softly, once Madeleine's house was safely behind them.

'Don't ask me,' Jessica answered, squeezing his hand. 'Did you notice what he said at the end, "They're coming for you"?'

'As in *us* – not him. Makes sense, though. He's on speaking terms with the darklings these days.' Jonathan waited until they'd caromed from the long top of an eighteen-wheeler on Kerr Street, then added, 'But I guess we're safe, you and me.'

'Oh, *that* makes me feel a lot better.'

He glanced at her. 'I just mean, we're safe as long as we stick together.'

She didn't say anything, just squeezed his hand again.

They climbed the buildings of downtown like stepping-stones, bounding to the summit of the old Mobil Building. This was where they had hidden in the days before Jessica had found her talent, back when the darklings were desperate to kill her – before she discovered who she was.

Jonathan looked out across Bixby, laid out before them in the even, deep blue glow of the secret hour. He looked in the direction of Jenks, trying to see the rip, but its red tinge didn't show on the horizon.

Not yet, anyway. It was growing every time an eclipse fell.

'We haven't been up here in a while,' Jessica said.

'Yeah. I was kind of missing Pegasus.' He looked up. The huge neon Mobil sign in the shape of a flying horse hovered over them protectively.

'That's not all I missed,' Jessica said, a smile playing on her lips. 'You remember what happened here, right?'

Jonathan nodded. 'You mean, us hiding from the darklings?'

'Yeah. But not *just* that.'

He thought for a moment. They hadn't really been up here since those early days. He shrugged.

Jessica let out a groan. 'I can't *believe* you. This is where we first kissed!'

'Oh, *right*!' He swallowed. 'But that was around the same time, yeah? I mean, I just said how we were hiding here, and that was when we . . .' Jonathan stumbled to a halt, realizing that explanations were only making things worse.

He took her hands, hoping that his midnight gravity would bring her smile back.

She just stared at him. 'I can't believe you forgot.'

'I didn't forget. I just didn't know what you were talking about.'

'Ugh. That's even worse!'

'Why?'

'Because it's like you've totally forgotten.' She pulled her hands away, looking out over the blue-lit city. 'We haven't exactly . . . This last week we've hardly touched each other.'

'No, I guess not.' He sighed. 'It seems like we're always in crisis mode.'

'I guess it's not that big a deal, compared to the whole town getting sucked into oblivion. But shouldn't that make us closer or something?' She looked at him for an answer, like this was a particularly tricky problem from physics class.

'Look at it this way, Jessica,' he said, putting his arm around her. 'Once Samhain comes, we'll get to spend a whole day flying together.'

'*Jonathan!*'

'What?' He held up his hands in surrender. 'I'm just saying.'

She groaned, turning away from him. 'I *knew* you were thinking that way.'

'What way?'

'You're *excited* that this is going to happen, aren't you?' she cried. 'You'd probably be happy if it went on forever: blue time, all the time. No more Flatland. What could be better?'

He rolled his eyes but couldn't bring himself to contradict her aloud. After all, he'd been thinking that exact thing as midnight fell.

But that didn't make him a terrible person, did it?

Jonathan took a deep breath. Usually with Jessica, explaining things just seemed to make an argument go downhill. But for some reason, he always tried anyway. You had to keep talking to each other or nothing ever got resolved.

He began nervously. 'Listen, Jess. Haven't you ever imagined the world ending? I mean, kind of *fantasized* about a nuclear war or a plague or something wiping out everybody – except you and a few friends? And of course it's all tragic and everything, but suddenly the whole world belongs to you?'

'Mmm . . . no, actually.' She frowned. 'In my fantasies I'm more of a rock star who can fly. And has no little sister.'

He smiled, took her hand, and nudged them both a few feet into the air. 'Well, one out of three isn't bad.'

'Are you saying I'm not a rock star?'

'You don't even sing.'

'I do in the shower.' A smile finally crossed her face as they settled back to the rooftop, but then she pulled away again. 'Jonathan, the problem is that this *isn't* a fantasy. It's real. I feel bad even joking about it.'

'But Jessica, *we* didn't make this happen. It's not our fault. All we can do is try to save as many people as we can.'

'And enjoy the extra flying time?'

'No! If we can stop it, we will. But maybe we should leave the planning to Rex. It's what he's good at, even if he's been a weirdo lately.'

'Even if it means keeping Flatland on its current schedule?'

'*Yes.*' He was silent for a moment, looking for words. 'I don't hate the world the way it is, Jessica. I don't want my dad and your family and everyone else sucked into some nightmare. I know the difference between a stupid fantasy and the *real* end of the world. Okay?' He paused, not quite believing what he was about to say. 'And whatever Rex comes up with, I'll follow his orders.'

'You promise?'

'Sure. I promise. Even if he's acting totally crazy. Anything to stop this.'

She looked at him, then finally nodded. 'Okay.'

He took her hand, felt his midnight gravity connect them. 'Let's not worry about Bixby right now.'

She smiled faintly and leaned toward him. His eyes closed as their lips met, and for a moment the rest of the world really did fall away. Jonathan pushed them up into the air until they seemed suspended in a dark blue void, with only each other to cling to.

When they parted, he said softly, 'Whatever happens in the long midnight, we'll be okay – you and me. You know that, right?'

She shook her head, a sad look crossing her face, then silenced him with another kiss.

22

FIREWORKS

'If Rex doesn't show up on time, I'll kill him.'

Jonathan looked tiredly at Dess, then at his watch. 'He's got another minute.'

'One minute to live, you mean.'

'Not really,' Jonathan said. 'Either Rex gets here in one minute, in which case he's on time and you don't kill him. Or he's late, which means he won't be here, so you *can't* kill him. Either way he has more than one minute to live.'

Dess cast a cold glance at Flyboy. He was making logical sense, which was *totally* unfair at this time on a Saturday morning.

'Jess,' she said. 'Tell Jonathan to stop making sense.'

Jessica, her head leaning sleepily on Flyboy's shoulder, started to answer, but a yawn consumed her words. She wound up waving her hand noncommittally.

'Wait a second,' Jonathan said. 'Is that them?'

Jessica sat bolt upright. 'What? In *that* thing?'

Dess felt her jaw dropping. 'No way!'

A pink Cadillac was rumbling toward them through the field, its vast frame bobbing across the furrows.

'Rex said he had a new ride,' Dess said with quiet awe. 'But I didn't think he meant his *mom*'s car.' She felt a smile break across her face. Teasing him about this was going to be so much more fun than killing him.

Rex's mother worked selling Mary Kay cosmetics door to door, and in recognition of her millionth facial or whatever, she had received a pink Cadillac. But Dess had never actually seen the fabled machine before; Rex refused to ride to school in it, and she'd never imagined him actually *driving* it.

Yet there he was, cruising through Jenks at daybreak like he owned the whole town.

It rolled to a stop next to Jonathan's car, and Flyboy barked out a short laugh as the front window came down. 'Wow, Rex. *Ding-dong!*'

'That's Avon, actually,' Melissa said as she stepped out of the Cadillac's passenger side. 'You're not even trying.'

'Oh, right,' Jonathan said. 'Well, it's not like I have to try *that* hard. I mean . . .' He spread his arms to indicate the car. 'It's so *pink*.'

Flyboy's voice trailed off as Rex stepped out, looked down at the car, and said, 'Hey, yeah, it is. I hadn't noticed.'

Then he turned back to them and cracked a smile.

Dess breathed a sigh of relief; that was the first joke he'd made in days. His messed-up morning hair made him look more human than he usually did. Maybe the effects of Maddy unleashing the darklings in his brain had worn off a little.

'How did you get your mom to lend it to you?' she asked. Since his father's accident, Rex's mother hardly ever showed her face in Bixby. Dess couldn't imagine her handing over the keys for an early morning joyride.

'She dropped by for a visit night before last,' Rex said. 'And I got the idea of pulling her starter cable out.'

Dess's eyes widened. 'Excuse me?'

'It was easy. I snuck out while she was in the bathroom and pulled out the starter cable.' Rex gave his new evil smile. 'She was in a hurry to get somewhere else, like always, so I called her a cab. She's already rented another Caddy, so this one's mine until I tell her it's fixed.'

Dess and Jonathan exchanged a glance, and she saw that even Jessica had woken up enough to be impressed.

'Rex,' Dess said. 'That is so cold-blooded.'

'True.' He nodded. 'But I needed a car. We have important things to take care of.'

'Like getting us all out of bed at six-thirty on a Saturday morning?' Flyboy asked.

'Exactly.' Rex looked at his watch. 'Come with me.'

He led them across the field toward the rip, and Dess found herself glad that she'd worn a skirt that didn't fall below her knees. At this time of morning the long grass was heavy with dew, and her sneakers got soaked as fast as if she'd been strolling through a car wash.

As they marched, the sun began to crest over the distant tree line, its glaring eye finally putting a dent in the fierce pre-dawn chill.

'This better be good, Rex.'

'Don't worry, Dess,' he said. 'I think you'll find it interesting.'

'At six-thirty in the morning I was hoping for better than "interesting," Rex.'

'I'm sure Jessica won't disappoint us.'

Dess looked at Jessica, who just shrugged back at her.

Suddenly Dess noticed that Melissa hadn't walked with them. 'Hey, where's the bitch goddess? She's not back at your Caddy *sleeping*, is she?'

Rex shook his head. 'She'll be along in . . . two minutes.'

'Great. More split-second timing.' Dess sighed. 'Hope this goes better than your last little scheme.'

'There's just one thing, guys,' Jessica said nervously. 'Cassie Flinders lives right over there. What if she sees us?'

'She won't remember us.'

'Are you sure about that?'

Rex raised an eyebrow. 'Why would she?'

Jessica looked over at the Flinderses' double-wide with an unhappy expression on her face. 'Well, I wasn't going to mention this, but she and my sister have been . . . hanging out. I was afraid to tell you guys in case . . .' She didn't finish.

In case the bitch goddess decided to rip your little sister's brain in half, Dess thought.

She looked at Rex, wondering if he was about to do one of his psycho transformations. But after a pause he only shrugged. 'Everyone will know about the blue time soon enough, Jessica. It doesn't matter.'

'Wow,' Jessica said, looking stunned. 'That's actually kind of a relief.'

Flyboy put his arm around her, smiling, but the idea of Rex not caring about secrecy sent a minor shudder through Dess. As she turned away to study the rip, the realness of how Samhain would change everything sank in yet another notch.

The rip wasn't glowing red here in normal time, but Dess could see its current shape in the color of the grass, as if the contortion were a giant piece of lawn furniture. Maybe the dark moon was mutating the chlorophyll or something. She noted the rip's geometry: a long, thin oval pointing almost due east and west.

She took out Geostationary and noted the coordinates of its center. Almost exactly on the 36th parallel.

Maybe not worth getting up at six-thirty in the morning for, but interesting.

'Okay, good. No daylighters around,' Rex said.

'That's because they're all *in bed*,' Dess pointed out.

Rex ignored her. 'I want to do a few experiments here today, and I want all of you to see them. When Samhain comes, all of Bixby – at least – is going to be swallowed by this contortion. And as we've noticed, the rip isn't exactly the same size as the blue time. You've all seen those leaves falling at midnight?'

'Yeah,' Dess said. 'But what's the point? It's not midnight now.'

'Not yet,' Rex said.

'No.' Dess looked down at Geostationary. 'And it won't be for another 62,615 seconds. So why are we here so—?'

'Whoa!' Jonathan interrupted. 'What's up with Melissa?'

Dess turned to see the Cadillac galloping across the field. It climbed up the railway embankment and straddled the tracks, its tires spitting gravel and dust as it bore down on them like a maniacal pink freight train, headlights flicking on.

'Has she gone crazy?' Dess shouted.

'Nope,' Rex said, glancing at his watch. 'She's right on time. But we might want to get out of the way.'

The four of them skidded down the slope of the embankment, and the Cadillac seemed to roar its approval, bolting forward with a burst of acceleration, the spinning tires churning up a giant cloud of dust.

Dess felt a tingling in her fingertips, stronger than she had in the lunchroom, and suddenly knew what was about to happen.

'It's back,' she said softly.

'You got it,' Rex answered.

Dess looked up at the charging Cadillac with alarm. 'But won't she . . .?'

The inky blue of an eclipse swept in from the east, across the cloudless sky and open fields, stilling the icy wind and blanketing the world in silence. The dark moon shot into the sky, like a huge flying saucer hovering just out of reach.

Yet the Cadillac kept rolling across the red-tinged oval of the rip.

Its engine died, the headlights going dark, but it didn't freeze like it should have. The car continued to coast until it finally skidded to a halt in a shower of dust and gravel.

Dess blinked as she took in the sight: instead of throwing Melissa through the windshield, the pink Cadillac had maintained its momentum.

'Is she okay in there?' Flyboy asked.

Rex nodded. 'She's fine. As I suspected, the rip brings *everything* into the blue time, not just people. I figured if dead leaves could still fall, then dead metal would cross over too.'

'It's awfully lucky you figured right.' Dess didn't much care for Melissa anymore, but it wasn't like she wanted her back in the hospital. Her current scars were creepy enough.

'She was wearing a seat belt,' Rex said calmly.

'Wait a minute, Rex,' Dess said. 'How did you know there was going to be an eclipse?'

He was silent for a moment, his violet eyes narrowing. 'There's a pattern. I can see when they're coming, all of them between now and Samhain. This one should last for a while longer.'

'You can see a pattern?' Dess cried. 'Then write it down for me.'

He shook his head. 'I can't express it in numbers, not without my head exploding. But she can give it to you.' He pointed toward the Cadillac.

The driver's side door opened, and Melissa got out shakily, grinning from ear to ear. 'That was cool!'

Dess shook her head. No *way* was Melissa touching her again.

'I thought you were afraid of driving fast,' Jessica said.

The bitch goddess shrugged. 'You have to face your fears to conquer them, Jess. That's what Rex has been telling me lately.'

'You two are both nuts,' Dess said softly.

Rex raised an eyebrow. 'This experiment wasn't just for kicks, Dess. We had to make sure that when midnight falls on Samhain, it won't kill everyone who happens to be in a car. Which is one less thing to worry about.'

Everyone was quiet for a second, and Dess realized she hadn't even thought about that. If the rip really did expand to consume a million people, and only one percent of them were driving at midnight, that would have been *ten thousand* Melissas going through their windshields all at once.

She swallowed. This thing just got bigger and bigger the more she thought about it.

'So cars are okay,' Flyboy said, pushing himself up into the air. 'But what about planes?'

Rex thought for a moment. 'Small aircraft can do dead-stick landings. But the big airliners will be a problem.'

'We could phone in bomb threats to all the airports on Halloween,' Jonathan suggested from above.

'*Bomb* threats?' Jessica cried. 'Wait a second, Rex. Why are we even talking about all this? Didn't you say we were going to try to *prevent* Samhain? I thought the point was to make sure that half of Oklahoma *doesn't* get sucked into the blue time.'

Rex took a slow breath, then shook his head. 'We can try to stop some of what's going happen – the worst accidents, some of the panic. We can prevent most of unnecessary deaths.'

'The "unnecessary" deaths, Rex?' Dess said. 'Are you saying that some deaths are *necessary*?'

He fixed her with a cold stare. 'The predators are coming back, Dess. We have to get used to the fact that we can't save everyone.'

She stared back at him. This new darkling-infected Rex seemed perfectly happy thinking the unthinkable. The old Rex would have been appalled by the thought of *one* death, but here he was, talking about thousands like it was just the Bixby Tigers losing again.

'All we can do is follow the old traditions,' Melissa said. She was leaning against Rex, her legs still unsteady after her maniacal ride.

'Like what?' Dess asked. 'Dressing up in costumes?'

'Be my guest,' Rex said. 'But that's not the tradition I was thinking about. We have to organize people, bring them together and teach them how to protect themselves. In the meantime we have to keep the darklings away as long as we can.' He looked at Jessica. 'Maybe that's why you're here.'

'Why I'm where?' said Jessica.

Rex's eyes narrowed. 'Here in Bixby, Jessica. Here on earth. You're the flame-bringer, after all, and we're going to need a *really* big bonfire.'

Rex had brought three experiments for the rip.

First he had Jessica light a candle and step away from it. Normally it would have sputtered out when she took her hand away – without the flame-bringer, fire couldn't exist in the blue time.

Yet as Jessica stepped back, first one yard, then a few more, then finally walking to the other side of the glowing red boundary, the candle stayed alight. Her eyes widened. The rip really did have different rules. Like the pink Cadillac, a fire would keep going once it was started.

'That's the price the darklings pay for making the blue time weaker,' Rex said. 'If normal people can move through the rip, so can flame.'

'So anyone can start a fire?' Dess asked.

'I doubt that.' Rex flicked his lighter a few times; it didn't even make a spark. But when he held down its button and placed its jet of gas to the candle, it came back alight. He smiled, lifting the tiny yet blinding flame. 'But once Jessica's started it, a fire can spread on its own. People can pass it to each other.'

'Whoa, Jess,' Jonathan said. 'See if your flashlight works the same way.'

Jessica waited until all their eyes were covered, then whispered Enlightenment's name and switched it on. Squinting through her fingers, Dess saw its white beam cut through the blue time in a blinding wedge.

But when Jess put it on the tracks and stepped away from it, the light sputtered and died.

'I didn't think so,' Rex said. 'The chemical reaction in a battery is too complicated to sustain itself – like a car engine. But if Jessica lights a bunch of torches, we can protect a lot of people at once.'

'Yeah, eventually. But this happens at *midnight*, Rex,' Jonathan said. 'People will be scattered all over Bixby or however far the rip spreads. So how do we organize everyone without radio or phones?'

'We *don't* organize everyone, Jonathan. We save who we can.'

They were all silent for a moment.

Dess realized that an awful feeling was growing in her stomach. For the first time she was starting to take this end-of-the-world thing seriously. This wasn't like saving one little kid. The lives of uncountable strangers depended on the five of them.

How many people could one darkling eat in a night? How many darklings were there altogether? The math almost made her head spin. Numbers were one thing when they were abstract: coordinates or computer bits or seconds between now and midnight. But when they represented human lives, the thought of all those numerals in a row suddenly became obscene.

Yet Rex stood there, calmly planning the long midnight.

'First we'll need a way to get the maximum number of people awake,' he was saying. 'Then we should create some sort of signal that's visible from all over town. Hopefully that will gather people together. And finally, we'll need a way to defend them all from the darklings.' Rex produced a bottle rocket. 'I was thinking fireworks might do all three things at once.'

Dess nodded. Rex might be cold-blooded about this, but at least he was making sense. When Jessica had first discovered her talent, she'd tried to shoot Roman candles in the blue time out of curiosity, but the flaming balls always sputtered out after flying a few feet. Inside the rip, though, they would keep burning – an instant antidarkling flamethrower.

Jessica was just standing there, looking stunned by what they were talking about. But when Rex stuck the rocket's stick into the gravel, she got herself together. Kneeling, she lit the fuse, then stepped back as the blinding sparkles made their way up into its tail . . .

With a *whoosh* it shot into the sky, rising twenty feet or so before its flaming trail choked off suddenly.

'Was that a dud?' Jonathan asked.

'No.' Dess shook her head. 'The rip is three-dimensional. It extends only so far up.' She could see the rocket frozen at the edge of the rip above them, waiting for the eclipse to end before resuming its flight.

Rex started talking about airliners again, how they would be too high to be caught by the rip on Samhain.

Dess had heard enough about airplane crashes. She turned away and walked to the edge of the rip, wondering if it was still growing.

What she really wanted Rex to do was get over his darkling number phobia and write down the exact dates and times of all the coming eclipses. If he could glimpse a pattern with his math-impaired brain, Dess knew she could analyze what was happening. Then maybe the five of them could do something more useful for Bixby than setting off bottle rockets.

Like finding a way to stop this thing.

Suddenly Dess heard the scrape of gravel behind her. She whirled around – it was Melissa.

'Don't touch me,' she spat.

Melissa held up her hands. 'Relax. I'm not going to force you.'

'Force me? You're not going to *anything* me.'

'Listen, Dess, I was there when Madeleine opened up Rex's mind. I saw what he knows. I can give it to you.'

Dess shook her head.

'I'm sorry for what I did to you, all right, Dess? But we need you now. I know you see how serious this is.'

Dess looked away. Of course, the mindcaster had tasted her nausea.

'There might be a way to stop this, Dess. But only you can find it.'

The image of darklings rampaging through Bixby came into Dess's mind, and she wondered for a moment if Melissa had placed it there. Of course, even if the mindcaster was manipulating her, the awful picture would become a reality in thirteen days unless they found a solution.

'The answer might be waiting for you right here, all around us,' Melissa said. 'But this eclipse is ending soon.'

Dess took a slow breath, realizing that she had the choice of facing the mindcaster's touch or of going along with Rex's dire calculations. She could either open her mind now or watch the slaughter.

It wasn't fair, having to save thousands of people. Not fair at all.

'Make it quick,' she said through gritted teeth, and held out her hand.

Melissa closed her eyes.

At the first contact of their fingers something massive and dark came into Dess. Images swept through her, a wire frame of the earth, red fire spreading along its lines of longitude and latitude. She saw the days between now and Samhain midnight, a steady beat of eclipses until the blue time shattered, the rip streaking across the earth for thousands of miles. She saw how long it would last, twenty-five hours of frozen time – humans within struggling to survive while everyone outside stood frozen and unaware.

Then she saw the rip's true shape . . . and the beginnings of a solution.

Dess pulled her hand away from Melissa's touch, realizing that she was hearing a sound in the distance. It was a soft spattering noise, like a light rain on a steel roof.

She turned away without a word and walked down the tracks to where the Cadillac had roared up onto the embankment. At the glowing-red edge of the rip, a dark curtain of something was falling lightly through the air.

Dess held out an open palm . . .

Dust gradually collected on her skin. Then a hard *ping* came from the metal rail next to her – the fallen piece of gravel skittered across the tracks.

She stepped back a few yards and looked up, her eyes making out a smudge against the dark moon. Like the arrested bottle rocket, the dirt and gravel churned up by the huge pink car still hung overhead, suspended in frozen time. But carved into the dust cloud was a long, oval shape . . .

Dess nodded; suddenly it all made perfect sense. The Cadillac's tires had put a lot of debris into the air just as the eclipse had arrived, flash-freezing it up there until normal time started again. But the dust *inside* the rip had swirled down to the ground, falling in regular gravity. So now Dess could see the whole thing in three dimensions. Its blimplike shape had been cut into the cloud, like a long, oval space carved into a mountain.

But why was the dust still raining down?

Dess walked back to the edge, put her palm out again, and found that now the dirt was falling a bit farther along the tracks.

Of course . . . The rip was *growing*, tearing the blue time in half. And as its edges traveled outward, more of the suspended dust fell to earth.

Dess looked up, her heart beating harder. She was actually *watching* the rip expand. She peered into the vague blur of suspended dust, trying to see its exact dimensions and cursing the dim blue light. If Rex was going to perform dramatic experiments, why hadn't he released a cloud of Ping-Pong balls right before the eclipse so they could see what was really going on? Then Dess could calculate how fast the tear in the blue time was spreading and in exactly what direction.

She scrambled down the embankment to the longer edge of the rip and put out her hand. Hardly any dust was falling here.

'Dess?' Rex called.

'Hang on.' She climbed back up to the tracks. Yes, the rip was spreading much faster at the oval's narrow end.

She ran by the four of them, all the way past the Cadillac to the other end of the rip. Glancing up, she got an eyeful of dirt. The dust fall was harder here too. But why would it follow the direction of the railroad tracks?

She closed her eyes, letting the knowledge that Melissa had given her take shape.

'Of course,' she said aloud.

'Of course *what*?' Rex called.

Dess waved him silent. She could see it now – so obvious that she wanted to thump herself on the head for not realizing it before. Until now she had imagined the rip expanding like the universe – a great big bubble, a sphere. But what if it were long and narrow instead?

The rip was heading in two directions, stretching along a single axis, just like a real tear in a piece of fabric. But what was at either end?

Dess visualized the map of the county she carried in her head and instantly knew exactly what was going on and why this godforsaken spot lay right in the middle of the rip. Jenks was halfway to nowhere, precisely poised between the center of town and the deepest desert.

The blue time was opening up long and straight, like some sort of darkling highway, a conduit between predators and prey. It was reaching west out into the mountains, where the oldest minds lived, the ones who hadn't had a decent meal in thousands of years. And at the same moment the rip was traveling east, directly toward the populated center of downtown Bixby.

'Dess?' Rex said, frustration creeping into his voice.

She still didn't answer. If he wanted to get all scary, let him.

Her eyes closed, Dess let her mind follow the direction of the tracks, recalling the images of wire frame globes that Melissa had given her.

What if the rip just kept growing year after year, shooting across the country like a lit fuse every Halloween?

It was tearing along Bixby's ill-fated latitude: 36 degrees. That line led east through Broken Arrow, which was why the

Grayfoots were evacuating. Then it whipped through a lot of small and medium towns after that . . . until eventually reaching Nashville, which sat at exactly 36.10 degrees. From there, it would go on to swallow Charlotte, North Carolina, at 35.14. Westward, the rip would cruise straight through downtown Las Vegas, which was centered at exactly 36.11. And it would pass a hundred miles north of Grandpa Grayfoot's new digs in LA.

'Dess?' Rex called. 'What *is* it?'

'We might be able to save more people than you think, Rex. Or at least delay the darklings long enough to get Bixby organized.'

He walked over, his violet eyes flashing, a smile on his face. Suddenly Dess knew he'd planned the whole thing to work this way – Dess too tired from getting up so early to resist Melissa touching her.

Well, it had worked.

'How do we do it?' he said.

'We need to build two big bonfires – or better yet, fireworks displays. The one out here will bottle them up for as long as we can.'

'Bottle them up?'

'Yeah. The rip will open up long and narrow, Rex, like a road. It leads right through here, straight from the mountains to downtown. If we stop them in Jenks for a while, make them go around us, we may have time to organize people back in Bixby.'

As Rex's eyes followed the path of the tracks back toward the mountains, a thoughtful look crossed his face, as if he was accessing the numberless darkling math stored in his mind. 'Yeah. You could be right.'

The world shuddered then – the dark moon falling like a rock, the red-tinged blue time fading – and the cold wrapped itself around Dess, driving its way into her bones. She shivered with excitement.

They had a way to stop the darklings . . . for a while, at least. Maybe they could give the people of Bixby time to understand what was going on and a fighting chance to survive their night in hell. Maybe thousands didn't have to die.

Above Dess's head the bottle rocket was suddenly released from frozen time. It shot farther into the sky, where it exploded with a tiny *bang*.

23

SLUMBER PARTY

Noises came from inside the hardware store, the clattering of falling metal and a million small things spilling.

'Jesus, Flyboy,' Dess yelled in through the window. 'It's good you're not a *real* burglar.'

'Never said I was,' he shouted back. Another crash erupted.

Even though it was the blue time, Jessica flinched a little at all the ruckus. It felt like they should at least try to be quiet, given that they were breaking and entering.

Again.

'Found them!' Jonathan's voice came.

She and Dess walked around the corner to the front of the store. Through the glass doors she saw Jonathan trying the keys from a big ring, one by one.

'Should have just climbed through the window,' Dess muttered as the process stretched out.

'Some of the stuff on your list is too heavy,' Jessica said, stifling a yawn and happy to be going in through the door. She could hardly keep her eyes open, and she still had to get back to Constanza's tonight.

Since Rex's demonstration out in Jenks, the five of them had spent every midnight gathering the materials they needed to bring the darkling invasion to a halt. Mostly that meant breaking into every store in town that sold fireworks and making off with the stock. The nightly burglaries in the blue time were getting tiring. And obvious too – the *Bixby Register* had run a story about the unknown vandals collecting a dangerous cache of fireworks. According to the article, the sheriff's office had actually figured out it was a bunch of kids planning something big for Halloween.

Of course, no one had a clue *how* big.

Tonight Rex and Melissa were knocking over the last fireworks stall in town while the other three picked up a few items from Bixby Hardware and Keys, after which, hopefully, Rex would let them get a few nights' rest. Halloween was only six days away.

Jessica scowled at the big paper skeleton taped to the glass door, swinging lightly from Jonathan's attempts with the keys. There were decorations up everywhere in school, orange and black bunting running down the hallways, pumpkin faces glowering at Jessica from the cafeteria walls. Every time she saw a witch or black cat on a classroom door, it reminded her of what was coming.

'Come on!' Dess said, just as the lock clicked.

'Ladies,' Jonathan said, opening the door with a bow.

'Good, let's hurry,' Jessica said, walking in among the rows of tools and appliances and paint cans. 'Constanza thinks I'm in the bathroom.'

Jonathan snorted. 'That would psych her out, wouldn't it? If you just disappeared in there?'

'Yeah, very funny,' Jessica said tiredly as Jonathan began to gather up a big plastic tarp.

On Monday morning, the day after tomorrow, Constanza was flying to LA. Supposedly it was only for a week. But as she mentioned to Jessica at least once every day, she might never set foot in Bixby High again.

Tonight could be the last time Jessica would ever see her.

Jessica pulled her coat tighter, wondering how many more people she would lose in the next week.

'Hey, check this out,' Dess said.

Jessica turned. 'An empty paint can?'

'Formerly a lowly paint can.' Dess swung it by its wire handle. 'But in its new incarnation, it will be a major explosive device.'

Jessica swallowed. Some of the stuff Rex was planning was on the edge of crazy. But there was no backing out now.

She pulled Dess's list from her pocket and started walking among the blue-lit shelves, searching for nails and wires and metal tools – sufficient fresh, clean steel to make a hundred weapons.

Jessica wondered if it would be enough.

A half hour later Jonathan tapped her on the back.

'Come on.' He offered his hand. 'We should leave soon if I'm going to get back here in time.'

'Thought you said it would be funny if I just disappeared.'

'Sorry.' He touched her hand softly, midnight gravity shivering through her body for a moment. 'You could have stayed there. Dess and I could have done this on our own.'

'Glad to help.' She shrugged. 'Slumber parties aren't much

fun when your host is a stiff.' Jessica looked into his eyes. 'Plus I hate midnights when I don't get to fly.'

He held out his hand, smiling. 'Let's fly, then.'

'Okay.' She took it, feeling the connection take hold, her body light as the air. 'See you tomorrow, Dess.'

Dess looked up from the open front door, where she was piling the stolen merchandise. 'Sure, Jess. And Flyboy? If you don't get back before midnight, I'm leaving all this stuff in your car with a big note to the sheriff.'

'Don't worry, I'll be back.'

They flew toward Constanza's, shooting down an empty stretch of highway to the colony of large houses on a circular road. Jonathan jumped with Jessica up to the roof, just outside the open window of the second-floor bathroom.

Jessica glanced at her watch; Jonathan still had plenty of time to make it back to the store before midnight ended. 'Thanks for the lift.'

'Listen, I know you needed to see Constanza tonight.' He stood. 'Seeing as how she's your only normal friend and everything.'

Jessica looked up at him, wondering if he was being sarcastic.

'I mean it, Jess. It's okay to need somebody who's not a midnighter.' He swallowed, looking uncomfortable. 'And I'm sorry I never made friends with her.'

'Thanks.' Jessica sighed. 'After what's coming, she won't be back, will she?'

'Yeah, I guess. But at least she'll be safe in Los Angeles.'

'Sure.' She sighed again. 'I just hate goodbyes.' Before she'd moved to Bixby, the last three months in Chicago had been nothing but farewells. And now she seemed to be losing everything again.

'Well, I'm not going anywhere,' Jonathan said. 'You can count on that.'

Inside, Jessica changed back into her pajamas, waiting for midnight to end. When the blue light faded, the house shuddering to life around her, she flushed the toilet and stepped out into the upstairs hallway.

'So, *as* I was saying,' Constanza began as Jessica opened her door. 'This shirt can be retired, right?'

Jessica looked at the black pullover with red shoulder pads. 'Yeah. Way too eighties.'

'Eww.' Constanza threw the shirt into the discard pile, then turned to the three giant suitcases that lay open on the floor. They were packed crushingly full of dresses, shirts, skirts, and what seemed like dozens of shoes.

'Won't your parents be suspicious? I mean, you're supposedly only going for a week.'

Constanza snorted. 'I always pack this much for a week. You wouldn't believe all the great stuff I'm leaving behind But I think that's it.'

'So . . . we're done?' Jessica said hopefully. They'd been packing pretty much all day.

'Done for tonight.' Constanza stood up, surveying the wreckage of her room. 'Thanks so much for helping me, Jess. I *hate* packing.' She looked longingly into her huge closets. 'All these clothes crying out to me. So many left behind.'

Jessica felt herself smiling. The whole last week had been spent preparing for a battle that seemed unwinnable. It felt good to have accomplished something concrete, even as minor as packing Constanza's bags. And it was a relief to make a few choices that nobody's life depended on.

'Glad I could help you. It was fun, if exhausting.'

'Ernesto *said* he was going to help, but he's long gone.'

Jessica frowned. 'None of your cousins are still around, are they?'

'No. And even if they were, Grandpa's being extra insane about anybody setting foot in Bixby before the move.'

Jessica nodded. This close to Samhain, only Constanza's unlucky parents would still be here. Their house was on the opposite side of Bixby from Jenks but still in the path of the rip. If the darklings broke through, her folks would be in serious danger.

'Isn't it going to be weird?' she said. 'Not seeing your parents . . . as much?'

Constanza shrugged. 'I'm almost seventeen. I figure I'd be out of their house soon anyway. At least this way they'll be able to see me on TV.'

Jessica had to smile.

'But you know, leaving them behind doesn't really make me sad,' Constanza continued. 'They'll always be around, one way or another. It's more my friends I'm going to miss. You especially.'

'Me? *Especially?*'

'Of course, silly. I mean, sometimes I feel like I've hardly gotten a chance to know you. It's only been what? Two months since school started?'

'I suppose so,' Jessica said quietly. It felt like years sometimes, but she'd only arrived in Bixby in late August. She sat next to one of the suitcases, staring at the profusion of clothes and shoes inside. 'Two months can seem like a long time, I guess.'

'That's *so* true.' Constanza leaned closer. 'In fact, my theory is that two months in friendship time is actually longer than a year, you know?'

'Um . . . not exactly.'

Constanza bent and picked up a stack of shirts that hadn't made the cut. She took them to one of the room's huge, now half-empty closets. 'Listen, Jess, I *know* you're all sad about me leaving. You've been moping around ever since I told you about LA. But sometimes these short friendships are totally the best.'

Jessica raised an eyebrow. 'They are?'

Constanza slid the shirts back onto hangers thoughtfully, one by one. 'Sure! Didn't you ever have a best friend at summer camp or something? You make friends quick, and you know you're only together until the end of summer, so it's *super* intense?'

Jessica nodded. 'Yeah, I guess I know what you mean.'

Constanza reached over to brush a lock of Jessica's hair out of her face. 'But those are always the people you remember for the rest of your life. At least I do. Even though I usually forget to write to them or whatever.'

Jessica swallowed, a lump rising in her throat. She couldn't believe that tears had sneaked up on her and knew she'd feel like a total dork if she cried. She tried to focus her mind on Jonathan's words: Constanza was one of the lucky ones. She wouldn't be here for Bixby's big Halloween surprise.

Constanza sighed. 'Maybe it's because when friendships end like this, instead of growing apart, you get ripped apart. So you never get to the phase where you don't like each other anymore.'

Jessica blinked, and one tear traveled down her cheek.

Constanza reached out with an elegant finger and softly brushed it away.

'Come on, Jess. That's enough of being sad.' She laughed. 'I'll be back in Bixby whenever my shooting schedule allows. Still have to see the parentals, you know.'

'Okay. Sorry.'

'Don't be sorry.' Constanza turned her smile up to its full wattage. 'But now that we're all packed, we've got to have some fun so I can remember you happy.'

Jessica nodded, letting Constanza's mood lift her out of the sadness that had haunted her all week. Dess kept saying that her plan should work, that maybe they could save everyone in Bixby, or almost everyone. And after twenty-five hours of midnight, the blue time would retreat again.

Maybe once the darklings realized they had a fight on their hands, they wouldn't keep coming back every Halloween.

Jessica decided that tonight, at least, she would have a good time.

'Okay, this is me being happy.' She forced a smile.

'That's the spirit,' Constanza said. 'We can still talk on the telephone, after all. It's not like it's the end of the world.'

24

TRICK OR TREAT

'Looks like Halloween might be canceled,' Don Day said from the other end of the couch.

Jessica looked up from the book she'd been trying, and failing, to read. As usual the Weather Channel was on. A man in a bow tie was coaxing a swirling mass of white out of the Gulf of Mexico and onto the Texas plains.

It was headed straight for Oklahoma.

'Is that rain?' she said. 'For *tonight?*'

'It was a hurricane, but by now it's just a tropical depression,' her father said in his Weather-Channel-lecture voice. He leaned forward to peer out the back window. 'By the time it gets here, it'll only be a thunderstorm.'

'Only a thunderstorm . . .' Jessica watched in horror as the satellite image repeated its course across the TV again and again, stopping at the border of Oklahoma every time. 'Um, when's it supposed to get here?'

'Sometime tonight. It might rain out all the fun.' He gave her a puzzled look. 'You're not going trick-or-treating, are you?'

'Duh. Of course not.' She rolled her eyes dramatically. 'I'm probably doing trig homework all night. But thunderstorms are kind of scary, you know, especially on Halloween.'

Especially at midnight, and particularly when you were trying to keep two hundred pounds of fireworks dry because you were fighting off an invasion of monsters. In the last two weeks of planning, no one had brought up the possibility that it might *rain*.

'So, Dad,' she said a minute later, trying not to sound *too* interested. 'Are they saying the storm should be here by, like, midnight?'

He shrugged. 'It's hard to tell what's going to happen once a hurricane, or even a tropical depression, hits land. Could take until tomorrow morning. Might break up into nothing. Or it could keep going strong and get here by nine or ten.'

'Whatever!' Beth announced from the doorway. 'I'm going trick-or-treating even if it's raining golf-ball-sized hail. Or even golf balls.'

Jess looked up at her little sister and had to suppress a snort of laughter. Eight coat hangers stuck out from Beth's shoulders at all angles, covered with black paper and bobbing wildly. Her face was mostly blackened with makeup, exaggerating the whites of her eyes, and she was wearing plastic vampire fangs.

'What are you supposed to be?'

'I'm a tarantula, stupid.' Beth took a step closer to the couch, angling one of the legs so that it menaced her father.

'Ow,' he said as it struck his head, eyes still trained on the Weather Channel.

'You're calling me stupid. Look in a mirror.' Then Jessica frowned. 'Where'd you get that idea?'

'From Cassie. We're both going as tarantulas. She has this thing about spiders.'

A chill ran down Jessica's spine. 'She's coming over here tonight?'

'What? Don't you like Cassie, Jess?' Beth said sweetly.

'Yeah, she's wonderful.' Jessica lowered her eyes to stare at her book. Cassie had been over a few times since that first awful Spaghetti Night. The two of them had left Jessica alone so far, but tonight she had a feeling they were going to show up at exactly eleven-thirty, when she had to slip out of her room.

At least in one way it was a good thing: it would be a lot safer for Cassie here than in Jenks. Once midnight fell, the rip was going to start expanding, zooming down the 36th parallel. Hopefully it wouldn't grow wide enough to swallow houses on the north side of Bixby. But even if it did, the darklings might not make it this far.

That's what Jessica had been telling herself all week, anyway.

'Well, you won't have to put up with us in any case.' Beth swiveled her hips so that one of the tarantula legs banged against Jessica's head. 'I'm going over to her house.'

'What, in *Jenks*?'

Beth looked at Jessica with surprise, and even her father's eyes lurched away from the Weather Channel.

'Um, yes, Jess. Because that's where Cassie, like, *lives*.'

'When are you getting home?'

'Jess, you're being weird. Dad, tell Jess she's being weird.'

'Jessica?' her father said.

'Well, trick-or-treating in a strange part of town and everything.'

They both looked at her in puzzlement a little bit longer, and then a knowing smile broke out slowly across Beth's face.

Their father turned back to the TV, which was filled with images of the storm roiling the Texas coast. 'Lighten up, Jessica. It's Halloween. Cassie's grandmother promised they'd be in bed by eleven and that they wouldn't eat too much candy.'

That last word seemed to remind him of the open bag of candy corn on the coffee table, and he leaned forward to grab a handful.

'Mom said not to eat that,' Beth said.

'Mom's not home yet,' he answered.

'But it's dangerous!' Jessica cried.

'What?' her father said. 'Candy corn?'

'No. Being out there in the country. With a possible storm coming and . . . everything.'

Beth was still smiling. 'You don't want me in Jenks tonight, do you?'

Jessica ignored the words, staring at her book, trying not to chew at her lip. Her little sister was headed right into the path of the darkling invasion, but she couldn't think of a single way to stop it. Beth had that smug look on her face – this time she really was ready to spill everything she knew if Jessica got in her way.

And this was *not* the night to get grounded.

'Come on, Dad, let's get moving,' Beth said. 'The Weather Channel will still be here when you get back. Like it ever changes.'

'The weather changes all the time, smarty-pants,' he said, scooping his keys and another handful of candy corn from the coffee table and rising to his feet.

Jessica found herself wishing that she'd become all predatory, like Rex, so that she could slip outside right now and pull the starter cable out of her father's car. But she didn't actually know what starter cables looked like and wasn't a hundred percent sure she could even get the hood open.

What else could she do? Explain that the food chain was about to turn upside down? That Bixby was about to be invaded? They'd only think she was kidding or crazy.

She would have to deal with this at midnight. Along with everything else tonight, Jessica was going to have to make sure her little sister was okay.

'See you later, Jess,' Beth taunted from the front door.

Jessica didn't answer, and the door slammed with a booming note of finality. She looked at her watch, her stomach slowly winding itself into knots.

Only five forty-five, and already Samhain was off to a brilliant start.

25

RAIN

'Can you still taste him?'

'Relax, Flyboy.' Melissa shook her head. 'He's headed off down Division.'

Jonathan let the car speed up again but glanced in the rearview one more time. Relaxing didn't seem like such a good idea at the moment. Cops were crawling all over Bixby tonight, hoping to catch Halloween vandals and impose curfew on any kids who'd stayed out late after trick-or-treating. And of course, the sheriff's department were dying to find whoever had stolen all those fireworks before they were put to use.

The fact that Jonathan's trunk contained about half of the collection of firecrackers, smoke bombs, Roman candles, sparklers, and rockets of every description certainly didn't fill him with relaxing thoughts.

'Just let me know if he comes this way again.'

'Don't worry about the cops. I can taste those rednecks a mile off.'

He leaned forward to look up into the roiling sky, a flicker of lightning illuminating the clouds from within. 'What do you figure about that rain?'

'In general, Jonathan, storm fronts don't have minds. So I have no idea.'

He let out a short laugh, only half sure that she was kidding. Melissa wasn't usually Jonathan's favorite traveling companion, but he was glad she was with him tonight. He was too nervous to ride around alone, especially with the police hunting for what was in his trunk.

'All excited about tonight?' she asked.

'Nervous.'

It was Melissa's turn to laugh. 'Jonathan, I know you're not completely dreading this.'

He sighed. There was no point in bluffing a mindcaster. The night before had been one long flying dream, a half-anxious, half-thrilled rehearsal in his mind.

Jonathan shrugged. 'It's something different.'

'That's what I like about Bixby: always something different.'

'What about you?' he asked. 'A whole day without . . . what do you call it? Mind noise? Isn't that your dream?'

'You'd think so, wouldn't you?' Melissa said. 'But as the rip grows, all those other minds will be sucked in, polluting our *midnight*. Frankly, Flyboy, I wish the secret hour would just stay between the five of us forever.'

'Yeah,' Jonathan said softly. He hadn't thought of it that way, but in addition to all the death and destruction, midnight was about to become something public, something less special. 'Me too.'

They pulled onto Jessica's street, five minutes early.

She was already outside and ran to the car, pulling open the door even before he'd rolled to a stop. She threw herself into the backseat and said, 'Okay. Go.'

'Relax, Jess,' he said. 'We're ahead of schedule.'

'I need to get out there early, okay?'

For a moment Jonathan wondered what she meant, but then, slowly but surely, the only possible explanation crept into his mind.

'Beth?'

'Just . . . drive.'

'She gave you trouble tonight?' Jonathan shook his head. 'It doesn't matter, okay? By the time the sun comes up tomorrow, thousands of people will have seen the blue time for themselves. The secret's over!'

'I know all that.' Her voice was tight, afraid. 'But we have to get moving. Beth's in trouble.'

He put the car back in gear, easing into the center of the street. 'She's not still out trick-or-treating, is she?'

'Much worse. She's in Jenks.'

'*What?*'

'She's spending the night with Cassie Flinders.'

Melissa put a hand to her head. 'Guys . . .'

Jonathan's eyes widened. 'But that's right next to the rip!'

'I *know*!' Jessica cried.

'Guys!' Melissa said, her head tipping back, eyes closed. 'Shush your minds!'

Jonathan brought the car to a stop at the next light, looking both ways and then into the rearview mirror, trying to think quiet, relaxed thoughts . . . and failing.

'Turn left,' Melissa suddenly whispered. 'Don't wait for the light.'

Jonathan spun the wheel and accelerated, whipping the car onto Kerr Street.

'He saw us. He knows your car . . .' She twitched. 'Crap. It's St. Claire.'

Sheriff Clancy St. Claire – Jonathan's knuckles went white on the steering wheel as he imagined the lawman's grinning face. The sheriff could recognize Jonathan's car from a mile away.

'Which way?' he hissed.

Melissa shook her head. 'Don't know yet. Can't feel any other cars, but he's calling it in.'

Jonathan breathed through clenched teeth. They didn't have much time to get clear of St. Claire. Soon there would be another cop car involved in the pursuit and then another – Bixby police never did things in small numbers. By the time midnight rolled around, they'd all be in handcuffs and miles out of position. Totally unable to help Beth or anyone else, for that matter.

'Hang on,' he said, and pushed the gas pedal to the floor, speeding down Kerr. A few seconds later lights spun in his rearview mirror, the whoop of a siren splitting the night.

'Oh, no,' Jessica said softly. It occurred to Jonathan that she'd been taken home by the cops right after she arrived in Bixby – part of her introduction to the hazards of the mid-night hour.

'Don't worry, Jess. We'll get there.' He spun the wheel again, turning onto a small residential road called Mallard and hoping there weren't any trick-or-treaters still out. Fortunately he'd flown over Jessica's part of town dozens of times and could visualize it perfectly from a bird's-eye view. Mallard took a winding route toward downtown, then branched into two roads a mile before hitting the highway.

If he could just get to the fork before Clancy caught sight of them again, they'd have a fifty-fifty chance of getting away. Which was better than nothing.

They swerved along the winding street, shooting through the narrow straights between parked cars. Jonathan had to force himself to look ahead instead of checking the rearview mirror.

Then – with a sudden *whack!* – something struck the windshield, and Jonathan felt the steering wheel slip from his fingers. Tires squealed for a moment before he pulled the car straight again.

'What was that?' Jessica shouted.

'I don't . . .' Jonathan started, then saw a delta of yellowish goo oozing upward on his windshield, spreading wider as it was pushed by the wind of their passage. A tiny white fragment clung to the ooze, fluttering for a moment before it was ripped away.

'Just kids,' Melissa said. 'And I think they've got a few more eggs for St. Claire's car.'

Lightning flickered in the distance, illuminating the goo as it crawled across the windshield.

They reached the fork, and Jonathan veered left. Another mile ahead was the highway that led toward Jenks.

'Wait! Stop!' Melissa suddenly shouted.

'Do *what?*'

'Pull over and park! Clancy's backup just turned onto this street. They're right in front of us!'

Jonathan squashed his foot down on the brakes, bringing a screech from the tires. He swerved the car in behind a camper van and switched off the lights and motor.

'What are you doing?' Jessica cried from the backseat. 'We can't just sit here!'

'We're not just sitting, Jess!' Melissa hissed. 'We're hiding!'

'It's okay, Jess. We'll get there.' Jonathan hoped it wasn't an empty promise.

He slid himself under the wheel, one hand still clutching the dangling car keys. He wondered how fast he could get the engine started again if the other cop recognized his car.

Of course, if they pulled in behind them, they'd all be stuck here behind the camper van . . .

'Here they come,' Melissa whispered, huddled against the passenger door.

Jonathan heard the swoosh of tires whipping by and listened for the sound of them slowing. But no lights flashed, no siren sounded, and gradually the car faded into the distance.

'They're gone,' Melissa said. 'And Clancy's headed the other way. He thinks he's got us now.'

Jonathan let out a slow sigh of relief, but as he pulled himself back up into his seat, his heart sank.

A few raindrops had already spattered on the windshield. As he watched, they began to fall more swiftly, diluting the egg goo and catching the flicker of lightning like a hundred glowing eyes.

Thunder rumbled again, this time right over their heads.

He looked at his watch. They still had time to get to Jenks, but by midnight it would be raining like crazy.

'Perfect night for fireworks,' he said, turning the engine back on and putting the car in gear.

26

THE BOMB

Rex threw himself at the roof door again, ignoring the horror that trembled through his body at the sharp smell of its bright, unrusted steel. As his shoulder hit, the door pushed outward another few inches.

'Can you fit through there yet?' he asked.

Dess looked at the narrow gap between the door and its frame. 'No way.'

Rex stepped back and hissed through his teeth. He and Jonathan had been up here just the night before to dump off most of the fireworks, and this door had been unlocked. Now it was secured with a chain an inch wide and a padlock as big as his fist.

Rex hit the door again, his shoulder banging against steel with a dull thud, pulling the chain tauter and winning another inch of space.

'Still too small,' Dess said.

Rex cursed. The fireworks show at Jenks wouldn't keep the darklings at bay for a whole twenty-five hours. They couldn't afford for this part of the plan to fail.

They'd chosen an empty building on the west side of town, tall enough that it could be seen from pretty much everywhere in Bixby. Once the rip reached downtown, anyone who was awake would notice that their IVs, radios, and phones weren't working. Hopefully when they stumbled out of their houses and into the blue time, they would spot the shower of rockets shooting up from this roof. Anyone who made it here could shelter under the protection of the flamebringer until the long midnight ended.

But the first trick was to make sure as many people as possible were awake at midnight. And to do that, they had to get out to the roof, where Dess's makeshift bomb lay hidden.

Thunder rolled overhead, and Rex smelled a change in the air.

'Oh, crap.' He thrust his hand out through the crack in the door, and a few drops struck his palm. 'Perfect. It's raining.'

'You guys covered the fireworks with plastic, didn't you?' Dess asked.

Rex just looked at her. There'd been so much preparing and planning this last week, rain was one thing that had slipped his mind. The fireworks were on the other side of the door, outside, hidden under some old cardboard boxes. They'd be reduced to a soggy, useless mass if they didn't get out there soon.

'Didn't you hear the weather report?' Dess cried. 'They've been predicting rain all week!'

'I can't watch TV anymore.' Since Madeleine had unleashed the darkling part of his mind, the clever, human flickering box in his father's house gave him fits to look at.

Dess groaned.

Rex took a few steps back, as much of a running start as he

could get in the small stairwell shed, and threw himself against the door again. It budged outward another inch against the chain. Still not enough gap between door and frame to squeeze out onto the roof.

The rain outside was falling harder now.

Rex noticed that the metal was bending outward from the center, where the chain held it. Maybe if he focused on pounding the bottom half of the door, he could open up enough room to crawl through.

He drew his foot back and kicked the metal, sending another booming sound echoing down the stairwell.

Dess looked down the stairs. 'Jeez, Rex. Make some more noise, why don't you?'

'I didn't smell anyone on the way in.'

'But if someone locked that door today, they might still be around.'

'So?' he said. 'At least they might have the key.'

'They might have a gun too.'

'Humans don't scare me anymore.' He gave the metal another kick; it scraped outward a little farther. Inside his cowboy boot Rex's foot stung, but he ignored the pain, focusing on raising up the darkness inside himself.

Black spots appeared in the corners of his eyes, and he felt his body shifting within his skin. Pain turned to anger, and he began to thrash at the door harder and harder, ignoring the damage it was doing to his foot.

Wild thoughts eclipsed his human mind: the flat metal expanse was his enemy, the clever alloys inside it an abomination. He had to escape this human structure and get out under the open sky.

The door buckled and twisted under his assault, its bottom

hinges tearing from the wall. Flakes of paint flew from the battered metal, which cried out dully with every kick. Finally the ring that held the chain snapped off, and the entire door tumbled outward onto the roof, like a drunk passing out cold.

'What the hell, Rex,' Dess said softly. 'Are you okay?'

Rex got himself under control, letting the darkness fade, taking deep breaths and feeling the pain swell in his right foot.

'Ow,' he said softly, turning to the stair rail to peer down. If anyone was in the building, they must have heard that.

But no sound of approaching feet met his ears.

'Come on,' she said. 'We're behind schedule.'

He followed Dess out onto the roof, every limping step pure agony. The cold rain fell on his face and hands, stronger now.

The fireworks were still there under the rain-spattered boxes, still dry. Ignoring his foot, Rex helped Dess drag the whole pile across the black tar and through the door into the shelter of the stairwell.

He checked his watch: four minutes to midnight.

Dess started throwing the boxes down the stairs, clearing some room in the tiny stairwell shed. The bomb sat atop the other fireworks, a paint can with a three-foot fuse protruding from its top.

'There's my baby,' Dess said with a smile.

Rex had watched her make the bomb, the terrifying smell of its contents almost panicking him. The soldered-shut paint can was stuffed full of gunpowder emptied from a dozen packages of M-80s. Its purpose was simple: to create as loud a boom as possible. Dess had calculated that its shock wave would set off car alarms for miles in every direction, waking people up all over this side of town.

Of course, for that to work, they had to set it off in the next four minutes, before the long midnight fell.

'I'll take it from here,' he said.

'No way. My toy.'

She lifted it with both hands and carefully carried it out into the rain. Still limping, Rex followed her to one corner of the roof, where a cell phone repeater sat, a five-foot-tall antenna that faced out toward the suburbs. Dess balanced the bomb atop it. She'd explained to Rex that it had to go up high so the roof wouldn't muffle the shock wave before it could travel out across Bixby.

'Okay. Let me do this part,' he said.

Dess looked at the bomb for a long moment, then nodded. 'Fine by me. But if that fuse starts to burn too fast, run like hell.' She paused. 'You know what? Run like hell no matter what.' She stepped back.

Rex took a deep breath and pulled out his lighter. His foot was throbbing dully now, keeping time with his quickening heartbeat.

He reached down and lit the long, dangling fuse. It sputtered to life and began crawling slowly upward toward the paint can.

'Okay, let's go,' Dess said.

He watched the fire climb for a long moment to be sure the rain wouldn't put it out, finding himself fascinated by the shower of sparks that were carried off in a little trail by the wind.

'Rex!' she called from the other end of the roof. 'Come on!'

Then thunder boomed overhead, and for a split second Rex thought the bomb had gone off. He stumbled backward onto his bad foot and, swearing at the pain, turned to limp after Dess. They huddled against the far side of the stairwell shed.

'Are you sure we'll be okay back here?' he asked.

'According to my research, Rex, bombs can kill you in two ways. Stray bits of flying stuff, which this shed is solid enough to protect us from, and the shock wave. My little baby isn't strong enough to crush our heads, but make sure you cover your ears unless you want to go deaf.' To reinforce this point, she placed her own palms flat against her head.

Rex checked his watch. Only a little more than one minute left.

Then a terrible thought occurred to him. They'd used the slowest-burning fuse they could find, three feet of it for the maximum amount of time. But kicking through the door had already put them behind schedule . . .

'How long did you say that fuse would take?' he asked.

'About two and a half minutes.'

'Good. There's just about a minute to go before midnight.'

'Really?' She looked at Geostationary. 'Sixty seconds? Crap, Rex, we took too long!'

'But the bomb will go off before midnight.'

Dess shook her head. 'Shock waves travel at the speed of sound, Rex, which is *slow* – almost eight seconds to go one mile. The shock waves have to get out to the suburbs, and then car alarms have to go off long enough to wake people up. That'll all take extra seconds we don't have!'

Rex took a breath, then peeked around the corner of the shed.

About a third of the fuse had burned. Dess was right; he'd lit it too late.

After a second of panicked deliberation Rex swore loudly, then hobbled back toward the bomb, pulling out his lighter.

'Rex, what the hell are you doing?'

'Dealing with it!'

He stumbled up to the bomb just as the fuse reached the halfway mark. Thrusting his lighter out, he aimed its flame at a point only a few inches from the top of the can. The lighter sputtered out once, a direct hit from a big raindrop extinguishing it.

'Come *on*,' he muttered, flicking it back to life.

'Get back here!' Dess cried.

Finally the flame caught. A foot-long section of fuse dropped to the roof, lit at both ends now. The shorter piece attached to the can sparked and hissed in the rain, then steadied and began to crawl its last few inches.

Rex didn't stick around to watch. He spun on his left heel and ran back toward the stairwell shed, his hands already over his ears.

Just as he rounded the corner, his boot skidded on the rain-slick roof, sending him sprawling painfully to the tar. He crawled the last few feet and huddled beside Dess against the side of the shed, eyes closed and ears still covered.

'Rex, you moron!' Dess shouted. 'You almost gave me a heart atta—'

The bomb exploded with a vast noise – a physical blow more than a sound, like a sack of potatoes hitting Rex in the chest. Even his closed eyelids felt the concussion, and a single, awesome flash of light shot through them.

For a moment all other noises disappeared, as if the bomb's roar had sucked sound itself from the rest of the world. But slowly the murmur of the rain returned, and Rex dared to open his eyes.

He glanced at his watch: twenty seconds to midnight.

Rising to their feet, he and Dess peered around the corner. Nothing was left of the paint can, of course, and the cell phone antenna was a blackened wreckage, bent and twisted metal sticking out in all directions.

'Whoa, cool!' Dess said.

Rex limped after her to the edge of the roof, training his darkling hearing on the city below . . .

The sweet sound of car alarms rang out across Bixby, a hundred whoops and screams and buzzes all mingled in a great, untidy chorus. Rex imagined people turning over in their sleep, glaring accusingly at their alarm clocks and wondering what all the noise was about. Even the sleepiest would still be awake in ten seconds when midnight fell. Perfect timing.

Here in town they wouldn't feel the blue time strike right away, of course: the rip still had to travel to downtown from Jenks. But for those the bomb had awakened – and all the others already up watching late-night TV or reading in bed – that delay would only seem like an instant. Suddenly at midnight the world would turn blue, everything flickering with the red tinge of the rip, TVs, radios, and car alarms all silenced at once.

Those who went out to investigate would find the dark moon risen overhead, the last few seconds of rain settling to earth. And soon they would see the fireworks display downtown, the only movement visible on the frozen horizon.

Hopefully many of them would start to make their way downtown then, searching for some kind of explanation. By that time Jonathan would be flying among them, telling everyone to get to this building as fast as possible. And as long as the midnighters' defenses at Jenks had held off the main darkling force long enough, they'd have time to get here.

As he and Dess waited for the last few seconds of normal time to elapse, Rex took a deep breath. For the next twenty-five hours humanity would be a hunted species, dispossessed of all its clever toys and machines, toppled from the summit of the food chain. Those who understood that quickly enough would run and would live; those who refused to believe would perish.

In the darkling part of his mind, Rex thought for a moment that perhaps this wasn't such a bad thing. Without predators to cull the herd, humanity had spread across the earth unchecked, crowding the planet beyond its resources, prideful and arrogant.

Maybe one night a year of being hunted would do them good.

He shook his head then, shivering in the cold rain. Darkling notions had teased his mind all week, but he knew he couldn't let himself think that way – he had a job to do. The people of Bixby didn't deserve to be slaughtered just because the world was overpopulated. No one did.

He listened to the car alarms and forced himself to hope that everyone down there was listening too.

Just before midnight fell, a peal of thunder started to roll, sounding directly over their heads. And then the earth shuddered, the blue time descending over everything, freezing the rain into a million hovering diamonds around him, cutting off the thunder, the car alarms, everything.

'Can you see it from here?' Dess asked.

Rex looked toward Jenks, and his seer's vision picked out the slim red glimmer of the rip. It was starting to swell.

'Yep. The red time is on its way.'

'Good going on that fuse.' Dess breathed out a slow sigh. 'Guess now we just sit back until the fireworks start.'

As per the plan, the other three midnighters were out in Jenks. Soon they would light the first fireworks display to forestall the main force of darklings. Once that was going strong and before the darklings started to flow around them and into town, Jonathan would fly Jessica and Melissa back here, where the five of them would make their stand.

At least, that was the way it was supposed to work.

'Whoa, Rex! Look at that!'

Dess was pointing back toward downtown. Rex turned, following her gaze to the Mobil Building, the tallest in Bixby. The neon winged horse at its summit hunkered just under the low ceiling of heavy clouds, strangely illuminated against their dark bulk.

Rex's heart began to pound. 'Oh my God.'

'Have you ever seen anything like that?'

'No, but I've always wanted to. Melissa and I have been looking for one of those since . . . forever.'

A frozen bolt of lightning reached down from the cloud, its motionless fire forking into a hundred tendrils that caressed the metal framework of the neon horse. In Rex's midnight vision the arrested lightning was mind-bogglingly complex, every inch of it divided into a million burning zigzags.

He remembered all the times he and Melissa had set off on their bicycles as kids, tunneling through the rain toward some frozen flicker of light on the horizon. They'd never made it before the secret hour finished, always having to plow back through the resumed storm empty-handed.

But they'd kept trying; one of the first fragments of lore Rex had discovered was all about frozen lightning, though it had never explained what you were supposed to do when you found it.

Still, there was something in his mind . . .

He felt the fissures that Madeleine had made, the still-tender wounds of her attack, begin to throb. He saw it now, thrown whole into his mind by the sight of the frozen lightning. *This* was the last remnant of what the darklings had hidden from him.

Rex blinked. 'Oh, no.'

'What?'

He couldn't answer, a shudder passing through him. Suddenly he knew what tonight was really all about and what had to happen before the rip reached downtown and set the lightning free again. He knew the instructions that the Grayfoots had never received before their halfling had died.

And finally he understood the real reason why the darklings were so afraid of Jessica – why they had always wanted her dead.

He looked out at Jenks; the glowing red of the rip was still moving toward them. 'We can stop this.'

'What, Rex?'

'We need Jessica here.'

'But they haven't even lit the—'

'Shhh.' Rex dropped to his knees and let his head fall into his hands. In planning tonight he'd put Melissa on the front line for two reasons. She could guide Jessica and Jonathan safely there and back, through cops or darkling invasions as needed. And Rex had also known that if anything went wrong, she could taste his thoughts for miles across the secret hour, just as she had when they were eight years old, when she'd made her way across Bixby wearing only pajamas covered in pictures of cowgirls.

Now he needed her to hear him again.

'Rex?' Dess said softly.

He waved her silent and focused himself, setting all of his will to the task of summoning his oldest friend.

Cowgirl . . . he thought. *I need you now.*

27

IN THE RIP

Silence . . .

Midnight fell, extinguishing the mind noise of Jenks, turning the world blue and still and . . . *red.*

Here in the center of the rip everything began to glimmer purple – red and blue mixing together, time arrested, yet . . . not. The rain pattered down for a few more seconds, then petered out; the rip hadn't expanded enough to include the heavy clouds above their heads. Melissa wondered if when it reached them, the rain would start again.

Weather in the secret hour. Just when I thought I'd seen everything.

'Where is she?' Jessica asked.

Melissa closed her eyes, trying to ignore the flamebringer's coppery, panicked taste. She sent her mind across the rip, feeling it growing, stretching in the opposite directions toward downtown and the mountains. It was moving slowly now, but she could already feel its speed increasing.

No little sisters in it, though.

'Sorry, Jess. I can't feel her.'

'Why not?'

'Your sister's not inside the rip. Not yet, anyway. She must still be frozen, so I can't taste her mind.'

'But Cassie's house is right there!' Jessica pointed down at the double-wide at the edge of the tracks. The red-tinged boundary had already swallowed it.

'Yep. And I can taste her grandma in there, still sleeping,' Melissa said. 'But nobody else is home.'

Jessica's face twisted into an expression of fury, her mind all fiery peppers and burned toast.

'That little creep snuck out!' she cried.

Melissa raised an eyebrow, suddenly relieved she didn't have an older sister of her own. Madeleine's interfering had included making sure that none of her pet midnighters in Bixby had siblings – and this was why.

'Calm down, Jess,' Jonathan said. 'She can't be too far away. Once the rip reaches her, we'll deal with it.'

Jessica looked at Melissa. 'And you're sure you'll recognize her mind?'

'I know Cassie's taste. They'll be together, won't they?'

'What if they aren't?'

Melissa sighed. 'I have an idea what your sister tastes like, okay? I've been to your house at midnight.'

Jessica stared back, her fury twisting into new shapes as she realized what Melissa was admitting. 'Damn you!' she said, and turned and stalked away.

'I never touched the shrimp,' Melissa said to Flyboy. 'Just the parents.'

He offered a shrug, then went to calm the flame-bringer down.

Melissa let out another sigh, feeling weighed down by her long, rain-soaked dress. She and Rex should have admitted what they'd done to Jessica's parents a long time ago. They always figured that it would come up eventually and at a time like this, when everyone needed to stay calm.

They had the fireworks already in place, rockets stuck into the gravel, flares and sparklers divided into separate boxes, all of it covered with a tarp from Jonathan's trunk. Melissa decided to make herself useful while the other two were stressing. She flicked the tarp to knock the rainwater off, then pulled it from the fireworks.

The arsenal looked formidable: candles and hurricane lamps so that Jessica didn't have to light every fuse herself, Roman candles and rockets to bombard the main force of darklings when they arrived, and highway flares that would last for hours, giving the residents of Jenks a fighting chance after the three of them had retreated downtown.

How long now?

Melissa closed her eyes again and swept through the expanding space of the rip. More humans were inside it now, startled by the sudden silence of their TVs and the strange shimmery light that had come over everything.

It was really happening; the blue time was swallowing everyone.

Then she felt a far-off twinge, a familiar mind cutting through the confused babble of normal humans and the mutterings of awakening slithers.

Cowgirl . . .

Rex was calling.

She smiled at first, but as she focused on the distant beacon of thought, Melissa tasted the emotions animating his cry. He was anxious, begging for her to respond, needing something . . .

'Oh, crap,' she said.

'What?' Jessica called. 'Is she okay?'

Melissa shook her head. 'Still no Beth. It's Rex. He needs us to get downtown.'

Jonathan frowned. 'Sure, but not until we—'

'It feels like he needs us *now*. Something's gone wrong!'

'Forget it,' Jessica hissed.

'Listen, just because your sister—'

'No way, Melissa,' Flyboy said. 'We can't leave Jenks undefended just because you've got a *feeling*. They're right in the path of the invasion here. We have to light these things before we head into Bixby.'

'So let's light them,' she said. 'He needs us!'

'Not until I find Beth.' Jessica grasped Jonathan's arm with a white-knuckled grip.

Melissa realized that arguing wouldn't get her anywhere. The taste of the flame-bringer's mind was set. 'Okay,' she said. 'You and I can stay here until I taste your little sister. Then I'll go get her while you light up the fireworks.'

Jessica crossed her arms. 'We'll both go get her.'

'Whatever. But Flyboy, you have to head downtown now. You can get there in five minutes if you go alone.'

'But why?' Jonathan asked.

'Because Rex needs us!' Melissa shook her head. 'I don't know exactly why; he's too far away for me to taste his mind that clearly. Just go and see what he needs.'

Jonathan looked at Jessica, and Melissa tasted the sickly sweet coupleness passing between them. 'I'm not leaving you,' he said.

Jessica frowned, and Melissa tasted a twinge of her guilt

that their plans were revolving around her as usual. 'But maybe Rex—'

'We said we'd stick together tonight!' he cried.

Melissa groaned inwardly, wondering how long this discussion was going to last.

Jessica took his hand. 'Listen, Jonathan. You promised me you'd do what Rex said, remember?'

'Yeah, but not—'

'Just go. I'll be fine. I'm the flame-bringer.'

For a moment Melissa felt the alternatives evenly balanced within Jonathan, like a coin on its edge. But then Jessica squeezed his hand, her expression set and unblinking, and he nodded.

'Okay. I'll be back in ten minutes.'

He kissed her, and the electric taste of their contact swept through Melissa's mind. And then he was gone, leaping out of the rip and over the trees, zooming toward downtown.

Jessica turned to her and said coldly, 'Is Beth inside yet?'

'Listen, Jess, about your parents . . .'

'I don't care. Just look for my sister, *please*.'

Melissa nodded, tipping back her head to taste the growing area within the rip. She tried to ignore the stirrings deep in the desert, the salty taste of anticipation, of ancient hungers ready to be sated at last.

So far, the oldest minds were still hiding in their mountain lairs. They had waited for thousands of years for this night; they could delay another few minutes until they were sure everything was working. Then they would charge toward Bixby, consuming every human in their way, a linear feast.

Melissa tasted something familiar at the edge of the rip – the quiet, self-assured thoughts of Cassie Flinders. She was surprised at how the world had suddenly changed but unafraid. She'd been inside the rip once before, after all.

A moment later Melissa tasted the other mind beside Cassie, a frightened, mewling, panic-stricken ball of little sister.

'Got her.'

'Where?'

Melissa turned her head, sensing the direction. '*Of course.* The cave where Rex found Cassie. They snuck out to go back there, figuring it was a magic spot or something.' Melissa shook her head. 'Funny. I really thought we'd fixed her memories.'

'She must have drawn a picture of it,' Jessica said.

Melissa nodded slowly, remembering the drawings all over Cassie's walls. She hadn't thought to check for that. 'The little sneak. Okay, let's go.'

'No. Just me. I remember the way.'

Melissa frowned. 'Listen, I know you don't like me, but I can—'

'It's not that.' Jessica glanced at the row of houses by the railroad; more of them had been swallowed by the expanding rip. 'They need you here.'

'But what am I supposed to do without you?'

'Light the fireworks when the darklings come. There are other people in Jenks who need protection. Listen, Melissa, I know I'm being selfish. I shouldn't only be thinking about my sister. So you stay here.'

'But I can't even . . . Oh, right.'

Jessica had taken out a lighter and thrust it into one of the hurricane lamps. She adjusted the wick until it was burning bright, then handed Melissa a sparkler.

'Let's just make sure this really works,' she said.

Melissa nodded and thrust the sparkler into the flame of the lamp. It burst to life, shooting out a blinding shower.

'Damn, that's bright!' Melissa said, dropping it to the wet gravel and stamping on it until it sputtered out. A swarm of spots remained brutally burned into her vision, but she founded herself smiling.

Maybe Samhain really *was* a holiday if Melissa was going to do some flame-bringing of her own. 'Okay, get moving! I'll be fine here.'

Jessica nodded, cramming highway flares into her jacket pocket. She skidded down the embankment and thrashed her way into the trees. Melissa closed her eyes, following in her mind as Jessica found the path that Cassie, and then Rex, had taken three weeks before.

She let her mind drift back to the cave. Cassie was getting nervous now, and Beth was a basket case. Their flashlights had extinguished when the blue time had fallen, and though most slithers had left this area permanently after the flame-bringer's last visit, Cassie still imagined she heard snakes in the darkness. They were making their way slowly out of the cave.

Which was a bad idea. There were young darklings not too far away, probing the edges of the rip, wondering if they could take a few quick prey before their elders arrived in force. Melissa just hoped that the scent of the flame-bringer would keep any midnight creatures away from Cassie and Beth.

She turned her focus back toward the city, where Rex's

mind still tugged at her. He was growing more anxious as the rip built up speed, heading toward him down the Bixby-bound railroad line. It was moving at running speed now.

Then it became a little clearer: he needed help to get there before the rip arrived.

Don't worry, Loverboy, she called. *Jonathan's coming.*

Opening her eyes, Melissa looked down at the trailer houses along the railroad right-of-way. Someone had wandered out of the house next to Cassie's, an old man wearing only a T-shirt and undershorts. He was looking around wide-eyed at the blue-red world, tasting of fear and wonderment.

'You ain't seen nothing yet,' she murmured.

Then she twitched, a taste reaching her from the deep desert again.

They were coming . . . daring to issue from the mountains now. They flew slower than their offspring, their muscles creaking with age, with millennia of disuse. But their ancient hunger drew them toward Bixby, with its hated spires of metal and glass.

Finally we hunt again.

Melissa shivered, then something reached her from in the middle distance – a human mind awakening in the desert, at the farthest end of the rip from Bixby. Someone was *camping* out there, she realized with horror, out with the spiders and the rattlesnakes. And tonight with much worse things . . .

They were already waiting for him, a trio of young dark-lings.

Melissa felt it all, the tastes surging into her mouth like stomach acid. They tore into his tent the moment the rip arrived, only seconds after the earth's shudder had pulled him out of his slumber. He fought back against them, swinging a flashlight whose stainless steel case brought a howl of pain from the youngest darkling. But it wouldn't light, and it had no thirteen-letter name, and soon their claws had cut across his face, then his chest, then finally found his throat.

And then the darklings were *eating*, slaking their thirst with the man's still-warm juices, reveling in his last gasps, fighting over scraps . . .

Melissa felt bile rising in her throat, and her brain spun with the darklings' killing frenzy. She struck her own head with her hands, trying to drive the images out, and stumbled half blind across the tracks, dizzy and close to vomiting, her mind caught in the whirlwind of hunger and death.

Then pain shot through her outstretched hand, a sharp sensation of burning, and she heard glass breaking.

She wrenched her eyes open, tried to tear her mind back into her own body.

Fire was everywhere, its white light blinding in the secret hour. She'd overturned the hurricane lamp, and it had shattered, spilling its oil across the fireworks. Through the dazzling flames Melissa saw fuses beginning to sparkle.

It was too soon; the darklings weren't here yet. She had to put the fire out before the rockets and flares and sparklers began to explode, wasting all their ammunition.

Melissa threw herself down on the gravel, rolling across the flaming oil, trying to stifle the flames. Her long black dress was still soaked, wet from trudging through the falling rain from Jonathan's car. Waterlogged enough to protect her body. But her hands burned, and she inhaled the bitter smell of her own hair igniting, its damp, sizzling strands shooting across the corners of her vision. A rocket shot into space beside her, climbing until the upward edge of the rip silenced it.

Melissa rolled back and forth, spreading out her dress as far as she could. She smelled its singed cotton, felt the muffled hiss of a bottle rocket trapped under her, its detonation like a quick jab to her ribs.

When she opened her eyes a moment later, they stung with smoke, but she saw that the fire was mostly smothered. The last flaming tendrils of oil spread across the wet gravel, sputtering out.

Melissa sighed with relief. Her hands and face were blistered, her hair felt like a total disaster, and she smelled like a wet dog that had been set on fire. But she'd saved the cache of fireworks. Jenks wouldn't die because of her mistake.

A second later she frowned, realizing her new problem.

The hurricane lamp was destroyed, her only fire extinguished, and Jessica was off chasing her little sister. Until the flame-bringer returned, Melissa was defenseless.

She sent out her mind and soon found a coppery taste on the midnight landscape – the familiar, metallic flavor of flame-bringer. Jessica was still moving, thrashing through the rain-heavy trees on her way to the cave. She hadn't reached her little sister yet.

Off to the east Jonathan was just now closing in on Rex, climbing toward the last-stand building in leaps and bounds.

And from the deep desert darklings were coming, old ones. Lots of them.

'Come on, Jessica and Jonathan,' Melissa said, rising to her feet. 'Hurry the hell up!'

28

FLYBOY, FLY

'Where are they!' Rex shouted.

'Who?'

'Jessica! Melissa!'

Jonathan spread his hands. 'They're still back in Jenks.'

Rex let out a half-animal howl, his hands twisting into claws. Dess looked up from where she knelt inside her thirteen-sided arrangement of fireworks and shrugged. 'He wanted you to bring Jessica,' she said.

'Yeah, I'm getting that.'

Jonathan was soaked. Barreling through the suspended rain at seventy miles an hour had been like swimming in his clothes. If the secret hour wasn't so warm, he probably would have died of exposure by now.

And some thanks I get.

'Why didn't you bring them?' Rex cried.

'Listen, Melissa didn't know exactly what you wanted, so she said I should come and see.' He coughed into a fist; he'd inhaled a lot of water on the way here. 'Plus Jessica had to sort of look for her, um, sister.'

'Look for her *what*?' Dess said.

'We need her here!' Rex hissed.

'Okay. Should I go back and get her?'

'*Yes*. But I'll come with you.' Rex made his way across the roof toward Jonathan, limping, his teeth clenched with pain.

'Are you okay?' Rex didn't answer, and Jonathan held out his hand. 'Are you sure you can fly?'

Rex shot him a look, and for a moment Jonathan thought he was going to get all scary-faced.

'Don't worry about me.'

'Hey, Rex,' Dess called. 'Sorry to do the math, but if there's four of you out there, how are you all going to get back?'

Jonathan nodded. As far as he knew, he could only fly with two midnighters in tow – one holding each hand. With four of them out in Jenks, someone would have to stay behind.

'If we can get Jessica back here in time, it won't matter.'

'What won't matter?' Jonathan asked.

Rex took his hand in a deathlike grip. 'I'll explain on the way.'

He looked into Rex's eyes; the exhaustion and madness had only gotten worse in the last week. What if the guy had snapped, and this was all a wild-goose chase? What if Rex decided he was a winged darkling in mid-flight and let go of Jonathan's hand?

What if he really *was* a darkling?

Jonathan paused, but then remembered his promise to Jessica and decided to follow the seer's orders, no matter how crazy he seemed.

'Fly,' Rex said, his voice cold.

'Okay. But I have to warn you, you're going to get really wet.'

They jumped from the building's edge, cutting two tunnels through the suspended rain, building speed as they fell. Water spattered against Jonathan's face, forcing his eyes closed to slits. Flying through frozen rain was like standing under a shower and staring straight up into the faucet.

Before the other buildings rose up around them, Jonathan caught a glimmer of red in the distance – the rip was moving faster now.

'Can we make it?' Rex shouted, covering his mouth with his free hand to keep the water out. 'All the way to Jenks and back before the rip gets here?'

'I don't know. Normally it would only take ten minutes or so. But this damn rain—' He broke off, coughing up water from his lungs.

Rex grunted as they hit the next roof over, and as they pushed off again, his fingernails dug into Jonathan's flesh, his face twisting with pain.

'Ow, Rex!' The pressure eased. 'Why do you need her back here anyway?'

'It's complicated.'

Jonathan shot Rex a sidelong glance. He should have known that the promised explanation wouldn't be forthcoming.

He sighed. No point in arguing now. How did Dess always put it? *Seer knows best.*

'Ten minutes? That's cutting it close.' Rex winced as they hit the next roof, taking two long strides across its rain-slick surface, then leaping into the air again. 'Dess says the rip will reach downtown in less than twenty.'

'Yeah, and that's assuming we find Jessica right away,' Jonathan said. 'I mean, she might still be out looking for her sister.'

'Don't worry, I can find her,' Rex said.

'Huh?'

The seer didn't answer as the outskirts of downtown rose up around them. They had landed at street level finally and angled onto the highway. Jonathan imagined the cars around them springing to life again in twenty minutes, all weaving to a stop, people struggling to control them with brute strength, their power steering and brakes suddenly heavy as lead.

Rex made a strangled noise with every bound.

When they reached a light patch in the frozen storm, Jonathan spoke up again. 'Listen, Rex. Why don't you let me go on alone? You could still make it back there in time. You're killing yourself on that sprained ankle.'

'It's broken, actually.'

'What the hell?' Jonathan looked down at Rex's right cowboy boot. It was turned wrong somehow. The next time they landed, he watched Rex hold the foot up off the ground, taking all his weight on his other side.

'You have to stop, Rex. I'll take you back to Dess first You're going to tear your foot apart!'

'No. You need me to track Jessica.'

'*Track* her?'

'She smells like prey to me now. You all do.'

Their next bound took them over a frozen pickup truck piled high with sharp, deadly scrap metal, giving Jonathan a moment to think before he answered.

Rex had really lost it; he was certain now. For once his plan had actually made sense, yet the seer seemed determined to screw everything up.

Except for the parts that Beth has already *managed to screw up.*

He let out a sigh through clenched teeth, wishing he hadn't promised Jessica that he'd do what Rex said. Of course, following orders didn't mean he couldn't try to make sense of them. 'So, wait. *Why* do you need Jess downtown?'

'Lightning,' Rex said in a strangled voice, then cried out as the ground rose up and struck them again.

He refused to say another word the rest of the way.

29

12:00 A.M.
LONG MIDNIGHT

BETH

'Beth!' Jessica shouted for the hundredth time. 'Where *are* you?'

The cave had to be around here somewhere, she was positive. But three weeks ago Jessica and Jonathan had flown here, not walked. Somehow the path had disappeared right under her feet, fading out into scrub and tree roots. Everything looked weird and unfamiliar here in the rip, the edges of the leaves glinting with purple and crimson fire.

She checked her watch. It had been almost ten minutes since she'd left Melissa behind. Soon the younger darklings would be closing in.

She pulled out her flashlight and whispered its new name: *Foolhardiness*.

The beam surged through the forest, driving away the violet shimmer of the rip. Jessica heard movement ahead, a slither – or something larger – fleeing before the white light.

'Beth!' she cried. 'Where are you?'

Finally an answer came. Not to her ears, but in words that sounded distantly in her mind.

To your right, fast. They need you.

Melissa. The mindcaster's taste washed across Jessica's tongue – a strange sensation, given that she'd never thought of Melissa as having a taste before. But there it was, bitter and caustic, like chewing some pill you were supposed to swallow.

Jessica began to run, veering right until a high-pitched scream reached her through the trees. She barreled toward the sound, ignoring the branches whipping at her face and clothes. The rip had cleared the suspended raindrops from the air, but the trees were still heavy with water – dumping gallons on her as she crashed through them.

Another scream came from dead ahead. Close.

She burst out into the familiar clearing, saw the finger of stone thrusting into the air, then stumbled to a halt, eyes wide. A *thing* was wrapped around the cave entrance, like a great jellyfish attached to its prey, its tendrils sinking into the rock itself. It had no head that Jessica could see, just a tangled knot of stringy appendages, all matted together like hair caught in a bathtub drain.

A small human figure stood just inside the mouth of the cave, pale and shaking, the creature's tendrils wound around her arms and legs.

Jessica ran toward it, playing Foolhardiness's white light across the creature.

But its tendrils didn't burst into flame; instead they sizzled angrily with blue fire, coiling tighter.

Rex had warned them that they might see new things tonight, things born well before midnight had been created, so old that mere white light wouldn't be enough to slay them.

In which case, he had said, there was always fire.

Jessica pulled a highway flare from her pocket and, in a move she'd practiced all week, flicked its top off, banging the two pieces against each other in a glancing blow.

'Ventriloquism,' she said, and the flare burst to life, its radiance white-hot and blinding.

In its radiance she saw one of the thing's legs reaching for her, snaking across the ground. She knelt, thrusting the flare at it. The tendril sizzled, a low flame racing across it, bringing up a gagging smell of burned hair and dust.

It retreated, slithering away from her, but another reached through the air.

'Haven't had enough?' Jessica said, fending it off. The arm darted around her, just outside the reach of the hissing flame. In the corner of her eye she saw another arm stretching its way from the creature.

She swallowed. Since she'd become the flame-bringer, the darklings had been so afraid of her. But apparently these old ones didn't cut and run.

This was their night, after all.

Jessica lunged forward, swinging the flare into the closest tendril. A gout of flame exploded, bringing a low, mournful scream and another rush of the burned-hair smell.

She looked around for the other arm . . .

At that moment something wrapped itself around her leg, soft and feathery but bitter cold. The chill climbed through her, shooting up her spine, bringing with it a tidal wave of emotion: old fears and nightmares rose in her, forgotten terrors dredged up to the surface of her mind.

Suddenly Jessica felt lost, filled with the certainty that she was failing out of school, was leaving her old friends forever, going to a place where reality was warped and strange. The panic of finding a new classroom after the tardy bell had rung paralyzed her, cold as the stares of a thousand unfriendly strangers.

Everyone in Bixby hated her, she suddenly knew.

Open your hand, Jess, a distant voice implored.

She obeyed unthinkingly, hoping to please the voice in her head, her fingers releasing the flare. Her only weapon fell from her grasp.

Then, like a phone line going dead, the cold disappeared, all her terrors vanishing in the space of a heartbeat. And again the screaming sound filled the air, slow and piercing and mournful, like the Bixby firehouse's noon siren.

Jessica looked down; the flare's burning end had cut the tendril as it had fallen, releasing her from the creature's spell.

'Thanks, Melissa,' she whispered, kneeling to retrieve the flare. She held it in front of herself, charging toward the thing wrapped around the mouth of the cave.

Tendrils began to writhe as she approached, slithering from the arms and legs of the small, pale figure in the cave's entrance, abandoning their grasp of the stone spire. A smaller set of extremities whirled around the thing's matted center like the blades of a helicopter, hissing with the sound of escaping steam. It rose slowly into the air.

Jessica hurled the flare directly at the creature and in the same motion reached into her pocket for another. As she worked to light it, the darkling thing burst into flame above her, the smell of dead rat and rotten eggs filling the air. It unleashed its mournful howl again, still rising, then flying across the sky. The flame seemed to be riding the creature, somehow unable to consume it. And then the burning mass passed over the horizon of trees.

Jessica held the new flare out, lighting the mouth of the cave. The small figure had fallen to the ground and lay huddled and sobbing. Another pale face appeared out of the darkness.

'Beth?' she said, squinting through the smoke of the flare.

'It's me – Cassie.' The girl took another step into the light, then knelt next to the fallen figure, turning her face up.

It was Beth, so pale she was almost unrecognizable.

Jessica dropped the flare and fell to her knees. 'Beth!'

For a moment the only answer was a wild fluttering of eyelids. Then Beth sucked in a sudden, sharp breath, and her eyes opened.

'Jess?' she answered.

'I'm here. Are you all right?'

'Yeah. Sure. What a nightmare. Was I screaming or just . . .?' Beth's eyes opened wider as she took in Cassie, the burning flare, the red-tinged blue time all around them. 'What the hell, Jess?'

'What are you *doing* out here?' Jessica cried.

Cassie's expression was dazed, but she answered calmly. 'We snuck out tonight. We figured something was going on out here at midnight.'

'You guys were right about that.'

'What was that thing?' Cassie asked.

'What thing . . .?' Beth said weakly.

'I have no idea. I mean, it was a darkling, but not the usual kind.'

'A darkling?'

Jessica shook her head. 'I'll explain later. Beth, can you stand up?'

Beth rose slowly to her feet. The highway flare cast wildly

jittering light into the cave behind them, and both the girls' faces looked ghostly in its harsh shadows.

'I remember the flashlight conking out,' Beth said, then looked at Jessica. 'Why are you here? What's going on?' Her voice had regained some strength.

'*Later*, Beth. Can't you see we have to go?'

'Go where? I mean, what is all this? Is *this* what you sneak out to do every night?'

'Beth!' Jessica reached back and grabbed her sister's hand. 'I'll tell you later! Come on!'

'But you won't!' Beth planted her feet, not letting Jessica take another step. 'You never tell me anything!'

Jessica groaned. Her little sister apparently didn't remember the creature that had taken hold of her; she didn't realize how close she'd come to being lunch meat. Even Cassie had folded her arms across her chest.

Part of her wanted to scream, but another part wanted nothing more than to stop in her tracks and tell Beth everything. Finally no secrets between them.

Jessica put her hands on her sister's shoulders. 'Okay. *This* is what I couldn't tell you about. This is what's weird about Bixby. It changes at midnight, becomes . . . something terrible. And we have to deal with it, me and my friends.'

Beth's eyes were still glazed. 'It's like some kind of nightmare . . .'

'Yeah, except that it's real.' Jessica shook her head. 'Especially right now. You picked the wrong night to spy on me.'

'Spy on you? I was *worried* about you, Jess. You were keeping secrets and lying all the time . . .'

'I'm sorry about that,' Jessica cried. 'I really am. But can't you see why now? You wouldn't have believed me anyway! '

Beth looked around at the purple light of the world, the silenced wind and rain, and nodded. 'Yeah. You got that right.'

'I never wanted to lie to you, Beth. But I just didn't have a way to tell you. And we have to go right now. Just come with me and I'll tell you everything. I promise I'll *never* lie to you again. Just trust me, please?'

Beth looked at her, and Jessica wondered if she was really listening or whether her suspicions were still whirring away, looking for something to doubt, to scorn or mock. Maybe everything was too broken between them.

But then, slowly, Beth nodded. 'Okay. I trust you.'

Jessica smiled, relief washing through her. 'Truth later? But do what I say now? No matter how weird it is?'

'Sure. Truth later. But can we get out of here? This place smells funny.'

'No problem.'

Jessica led them out of the cave, Foolhardiness in one hand, the hissing flare in the other. As they crossed the clearing, her eyes searched for the path back to the railroad embankment.

'Hey, can I ask a question?' Cassie said.

Jessica turned. 'Do you *have* to?'

'Kind of.' Cassie pointed into the air. 'What's that?'

Jessica spun around, Foolhardiness sweeping across the sky. Its beam found Jonathan and Rex hurtling down toward them, hands across their eyes against its light. She flicked it off.

Rex landed sloppily, skidding to a stop, but Jonathan bounded from the edge of the clearing, soaring to where they stood. He corkscrewed to a halt and wrapped Jessica in his arms, his midnight gravity flooding into her along with the sudden feeling that she might cry with relief.

He pulled back to look at her. 'Are you okay?'

'Yeah.'

He turned. 'Hey, Beth. How's it going?'

'Uh, hi, Jonathan,' Beth said, her voice small again.

Jessica took both his hands. 'I think they're okay, but there are some weird-ass darklings out tonight.'

'No kidding. But Jess, you and I have to go now. We have to get back downtown.'

'Why? Melissa hasn't even set off the first round yet.'

Rex hobbled up to them, wincing with every step. 'We can stop all this, Jessica,' he panted. 'Right now, save everyone.'

'What? How?'

'There's a bolt of lightning caught by midnight. It's striking the Pegasus sign over the old Mobil Building. You need to get there before the rip does.'

'And do what?'

'Put your hand into the lightning.'

'*Do what now?*'

Rex raised his hands in surrender. 'I can't explain how I know this. It's something I got from the darklings, combined with an old piece of lore. But you can force the rip closed again, I'm certain of it. That's why the darklings were so afraid of you. All along *tonight* is what they feared.'

Jessica blinked. 'But what about my sister and Cassie?'

'I'll take care of them. Just give me that.' He took the hissing flare. 'Melissa needs it. The fire you left her got put out.'

'But there's darklings everywhere!'

'I know.' His voice broke. 'They're closing in on her now.'

Jessica grabbed Jonathan's hand. 'We can fly there—'

He waved her silent. 'You have to go downtown *now*. There's no time to waste.'

She stared at Rex. He didn't look capable of walking another step, much less fighting off any darklings. But his pleading expression silenced any argument.

'*Now*, Jess!'

In the next split second Jessica realized that she was here again – not knowing what to do, having to believe what the others told her. From the moment she'd set foot in Bixby, the rules of reality seemed to shift every week, as if the blue time were one big practical joke the universe had decided to play on Jessica Day. As usual, there was never time for a full explanation, never time to think anything through.

She could only trust that Rex, whatever the darklings had done to him, was still human enough to want to do the right thing. She had to believe that even though Bixby had been deceived and manipulated for thousands of years, this orphaned generation of midnighters was different. Most of all, she had to remember that Rex Greene would never leave Melissa in danger for an extra second unless thousands of lives were at stake.

'All right.' She turned to Beth. 'Follow Rex, okay? Just do what he says. He'll keep you safe.' Jessica smiled. 'Trust me.'

Beth sputtered wordlessly for a moment, then finally blurted, 'Your boyfriend can *fly*?'

Jessica smiled. 'Yeah, actually, he can.'

She turned to Jonathan, extending her hand. 'Okay, let's go.'

30

BONFIRE

'Come *on!*' Rex shouted.

He took another painful step, one gloved hand clenched around a tree branch, pulling himself along to reduce the weight on his injured foot. Even so, a strangled cry escaped through his teeth – this was much worse than the flight here. Without Jonathan's midnight gravity moving through him, Rex felt every ounce of his tall frame. The hissing flare in his free hand brushed against a wet branch, scattering blinding white sparks across his vision.

'You're Rex, right?' Cassie said from behind him. He didn't answer, but she went on. 'I'm starting to remember now.'

'He looks just like you drew him,' Beth whispered.

'You're the one who saved me, right?' Cassie asked. 'A few weeks ago?'

'I'm the one who's saving you *now!* Can we focus on that?' The darkling hiss in his voice silenced her and brought a fresh burst of fear from Beth. He tried to concentrate on the painful task of walking, not the defenseless scent of the two girls behind him.

Melissa . . . he called.

Again there was no response. Rex forced despair from his mind, hoping she was simply too busy fighting to answer. The last message he'd received from her had shown the hurricane lamp breaking, its flames extinguished, and the acid taste of darklings on their way.

He moved faster through the trees, ignoring the pain. The narrow trail before them danced in the jittering white light, and he recognized a low, twisted mesquite tree. Another hundred yards and they would reach the railroad tracks, only a few minutes away from Melissa and the cache of fireworks.

A hunting cry cut through the trees, and the flutter of leathery wings came from all directions. Rex paused, lifting the flare and shielding his eyes from its glare. Slithers darted in the corners of his vision, and larger shapes shifted among the crooked lines of branches, wary of the white light sputtering in his hand.

Rex could smell their hunger, finally unleashed after millennia, and knew that tonight there would be no respect among predators, no safety for him. This was their night at last – Samhain.

'What *was* that?' Cassie said.

'Monsters.' Rex pulled Animalization from his belt, thrusting its hilt into her hand. Of all the metal Dess had carefully prepared, it was the only weapon he'd brought on the frantic flight with Jonathan. Of course, there were plenty of weapons at the railroad tracks, if they could only get there.

'You remember this?'

She stared down at the knife, eyes wide, head nodding slowly.

'It's called Animalization.' He winced as the tridec left his lips. 'Say it.'

As Cassie carefully sounded out the syllables, Rex heard something flying through the trees toward them. Something bigger than a slither.

'Duck!' he cried, raising the flare as he crouched.

A roar came through the forest like a sudden storm, bringing the overwhelming smell of predator. A huge winged creature burst into view, tearing at the treetops with four outstretched arms. It uttered a shriek at the spitting white light of the flare, then passed overhead, trailing the sound of breaking branches like snapping bones.

A sudden downpour descended in its wake, sheets of water dislodged from the rain-soaked trees by the creature. A vortex of wet leaves and branches swirled around the three of them, and the flare sputtered in Rex's gloved hand, its flame almost smothered by the deluge. Just in time he dropped to his knees and sheltered the burning weapon under himself, protecting its flame from the watery onslaught.

At that moment the air was full of slithers streaking past, their timing perfect to take advantage of the flare's concealment. One stung Rex in the middle of his back, sending a bolt of ice down his spine. A burst of blue sparks shot into the night from Animalization in Cassie's upraised hands, and he heard Beth cry out.

Rex lifted the flare again, exposing it to the dwindling tempest. A slither was caught among its white sparks and burst into flame in midair, disintegrating like a shovelful of embers flung through the trees. The others split into a panicked mass and whirled off into the forest trailing a chorus of screams.

But as the torrent of dislodged water subsided, the flare sputtered weakly, barely staying lit. It burned unevenly now, half extinguished by the remains of wet leaves wrapped around it.

Rex heard the many-armed darkling circling, ready to come at them again. He saw Beth staring dumbfounded at a purple welt on her hand. 'You two okay?'

'It bit me!' Beth shouted angrily.

'They're afraid of fire?' Cassie asked.

He nodded, gesturing with the flare. 'They're trying to put this out.'

'Why didn't you say so?' She started scrabbling among the leaves. 'We can start a fire.'

'It's too wet!'

'Not under here.' She pushed aside handfuls of glistening damp leaves. 'My grandma says you can always find dry leaves at the bottom of a pile. And they're better for burning 'cause they're rotten.'

Rex raised his eyebrows. In the jittering white light the exposed patch of leaves did look dry. The flare still sizzled wetly in his hand, as if it might not withstand another pass by the creature. He reached down to thrust its blinding tongue into the pile. Flames curled the leaves' edges, and a rich smell like an autumn burn-off struck his nose.

'Bonfires,' he said, remembering his images of ancient Samhains.

'Not exactly a bonfire yet.' Cassie cleared more leaves, adding to the smoking pile.

'It's coming back!' Beth said. The darkling was closing in

again, the sound of snapping branches building as it neared them.

This time, Rex realized, its attack would be less effective. The beast had already shaken most of the water from the rain-soaked leaves. They could hold out here indefinitely, or as long as they could feed their little bonfire. If they moved from this spot, though, the creature could douse them with fresh tree-loads of water.

But they had to reach Melissa and the fireworks, not sit here huddled around a shred of safety.

Rex felt his teeth bare, smelling the arrogance of the young and clever darkling. It thought he could be frightened into immobility, like some cornered prey.

It was wrong.

'Take this!' he cried, handing the flare to Beth. 'Keep it covered!'

He snatched the knife back from Cassie, readying himself to spring, feeling the hunting frenzy rising up in him. The darkling approached again, tree branches rocking and shaking free more water, and Rex leapt into the air toward its black silhouette with a scream in his throat, hardly feeling his injured ankle. He thrust the knife out before him, plunging the steel blade into the creature's flesh.

Blue sparks spat from the wound back into his face, and the creature's arms wrapped around him, flailing to claw at his back and legs. Rex felt himself carried along on a few powerful strokes of its wings – away from the two girls. He howled, twisting the knife as hard as he could. The beast let out a cry, its grasp loosening. Rex kicked at it with his good foot . . .

And then he was tumbling from its arms, crashing through

branches and undergrowth, slashing blindly at the slithers shooting past. He landed heavily on a bare patch of ground, his breath knocked out of him as if the earth were a huge fist. He lay there for a moment, staring at the blue fire coursing through the knife. Somehow he'd held on to it.

But the forest was alive with sounds: big things pushing through the branches, slithers on the wing. Coming for him.

Rex rose painfully, his bruised ribs creaking, the slither bite shooting pain down his spine. A shape shot toward him out of the forest, and he brought the knife up to slice into a wing. The slither kept flapping, jerking away like a broken kite into the trees.

In the distance he saw a flicker of red. Cassie was getting her bonfire going. But it seemed incredibly far away.

Rex . . .?

'Melissa!' he cried aloud, sensing that she was nearby. Whirling around to look for her, he realized that his brief flight with the beast had taken him closer to the railroad tracks.

'Rex!' a cry answered.

Following the sound, he saw a sheet of blue sparks through the branches and charged toward it. He was unprotected by the flare now, and the looming shapes in the trees were moving toward him. His ankle throbbed with every step, and the metal on his boots sparked as crawling slithers struck at his legs. But Melissa was so close.

The blue sparks glowed through the trees again, revealing the silhouette of a great cat raised up on his haunches. The creature was young and eager for a kill, full of the fervor of Samhain. Then Rex spotted a human form just past the darkling: Melissa tossing up handfuls of metal, hurling the bolts and screws that Dess had created into the cat's face, driving it wild with fury. It let out a cry, swiping a claw at the tiny missiles.

Then it dropped into a crouch, ready to launch itself at her.

Rex felt his body changing, transforming more than it ever had before, the full fury of the beast inside him unleashed at last. Suddenly his injured foot seemed beside the point, the great cat's size and strength meaningless – nothing mattered but saving Melissa.

He found himself crashing through the trees with a hunting scream, taking a wild leap onto the back of the darkling He plunged Animalization into its shoulder, and the creature let out a howl. Its coiled muscles exploded under Rex, a jump that carried both him and the beast straight up into the air.

It twisted beneath him, trying to bring its powerful claws around. But Rex hung on with a wild, inhuman strength, his metal-encircled boots sparking against its flanks. He and the darkling spun around each other in midair like some bizarre rodeo ride.

The taste of Melissa entered his mind . . .

Get off it, Rex!

It made no sense, letting the beast free to shred him, but this was *Melissa*, and his human half obeyed the frantic demand without thinking. He pushed away with all his strength, leaving the knife embedded in the darkling, trying to shield his face from its flailing claws.

Rex fell hard on the damp ground, battered ribs letting out a *crack*, his ankle screaming with the pain he'd ignored. The beast inside him had faded a little. It had wanted to fight to the death, but he'd listened to Melissa instead . . .

He struggled to his feet with empty hands spread wide, defenseless.

The darkling lay a few yards away, its paws twitching like a dreaming cat's. Then it let out a horrifying scream. For a moment Rex didn't understand, until he saw the metal shaft protruding from its flank: some kind of spear, its steel still sizzling with blue fire. The creature twitched once more, then stopped moving.

Melissa emerged from behind its bulk, looking stunned, her hands black with the creature's blood.

'Uninterrupted Vivisectional Preoccupation,' she said.

Rex blinked. She had set the spear on the ground and let the darkling fall on it.

'Thanks for distracting it,' she said.

Rex heard slithers flapping away from them in all directions, momentarily scattered by the dying howl of the great cat. He took a painful step, put a gloved hand on her shoulder. 'No problem. But what are you *doing* out here?'

'I got bored of waiting and figured you needed some help.' She held up a backpack. 'I brought fireworks. So, um . . . where's the fire?'

Rex looked back the way he'd come; the red glimmer was just visible in the distance. 'That way.'

A puzzled expression crossed Melissa's face. Her eyes closed for a moment. 'You left our only fire with a couple of *thirteen-year-olds?*'

He nodded. 'Pretty much.'

Melissa shook her head with disgust. 'Daylighters in the secret hour.' She sighed, tossing him a long metal shaft marked with spirals of solder. The steel burned even through Rex's gloves, but its heft felt good in his hands.

'Thanks,' he said. 'How's Jessica doing?'

'Don't worry about her; worry about us.' She lifted another spear onto her shoulder. 'There's a lot more darklings on their way.'

They crashed through the trees toward the bonfire's glow, swinging their spears at the slithers that struck through the air. Every step shot through Rex's injured foot and his throbbing ribs, but the pain had faded into a mindless blur. He had reached Melissa, and his human half was willing to let the beast take over.

The bonfire ahead was building, the smell of smoke swirling through the forest. More of the four-armed darklings thrashed at the trees around it, as if trying to batter it into submission. But the wind of their wings only seemed to drive the fire brighter.

As they grew closer, the slithers stopped coming at them, wary of the whirlwind of sparks and burning leaves.

'Cassie! Beth!' Rex shouted.

'Rex?' came a cry. He saw Cassie silhouetted against the flames, the highway flare still sputtering in her hand.

'We're coming!' he yelled back.

'What about them?' Melissa asked, coming to a halt.

As she spoke, the bloated forms of five huge darklings rose from the forest floor. Their mouths glistened, and the clusters of eyes that dotted their bodies glowed dully in the purple light of the rip. Their long, hairy legs were splayed like the bars of a cage around the fire.

'Spiders,' Melissa said. 'Your favorite.'

'Not a problem.' Rex held out his hand. 'Give me the backpack.'

He unzipped it and dug his hand in, feeling a collection of bottle rockets, Roman candles, and firecrackers threaded in long strings. 'Any highway flares?'

'Sure. At the bottom.'

His hand closed on the flares, and he handed three to her, keeping another for himself. 'One for each of us. After I deal with those things, we'll light up and make a run for the tracks.'

'There's *five* of them, Rex. And they're just standing there, staring at that fire like it's no big deal. They're not going to be afraid of *you*.'

Rex smiled, feeling the beast well up in him. 'They should be.'

He turned, spear in one hand and backpack in the other, and limped toward the great spiders. They stood impassively, eyes aglitter with firelight. They were old, he could tell now. As he grew near, Rex felt their minds moving through him, the taste of ash and sour milk coating his tongue.

Abomination. You will die tonight.

'We'll see.' He broke into a painful, ungainly run.

The spear left his hand first, shooting through the air toward the closest darkling. Two of its arms rose to ward it off, flailing like hairy tentacles. The spear glanced off one of them, coming to rest in the soft earth at its feet.

But the still-unzipped backpack was already soaring over the darkling's head. It traveled in a long arc, over Cassie and her sputtering flare, its contents already spilling from it as it flew. It all landed with a burst of sparks and smoke in the center of the bonfire.

Watch this . . . he thought at the darklings.

A moment later the scattered fireworks began to explode,

balls of fire spitting out in all directions, the shriek of long strings of firecrackers expelling clouds of smoke, rockets bouncing among the branches. The burning tongue of a Roman candle reached out to ignite one of the spiders, and the beast screamed in pain as flame spread across its hairy surface. One of the winged darklings caught a bottle rocket and began to flail its wings, then crashed into the beast beside it, the two creatures wrapping around each other in a frantic, blazing embrace.

Beth and Cassie dropped into the wet leaves, hands over their heads. The great spiders shifted, their arms shuddering, their terror washing through Rex's mind with an electric taste.

He rolled under the nearest darkling, pulled his spear from the ground, and thrust it into the beast's belly. A foul smell spilled from the wound as the beast reared up, its mouth opening wide, its teeth as long as knives.

As Rex raised his spear, a squadron of rockets skittered randomly across the ground in the corner of his eye. Then one hit his shoulder, leapt into the air spinning head over tail, and shot into the gaping mouth of the darkling. The creature made a choking sound as Rex rolled toward the bonfire, rising to his knees to scrabble over to where the girls huddled.

'Are you okay?'

'Those *things* . . .' Beth sobbed.

'Don't worry. They're leaving.' He looked up.

The beast behind him was trying to transform, wings sprouting from its back as the legs were sucked into the body. But then Rex heard a huffing sound – the rocket in its gut exploding – and tasted the beast's panic in his mind. Its glittering eyes dulled, and a gout of flame burst from the spear wound in its belly. The wings began to crumble . . .

Rex covered his head as the creature exploded, a mighty rush of scorching heat, the light blinding even through his slammed-shut lids. The earth bucked beneath him, a roar like a jet taking off filling the air.

And then the sound was fading, until all he heard was the screams of midnight creatures retreating in all directions.

When Rex opened his eyes, he saw Melissa kneeling nearby, lighting the highway flares from the remains of the fire. Burning leaves were spread far into the trees, but a few glowing embers and a broad dark patch of ground were all that was left of Cassie's efforts.

'They're gone, Rex,' she said. 'Looks like you ruined their Samhain.'

He nodded, his vision swarming with glowing spots. 'Yeah. I guess bonfires have gotten a lot nastier since their day.'

'We can do even better with the stuff back at the tracks. And we need to get there fast.' She stood, two hissing flares in each hand.

Cassie was already standing, pulling Beth to her feet. They were covered with ash and wet leaves, their faces blank with shock. But Cassie took the flare that Melissa handed her. 'Are they all gone?' she asked.

Melissa closed her eyes. 'Not hardly. We have to run, girls.' She pointed toward the tracks. 'There's tons more fireworks waiting for us that way.'

'Just give me a minute,' Rex said. His torso was bruised all over, his ankle aching, his vision and hearing swarming with echoes of the explosion. His lungs felt scorched, as if he'd inhaled too much bonfire smoke.

He didn't hear Melissa's words at first.

'*Rex?*' Her hand pulled at his jacket.

'Just a second.'

'We have to go *now*.'

'I can barely stand.'

'Look.' She reached up and bare fingers brushed his neck, her mind entering him in a wild rush. He saw what was coming . . .

'Oh, crap.' Rex shuddered. He'd been a fool, all his plans empty gestures. 'I never knew.'

Melissa took her hand away and lifted his weight onto her shoulder, pulling him forward. 'We can help Jenks, anyway.'

They set off through the trees, Rex's battered body responding once more to the commands of his will. He didn't bother to look back, but the jittering of the branches ahead showed that the girls were following, their flares casting wild shadows through the forest. The tracks were only a few minutes away, but it all seemed futile . . .

Rex shut his eyes and ran, ignoring the pain, trying to erase the image that Melissa had given him. A flood of darklings, a wave that darkened the sky, a vast horde beyond anything in the lore. Their fireworks would present nothing but a trivial detour to the onslaught.

Jessica Day was their only hope.

31

LIGHTNING

They bounded down the railroad tracks, following the rip. It stretched out before them, a red arrow pointed at the heart of Bixby.

'Can we make it in time?'

Jonathan nodded. 'It's clearing the way for us, knocking down the frozen rain as it goes. But watch out when we get ahead of it. Water sucks.'

'Jonathan!'

A man stood on the tracks ahead of them, dressed in a bathrobe and wearing an expression of disbelief. They took an extra-high jump so as not to hit him, and his pale face lifted to watch them pass overhead.

'Okay, that was weird,' Jessica said.

'There are more of them. The rip is getting crowded. And not just with humans.'

As they neared Bixby, houses became more frequent. They saw more people wandering around, first alone or in twos and threes, then in crowds gathered on the street. Some of them stared up in wonder at Jessica and Jonathan, but many didn't even notice as they soared overhead, too dazzled by the blue-red world around them.

'You think Rex is right?' she said. 'Can we really stop this?'

'If he isn't, most of these people are in big trouble. They're just standing here, right in the middle of the rip.'

'At least the darklings aren't here yet.'

He pointed ahead. 'Some of them are.'

Before them was another of the creatures made of wispy, grasping tendrils. It hovered over a small group gathered in the backyard of a house, what must have been a Halloween party going late. Everyone was in costume – knights and devils and cowboys and even a white-sheeted ghost all standing almost motionless. The darkling thing had a tendril wrapped around each of them, and Jessica saw that their hands were shaking, as if each was trapped in their own silent, private horrors.

'My God, should we stop?'

'No time,' Jessica said. They had to halt this invasion. All of it, everywhere, not just in this one backyard. 'But slow down a little.'

She pulled a flare from her pocket and put one end into her mouth, yanking the top off. Then she banged it against the friction pad clenched between her teeth, sparks flying into her face, the first hiss of the flare burning her eyebrows before she could whip it away.

At the top of their next bounce she threw the flare down into the matted center of the thing. It ignited, the scream echoing across the blue time, its tendrils beginning to slip from the costumed people.

Jessica looked over her shoulder as they flew onward and

saw that the crowd had sprung to life and were pulling at the thing's arms with a sudden and terrifying madness, as if trying to rip it apart.

'There's more,' Jonathan said softly.

Ahead of them two of the old darklings were stretched across the railroad tracks, like hovering spiderwebs.

'Go around them?' he asked.

'They move too fast.' Jessica pulled out another flare, then realized that it was the last one she was carrying. 'Crap.'

She yanked off its top with her teeth, managing to light it without burning her face this time. She thrust it out before them as they soared into the joined webs of tendrils.

At the touch of the flame the two darklings screamed, but Jessica felt cold feathers brushing her legs, her arms, her neck – slithering around her waist for a fleeting moment. Fear welled up in her again, a paralyzing horror that she had made the wrong decision. It was crazy leaving Jenks defenseless, her sister doomed. And suddenly she knew: the darklings had opened up the blue time because of her, because they hated Jessica Day so much . . .

The end of the world . . . it's all my fault.

Only the feeling of Jonathan's hand in hers kept her from giving in to the awesome despair that racked her being. He wouldn't abandon her, she knew. But they were wrapped around Jonathan as well; she had to fight.

Jessica gritted her teeth and slashed with the flare, carving into the matted tendrils, ripping herself free.

One by one, the fears fell away.

Then the feeling vanished, and she was filled with weightlessness again. The tracks reared up, and she reflexively took another bounding step. She glanced backward; the two darklings lay in a smoldering wreckage, scattered along on the tracks.

'No!' Jonathan yelled, his hand wrenching hers.

'Ow! What's wrong?' she cried.

'Huh?' He looked at her, dumbfounded. 'Wait a second. I caught you . . .?'

'Caught me? I wasn't falling.'

'But I thought . . .' He stared at their joined hands.

'Oh.' Jessica's eyes widened. 'Is *that* your worst nightmare, Jonathan? Dropping me?'

He blinked. 'Of course. But . . .'

Jessica felt a smile spread across her face. 'That is *so sweet*!'

They landed and launched themselves into the air again. Jessica saw a glowing red boundary rising up before them. 'What the—?'

'It's the front end of the rip,' he cried. 'Get ready!'

Jessica started to answer, but a wall of water struck her in the face.

She'd never flown through frozen rain before. Her first time in the secret hour, Jessica had walked around in a midnight shower, a magical experience no worse than dashing through a sprinkler in summer. But at seventy miles per hour, hitting the motionless storm was like having a fire hose trained on her.

The water soaked her already damp clothes, filled her mouth so she could hardly speak or breathe, and reduced their path to a blur before them. The highway flare sputtered in her hand, hissing like an angry snake. She could hardly see the ground rushing up at them.

She took a blind jump, and they began to spin.

'Stop! I can't see anything!' she shouted into the wall of rain.

'Can't stop for long – the rip's too close.'

Jessica looked backward, which shielded her vision from the water. A huge sheet of red was streaking across Bixby, moving almost as fast as they were.

Turning back to face the deluge, she found she could finally make sense of the watery blue chaos. Through slitted eyes Jessica saw that they were entering downtown. On their next jump they bounded up onto the roof of a six-story building, then jumped higher.

Before her the tallest building in Bixby waited, a huge and winged shape glittering at its summit.

'Is that . . .?'

'Don't you recognize Pegasus?'

'Wow.' She had seen the giant horse from up close before, but never illuminated like this. A long finger of lightning reached down from the heavy clouds above, wrapping the sign in a thousand bright filaments.

They came down on another rooftop, skidding to a halt across wet black tar. Her soaked sneakers stumbled through a clutter of small shapes.

'Yo! Watch the fireworks!'

Jessica wiped water from her eyes. 'Oh. Sorry, Dess.'

'Where's Rex and Melissa?'

'Long story,' Jonathan said. 'We're on our way up there.' He pointed at the lightning-sheathed Pegasus sign.

'What the hell for?'

'Rex thinks we can seal the rip.'

'What, with *lightning*?' Dess swore. 'You *do* know Rex is crazy these days, right?'

Jonathan looked at Jessica, who felt doubts rising in her again.

But she set her teeth. 'We can't let this go on. We have to try.'

'Don't ask me. But can I have that?' Dess pointed at the hissing flare. 'Just in case you guys are crazy too?'

'Sure.' Jessica handed it over.

'Come on.' Jonathan was already perched on the edge of the roof. 'The rip's right behind us.'

'Good luck,' Dess said.

'You too.' Jessica ran to Jonathan and took his hand. She looked up at the glittering winged horse above them.

'Let's try to make it in one jump,' Jonathan said.

'Can we get that far?'

'I hope so. Three . . . two . . . one . . .'

Jessica pushed off as hard as she could, and they soared into the air. At the peak of their arc, she was almost at eye level with the giant horse, higher than she'd ever flown before. But as they came closer, she realized that they were falling short.

'Uh-oh.'

'We'll make it!' Jonathan flailed against the rain like an injured bird, then reached out one hand, and as they hit the building, his fingers found the edge of the roof. Jessica smacked into the wall below him, bouncing off and outward. For a moment the canyon of the street below yawned beneath her, and her hand seemed to be slipping through Jonathan's wet fingers.

But his grip remained firm, and he managed to cling to the building, letting her almost weightless body rebound in a circle over his head. She landed on the building's edge and pulled him up behind her.

'Made it!' he cried.

She looked back the way they had come, and her eyes widened. 'Jonathan . . .'

The rip was barreling toward them, taller than a skyscraper now, wider than a football field. As the boundary of red time struck the rain, it released vast sheets of water, like a huge crimson tidal wave plowing through downtown Bixby's streets.

In its wake flew a horde of darklings, a thousand winged shapes of every size, vast whirlwinds of slithers glittering red and black, screaming their rat-squeak cries. A knotted mass of the tendril creatures flew at the center of the horde, their appendages intertwined like braided hairs.

'Rex didn't make it,' she said softly. 'Beth . . .'

'No, look.' Jonathan pointed. Miles away, a tiny plume of fire rose into the sky over Jenks, showers of sparks and explosions in every color. 'He and Melissa must have stopped some of them. Maybe there are more than we thought.'

Jessica nodded slowly. Their carefully prepared plan had been woefully inadequate – a few fireworks against an army of monsters.

She tore her eyes away, dropping Jonathan's hand and running toward the giant horse. Its lowest hoof reached down almost to the rooftop – a strand of the arrested lightning wrapped around its metal support, bright and humming with contained power.

She reached toward it, her palm out, like testing the heat of a fire. Huge energies moved inside it, the hairs on her arms standing upright, her whole body tingling. It was like the glorious buzzing feeling when she'd first brought white light into the blue time, but a thousand times more intense. It made her heart pound harder, her vision swim.

Frozen or not, this was really *lightning*, she realized. An awesome force of nature, inconceivably deadly. Like sticking her hand in a light socket, but a million times more powerful. What was supposed to happen to her when she reached into it?

All she knew was what would happen if she didn't: thousands dead, the old ones feeding on their victims freely, humanity at the mercy of its oldest foe.

'I have to do this,' she said softly.

'Are you sure?' Jonathan was right behind her.

'Stand back.'

He shook his head, reaching for her, pulling her into a kiss. Jessica felt it in her lips then, the energy of the trapped lightning all around them mixed with the dizzying glow of Jonathan's midnight gravity. Her skin seemed to tighten, its surface running with wild currents and heat.

Jonathan pulled away, stepping back from her. 'Okay. Be quick now.'

'Farther, Jonathan.'

He nodded, leaping to the edge of the roof. Behind him the crimson wave was almost upon them, a towering sheet of falling water and screaming predators.

Suddenly a hissing squadron of rockets rose up to meet them, bursting into showers of white light. Darklings wheeled and spun to avoid them.

'Dess,' she whispered. The other building, only one jump away, was now inside the rip.

Jessica Day thrust her hand into the lightning . . .

The frozen storm surged through her like an explosion. Thunder filled her ears, and wave after wave of pitiless energy rolled through Jessica until her body seemed to disappear and she could feel nothing but the primordial power locked inside that one instant of lightning. It built inside her, white spots flooding into her vision, her ears popping, the taste of metal skating across her tongue.

She felt like it was going to tear her apart.

Then the white heat burst out in a flood, shooting toward the approaching wall of the rip, cutting through its face and into the hordes of darklings and slithers, fire spreading from one midnight creature to the next in a mad zigzag pattern.

The mass of flying beasts began to wheel and howl.

Another torrent of lightning erupted from Jessica, then two more – four lines of fire radiating in the points of the compass, coruscating across the frozen darkness of the blue time.

Finally she felt the wild energies inside her body lessen, falling away like the shriek of a kettle picked up from the stove. The blinding light began to fade, and Jessica could feel her own breathing again and hear the beating of her heart.

The rip was almost gone, folding upon itself to make a narrow beam of red. The darkling horde was cut into fragments, reduced to scattered clouds of slithers and a few maddened darklings fleeing back toward the desert.

Jessica looked around; four streams of soft white light flowed from her, cutting into the distance toward the north, south, east, and west. The energies in her body dwindled further as she felt them spreading out across the entire globe, wrapping themselves around the earth in some sort of pattern.

Something Dess would want to see, she thought hazily.

But her consciousness was fading away.

Then she saw it through the supports of the giant horse, heading toward them from the east. The light of normal time, sweeping across the world like dawn. The dark moon overhead was falling fast.

Samhain hadn't lasted a whole day, not even an hour . . .

'Jessica.' Jonathan was walking toward her across the roof. 'You're . . .'

'Be careful,' she said weakly. White heat still burned in her hand. She lifted it heavily before her eyes and stared into the trapped lightning there.

But why was the midnight hour over already?

She pulled her eyes away from the fire pulsing in her palm and looked out at the horizon. She saw the storm unfreezing, the blue light of midnight swept out of the world.

Just as normal time reached her, Jessica felt herself fading . . .

'Oh, no,' she said, casting one last glance at Jonathan's stupefied face.

An interrupted peal of thunder rolled as midnight ended.

And then everything was gone.

EPILOGUE

The car slid to a halt in front of the house across the street, setting the neighborhood dogs barking wildly.

Nice move, Flyboy, Melissa thought. Dess had told him to keep it quiet tonight. Her parents were still in major curfew mode since the Great Bixby Halloween Hysteria.

He waited for a moment, then reached to honk the horn.

'Don't,' Melissa said. 'She's coming.'

He glowered for a moment, his impatience bitter in the air. Of course, there was plenty of time before midnight to get to Jessica's house and still make it out to Jenks. But Jonathan was in a hurry to get tonight over and done with. It was all too emotional, and underneath his tension Melissa sniffed a sliver of fear . . .

'Don't worry, Jonathan. She won't change her mind about leaving.'

He looked at her, bristling, then sighed.

'She better not, anyway,' Melissa said. 'I don't think I can live with my parents much longer. Not with Rex's new rules on mindcasting.' Her parents had never been psychos like

Rex's dad, but the subtle web of deceits she had woven around them over the years was beginning to collapse. Melissa had spent the last sixteen years shrinking from their very touch; she doubted she was ready for any heart-to-heart talks about her private life.

In particular, they'd started asking about her missing car. It was definitely time to get out of town.

Dess appeared, slipping from her window and crossing the threadbare lawn at a deliberate pace. Melissa felt her annoyance at Jonathan's noisiness and saw her taking her time.

'Hey, Flyboy.' Dess pulled the back door open and slid her backpack across, then jumped in herself. She didn't say hello to Melissa, but there was no real animosity in it, only habit.

Jonathan glanced over his shoulder at the backseat. 'You really think we'll need that stuff? I mean, are there even any darklings left?'

Melissa found herself defending Dess. 'A few got away. And the really cautious ones never even showed.'

'Sure,' Flyboy said. 'But they're not in Bixby anymore. And the four of us will be there.'

Dess shrugged. 'When dealing with midnight, better safe than sorry.'

Jonathan gave her his new wounded stare. 'Guess that makes me sorry.'

Melissa scowled as the sour milk taste of guilt rolled out of his mind. Two weeks later and he was still wallowing in the idea that what had happened to Jessica was his fault. She sighed softly, wondering what it was going to be like to deal with Flyboy all alone for twenty-four hours a day.

Maybe without Rex around to challenge his freedom, he'd chill out . . .

At the thought of leaving Rex behind, Melissa shivered a little and pulled her mind back to the present. The future could sort itself out now that they actually had one to look forward to.

Jonathan pulled out onto the street, swinging the car into a wide one-eighty that kicked up dust on Dess's dying lawn. Then he shot down the unpaved road, tires spitting gravel and sand. As usual these days, he wasn't in the mood to talk or watch out for cops.

Melissa settled into the front passenger seat, casting her mind across the empty spaces on the edge of town, staying alert. Since the Hysteria, curfew had a whole new meaning here in Bixby.

The official story was, of course, a big joke. A freak collision of air masses over eastern Oklahoma had caused a record number of lightning strikes and brain-rattling waves of thunder. Power had been knocked out across the county, and random electrical fields had disrupted even battery-operated devices and cars. These natural phenomena – along with statistical spikes of heart attacks, fireworks thefts, and costumed Halloween pranks – were the official reasons for the panic.

None of which explained the mutilated body of the camper found in outer Jenks or the seventeen people still missing. But it was a good enough rationalization for anyone who hadn't been awake and inside the rip that night.

Of course, a few conspiracy types had much better theories. Melissa's favorites were an electromagnetic pulse from an experimental plane using the new Bixby runway (which wasn't even built yet) and psychedelic mushrooms growing in the town water supply.

It was all part of a need to understand or, more accurately, to explain away what had happened. Anything not to have to face the truth – that the unknown had come visiting.

One certainty remained, though: Halloween would never be the same in Bixby again.

They reached Jessica's house just before eleven.

All the inside lights were off, both cars sitting in the driveway. There was no For Sale sign on the lawn yet or any other way to distinguish the Day house from the others on the street. But it looked different somehow, even before she cast her mind inside. Sadder.

'Are they really moving?' Dess asked.

'That's just a rumor at school,' Flyboy said. He looked to Melissa for confirmation.

She nodded, her mouth filling with the burnt-coffee taste of anguish that still clung to hope. 'They don't really know. Still waiting for some kind of hard evidence, I suppose.'

'Waiting sucks,' Dess said, and Jonathan nodded.

And then they waited.

She made her way out the window about fifteen minutes later, dropping ungracefully into the bushes. Her jacket looked too big on her, and she walked hunched, her hands jammed all the way down into the pockets.

When she was halfway to the street, Jonathan flashed his headlights once. She spun toward the car, and a sudden jolt of fear shot through the air. For a second Melissa thought that she was about to chicken out and crawl right back into her bedroom.

But a moment later she was at the car window. Her anxiety pulsed in Melissa's mind, her suspicion almost hiding the tight ball of grief in her stomach. Suddenly Melissa realized how brave Beth was to have agreed to this at all.

'Hey,' Jonathan said.

'That's Dess, isn't it?' the kid said.

Dess nodded. 'Yeah. How'd you know?'

'You look just like Cassie's picture.'

Dess didn't answer, giving off the prickly taste of a lump rising in her throat.

'You cut your hair,' Beth said to Melissa.

The mindcaster pushed her fingers through her one-inch buzz, a nervous habit she'd learned from Rex. 'It's what I get for playing with fire.'

Beth got into the back with Dess, sitting on the backpack with a *clink*.

'Ouch!'

'Just give it here,' Dess said.

'What's in there?'

'Magic stuff.'

Jonathan turned to give Dess a death glare, but the kid handed over the backpack with the utmost care.

Rex limped up the stairs of Madeleine's house, trying not to think of what was going on in Jenks. There were bigger issues to consider, lots of questions to be answered before the others left. He clutched his latest letter from Angie and its accompanying sheaf of photocopies – biface spear points from a museum in Cactus Hill, Virginia. She was researching Stone Age culture there, helping Rex search for a link to ancient finds in southern Spain. Rex had serious work to do tonight, more important than watching over ritual farewells.

Besides, Madeleine needed feeding.

In his other hand he carried a thermos of hot chicken soup. Not too hot, of course; she could drink on her own now, but like a baby, she didn't know enough not to burn her lips. Fortunately Rex knew a lot about caring for invalids.

He didn't mind taking care of Madeleine, actually. Here inside the crepuscular contortion that had protected her for fifty years, the human presence of the outside world didn't bother him as much. No cable TV, no cordless phone filling the air with its buzz. The place stank of thirteen-pointed steel, but rust had long ago consumed the alloy's bite. The midnighters who had named those weapons were all dead, except for Madeleine.

Not merely alive: Melissa said that her mind was slowly repairing itself, rebuilding from what his darkling half had done to her, a survivor to the last.

When he opened the door to her room, Rex was surprised to see her sitting up, a gleam of intelligence in her eyes. The smell of weakness and death had lifted a little.

'Madeleine?'

She nodded slowly, as if remembering her name. 'What day is it?'

Rex blinked. The dry, rough-edged words were her first in a month. 'Samhain has come and gone. The flame-bringer stopped it.'

She let out a rattling sigh, a smile fluttering on her lips. 'I knew that girl was special. I was right to call her here to Bixby.'

Rex couldn't argue with that. Since Samhain he had been forced to admit that Madeleine's manipulations over the years had saved a lot of lives. Her orphaned set of midnighters had done more for Bixby than all the previous generations put together. However broken the two of them were, they could congratulate themselves on that.

He sat down next to her, twisting the top from the thermos.

'Where is Melissa?' she croaked.

'She's leaving.' The two simple words sent a spur of pain through him. But of course it was the only way.

'Where?'

He shrugged. 'Eat.'

She took the thermos in trembling hands, held it to her lips, and drank. Rex watched her wrinkled throat move with each greedy swallow. Apparently rebuilding her damaged mind was hungry work. He looked down at the spear points, reading the lore symbols in Angie's cramped handwriting. It was easier on his brain than modern letters. Melissa found it maddening how much he enjoyed the letters from his new pen pal.

Finally Madeleine rested the thermos in her lap, catching her breath. 'You're a fool to hate me, Rex.'

'I don't hate you. I pity you when I bother to think about it.'

'I did it all for you, Rex. Don't you see?' Her eyes gleamed, and he could see what remained of her colossal egotism. 'I wanted to make Bixby as it was in the old days.'

He shook his head. 'That Bixby was a nightmare. It's our day now.'

She snorted. 'What would you know about it? A half-darkling, half-midnighter and so concerned with *daylighters*. It's perverse.'

Rex smiled, glad to hear her diagnosis. She could see that the beast inside him was under control, subservient to his human side. Maybe she wasn't the only one repairing herself.

'Did you say Melissa was leaving?'

He nodded.

'But why? I cowered in this house for fifty years rather than leave the contortion. She'll be blind and deaf out there, without a hint of taste. A daylighter, Rex – a *nothing*.'

'No, she won't be.'

He swallowed, fear moving through him again at the thought of her leaving. It wasn't Melissa he was worried about, of course. It was Rex Greene. Would he still be able to hold himself together once his oldest friend was gone? Maybe he should join the others, leaving Dess all alone in Bixby, leaving his father and the old woman to die. They deserved whatever they got, and without Melissa's calmness of mind, without her touch . . .

Rex shook his head, steeling himself. He took the thermos from Madeleine's hand and wiped stray soup from her chin. Perhaps Melissa was right, and it was tending to his father and an old woman that had kept him sane all along. His cares kept him human.

Madeleine hadn't heard him; she was still mewling. 'Why, Rex? Why would she leave? This is *Bixby*, after all.'

He drew himself up and gave her a predatory smile, knowing that the news would silence her.

'Because Bixby isn't special anymore.'

They reached Jenks without any trouble, and Jonathan drew to a halt in the same field that Rex had raged across in his mother's pink Cadillac. As the four of them made their silent way toward the rip, he stared down the railroad tracks, which still bore the scars of Halloween – a few cross-ties were blackened from burning oil and rocket exhaust, and the soggy relics of firecracker-red paper clung to bits of gravel everywhere.

But the surrounding grass had recovered from the rip's strange light, Jonathan noticed, a healthy green again. Maybe the dark moon wasn't so tough after all.

There wasn't much left of the rip anymore, just a sliver. A few more nights and it would fade into the lore completely. When they reached it, Dess pulled out Geostationary and began to make a small, precise circle of stones.

Beth stood close to him, watching her. 'What's that thing?' she said softly.

'A GPS device,' he answered. 'It's not magic or anything.'

'What's it supposed to do?'

'It's for finding places. You have to be in exactly the right spot for this to work.'

Beth looked at him, her stare suddenly fierce. 'I've got my mom's cell phone, you know.'

He blinked. 'That's . . . good.'

'So you guys better not try anything weird.'

Jonathan sighed. What they were about to try was, pretty much by definition, weird. 'Don't worry, okay? We're all friends here. You said you wanted to do this.'

Beth only swallowed and for a moment looked like she was about to cry.

'She wants this too,' Jonathan added, wishing he were somewhere else. He'd been the one to break the news to Beth, to argue against her suspicions, her angry disbelief. After the hours spent convincing her to come out here, Jonathan was all out of words. He reached out and put his arm around her, drew her closer.

'Really?' she said, her voice breaking. 'And this is for real?'

He smiled. 'Well, I ain't dreaming.' She felt unbelievably small and fragile, shivering in the cold.

'Come on,' Dess said. 'Stand right here.'

Jonathan guided Beth up onto the tracks and into the circle of stones. The frightened expression on her face made something loosen in his throat, and his voice grew hoarse. 'Don't worry. It'll be okay.'

He stepped back, waiting, hoping that this would work.

Midnight fell a few moments later, the moan of the cold wind switching off like a light, the blue time sucking the color from their faces. Jonathan felt the awful weight of Flatland lift up from him.

Same old midnight – damaged, unleashed from its proper boundaries, but not destroyed.

For a moment Jonathan wondered if they'd waited too long to try this and the rip had faded out. Beth just stood there in her circle of rocks, as motionless as any stiff.

But then her eyes blinked. 'That was weird.'

'No kidding,' Jessica said from behind her little sister. She'd asked them to face the kid toward Bixby and had wisely chosen not to be standing in Beth's view. She kept her right hand in her jacket pocket as well.

It still freaked Jonathan out how Jessica always *folded* out of the air as midnight fell. Even darklings and slithers had to escape from the sun, hiding in caves or burying themselves. But the flame-bringer had become something altogether different, a whole new kind of midnight creature.

She wasn't frozen during daylight . . . she simply *wasn't*.

Rex called it 'temporal dependence.' Jonathan didn't know what to call it. During the day it felt like Jessica was gone, like that first night when he thought he'd lost her to the lightning. He'd searched the roof for hours before trudging down the twenty-six flights of stairs to the ground floor, exhausted by

Flatland, crushed by grief. It had been a whole terrible day before midnight had fallen again and he'd flown back up to Pegasus, hoping to find some kind of sign.

And she was standing there . . . still in shock, not realizing a whole day had passed without her. Alive.

But his joy had faded when midnight had ended again and they realized that Jessica was trapped now inside the secret hour.

Jonathan looked at her, feeling that fractured rush of relief again. For the last two years his life had been split in half, between glorious midnight and the crushing gravity of daylight. These days it was even worse: Flatland was much flatter without Jessica and the secret hour suddenly more precious.

Midnight stretched across the whole world now, after all. They could fly anywhere . . . in their one hour.

Beth turned around slowly, huddling in her jacket as if the air were still cold. She stared at Jessica.

'Come on, Flyboy,' Dess said. 'Let's give them some privacy.'

He caught Jessica's eye, and she nodded.

Walking away felt like a kick in the stomach, giving up these minutes with Jessica. *This* was what he'd always tried to avoid since the day his mother had departed and not returned: this feeling that if you lost someone, your world could come crashing down. And it had happened again.

But at least Jessica hadn't disappeared completely. She was only gone for twenty-four hours a day. And Jonathan knew he would hold on to that one hour left to them for as long as he could.

'Jess?' Beth said in a small voice.

'Yeah, it's me.' Jessica felt tears on her face. She'd known the exact spot her sister would shimmer into view, but it still made her breath catch.

'You're really . . . here.'

Jessica nodded. She wanted to gather her little sister into a hug, but for these first fragile moments she'd decided to keep her right hand in her pocket. 'Yeah. I've been here all along.'

'Why didn't you come home?'

Jessica bit her lip. 'I can't. I'm stuck here.'

'What? In *Jenks*?'

'No, in midnight. I only exist for an hour a day. I'm part of midnight now.' Jessica shook her head sadly. Maybe she'd been part of midnight since she'd woken up that first time in the secret hour. It had nibbled away at her life since then, until only this one sliver was left.

She felt a mental nudge from Melissa, standing close by, and stood straighter, swallowing her self-pity. Jessica had made her choice on that building top, after all, knowing that sticking her hand into the bolt of lightning would change everything.

'Why didn't you *tell* me what was going on?' Beth said. 'The whole time, you could have let me know.'

Jessica was ready for this. 'Are you going to tell Mom and Dad?'

'Tell them . . . ?'

'About this. Are you going to tell them you saw your missing sister appear on some railroad tracks in Jenks?'

Beth thought for a moment, then shook her head. 'They'd probably send me to a shrink.'

'Exactly.' Jessica nodded. 'So you have to keep it secret. Like I did. That's just the way it works. But Beth, at least you'll know I'm . . . somewhere.'

'*Somewhere* isn't good enough, Jess! You're leaving me all alone.'

'I'm not. You've still got Mom and Dad.'

Beth clenched her teeth. 'Mom cries all the time. She thinks it's because she was working so much that you disappeared. And Dad's an even bigger zombie than before.'

Jessica closed her eyes, her tears hot on her cheeks in the cool of the blue time. The thought of her parents missing her, not knowing what had happened, was too much to bear. 'They need you, Beth.'

'They need *you*. Maybe they could come here and stand here like I did. I'll think of some way to get them out to Jenks. I'll *make* them come . . .'

'No.' Jessica took a step forward, put her left arm around Beth. 'The rip is fading. And besides, I won't be here anymore. Jonathan and Melissa and I are leaving Bixby.'

Beth kicked at the gravel, tears appearing in her eyes. 'You *are* leaving me.'

'Midnight's spreading, Beth. There are going to be more people like me, waking up and finding themselves in the blue time.'

'And lying to their little sisters?'

'Probably, at first.' Jessica nodded. 'Right now they need our help.'

'*I* need you too, Jessica.' Beth was sobbing now.

'I know.' She drew her little sister into a left-handed hug and sighed. 'I'm so sorry, Beth. Maybe it wasn't fair, bringing you out here.'

Beth shook her head.

'But you'll have to keep everyone in the dark, just like I did,' Jessica said. 'You'll have to lie about it.'

Beth raised her head. 'Not to everyone. There's Cassie.'

Jessica nodded slowly. 'That's right. She saw the rip, anyway. I guess you could tell her about me too.'

Beth sniffed once. 'Already did.'

'What?'

'When Jonathan was trying to convince me to come out here. I had her spend the night, and she hid in my closet. And listened.'

A momentary wave of annoyance, all too familiar, went through Jessica. But then it turned into a feeling of relief and she let out a chuckle. 'You little sneak.'

'There have to be more people in Bixby who know about all this, who've figured out how it works.' Beth pulled away a bit, staring fiercely into her sister's eyes. 'And believe me, Cassie and I are going to find them. Don't think you've gotten away from us yet.'

Jessica looked down at her little sister, a smile spreading across her face, suddenly certain that Beth was going to be okay, with or without her big sister around.

Dess let herself wander along the tracks, looking into the trees, searching for any sign of life. It was almost too quiet these days; she wouldn't mind the sight of a slither among the leaves. Certainly she was safe enough, between Counterfeiter in her pocket and the flame-bringer a few hundred feet away. Jessica hadn't tried out her new, softly sparkling right hand on any darklings yet, but Dess was pretty sure she didn't need a flashlight anymore.

Dess hadn't slain anything herself in ages now. Why had they *all* run away? Darklings were like tigers, she figured. You didn't want them eating you, but you didn't want them going *extinct*. The world was less interesting without them.

Of course, after a few thousand years in one crappy town, Halloween had probably looked like Christmas to the darklings who'd survived.

When Jessica had sealed the rip, the energies built up along Bixby's fault line hadn't disappeared – they'd spread across the globe.

Dess shook her head. After all her work on the geography of the secret hour, it seemed a shame to throw out all those maps. Still, she couldn't wait for Jonathan and Jess to start exploring the 36th parallel, finding out how far midnight stretched in the aftermath of Samhain.

Did it extend along the whole 36th parallel? And the 12th, 24th, and 48th as well? Was it wrapped around the entire globe, or did it only pop up at the intersections of multiples of twelve?

Or was midnight simply *everywhere* now? Were lucky midnighters waking up in every city and town, amazed at the blue and frozen world?

Dess heard the crunch of gravel and turned. Flyboy was bouncing along behind her, looking unhappy, like he needed someone to talk to.

She sighed. 'So when do you three leave?'

'Probably soon.' He pointed his chin back toward the girls. 'Now that this is over and done with.'

'It's going to be lonely, only seeing Jess an hour a day.'

'It's already lonely.'

Dess shook her head, wondering if he'd bothered to do the math on that little conundrum. Jess lived only one hour to his twenty-five, which meant she'd be hitting her nineteenth birthday just about the same time Jonathan was dying of old age. And sometime *way* before that, things were going to get . . . icky.

'Oh, well.' Dess smiled wryly. 'You've always got Melissa to talk to.'

He looked up from the tracks. 'Why do you still hate her? She saved Jessica that night, you know. *And* Beth. Maybe everyone in the world.'

'I don't hate her.' As the words left her mouth, Dess realized it was really true – her hatred of the mindcaster had quietly expired. 'Still, she's not exactly road trip material.'

'Maybe not.' He smiled. 'But without her, we'll never find all of them.'

'*All* of them? Flyboy, there's lots more than you think.'

Jonathan looked at her, then shook his head. 'Any idea how all this happened? I mean *why* it happened?'

Dess just snorted at that one. Let Rex bury himself in the lore, still trying to figure that stuff out, how the timequake and the lightning had chosen the same moment to strike. But Dess knew that was nuts. Not that she was against doing the math – explaining why and how things happened was the credo of the Discovery Channel, after all. But sometimes the numbers would never add up, no matter how hard you calculated.

After all, the chances of a bolt of lightning hitting the center of Bixby on the exact stroke of midnight on Halloween were . . . rather low. And if you thought for too long about why it had happened in exactly that way, you weren't doing your brain any favors. In which case it was better to leave the math the hell alone.

She looked into the sky and saw that the dark moon had reached its apex. 'Come on, Flyboy. Time for your party trick.'

'Okay.' He swallowed. 'You really think this will help?'

'Of course it will.' Dess led Jonathan back toward where the other three stood. She knew the two sisters had more stuff to work out, but sometimes apology math was funny: no number was ever high enough, and you just had to get over it.

They were holding each other, as if already out of words. Melissa stood off to one side, eyes closed. Prompting? Controlling? Or just eavesdropping? Dess wondered if this new non-evil style of mindcasting really helped or was just another crock.

Dess waited until she caught Jessica's eye, then pointed at Jonathan.

Give the poor kid this much at least.

Jessica nodded back and pulled away. 'Come on. I want to show you something about midnight. Something not horrible. It's a little weird but . . . trust me?'

Beth made a choked little sound, wiping at her face, then said softly, 'I trust you.'

Jonathan stepped forward, holding out both his hands. 'You saw us do this, right? On Halloween?'

Beth nodded, taking his hand carefully. As her smaller fingers closed around his, a look of surprise crossed her face.

'It's . . . dizzy.'

'It's a lot better than dizzy,' Jessica said, smiling. She pulled her right hand from her pocket; white sparks fluttered upward from it. The bracelet she wore glowed, its tiny charms aglitter. Dess squinted at the light.

Beth stared at it openmouthed. 'What *is* that?'

'Don't you remember? It's a present from Jonathan . . . plus some lightning.' Jessica took Flyboy's hand.

At first they took a weenie, ten-foot hop. Then a longer one took them to the middle of the field. Finally they opened up big time, heading for the motionless Arkansas River. Jessica's right hand sparkled in the distance, its trail of white light coruscating across the blue horizon.

Dess felt a smile spread across her face, and she was suddenly much less depressed. Beth had seen the blue time again; she'd gotten to fly.

'Yeah, I know,' Melissa said.

Dess let out a sigh. Alone with the bitch goddess one more time.

'I'm still sorry, you know. For what I did to you.'

Typical mindcaster trick, catching her off guard and getting all sentimental. Dess heard herself saying, 'Whatever. It's probably not your fault, the way you are.'

'We saved Rex that night.'

Not so sorry after all? Dess thought. But she couldn't argue with Melissa's logic. 'You'll miss him, won't you?'

Melissa nodded. 'I already do.'

Dess sighed again. Maybe there was one darkling left in Bixby.

They stood there in silence for a while, waiting for the others to come back.

'So how many more of us are out there?' the mindcaster finally asked.

Dess took a breath, glad to be talking about math instead of all this emotional crap. 'Well, let's say you have to be born within a half second of midnight, right? That would be one out of every eighty-six thousand four hundred people.'

'In a big city that's a lot, isn't it?'

'In New York about a hundred. In the world . . . a hundred *thousand*.'

'Crap,' Melissa said softly, like she hadn't thought through the scale of their little road trip yet.

Amazement radiated from the mindcaster, a tingle that shot down Dess's arms into her fingers, bringing back her smile. Even being stuck here in Bixby with crazy Rex and crazier Maddy, even with no darklings left to slay, even living in a major curfew zone for the next two and a half years, Dess couldn't complain about the cards she'd drawn.

Once the midnighters had gone their separate ways, Dess would no longer be stuck between the two couples, hemmed in by the constant clash of egos. And eventually she would be free of Bixby itself. No longer a fifth wheel.

After high school, Dess knew, she could get a job anywhere. Computers, spacecraft, all kinds of cool stuff that hadn't even been invented yet – all of it needed math. And with midnight spreading across the globe, thousands of polymaths would be waking up. Finally she'd have people to talk to with minds like hers, math geniuses in a frozen time where math kicked ass. Together they could map the expanded secret hour, have whole conversations in tridecalogisms, try to figure out how time itself worked. Change the world, maybe.

Screw the lore, with all its propaganda and lies and bitter history. Dess was going to be the one to write the axioms of midnight, the first principles of Dessometrics.

Inexhaustible. Unsmotherable. Extraordinary. That was her.

It was way cool, being the one who did the math.

Turn the page
for a special preview of another
amazing book from Scott Westerfeld

PARASITE POSITIVE

Out now

1. STAY AWAY, JOE

After a year of hunting, I finally caught up with Sarah.

It turned out she'd been hiding in New Jersey, which broke my heart. I mean, *Hoboken*? Sarah was always head-over-heels in love with Manhattan. For her, New York was like another Elvis, the King remade of bricks, steel, and granite. The rest of the world was a vast extension of her parents' basement, the last place she wanted to wind up.

No wonder she'd had to leave when the disease took hold of her mind. Peeps always run from the things they used to love.

Still, I shook my head when I found out where she was. The old Sarah wouldn't have been caught dead in Hoboken. And yet here I was, finishing my tenth cup of coffee in the crumbling parking lot of the old ferry terminal, armed only with my wits and a backpack full of Elvis memorabilia. In the black mirror of the coffee's surface, the gray sky trembled with the beating of my heart.

It was late afternoon. I'd spent the day in a nearby diner, working my way through the menu and waiting for the clouds to clear, praying that the bored and very cute waitress wouldn't start talking to me. If that happened, I'd have to leave and wander around the docks all day.

I was nervous – the usual tension of meeting an ex, with the added bonus of facing a maniacal cannibal – and the hours stretched out torturously. But finally a few shafts of sun had broken through, bright enough to trap Sarah inside the terminal. Peeps can't stand sunlight.

It had been raining a lot that week, and green weeds pushed up through the asphalt, cracking the old parking lot like so much dried mud. Feral cats watched me from every hiding place, no doubt drawn here by the spiking rat population. Predators and prey and ruin – it's amazing how quickly nature consumes human places after we turn our backs on them. Life is a hungry thing.

According to the Night Watch's crime blotters, this spot didn't show any of the usual signs of a predator. No transit workers gone missing, no homeless people turning psychotically violent. But every time New Jersey Pest Control did another round of poisoning, the hordes of rats just reappeared, despite the fact that there wasn't much garbage to eat in this deserted part of town. The only explanation was a resident peep. When the Night Watch had tested one of the rats, it had turned out to be of my bloodline, once removed.

That could only mean Sarah. Except for her and Morgan, every other girl I'd ever kissed was already locked up tight. (And Morgan, I was certain, was *not* hiding out in an old ferry terminal in Hoboken.)

Big yellow stickers plastered the terminal's padlocked doors, warning of rat poison, but it looked like the guys at pest control were starting to get spooked. They'd dropped off their little packets of death, slapped up a few warning stickers, and then gotten the heck out of there.

Good for them. They don't get paid enough to deal with peeps.

Of course, neither do I, despite the excellent health benefits. But

I had a certain responsibility here. Sarah wasn't just the first of my bloodline – she was my first real girlfriend.

My *only* real girlfriend, if you must know.

We met the opening day of classes – freshman year, Philosophy 101 – and soon found ourselves in a big argument about free will and predetermination. The discussion spilled out of class, into a café, and all the way back to her room that night. Sarah was very into free will. I was very into Sarah.

The argument went on that whole semester. As a bio major, I figured 'free will' meant chemicals in your brain telling you what to do, the molecules bouncing around in a way that *felt* like choosing but was actually the dance of little gears – neurons and hormones bubbling up into decisions like clockwork. You don't use your body; it uses you.

Guess I won that one.

There were signs of Sarah everywhere. All the windows at eye level were smashed, every expanse of reflective metal smeared with dirt or something worse.

And of course there were rats. Lots of them. I could hear that even from outside.

I squeezed between the loosely padlocked doors, then stood waiting for my vision to adjust to the darkness. The sound of little feet skittered along the gloomy edges of the vast interior space. My entrance had the effect of a stone landing in a still pond: The rippling rats took a while to settle.

I listened for my ex-girlfriend but heard only wind whistling over broken glass and the myriad nostrils snuffling around me.

They stayed in the shadows, smelling the familiarity of me, wondering if I was part of the family. Rats have evolved into an arrangement with the disease, you see. They don't suffer from infection.

Human beings aren't so lucky. Even people like me – who don't turn into ravening monsters, who don't have to run from everything they love – we suffer too. Exquisitely.

I dropped my backpack to the floor and pulled out a poster, unrolling it and taping it to the inside of the door.

I stepped back, and the King smiled down at me through the darkness, resplendent against black velvet. No way could Sarah get past those piercing green eyes and that radiant smile.

Feeling safer under his gaze, I moved farther into the darkness. Long benches lined the floor like church pews, and the faded smell of long-gone human crowds rose up. Passengers had once sat here to await the next ferry to Manhattan. There were a few beds of newspaper where homeless people had slept, but my nose informed me that they'd lain empty for weeks.

Since the predator had arrived.

The hordes of tiny footsteps followed me warily, still unsure of what I was.

I taped a black-velvet Elvis poster onto each exit from the terminal, the bright colors clashing with the dingy yellow of the rat-poison warnings. Then I postered the broken windows, plastering every means of escape with the King's face.

Against one wall, I found pieces of a shredded shirt. Stained with fresh-smelling blood, it had been flung aside like a discarded candy wrapper. I had to remind myself that this creature wasn't really Sarah, full of free will and tidbits of Elvis trivia. This was a cold-blooded killer.

Before I zipped the backpack closed, I pulled out an eight-inch '68 Comeback Special action figure and put it in my pocket. I hoped my familiar face would protect me, but it never hurts to have a trusty anathema close at hand.

I heard something from above, where the old ferry administration offices jutted out from the back wall, overlooking the waiting room. Peeps prefer to nest in small, high places.

There was only one set of stairs, the steps sagging like a flat tire in the middle. As my weight pressed into the first one, it creaked unhappily.

The noise didn't matter – Sarah had to know already someone was here – but I went carefully, letting the staircase's sway settle between every step. The guys in Records had warned me that this place had been condemned for a decade.

I took advantage of the slow ascent to leave a few items from my backpack on the stairs. A sequined cape, a miniature blue Christmas tree, an album of *Elvis Sings Gospel*.

From the top of the stairs, a row of skulls looked down at me.

I'd seen lairs marked this way before, part territorialism – a warning to other predators to stay away – and partly the sort of thing that peeps just . . . liked. Not free will but those chemicals in the brain again, determining aesthetic responses, as predictable as a middle-aged guy buying a red sports car.

More tiny feet skittered when I kicked one of the skulls into the gloom. It rolled with a limping, asymmetrical *ka-thump, ka thump* across the floor. As the echoes died away, I heard something human-size breathing. But she didn't show herself, didn't attack. I wondered if she recognized my smell.

'It's me,' I called softly, not expecting any response.

'Cal?'

I froze, not believing my ears. None of the other girls I'd ever dated had spoken at all when I'd tracked them down, much less said my name.

But I recognized Sarah's voice. Even raspy and desiccated, as dry and brittle as a lost contact lens, it was her. I heard her dry throat swallow.

'I'm here to help you,' I said.

There was no answer, no movement of rats' feet. The sounds of her breathing had stopped. Peeps can do that, subsist on pockets of oxygen stored in the parasite's cysts.

The balcony stretched before me, a row of doors leading to abandoned offices. I took a few steps and glanced into the first one. It was stripped of furniture, but I could see the outlines of tiny cubicles imprinted into the gray industrial carpet. Not a terrible place to work, though: Iron-framed windows overlooked the harbor, the views magnificent, even though the glass was broken and smeared.

Manhattan lay across the river, the downtown spires lighting up as the sun went down, painting the glass towers orange. Strange that Sarah would stay here, in sight of the island she'd loved. How could she stand it?

Maybe she was different.

Old clothes and a couple of crack vials littered the floor, along with more human bones. I wondered where she had been hunting and how the Watch had missed the kills. That's the thing about predators: They leave a huge statistical footprint on any ecosystem. Get more than a dozen of them in even the biggest city and the homicides show up like a house on fire. The disease has spent the last thousand years evolving to conceal itself, but it gets tougher and tougher for man-eaters to stay hidden. Human beings are prey with *cell phones*, after all.

I stepped back into the hall and closed my eyes, listening again. Hearing nothing.

When I opened them, Sarah stood before me.

I sucked in a breath and the most trivial of thoughts went through me: *She's lost weight*. Her wiry body almost disappeared in the stolen rags she wore, like a child in borrowed, grown-up clothes. As always when running into an ex after a long time, there was the weirdness of seeing a once-familiar face transformed.

I could see why the legends call them beautiful: that bone structure right there on the surface, like heroin chic without the bad skin. And a peep's gaze is so intense. Adapted to the darkness, their irises and pupils are huge, the skin around the orbitals pulled back in a predatory face-lift, revealing more of the eyeballs. Like Botoxed movie stars, they always look surprised and almost never blink.

For a brief and horrible moment, I thought I was in love with her again. But it was just the insatiable parasite inside me.

'Sarah,' I breathed out.

She hissed. Peeps hate the sound of their own names, which cuts into the tangled channels of their brains just like an anathema. But she'd said, 'Cal . . .'

'Go away,' came the raspy voice.

I could see hunger in her eyes – peeps are always hungry – but she didn't want me. I was too familiar.

Rats began to swirl around my feet, thinking a kill was coming. I stamped one of my rat-proof cowboy boots down hard to send them scurrying. Sarah bared her teeth at the noise and my stomach clenched. I had to remind myself that she wouldn't eat me, *couldn't* eat me.

'I have to take you out of here,' I said, my fingers closing on the action figure in my pocket. They never went without a fight, but Sarah was my first real love. I thought maybe . . .

She struck like lightning, her open palm landing upside my head, a slap that felt like it had burst my eardrum.

I staggered back, the world ringing, and more blows pummeled my stomach, driving the breath from me. And then I was lying on my back, Sarah's weight on my chest, her body as sinewy as a bag full of pissed-off snakes, her smell thick in my nostrils.

She pushed my head back, baring my throat, but then froze, something fighting behind her Botoxed eyes. Her love for me? Or just the anathema of my familiar face?

'Ray's Original, First Avenue and Eighth Street,' I said quickly, invoking her favorite pizza place. 'Vanilla vodka on the rocks. *Viva Las Vegas*.' That last one scored, so I added, 'His mother's middle name was Love.'

At this second Elvis reference, Sarah hissed like a snake, one hand curling into a claw. The fingernails, like a corpse's, keep growing as everything else is eaten away, and hers were as gnarled and black as dried beetle husks.

I stopped her with the password for our shared video store account, then rattled off her old cell-phone number and the names of the goldfish she'd left behind. Sarah flinched, battered by these old, familiar signifiers. Then she let out a howl, her mouth stretching wide to bare the awful teeth again. A dark claw raised up.

I pulled the action figure from my pocket and thrust it into her face.

It was the King, of course, in Comeback Special black, complete with leather wristband and four-inch guitar. This was my only keepsake from her former life – I'd stolen it from under her roommate's nose, dropping by a week after Sarah had disappeared, instinctively knowing she wasn't coming back. Wanting something of hers.

Sarah howled, closing her fist and bringing it down on my chest. The blow left me coughing, my eyes filling with tears. But her weight was suddenly gone.

I rolled over, gasping, trying to regain my feet. As my eyes cleared, I saw boiling fur in every direction, the rats in a panic at their mistress's distress.

She had started down the stairs, but now the anathema had taken hold of her mind. The Elvis memorabilia I'd placed on the steps did its job – Sarah twisted in midcourse at the sequined cape, like a horse glimpsing a rattlesnake, and crashed through the rickety banister.

I scrambled to the balcony's edge and looked down. She crouched on one of the pews, glaring up at me.

'Are you okay, Sarah?'

The sound of her own name got her moving, gliding across the waiting room, bare feet silent on the backs of the benches. But she stumbled to a halt as she came face-to-face with the black velvet King poster, a horrible wail filling the echoing terminal. It was one of those spine-tingling transformations, like when a forlorn cat suddenly makes the sound of a human child, Sarah uttering the cry of some other species.

Rats swept toward me from all sides – attacking, I thought for a moment. But they were simply freaking out, swirling without purpose around my boots, disappearing through holes and into office doorways.

As I ran down the staircase, the metal bolts that held it to the wall yanked at their berths in a screeching chorus. Sarah darted from exit to exit, mewling at the sight of the King's face. She froze and hissed at me again.

She knew I had her cornered and watched warily as I put the doll back in my pocket.

'Stay there. I won't hurt you.' I slowly climbed down the rest of the swaying stairs. It was about as steady as standing in a canoe.

The moment one of my feet touched the ground floor, Sarah ran straight toward the far wall. She leaped high, her black claws grasping one of a web of steam pipes that fed a long radiator. Her long black fingernails made pinging sounds on the empty pipes as she climbed up and along the wall toward a high window I hadn't bothered to cover. She moved like a spider, fast and jerky.

There was no Elvis between her and freedom. I was going to lose her.

Swearing, I turned and dashed back up the swaying stairs. A series of pops came from behind me, bolts failing, and just as I reached the top, the whole staircase pulled away, freeing itself from the wall at last. But it didn't crash to the ground, just sagged exhaustedly, a few bolts still clinging to the upper floor like rusty fingernails.

Sarah reached the high window and put her fist through it, smeared glass shattering onto a jagged patch of gray sky. But as she pulled herself up into the window frame, a bright shaft of sun struck through the clouds, hitting her square in the face.

The rosy light filled the terminal, and Sarah screamed again, swinging from one hand, the other flailing. She tried to hoist herself through the broken window twice more, but the punishing sunlight forced her back. Finally she scurried away, fleeing along the pipes and leaping to the balcony, darting through the farthest doorway from me.

I was already running.

The last office was the darkest, but I could smell the rats, the main nest of her brood. When I reached the door they turned to face me in awful unison, red eyes illuminated by the dusty shaft of sunlight filtering in behind me. There was a bed in one corner, its rusty springs covered with rotting clothes. Most peeps didn't bother with beds. Had it been left here by squatters? Or had Sarah salvaged it from some rubbish heap?

She'd always been a fussy sleeper, bringing her own pillow to college from Tennessee. Did she still care what she slept on?

Sarah watched me from the bed, her eyes half closed. It was only because the sunlight had burned them, but it made her look more human.

I approached carefully, one hand on the action figure in my pocket. But I didn't pull it out. Maybe I could take her without any more struggle. She'd said my name, after all.

The motionless rats made me nervous. I took a plastic bag from my pocket and emptied it onto my boots. The brood parted, scenting Cornelius's dander. My ancient cat hadn't hunted in years, but the rats didn't know that. Suddenly, I smelled like a predator.

Sarah clung to the bed's spindly frame, which began to shudder. I paused to pull a Kevlar glove onto my left hand and dropped two knockout pills into its palm.

'Let me give you these. They'll make you better.'

Sarah squinted at me, still wary, but listening. She had always forgotten to take her pills, and it had been my job to remind her. Maybe this ritual would calm her, something remembered, but not fondly enough to be an anathema. I could hear her breathing, her heart still beating as fast as it had during the chase.

She could spring at me at any moment.

I took another slow step and sat down beside her. The bed's rusty springs made a questioning sound.

'Take these. They're good for you.'

Sarah stared at the small white pills cupped in my palm. I felt her relax for a moment, maybe recalling what it was like to be sick – just *normal* sick – and have a boyfriend look after you.

I'm not as fast as a full-blown peep, or as strong, but I am pretty quick. I cupped my hand over her mouth in a flash and heard the pills *snick* into her dehydrated throat. Her hands gripped my shoulders, but I pressed her head back with my whole weight, letting her teeth savage the thick glove. Sarah's black nails didn't go for my face, and I saw swallows pulsing along her pale neck.

The pills took her down in seconds. With a metabolism as fast as ours, drugs hit right away – I feel tipsy about a minute after alcohol touches my tongue, and I damn near need an IV to keep a coffee buzz going.

'Well done, Sarah.' I let her go and saw that her eyes were still open. 'You'll be okay now, I promise.'

I pulled the glove off. The outer water-resistant layer was shredded, but her teeth hadn't broken the Kevlar. (It *has* happened, though.)

My cell phone showed one lonely bar of reception, but the call went straight through. 'It was her. Pick us up.'

As the phone went dark, I wondered if I should have mentioned the crumbling stairs. Oh, well. They'd figure out how to get up.

'Cal?'

I started at the sound, but her slitted eyes didn't seem to pose a threat. 'What is it, Sarah?'

'Show me again.'

'Show you what?'

She tried to speak, but a pained look crossed her face.

'You mean . . .' His name would hurt her if I said it. 'The King?'

She nodded.

'You don't want that. It'll only burn you. Like the sun did.'

'But I miss him.' Her voice was fading, sleep taking her.

I swallowed, feeling something flat and heavy settle over me. 'I know you do.'

Sarah knew a lot about Elvis, but she enjoyed obscure facts the most. She loved it that his mother's middle name was Love. She searched the Web for MP3s of the B-sides of rare seventies singles. Her favorite movie was one that you've probably never heard of: *Stay Away, Joe*.

In it, Elvis is a half-Navajo bronco buster on a reservation. Sarah claimed it was the role he was born to play, because he really was part Native American. Yeah, right. His great-great-great-grandmother was Cherokee. And, like most of us, he had *sixteen* great-great-great-grandmothers. Not much genetic impact there. But Sarah didn't care. She said obscure influences were the most important.

That's a philosophy major for you.

In the movie, Elvis sells pieces of his car whenever he needs money. The doors go, then the roof, then the seats, one by one. By the end he's riding along on an empty frame – Elvis at the steering wheel, four tires and a sputtering engine on an open road.

As the disease had settled across her, Sarah had held onto Elvis the longest. After she'd thrown out all her books and clothes, erased every photograph from her hard drive, and broken all the mirrors in her dorm bathroom, the Elvis posters still clung to her walls, crumpled and scratched from bitter blows, but hanging on. As her mind transformed, Sarah shouted more than once that she couldn't stand the sight of me, but she never said a word against the King.

Finally, she fled, deciding to disappear into the night rather than tear down those slyly grinning faces she could no longer bear to look at.

As I waited for the transport squad, I watched her shivering on the bed and thought of Elvis clutching the steering wheel of his skeletal car.

Sarah had lost everything, shedding the pieces of her life one by one to placate the anathema, until she was left here in this dark place, clinging to a shuddering, rickety frame.

Scott Westerfeld is a software designer, composer and writer. He lives with his partner, writer Justine Larbalestier, and they divide their time between New York City and Sydney. Visit his website at www.scottwesterfeld.com